"Sorry, Kinloch," his uncle replied. "I thought she would make trouble for us."

"She just did," Dougal admitted, and turned his attention to the girl still pushing against him. "That pistol could have gone off and killed someone!"

"Then he should not have pointed it at me," she said.

Sighing loudly, Dougal shifted his weight off her, holding her down with his arm stretched against her full bosom. Her breath heaved under his entrapment, and he closed his eyes for a moment; it was damned distracting, he thought.

"What do smugglers care about killing?" she said. "Kidnapping and murder, smuggling and breaking the king's law—it is nothing to such as you."

"Ruthless, we are," Dougal drawled. "Black-guards, we three."

"Wretches," she agreed.

"Kinloch, the king's men are just ahead on the road," Andrew called back.

Yanking the blanket over his head and the girl's, Dougal slid down as flat as he could. "Keep quiet and stay still," he told her tersely. He lay back in the straw with the girl pressed tightly against him. Like lovers, he thought, bundled and courting.

"Beast," she hissed. "Scoundrel."

Other **Avon Romances**

Coming Soon

And Don't Miss These
ROMANTIC TREASURES
from Avon Books

The Highland Groom

Sarah Gabriel

AVON

An Imprint of HarperCollinsPublishers

AVON BOOKS
An Imprint of HarperCollins*Publishers*
10 East 53rd Street
New York, New York 10022-5299

Copyright © 2009 by Sarah Gabriel
ISBN 978-0-06-123497-2
www.avonromance.com

First Avon Books paperback printing: January 2009

Avon Trademark Reg. U.S. Pat. Off. and in Other Countries, Marca Registrada, Hecho en U.S.A.
HarperCollins® is a registered trademark of HarperCollins Publishers.

Printed in the U.S.A.

10 9 8 7 6 5 4 3 2 1

For Jason and Jeremy,
brewmeisters extraordinaire,
and for all the wonderful readers
who make writing novels so worthwhile:
thank you.

So wondrous wild, the whole might seem
The scenery of a fairy dream.

—Sir Walter Scott, *The Lady of the Lake*

The Highland Groom

Prologue

May 1807
Scotland, the Central Highlands

Just before dawn on his thirteenth birthday, Dougal MacGregor climbed a hill behind his father, whose steps were long and sure. Tall for his age, Dougal kept pace and glanced around in the half darkness, where the trees and rocks looked as insubstantial as the surrounding mist. Though the climb was risky even in daylight, his father knew every step and misstep of the paths over the hills, having been born in the glen below; John MacGregor, laird of Kinloch, was a shepherd, a farmer, and a clever smuggler.

Proud to be Kinloch's son and the newest keeper of the family secret—his father would reveal it that very morning—Dougal hurried behind.

Where the hill met the mountain the way grew steep, but Dougal and his father had the strong legs and good lungs of Highlanders used to long miles. His late mother, Anna MacIan, had often said that the son was even more handsome than his brawny, dark-haired father. Dougal wanted to be as fine a man one day, watching over the people of Glen Kinloch in the same fair manner that his father did.

He wanted to be a smuggler like John, too. The free trade put coin in poor Highland pockets, though lately new laws and regulations made the enterprise more dangerous. But Dougal would rather run whisky over the hills and outwit the revenue men at every turn than go to school. Books and learning were not half as enjoyable as leading gaugers on a merry chase by moonlight to the shores of the great loch, where sloops waited to take whisky kegs down the loch to the river, and out of Scotland entirely. Dougal had accompanied his father and uncles on a few runs, when a swift and clever lad was a boon to the work.

But his father did not want that life for his son. John MacGregor was adamant that Dougal be educated. He declared dusty books and stiff collars in Dougal's future, not illicit exporting, and to that end, John had saved every spare penny, even most of his modest inheritance, so that someday his son could attend the university in Glasgow to become a lawyer. Education and personal wealth were the only ways to save Glen Kinloch, John often said; if the laird could guarantee their well-being, the people of the glen could remain in their own homes, tending their livestock and brewing whisky for their own use, without the need for smuggling.

For generations, Dougal knew, Highlanders had been forced from their homes due to the greed of wealthy men who often were not Scots, but bought acreage and overran the hills with wool-producing sheep or turned land into shooting preserves. Clan chiefs with funds could save their lands—but Glen Kinloch was a small, poor lairdship.

So dry books and neck cloths would be part of Dougal's future: in a few short years he would go to the city university and leave the glen, and all he loved, behind. Until then, he attended the little glen school whenever there was a dominie—currently they had a sour-faced man hired by Kinloch, who personally paid his fee. Quick to learn but disinterested, Dougal preferred tending the herds and fields with his father; even more, he liked the excitement of the smuggling runs.

That particular morning, he looked forward to learning the Kinloch secret, a legend so closely guarded by each generation of the laird's family that Dougal had heard only part of the story; it involved the rescue of a fairy long ago, a fairy promise, and the gift of a recipe for a magical whisky made only by the lairds of Kinloch. Now he would learn the rest.

"Come ahead, lad," John whispered, and led Dougal up the steep hill. Trees crowned the ridge, and far above, the mountain peak loomed through the mist. "Look for the markings that show the way." He paused, gesturing toward the ground.

Dougal knelt where clusters of heather sprigs were thick and newly green, not yet blooming where they spread over earth and gray rock. "What marks?" he asked.

"Fairy footprints. See, just there." John pointed. In the pale rock were marks of tiny feet marching all in a row, heading up the mountain.

Dougal blinked in awe. "Did the Fey come by here?"

"May have," John answered. "The fairies leave their mark wherever they walk or dance, and their footprints show the way to fairy places. Only a few can actually see the marks."

"I see them. You do, too."

"The MacGregors of Kinloch have the gift, and we know the secret of this place. Come ahead." He led the way upward.

The sky was lighter now, the rock walls of the hills rising to one side, and to the other, the vast expanse of the glen below looked like a bowl of mist. Dougal looked around. "Da—can the revenue men find us up here?"

"Not in this fog. And the gaugers rarely come up this high, being Lowlanders too weak for the climb."

"But I feel as if someone is watching us."

"It is only the mountain fairies. The Fey will not harm us. Come up to me," John said, beckoning as he helped Dougal climb over a cluster of boulders.

A glint on the ground caught his attention. Seeing a small, shining stone, Dougal stooped to pick it up. The crystal was of the sort called cairngorm; its peaty color glowed in the soft dawn light.

He dropped it into his jacket pocket and walked on. "Da, tell me again about the gift."

"The Kinloch gift? Long ago, the first laird of Kinloch and his wife were walking on this very mountainside, when they came upon an ailing fairy woman, about to give birth. They delivered her babe and gave her a dram of whisky made in their own still. Later her husband visited and gave them a gift—the secret of making a magical brew."

"Fairy whisky," Dougal said. "A magical brew that men would kill for."

John huffed. "Your uncles have been speaking out of turn again. True, our *uisge beatha* is legendary, and the secret of making it is known only to the lairds of this glen, who guard it at any cost. Others covet this whisky and would have it—but Kinloch's fairy brew must never be sold for coin. Only sharing it freely will keep our luck with the Fey. You must remember that always, when you are laird."

Dougal nodded solemnly. "I will. It is never to be sold, only given away, and I will guard the secret with . . . my life."

"And remember this—great riches will come if ever the fairy whisky is sold, but greater consequences will follow. Besides," John said with a shrug, "our own Glen Kinloch brew is excellent stuff, and earns us enough coin to live by."

Now and then Dougal had a sip of their regular Glen Kinloch whisky, though he had never tasted the secret brew. "What is so different about the fairy whisky?"

"It has powerful magic, and must be sipped with care. Even a dram can bring on a sort of madness. Not all are affected by the magic. Some consider it simply an excellent whisky." He winked. "Look there."

Blinking in surprise, Dougal saw a small glade of birches tucked in a level place on the slope. Dawn light slanted through mist and trees as he and his father entered. Their footfalls crushed grass, and the only other sound was the keen cry of a hawk somewhere overhead.

In the pale light, Dougal saw a hazy glow of blue: thousands of bluebells were scattered along the ground in a dense carpet beneath the trees. Their delicate bells drooped gracefully on slender stalks as he and his father walked among them. Dewdrops shed on his legs and kilt hem. He had seen wildflowers in profusion, but never like this.

John MacGregor took a silver flask from inside the folds of his plaid. Handing that to Dougal, he withdrew two more flasks. "Now we will collect the fairy dew, which gives the whisky a special magic. First we fill three silver flasks, and when we pour it later for the brew, we will have captured far more than these three seem to hold."

Dougal looked dubiously at the swath of bluebells. "Collect dew from these wee flowers? That is impossible. And it is a task for girls," he added with disdain.

John laughed. "We do not take it from the flower petals. Follow me." He waded through the bluebells toward some birch trees, pushing aside flower stalks with his boot to expose a natural well in the ground. "There is magic here, so it is said."

The opening in the earth was as wide across as a laundry kettle, edged with rocks and crowded by flowers and grasses. Walking closer, Dougal peered down to see the dark reflection of the water. Natural springs like this were common enough in Scotland. He frowned, still doubtful.

His father circled the well three times, murmuring in Gaelic. Then he looked at Dougal. "Walk thrice round the well and ask politely for your dearest wish, and the fairies will grant it to you."

Dougal looked at him. "Have you done so before? Did it come true?"

"I wed my dearest love," John murmured. "I have a fine son."

"What did you wish for today?"

Smiling, John shook his head. "Your turn."

Thinking for a moment, Dougal then traced careful steps around the well. *I wish to be a brave smuggler like Da, not a dull scholar*, he thought.

John lifted his arms. "MacGregor of Kinloch is here!" he said. "I ask that you help us collect the magical gift promised me and mine long ago. This is my son, who will one day be the keeper of this well after I am gone."

Hearing the sound of rushing water, Dougal glanced down to see bubbles churning in the well. A spout shot upward, the water dancing with rainbows. In the mist rising from the well, small lights soared up, circling around him. He stared in awe and delight, feeling delicious chills run all through him, so that his hair and skin tickled.

"The lights!" he said, looking up as they seemed to encircle him, then his father, flitting about and swirling away like leaves on the wind. "Do you see them?"

"I do," John said. "They are sent by the Fey to tell us that they are here, and their magic is strong. I am glad that you see them as well."

Dougal glanced around. "I have seen them before, but I thought it was a trick of the sunlight."

His father smiled. "Sometimes it is just that, and so we must look carefully to determine if it is indeed the Fey, with a message for us, or a gift of magic."

Then he dropped to one knee to fill his flask at the water spout. Dougal knelt and did the same, tipping the flask while the water leaped inside. When the three silver flasks were full, the bubbling spout subsided, and the tiny rainbow lights faded, too.

John stood, Dougal with him, and the carpet of flowers closed to cover the well. "And that," John said quietly, "is the magical fairy water that is used to make *uisge beatha an Kinloch an sìth*, the Kinloch fairy whisky."

Dougal nodded, feeling almost reverent. "Where are the fairies? I saw none." He had hoped to see a few, having no idea what they looked like.

"The Fey are here. The lights told us that. If they wanted us to see them, they would have appeared.

Now listen, and remember. Circle the well three times to make your wish, then ask the Fey to bring up the water. Fill three flasks, and always leave a token of thanks." John plucked a silver button from his jacket and set it beside the little spring.

Having only wooden buttons on his jacket, Dougal reached into his pocket for the small crystal he had found on the slope, leaving it beside the silver button. His father nodded in approval, and they turned and left the glade to walk down the steep hillside. As the sun rose higher, the mist burned away to reveal the long green glen with its meadow floor and sparkling river like an unrolled ribbon. Cozy houses were tucked in the hills.

"What did you wish for, Da?" Dougal asked as they neared home. Kinloch House, the old stone tower where he lived with his father, his aunt and uncles, and his little sister, Ellen, rose up from the low-lying fog, its stone crumbling at the edges, ivy softening the places where stones had broken. The place was three hundred years old and always needed repairs, but Dougal loved its familiar, quirky flaws.

"My wish?" John MacGregor shrugged. "I asked that my son be Kinloch's finest and best laird someday, so that he could save the glen from any harm to come."

"But Da," Dougal said, "you are the best laird the glen has ever had."

"I wish it were so, lad. What was your wish?"

"To be like you," Dougal said.

John laughed. "Go ahead now," he said. "Tell

your aunt Jean that we have returned with the fairy dew. Tell her to start baking and cooking, for we shall have a celebration. Tomorrow we will spread fresh barley to sprout, and begin our first batch of fairy brew together."

Months later, John MacGregor was pistol-shot by revenue officers in the evening and died at midnight. The laird of Kinloch had been carrying four kegs of whisky in panniers on the back of a pony when the excise men had seen him. A known smuggler, he was given no chance to explain before he was shot down. He had not died defending his people, or even while trading Kinloch's fine brew. Instead he had traded his life for a few casks of inferior peat reek whisky. The kegs were not smuggled; they were meant as a customary gift to the manse and the reverend.

His father's unfair end troubled Dougal deeply, giving him nightmares in the darkness and hardening his heart during the day. He alone knew that his father's wish at the fairy well had come true: the son was laird of Kinloch now.

In the years that followed, knowing that he could never become the finest laird—John MacGregor had been that—or the educated and wealthy gentleman his father had dreamed of for his son, Dougal found another way to honor his father as fiercely as the man deserved.

He became a smuggler the likes of which the hills had not seen for generations.

Chapter 1

April 1823
Loch Katrine, Scotland

"**D**id you hear that?" Patrick MacCarran glanced up the long Highland slope as a gust of wind stirred the tail of his dark frock coat, and sent a few loose pebbles scattering. "I'm sure I heard footsteps over the rocks somewhere above us."

Standing beside her brother, Fiona turned to look around and then up the steep hillside toward the towering mountain, with its limestone cliffs and dark scrub. "Bogles," she said. "Haunts or fairies. Or small stones shifting along the slopes in the wind."

"Or smugglers," he muttered. "Had I known we would climb so far into these hills in search of your rocks, I would have brought a firearm."

"I thought smugglers only came out at night."

"They're men, not bats," Patrick drawled. He walked away, looking around as if he suspected criminals to be hiding behind the boulders and tall trees farther up the hillside.

Fiona turned, looking down the slope toward Loch Katrine, which edged one side of Glen Kinloch, where she intended to stay for a couple of months as a teacher in the small local school. From her vantage point, the smooth surface of the loch was misted over, and fog drifted in patches over the hills that nudged against its shores. Here on the upper end of the long loch, the hills were remote and rugged; where the small glen met the loch, the landscape was beautifully wild. Fiona wanted to linger and explore further, but she knew that Patrick had scant patience left after the lengthy afternoon stroll they had taken.

And he seemed distinctly uneasy. She frowned, watching him. For the last few months, her youngest brother had acted as an excise officer at the distant southern end of Loch Katrine; now he seemed alert to trouble everywhere he went. Being a government agent in the Highlands had matured his character quickly, though she was grateful that his true lighthearted nature remained.

"Surely it was the wind, Patrick," she said.

"Or free traders evading customs officers such as myself," he said, inclining his head. "Fiona, are you ready to go back yet?" Sounding hopeful, he picked up her canvas knapsack to carry it.

"Not quite. I've found some excellent trilobites here, and I want to keep looking." A cool updraft lifted the ribbons of her gray bonnet and made the skirt of her gray woolen gown, pale as the mist, dance over her ankles and the tops of her leather boots. Raising a gloved hand powdered with dirt and rock dust—her cheeks and nose were no doubt dusty, too, but she did not mind—Fiona turned to look at the Highland slopes that surrounded them. The hillsides were brown and dreary, their spring greening only just begun, and the air had a wintry nip. Another gust of wind made her shiver slightly, and she glanced around. "This place is so . . . remote."

"Exactly. And that makes it is easier for smugglers to slip cargoes of their whisky through the hills down to the lochs and rivers," he answered. "I have said this before, but I do wish you had not been so eager to stay in this glen for the next few weeks. There are rogues about, I guarantee it."

"I have promised to teach here," she said. "And I intend to fulfill my part of the conditions in Grandmother's will."

"Those clauses may prove the bane of all of us, but for James," Patrick said. "Come back with me—you could be back in Edinburgh by week's end. You know Eldin would lend his barouche if you needed it. Our cousin has always been fond of you, when he seems to dislike most people."

"I do not need his charity or his barouche. I will stay until summer with Mrs. MacIan."

"Mary MacIan can barely see or hear, talks endlessly, and drinks whisky like a man."

Fiona laughed. "It is acceptable for Highland

women to take a dram with the men, or even on their own, as she does. I think she is a delightful sort, and quite unique."

"She's no fit companion if you mean to walk the hills around here. Promise me you will not wander about alone. There are rascals about in this god-forsaken place."

"As an officer of the government now, you suspect a smuggler at every corner."

"Not without reason," he said quietly. "I am concerned for your welfare."

"As I am for yours," she pointed out. "I know you were bored as a Signet clerk in Edinburgh, and that you were willing to take the risks when you were appointed as a customs officer along Loch Katrine. Sir Walter Scott confided to me, the last time we had supper together with Aunt Rankin before I came north, that the work of pursuing smugglers is stressful and dangerous," she went on. "And so as your older sister, I worry on your behalf."

"But I rather like the adventure of it. I've learned a good deal in my apprenticeship months here. And the region is populated with rogues, remember that." He frowned at her. "In the ten miles or so of Loch Katrine's length, from the southern end up to this more remote area near Glengyle, most families run private stills."

"Anyone can produce whisky, up to five hundred gallons or so; you told me so yourself. When we were small in Perthshire, there was a private distillery on the home farm to supply the estate. Father very much liked the brew they made," she said, glancing away as she made a rare reference to their father, who had passed away years ago, along with their mother, leaving the four children—the twins, Fiona and James, and the younger boys, William and Patrick—in the care of their relatives, as well as the overbearing guardianship of Lady Rankin, their great-aunt, on whose estate Fiona presently lived, just outside Edinburgh.

"Home distilleries are not the issue. The dispute is that most still owners manufacture far more than their allotted amount, and smuggle thousands of gallons a year for export, avoiding the taxes posed by the Crown."

"A few smugglers would not be interested in a glen teacher."

"Unless she wanders the hills and interrupts their business," he pointed out. "I promised our brothers that I would keep an eye on you."

"No need. I came here to teach, just as I have done in other glens." She drew herself to her full height, taller than most women, though not nearly as tall as her brothers. "I will be fine."

Patrick twisted his mouth awry, then nodded. "Very well, but I want to hear from you often. The mail runs out of here once or twice a week."

Fiona nodded. "Reverend MacIan reassures me that the glen is safe and quiet, and that the tenants are fine, hardworking shepherds and drovers, and farming families. Not smugglers."

"Those farmers raise barley crops and make

whisky. Did he mention that hardworking Highland men are free traders by night, moving cargo
on pack ponies and carrying loaded pistols through
these peaceable hills?"

"He said nothing of the kind," she said, and
walked farther up the slope, while Patrick followed. She stepped carefully over turf, looking
down at the rocks as she went.

"Nor would he. Even Mrs. MacIan remarked
today that whenever the laird is on the mountainside, it is wise to keep away. Best to take heed."

"I suppose she meant that the laird of this glen
is a disagreeable sort," Fiona said.

"One of the more notorious smugglers in this
part of Scotland is called the Laird," Patrick explained. "He is laird of peat reek whisky only.
The actual laird of this glen is a Mr. MacGregor,
I believe, who raises sheep and cattle and makes
whisky on the side. Just beware any mention of
this laird of peat reek. The law has been looking
for that sly lad for years."

"Peat reek? Is that the poisonous variety? The
whisky we tasted at Mrs. MacIan's was rather
nice, I thought."

"It was excellent. I see you are determined to be
stubborn about this," Patrick went on.

"I am not worried—I shall not encounter any
smugglers or peat reek lairds. I am just a glen
teacher. Oh look!" Fiona knelt again to study a section of rock, dusting it clean with a cloth. "What
a nice little ammonite fossil," she said, pointing to

a curled shape impressed on the rock surface. "I believe there is a massive limestone bed beneath this hill, with deposits of graywacke along with the Old Red Sandstone layer, with liberal evidence of a great, ancient flood. I cannot wait to tell James about it." She rubbed at the rock with a gloved finger.

"Your geological babble is lost on me, but James will love it. Fiona, sorry, but I must get back soon. I have a dinner engagement at Auchnashee. Perhaps you can explore here with James when he returns."

"James and Elspeth will be in Edinburgh for another month or so." Her twin brother, James MacCarran, Viscount Struan, was an accomplished geologist and professor of natural sciences, while Fiona considered herself a mere amateur with a keen interest in fossils. "He must finish his lecture series for the university before he and Elspeth return to Struan House. They want their child to be born in the Highlands rather than in Edinburgh, later this summer. Struan House is but a half day's drive from here, so I hope he will visit me here. I know you will be too busy to see me often—and I do not want you to feel anxious about keeping watch over me."

"We do have a good deal of work now, with the new laws in effect. Smuggling continues full pace along the loch, despite the changes in regulations."

"I thought the recent laws were going to make

your work easier." She stood, brushing her skirts with gloved hands.

"Nothing is ever as simple as we hope," Patrick said. "Taxes were lowered to create less incentive to smuggle whisky out of the Highlands, and the government has recruited hundreds more revenue officers to catch offenders in the hills. Penalties are stiffer, too—if a still is found and dismantled and no owner comes forward, the laird of that land is held responsible, regardless of his involvement. But I suspect many Highlanders enjoy the risks of free trading too much to stop altogether."

"I am sure they do, given their tendency to ignore authority," Fiona said, smiling a little; secretly she had always enjoyed the vein of rebellion that ran through Highland history. "You will be kept busy at the other end of the loch, so do not fret about me up at this end. And do not expect me to visit you, either. Cousin Nick's refurbished hotel will be lovely for tourists who visit the romantic Highlands, but I do not care to see him any more than necessary."

Patrick nodded his understanding. "I do not have much choice, since he's offered me free rooms at the hotel. And tonight I am invited to dinner with him and a few Edinburgh businessmen to discuss plans for the hotel. Did I tell you that Nick has decided to become a revenue officer?"

"What!" Fiona widened her eyes. "Nicholas MacCarran, Earl of Eldin, stooping to regular work? I cannot imagine it. He is far too concerned with his own comforts, and has grown too arrogant by far. I doubt he even cares if others break the law, so long as they leave him be. Nick cares about Nick," she added. "It was not always so, sadly, but after his family perished when he was away at school, he was no longer the lad we knew. But a law officer? Never!"

"It is a formal title only. He paid a fat sum for it, and will rarely ride out on patrol. He wants a veneer of authority here, and the Crown needs the money. This is a reminder that it does not do to trust the Earl of Eldin too far."

"Sad, really." Fiona sighed. "I liked him so well when we were children. But if we do not meet the collective conditions in Grandmother's will, Nick will inherit the bulk of the estate. You are right to watch him carefully." She walked onward, Patrick beside her. "I'd like to gather a few fossil samples higher on the hill before going back to Mrs. MacIan's house."

Patrick glanced behind them toward the loch. "Mr. MacDuff arranged to take me back by boat within the hour." He frowned. "But it does not do for a gentleman to escort a lady on a nature walk and then desert her on a hillside."

"But a brother can leave a sister if she insists that he go." Smiling, heedless of her skirts, she knelt once again on the damp turf and brushed at the dirt on a rocky surface.

"I know you find the old rocks interesting, but I think you will not discover here what you truly want to find."

"True, there are no fairies under these rocks." Fiona laughed ruefully. "I do wonder how I can possibly fulfill Grandmother's request to find real fairies and sketch or paint them for the book James has been putting together from her work. She wanted me to continue my charitable work, and that I can easily do. But fairies—and her order that I marry a wealthy Highland husband—well, it seems almost mad."

"Perhaps you should just leave here and return to Edinburgh. We can contest the will. I plan to talk to Grandmother's advocate, Mr. Browne, and to Sir Walter Scott, too, about that."

"Sir Walter says it is sound. If we do not meet those clauses, everything goes to Nick. It is quite simple, but quite . . . extraordinary for the four of us." Fiona stood again, facing Patrick.

"We could manage without the fortune," he said. "It would be easier than finding spouses with fairy blood, or drawing sprites and so on. Just invent some images and have done with it," he urged. "None of us would blame you if you decided to do that."

"When I make a promise, I keep it, no matter what. You have said almost nothing about what the will asked of you—nor has William said much."

"I am not eager to admit that I must find a fairy bride by order of my grandmother," Patrick replied. "And William, being a physician, must guard his reputation or be labeled a quack. He is supposed to collect spells of fairy medicine, or some such."

"James was fortunate to accomplish his request, but it was a wonderful coincidence that he met and married a woman who can claim fairy blood in her family. As for the rest of us—"

"May we be half so lucky. Fiona, I intend to oppose the will, if you and James and William will agree that we have a case. Then you need not go searching under flower petals and rocks for fairy creatures."

"Either way, I must stay here. I have agreed to teach at the glen school. The Edinburgh Ladies' Society is relying on me. No one else could take this teaching assignment."

"No one else wanted to come up here, Fiona."

"But it is a lovely place," she murmured, glancing around at the misted hills and the long, rock-studded slopes that ran toward the loch. "Sometimes I think I cannot bear to exist as another spinster in Edinburgh, attending charitable meetings and social gatherings, gossiping, netting purses, and finding silly ways to fill time. This charitable work is interesting, even adventurous, and I do need to make something of my life," she added passionately. "Something that does not involve netting purses and pouring tea!"

"We have all seen that the Edinburgh Ladies' Society for—what is it?—oh aye, for the Education and Betterment of the Gaels, has been good for you these past few years."

"True, and they are genuinely dedicated to helping Highlanders. I care very much about that cause," she murmured.

"They were genuinely delighted to find a lady who is not only fluent in Gaelic, but willing to travel to the back of beyond."

"If not for those opportunities, I might have given in to grief . . . after Archie's death," she said.

"Not you," he said. "You are a hardy soul."

Fiona shook her head in gentle denial. Not even her family knew how close she had come to succumbing to perpetual near-widowhood; she had been so young, and Archie had seemed to be everything to her. But now she knew better, and she would not make the mistake again of giving herself over so completely to someone, only to be abandoned when death took him, as it had taken both her parents when she and her siblings were all quite young.

"I've had marvelous opportunities to travel the Highlands to do my teaching, and have a wonderful hobby in the fossils—oh, Patrick, it is getting late," she added. "Go! I promise to return to Edinburgh by summer, with or without the fairy drawings."

"Or the required wealthy Highland husband?" Patrick lifted a brow.

"I can hardly find one of those here, or anywhere in the Highlands. I am a few years older than most, a spinster with dull academic interests—not much of a catch. Nor are there many wealthy Highlanders left, with what Scotland has suffered over the last century."

"You are a lovely girl, and you have rejected every suitor who has been interested."

"They are interested in what I might inherit. Otherwise, I am the sister of a viscount and the niece of a viscountess, and lack a fortune without that inheritance. Being no one in particular, I am unlikely to find a wealthy husband at all. Nor do I care about it particularly." She lifted her chin.

"You refused a marriage offer just last Christmas."

"I felt no spark toward the man," she said. "Nor was Sir Walter impressed with him, either. You know Sir Walter is convinced that we can all do what Grandmother asked of us. He was such an excellent friend to her, and to us. She truly believed that the old MacCarran traditions of fairy magic can be restored if we marry spouses with fairy blood."

"Nonsense, however well meant," Patrick said, "is still nonsense."

Fiona nodded and looked out over the hills, the breeze stirring her bonnet ribbons. "It is beautiful here. So mystical. Here, I could believe any legend."

"So could I," he said. "Well, I had best go, while you go on looking for fairies under rocks."

"Or at least fossils in rock. They will help prove the new theory that a catastrophic flood brought primeval waters as high as the level of these mountains."

"Enough," Patrick groaned, then set her knapsack on the ground. "I will leave this with you.

Please be careful when you walk back to Mrs. MacIan's cottage—and all the while you are here in Glen Kinloch."

"I will." She kissed his cheek, and he turned to depart, waving a hand.

Watching him for a moment, Fiona then bent to retrieve a small hammer and chisel from the canvas knapsack. Kneeling again, she angled the chisel point against a pale rock and smacked the handle with the hammer until a chunk split away.

Grandmother's intentions were good, she thought as she wrapped the piece of stone in a small cloth and tucked it into the canvas sack. But it was not so easy to find a Highland husband with a title and fortune, as indicated by Lady Struan's will. Besides, Fiona thought, she had managed to recover from the grief of losing her fiancé, Archibald MacCarran, her cousin and chief of their Highland clan. Eight years earlier, Archie had died a hero on a bloody field of Quatre Bras the day before Waterloo. Her twin, James, had been left with a permanent limp after the same battle. She, too, carried scars from that day, hidden in her heart.

Since then, she had pragmatically accepted her situation, though secretly she still dreamed of a husband, a family, a home in the Highlands— dreams lost along with her fiancé.

Perhaps her grandmother had wanted Fiona to find happiness again. *But I'm perfectly happy*, Fiona thought, brushing her fingers over another rock. Well, she was fine, at least.

No magical solutions involving fairies would help this MacCarran find the bliss of love again. After all, that was what she had lost—love's magic.

Enough, she told herself; the afternoon light on such a misty day would soon fade. She hefted the hammer and chisel again to resume her work. A few minutes later, she lifted her head, feeling a strange prickling along the back of her neck, as if she sensed someone watching her. Then she heard a sound like a crisp footfall.

"Who's there?" she called, looking around. "Patrick?"

Her voice echoed in the mist, echoing softly. Shivers ran down her back. No matter how she might dismiss such things, she secretly believed in the possibility of haunts, bogles, and fairies. Everyone thought of Fiona MacCarran as practical, calm, capable, neither a dreamer nor a fool.

But she was not as dull as they thought. She had private dreams and precious hopes, though she tried her best to accept her life as it was now.

Turning, she glanced around the empty hillside, realizing then how far she and Patrick had walked. The long loch was visible far below, and limestone cliffs towered above the hills, which were crowned by wreaths of mist. The day was dreary and cool with a silvery light—the atmosphere was beautiful, eerie, and lonely.

Just then she saw a glint among the rocks, and even thought she saw movement. Gasping, startled, she paused—then told herself the gleam came from the varieties of rock crystal so common in the area. The cliffs, she was sure, were primarily limestone and sandstone, and would house not only tiny crystalline structures, but many fossil remains.

Did the hills also hide fairies, and handsome, rich Highland lairds ready to sweep her away? Then perhaps her grandmother's spirit would feel pleased, and Fiona could help her brothers earn the fortune they needed far more than any of those dear fellows would admit, even to one another.

She had work to do, and fairies to seek out. Smiling a little, shaking her head in bemusement, she lifted her knapsack to her shoulder and walked onward.

Chapter 2

The woman moved like a dream through the mist, lovely as a fairy sprite in a gown and bonnet gray as the fog. Just a glance told him that she was all he could ever desire in a woman— graceful and beautifully shaped, with a mysterious allure that could endlessly fascinate a man. With such a woman, the days, and the nights, too, would be filled with the happiness that had so long eluded him. He wondered who she was—and how quickly he could convince her to leave the hillside, and the glen.

Dougal MacGregor, laird of Kinloch, leaned a shoulder against the cave entrance and looked down, watching the young woman take the steep slope upward to where the foothills met the great, dark mountain. Inside the cave behind him was a valuable cache, and within arm's reach, a loaded pistol with which to protect it. He stood still and silent, breathing slowly, waiting.

Whoever she was, he had to send her away from the mountain and Glen Kinloch quickly. She had come too far into the foothills, and wandered still higher, though her companion had left not long ago. For a moment, Dougal wondered what sort of fellow would abandon a lady in the wild hills of Kinloch, where rogues even worse than the laird of Kinloch roamed, day and night.

The lady must be a willful creature indeed; observing their conversation earlier, he had noticed how earnestly the young gentleman tried to convince his companion to go with him. She seemed to steadfastly refuse, sending the lad on his way, preferring for some unknown reason to remain so that she could collect and chip away at rocks. He did not know the lady, but the man had looked familiar—

"The new gauger," he muttered under his breath. The Lowland excise officer, whose name he could not recall, had accepted a post at the lower end of Loch Katrine. Dougal had seen him once or twice in the town, without meeting him. Why would that fellow escort a lady into these hills? Every customs officer in the region knew that whisky-smuggling scoundrels lurked here.

Being one of the worst of those scoundrels, Dougal frowned. Whatever had brought the couple into the hills overlooking Glen Kinloch, he would bet it was not tourism.

With a charming disregard for her skirts, the solitary young woman now sank to her knees and reached into the knapsack, taking out a small hammer. She struck hard at a pale rock, breaking off one or two pieces efficiently. *Chink, chink, thunk* echoed over the mountainside.

Bemused by the incongruous sight of a lovely girl wielding a hammer with such a sure hand, Dougal reminded himself that she had no business here—especially if she knew a customs man. He wondered briefly if she might be the teacher his cousin, Reverend MacIan, had hired for the glen school. Like others in the glen, he expected an older woman to arrive in the next week or two; he had not seen Hugh lately to learn the status of that.

Narrowing his eyes, he watched her. The young woman was no tourist enjoying the scenery; her path had purpose and her glances were observant. She dropped to her knees to examine the ground, then took a small notebook from the knapsack on her shoulder, and made notes or sketches.

If she and the gauger were spying in the area, that was of great concern. An accurate map would enable excise men to locate caves and niches where valuable goods were hidden.

Gaugers—and willful young ladies—had to be prevented from sketching and exploring here, Dougal thought. He would have to dissuade her, and quickly.

The girl headed upward again, lifting her skirt hems over sturdy boots—she was serious about her hill walking, he saw, having dressed for the occasion. Her path brought her closer to where he stood in the recess of the cave. In her fog-colored dress, with its jacket and bonnet of darker gray,

with her nimble grace, she seemed part of the mist
and the rock.

For a moment, Dougal thought of the sylphlike
fairy folk, the *Daoine Sìth* said to inhabit the hills
and hidden places throughout Scotland. If he possessed a romantic nature, which he did not even if
he allowed for fairy magic, he could believe she was
part of the magic in the hills he loved so much.

But he had seen the ones who inhabited the hills,
and she was none of those. Earthly, she was, and
beautiful. In that moment, she removed her bonnet
and looked up at the mountain.

Dougal pulled in a breath. That plain bit of hab-
erdashery was unworthy of her, he thought. Her
oval face was as serene as a Renaissance Madonna,
her features delicate, her eyes large. The dark
gleam of her hair was pulled smooth to frame her
face and coiled in heavy braids at the back of her
neck; he wanted to loosen that thick silk and sink
his fingers into it.

But he could not let his thoughts go there. The
sooner she left, the better for all.

Easing away from the cave entrance, Dougal set
out down the hill.

Absorbed in her work, Fiona knelt without heed
for the muddy splotches on her skirts, and uncaring
that breezes played her hair into loops that spilled
to her shoulders. Instead she focused her attention
on what she saw impressed in the rock under her
hand. Sweeping gloved fingers carefully over the

rock, she was pleased to find more excellent preservations of the exoskeletons of several tiny trilobites, the little sea creatures whose preserved tracks were clear evidence that the area had been covered by water, long ago.

"James will be so pleased," she murmured to herself. Using the hammer, she tapped all around the section with the traces. Limestone by nature was grainy and soft, as rock went, and the piece broke away easily enough. She tugged it free.

"Miss." The male voice was deep and rich, and startled the very devil out of her. Gasping, she looked up. A man stood on the rise above her, one booted foot propped on a rock, and his kilt draping over powerful thighs. Leaping to her feet so quickly that she almost tripped, she grabbed the protruding edge of a boulder before she could fall.

"Who—are you?" she asked breathlessly.

He stepped downward, moving through a thick veil of fog, and he extended a hand toward her. "Come up to me," he said, beckoning with his fingers.

Fiona gaped. Just above her on the steep, rocky slope, he looked fierce, powerful, and wholly not of this earth. Tall and dark-haired, dressed in a kilt of muted dark tones with a brown jacket, he was the very image of a Highlander from a century ago, as if he had stepped out of time. His legs were strong and well made, swathed in thick stockings to his flat knees; chestnut-brown hair sifted in waves to his shoulders, and his jaw was dusted with the shadow of a dark beard. His eyes, narrowed beneath straight black brows as he glared at her, seemed greenish.

"Who are you?" she managed again, heart pounding. She had heard stories of the *Sidhe*—an ancient fairy race of tall, magnificent beings. They sometimes appeared to humans, even stole them away. James's wife, Elspeth, claimed that her own grandfather and father had been taken by fairies, but Elspeth was a charming storyteller, and no one really believed it.

But as Fiona stared up at the handsome stranger who had appeared out of the mist, beings of the Otherworld seemed all too possible. "Are you one of the Fey?" she asked tentatively.

He gestured again with long, nimble fingers. "Miss. Come up to me."

She stepped back again, her gaze never leaving his—somehow she could not look away—and then she turned to run. But she stumbled on the rocky terrain, and the Highlander stepped down and grabbed her arm. He drew her toward him, his grasp strong.

"Come with me," he said.

"No!" She pulled her arm away. "You would steal me away!"

"I would what?" He looked down at her, the steep angle making him seem tall as a giant. "Just who the devil do you think I am?"

"One of the, ah, *Sidhe*." Then she realized how foolish she sounded.

His chuckle sent shivers through her—delightful rather than dreadful, for his laugh was warm and enticing. "Not terribly likely," he said.

Fiona felt herself blush. The man was perfectly real, of course, and she looked a perfect idiot. "What was I to think when you stepped out of the mist like that, looking like a ghost, or a legend?"

"I would credit you with more sense. Have you never seen a Highlander wearing the plaid?"

"Of course," she snapped. "But you could have given me some warning of your approach."

"Beg pardon, Miss." He inclined his head, dark hair sliding over his brow, and looked amused. "I did not mean to startle you." He released her arm.

Setting her bonnet back on her head, she stepped away. "I must go."

"I think you must come with me." He reached out again, but she evaded him, bending to pick up her knapsack and hammer. Before she could turn and run, he stepped toward her and took her arm, drawing her toward him, his grasp at once threatening and somehow protective.

She gasped. "I am expected by my companions. They are looking for me even now!"

"Aye?" Clearly he did not believe her. He turned with her in tow and walked across the slope rather than downward. Alarmed, Fiona tried to break free, but his strong hand guided her, even half dragged her, along the hillside.

"Let go!" Still clutching the hammer in her free gloved hand, she struck at his forearm, and heard a bruising thunk as the iron hit thick wool over taut muscle.

The man swore in Gaelic. "Give me that," he said, snatching it from her to drop it in the pocket of his jacket. "I mean you no harm. I just want you out of here. The hills are not safe."

"I was quite safe until you accosted me," she said, stumbling along beside him. "You have no right to order me out of here."

"This is my glen," he said. "I am MacGregor of Kinloch."

"You own the glen?"

"It is deeded to me. And I do not permit tourists to wander the area."

"I am not a tourist, Mr. MacGregor. I was invited to stay in Glen Kinloch."

"Tourist or visitor, the terrain is treacherous but for locals who know the paths through the hills. Rogues and smugglers are sometimes about, both night and day."

"Such as you?" She looked at him. He had confiscated her hammer, but her bag held some hefty rocks that she could use for a weapon, if need be.

"Give me that knapsack," he said then, as if he had read her thoughts. He took it from her shoulder and then shook the bag, its contents clunking. "What is in here?"

"Rocks."

"Ah, from my own glen?"

"I will put them back if it disturbs you."

"Keep them. I do not care about rocks. If you

are searching for gold or treasure, there is none here. We would all be wealthy in this glen if so."

"I do not search for gold. I am an amateur fossilologist."

"A what?" He seemed distracted as he pulled her along. "Never mind. Come this way. It is a shorter distance to the road, and to wherever you are staying. Is there a carriage waiting to take you back to Auchnashee and the hotel there?" He led her onward.

"Auchnashee? No," she said. The man had the manners of a beast, she thought, and did not seem like any privileged landowner she had ever met. "You claim to own the whole of this glen, Mr. MacGregor? Then you must be an earl or a viscount, to possess so much land."

"I do not own it outright. In Scotland the land, but for certain regions, is owned by the Crown and deeded back to the Scots. I hold the inheritable rights to Glen Kinloch, but I have no fancy title such as you are likely used to in the Lowlands."

"I am not used to any such thing," she replied.

"Your father must be someone of note, I am sure, to have such a fine lady for a daughter."

"My father died when I was small. My grandfather was a viscount, which passed to my twin brother. It is not much."

"It is enough, and your family is fortunate for it."

"True," she admitted. "We are."

He paused, looking at her keenly, head tilted. His irises were a clear hazel-green, framed in thick lashes and straight brows of deep black; they were striking and beautiful eyes for a man, especially a brusque and roguish one. He nodded.

"My father died when I was a boy. My sympathies to you and yours."

"Thank you," she said, surprised.

"My father left me a plain lairdship with a house and some land. Kinloch is a small glen, far from the main roads and the civilized world. Earls and such—few of that sort would live here."

"I know one or two who might like it here very much. In fact, an earl has purchased the hotel down the loch at Auchnashee," she said of her cousin.

"So I have heard. Some buy land for their shooting lodges and sheep runs, and to attract tourists to gape at our homes and our hills. But I will not sell. If you think to tell your friends about this place, do not bother. Come ahead, and hurry."

"Why hurry? Is someone after you?" She glanced over her shoulder.

"Bogles, ghosts, and the Fey," he answered wryly. "Or perhaps smugglers."

"Ha! Your own ilk." She dug in her heels and stopped again, forcing him to stop, too. "Give me my things and I will trouble you no further." She pulled, but he held her arm. "There are rogues here, so I understand, led by the laird of the smugglers, or some such. Are you one of his men?"

"If I was, would I say? Have no fear of me—I am only warning you to leave the hills now. People, especially tourists, do not venture through this part of the glen late in the day or evening, without reason."

"What is your reason?" she persisted, curious, despite the risk of a direct question; the answer might reveal something she was better not knowing.

"Since I own the land, I have the right of it. And you?" He tipped his head politely.

"I came out here to search for . . . fossils," she said. "The imprint of ancient flora and fauna left in masses of rock. They provide a geological record of the earth."

"I know what fossils are," he said, sounding impatient. "You can study those elsewhere in Scotland, not just here, just now. Come."

Tugged along by his strength, hurrying in his wake, Fiona concentrated on her path, for the terrain was rugged and uncertain. Thin, drifting mist obscured the way as they hurried along.

MacGregor stopped then, his fingers tightening on her wrist, and Fiona stopped, too. Hearing the clop of horse hooves and the rattle of a cart, she turned her head, trying to determine the sound and its direction through the fog.

"What is that?" she asked.

"A pony cart," he answered. "It is coming along the drover's track that runs from the slopes down to the road that runs beside the loch. This way," he said, tugging her along again, so that her booted toe hit a rock and she stumbled.

MacGregor caught her around the waist, and she fell against him, off balance. He felt so solid and sure that she leaned against him, but reason prevailed and she straightened away. He pulled her along over hillocks and stones, then stopped short, so that she bumped into his back. She paused with him, her shoulder pressed against his.

"Hush." He turned his head warily, fingers tightening on her wrist. Sensing danger, she moved closer to him, gazing about as he did, feeling blinded in the fog, which was deeper farther down the hill.

To the left, she heard the rumble of the cart, and then it came into view—a boxy wagon stacked with hay, pulled by a sturdy brown horse. Two men sat on the cross bench, one in a plaid, one in trousers, both in nondescript jackets; dark, flat bonnets were pulled low over their heads. The driver was a lean young man, his passenger robust and older.

"Are they farmers?" she asked. "Or smugglers with a load of illicit spirits?"

"Riding along a main road like that? Going home to supper, most like."

"I hear that smugglers go about day or night quite openly. And it is nearly twilight." She glanced at the fading light through the fog.

"Those are my kinsmen. Farmers and herders like me, and most of the glen folk."

"Not dangerous then?"

"Not to us. But those fellows, on the other hand—" He stopped.

MacGregor was looking in the opposite direction, and now she, too, glanced there. Far along the loch road, two men emerged from the fog. They wore dark jackets and trousers and stiff-brimmed hats. One of them carried a heavy object, either a pistol or a cudgel. Fiona gasped.

"Smugglers!" She edged closer to MacGregor. He exuded a reliable sort of strength, despite all. Strange though it seemed, she felt safe near him.

"The men walking along the road?" He sent her a quick glance. "Gaugers."

"Revenue officers? Then we have nothing to worry about."

"Aye," he drawled. Taking her arm in a new grip, he led her down the slope. Seeing the cart approaching from one direction and the king's officers from the other, Fiona angled her steps toward the men who would know her brother.

But MacGregor tugged her in the other direction. Then he gave a low whistle and began to hurry forward, rushing Fiona with him.

In that moment, she realized that the laird of Kinloch was not the upstanding landowner he claimed, but the smuggler both Patrick and Mrs. MacIan had warned her about. *Whenever the Laird and his men walk the mountainside*, Mrs. MacIan had said, *we all keep away*.

The Laird. Now Fiona wished she had heeded the cautions she had heard.

Too late, she told herself. The Laird himself had found her.

Chapter 3

MacGregor stopped short, and the girl bumped into his shoulder. He set his hand firmly on her arm, wanting her to know that he did not intend to release her. Not yet.

Narrowing his eyes, he estimated the king's revenue men to be two miles or so along the loch road. From the slope's high angle, he could see them, although he was sure that the mist and odd angles of the slope and jutting rocks would obscure their view of the two standing on the hillside. They probably had not yet seen the cart, but soon enough they would hear its creaking noises and look for its approach.

Taking the girl's arm, Dougal ran with her toward the road.

"Let go," she said breathlessly. "The excise officers will take me to Mrs. MacIan's home."

"I will see you back there myself. You would not be safe with them."

"I am hardly safe with you," she pointed out.

He whistled again, a soft trill like a curlew's call,

and the squeak of wheels slowed. His comrades knew his call. Dougal hurried down the slope with the girl in tow, and headed for the cart, where his kinsman rode on the cross bench.

"I do not need a ride—" she began.

"Hush," Dougal said, dragging her along toward the rumbling cart. The road curved around the base of the hill, and he could not see the men on foot. Good, he thought; they would not see the cart, either. Not yet, at least.

The vehicle rolled to a quiet halt in front of them, and Dougal nodded to the driver and the older man beside him, all the while pushing the girl ahead of him.

"Miss, this is Ranald MacGregor and his son Andrew. My uncle and cousin," he told her. "And this is, ah . . ." Then he realized that he did not know her name.

"Fiona MacCarran." She turned to his uncle and cousin and smiled so warmly at them that Dougal suddenly, sharply wished she would bless him with a smile like that. Instead she sent him a furious glare.

"Miss MacCarran," he said. "Into the cart. Now," he added, low and fierce.

She blinked. He had not noticed the color of her eyes before—they were a sparkling blue. Looking at her, he felt something essential and intangible within him shift somehow—and become a need, a craving. He frowned and offered his hand.

She ignored it and extended her hand to his

kinsmen. "Gentlemen, how good to meet you. I am Fiona MacCarran of Edinburgh, come to Glen Kinloch to teach at the glen school."

She had not introduced herself to him so sweetly as that, Dougal thought, scowling.

"Ah, the new dominie! And a bonny one, too." Ranald's hand looked like a paw closing over her slim gloved fingers.

Andrew, at fourteen easily struck dumb by a pretty girl, nodded. "We thought you'd be old and ugly, miss," he managed, blushing.

"She's neither of those, but she is a problem nonetheless," Dougal snapped. "Hurry, all of you." He took the girl by the waist, his hands fitting the taut shape. "In you go."

"No," she said, as he dumped her over the side into the hay.

Dougal tossed the knapsack inside after her and set a foot to the hub of the wheel to leap inside. Kneeling on the hay, a hand on the girl's shoulder, he saw his kinsmen gaping at him. "Gaugers on the road," he told them. "Two of them, a league or so away."

"Och!" Ranald said. "Hide! Cover yourselves with the old plaid that is back there. If they see the teacher with us, they will want to know why."

Dougal snatched a folded plaid in the cart bed and tossed it over both of them. As the girl gasped out in surprise, he took her by the waist and pushed her down beside him in the hay, pulling her close under the covering.

She shoved at his chest. "What are you doing! Let me go!"

"Soon. You are safer with us than with those gaugers."

"Even if one of them is my brother?" She pulled away.

"Ah, just as I thought. Your brother is the new gauger down the loch."

"You may regret holding me against my will." She shoved at him; Dougal caught both her hands in one of his and peered out from under the blanket.

"Do either of you recognize the gaugers up ahead?" he asked his kinsmen.

"They are too far away," Andrew answered. "What does it matter?"

"We have the sister of the new excise officer with us," Dougal answered.

"Och," his uncle growled. "That's trouble for us, then."

"What sort of trouble?" the girl asked in Gaelic.

"Hush," the three men said in unison.

"Keep her hidden, and yourself as well," Ranald said. "I see them coming now. Andrew, take the reins." Dougal felt the cart lurch as the horse stepped forward.

Dougal yanked the blanket over his and the girl's heads, and settled beside her under the sudden darkness. "Hush," he told her, his face close to hers in the darkness of the woven covering.

"I will not hide from my own brother, or his

men," she said loudly, and began to struggle, so that the blanket slipped from both their heads.

Click. Hearing a gun latch, Dougal glanced up to see a glinting barrel not far from his head. Ranald waved the pistol in his hand and looked at them, silvery eyebrows lowered over dark eyes. "Lass, no word from you, and do as the laird says."

"What the devil—" Dougal began.

"Mr. MacGregor," Fiona MacCarran told Ranald in a cool, clear tone, "put that pistol away." She spoke in Gaelic, and sounded eerily like a teacher Dougal had once had: a stern and lovely creature whom he had unabashedly adored.

He saw his big, beefy, fearless uncle hesitate. "Begging pardon, miss, but I mean to make it clear. You must hide and do as the laird says, or there will be difficulty," he answered in the same language.

"I will not hide. Those are officers of the law, and surely friends to my brother. And you are clearly scoundrels—indeed, smugglers," she added.

Dougal sensed a hot spark of indignation in her, saw the snap of anger in her eyes, heard it in her voice. Impressed with her ire, he might have debated the nature of gaugers versus smugglers with her—she seemed disposed to like one and not the other—but for his idiot uncle waving the pistol about. "Ranald, set that thing down!" he said.

In the next instant, Fiona MacCarran grabbed her knapsack and swung it hard enough to knock the weapon out of Ranald's fingers. Snatching the bag away, Dougal fell across her to hold her down, while Ranald swore, shaking his hand, and Andrew leaped out of the cart to grab the pistol. He jumped back to the bench to take the reins, while the horses sidestepped uneasily.

"Och, that's an excellent lass!" Ranald crowed as he stashed the gun under his jacket. "Go, Andrew—go!" His son slapped the reins and the cart rumbled onward.

"Are you mad, both of you?" Dougal pressed Fiona beneath him, one leg thrown over both of hers, while she writhed. "Uncle, what the devil was that for?"

"Sorry, Kinloch," his uncle replied. "I thought she would make trouble for us."

"And so she has," Dougal drawled, while the girl still pushed against him. "Stop. That pistol could have gone off and killed someone!"

"Then he should not have pointed it at me," she said.

Sighing, he shifted his weight off her, keeping her legs under his, holding her down with his arm stretched over her full bosom, his hand on her arm. Her breath heaved under his entrapment, and he closed his eyes for a moment; she was damned distracting, he thought.

"What do smugglers care about killing?" she asked. "Kidnapping and murder, smuggling and breaking the king's law—it is nothing to such as you."

"Ruthless, we are," Dougal drawled. "Blackguards, we three."

"Wretches," she agreed.

"Och, we are not so bad," Ranald said over his shoulder. "Not so bad as gaugers."

"So you say," the girl replied. "Others would say the opposite."

"Highland whisky smugglers," Dougal pointed out, "are not bad sorts, but often decent men interested in correcting bad governmental regulations."

"Correcting?" she asked. "Blatantly ignoring!"

"Most Highland whisky makers are only acting upon their born right to do as they please with their own damned barley," Dougal said. "The English Crown has no right to tax any product made from barley that a man grows himself, on his own land."

"It is hard to argue with that," Ranald said over his shoulder.

"And revenue men are only trying to earn an honest living and uphold laws that they believe in," the girl answered.

"Honest living! Ha," Ranald grunted. "Dougal lad, the lassie is Scots, is she not? She speaks the tongue of the Gaels. She should understand our natures as well."

"I do," she insisted in Gaelic. "I do understand and appreciate the Highland nature."

"If so," Dougal said, "you would not feel safer with customs men who would willingly take a life for the price of a bottle of the barley brew."

"So you *are* smugglers," she said.

"I never said so. But I promise you we are no

friends to gaugers who conspire to profit from the fees the government will pay them for bottles of whisky taken from Highland men."

"My brother is a fine customs officer, interested in bringing criminals to justice."

"If I were you," Dougal said, "I would not go about telling Highland folk about that brother."

"Keep it quiet for sure, in these hills," Ranald said over his shoulder. "I, for one, do not want to hear it again."

"Kinloch, the king's men are just ahead on the road," Andrew called back.

Yanking the blanket over his head and the girl's, Dougal slid down as flat as he could. "Stay quiet and still," he told her tersely, and lay back in the straw with the girl pressed tightly against him. Like lovers, he thought, bundled and courting. He almost laughed.

"Beast," she hissed. "Scoundrel."

"This is for your safety as well as ours," he murmured. "We must get past those revenue men, and we cannot do that if you are seen with us."

"I shall scream," she said fervently, and opened her mouth.

He set a hand over her lips, over smooth, creamy skin, and leaned close to whisper directly into her ear. "Will you?"

She looked at him—he could see those wide blue eyes by the dim light filtering through the weave of the plaid—and attempted to scream, but for the press of his hand.

"Hush." He had no desire to frighten her. "Please—"

She bit his hand. He yelped, broke his hold, then clamped down again.

"Listen to me," he hissed. "We must pass this road without incident. It is for the sake of many, do you understand?"

She nodded, finally. Dougal kept his hand over her mouth, unwilling to trust her and wary of being bitten again. He tucked her into his arms, the only way to keep her from moving. A glimpse of her showed the fear in her eyes—and suddenly he could not look at her.

"You there! Stop in the name of the king!" a man's voice called out harshly.

The cart pulled to a stop. Dougal lay still in the hay, holding the girl against him. Warmth generated between them and built under the plaid. His cheek rested against her hair; her hand curled on his chest. He could feel her trembling, breathing quickly.

She smelled like rain and roses. Closing his eyes briefly, he savored that airy sweetness. A long while had passed since he had held a woman in his arms, at least one that smelled like heaven and felt like a warm, perfect fit for his very soul. He sighed, part yearning, part regret.

Then her elbow jutted in his side, and he grunted. She mumbled under his hand, and he shifted his fingers a breadth away, his body pressed to hers close as a lover. He felt her lips against his cheek, lightly moist, warm breath raising chills in him. "What is it?" he asked softly. "Do not think to scream."

"Let me go," she whispered, "and I will not tell them you are smugglers. You have my word, I swear."

"That is what we call a fairy's bargain," he said.

"A what?"

"It is never wise to trust a stranger, especially a beautiful, charming woman who holds a man in her thrall." He began to place his hand over her mouth, but she pushed at his hand.

"Do you know much about fairies?" she asked quickly.

"Some. Shh," he murmured, finding the question odd. He covered her mouth again.

"Stop in the name of the king!" The shout echoed, closer this time.

Dougal froze, and felt the girl do the same. He held her tight, improperly so, his leg wedged between hers, her skirt wadded between their bodies. He waited, sensed she did, too. The plaid covered them both, but he rolled over her just enough so that she could not be seen, even if his shape could.

"Who are you, and what is in the wagon?" one of the revenue men called out.

"MacGregors from north of the glen," Andrew replied.

"Kin to the MacGregors who carry illicit whisky about these hills?" one man demanded.

"I do not know who you mean."

"If we ever caught any of them, we would recognize them," the other revenue man said, snorting in laughter. "They are a slippery lot."

"Sir, there are many MacGregors in this glen, and all around Loch Katrine. We are only bringing a kinsman to the healing woman in the hills above Drumcairn. Old Hector MacGregor from up the glen side is in the back. He is very ill."

As Andrew spoke, Dougal knew he should play the part of Hector, an elderly uncle who lived at the other end of the glen. He groaned a little and coughed.

"Don't believe the lad," one revenue officer said to the other. "They're rascals, the lot of them. Search the cart. You two sit there, and do not move or speak to each other."

"My father does not speak much English," Andrew said. "I will have to translate and explain to him what is going on here."

Hearing heavy footfalls, Dougal realized that the revenue men stood beside the cart bed now, no doubt staring at the blanketed form in the hay. The girl tensed beneath him, and he lay motionless with her, his breath brushing the soft curls along her brow.

"Aye, there's a man there under the plaid," one of them said. "See his boot."

Dougal coughed, adding an ugly groan at the end.

"Damn," the other man said. Thumps sounded,

and then came the rustling of straw as the gaugers poked dangerously close through the straw. Dougal moaned again and made a sort of retching sound.

"Drunk on his own peat reek," one of the men growled. "What else do you carry besides that drunken rascal? Kegs of whisky that we should confiscate?"

Ranald growled in Gaelic to Andrew, who answered and then addressed the officers. "Not everyone moves peat reek about, sir. My father takes offense to be so accused."

"Until we find crocks and kegs under the straw, eh?"

"We're carrying only hay and one sick old man," Andrew answered. "Hector is not drunk. He's ill, and we mean to get him some help."

"They're all thieves and liars in this glen," one of the officers snarled. He thumped the bottom of the cart bed so hard that Dougal knew, by the sound, that he used a gun butt or a cudgel.

Dougal emitted an unearthly groan, even to his own ears. The men cried out and must have jumped back. One of them barked something to Andrew and Ranald.

"I would not be touching him if I were you," Andrew answered.

"What's he got?"

Ranald muttered again to Andrew. "Fever, sir," Andrew said.

"That's nothing. Get him up. Let's see him."

"*Tinneas-an-gradh dubh,*" Ranald said quickly.

"Tinnie-gra-doo . . . what is that?" an officer demanded.

"It is the Gaelic for a terrible sickness," Andrew said. "He has had the *tinneas-an-gradh dubh* before, but not so bad as this. Please do not touch him, sir," he added hastily, when one of the men stepped closer.

Dougal coughed again, loudly, still clutching the girl to him. Her arms slid around him, probably to ease her position. Feeling her tremble against him, he rubbed her shoulder in reassurance, and felt her relax a little. Her bonnet tipped askew, and his lips touched the soft shell of her ear. She sighed beneath his hand, and shifted in his arms.

The movement was sultry—they were so damn close, he thought—and feelings rocketed through his body that required immediate suppression. He drew his hips back a little from her. She glanced up at him in the darkness of the plaid over both of them, and he stared into her eyes.

For a moment he could have forgotten where they were, what they were doing—who he was, and what he had promised himself about women, as if there was magic in her gaze. But he could not allow himself to be so distracted, not now, with king's men standing so near.

"Tinnie what? I've never heard of it," one revenue man said to the other.

"They're lying, so they can get illegal whisky past us. Search the cart."

Dougal knew the men had the authority to

search the cart, and everyone in it. The excise officers acted as deputies of the law, specially charged
with apprehending smugglers and collecting their
illicit goods, usually whisky, from which the officers could collect fees that made up the greater
part of their wages. Therefore the incentive to find
criminals throughout the Highland regions was
strong, and encouraged by the government. Dougal
frowned, listening.

"Sir, *dubh* means 'black' in Gaelic," the other
revenue officer replied. "Black something. It seems
bad. We'd best keep away, Mr. MacIntyre."

Dougal frowned. Tam MacIntyre was known to
be a tough, even cruel law enforcer, who had lately
been promoted to chief revenue officer at the other
end of the loch.

"*Tinneas-an-gradh dubh*," Ranald repeated.
"Bad."

"Bad, see," Andrew said hastily. "Mr. MacIntyre,
sir, we must pass. Only one woman can help Hector,
and we must get there. Please, he is suffering."

MacIntyre paused. Dougal felt the tension in the
silence. "Go on, then," he growled. "But if you see
that rascal Dougal MacGregor, tell him I am looking for him."

"I have not seen him for a while," Andrew said.

"He's probably out roaming the drovers' roads
with a load of peat reek," MacIntyre said.

"He has never been caught out at such a thing,"
Andrew said. "He is a fine laird, caring after his
glen and his tenants, his cattle and his fields."

"And his barley brew? Just tell him we've discovered another still up the glen side. We've dismantled it, but we do not yet know who owns it. The new law states that any illegal still found on a landowner's property is the fault of the landowner, regardless of who owns or runs the still. The punishment and the fine could be Kinloch's to bear on this one."

Ranald murmured something and spat.

"In English, you old goat, I know you speak it," MacIntyre said.

"The reverend hired a teacher to come to Glen Kinloch to teach us English," Andrew said. "Perhaps my father will learn it then."

"You need no teaching. You're a slick-tongued otter, and I do not trust a word you say."

Dougal coughed again, wretchedly so. MacIntyre's companion swore. "Let them pass, sir. If the old man dies here—"

"Very well," MacIntyre said. "But tell all your kinsmen and friends that we are watching them. We have more men, and new laws. Highland smugglers will not get away with their crimes so easily as before."

"Good evening sir," Andrew said abruptly, and snapped the reins. As the horse stepped forward and the cart lurched, Dougal kept his arms wrapped around the girl. His face was close to hers under the cover of the old blanket. He heard Andrew and Ranald talking, and then Ranald laughed outright.

"Kinloch, did you hear?" Ranald asked over his shoulder.

"I did," Dougal said. "Be quiet, you two, until we are far away."

"*Tinneas-an-gradh dubh*," Andrew repeated, hooting. "The black lovesickness!"

"Aye, the black lovesickness is upon him," Ranald crowed. "He's got it bad!"

"It will slay him for certain," Andrew added with exaggerated seriousness.

"We'd best see the lass home to save the laird from the lovesickness," Ranald said.

"Enough," Dougal called gruffly. Holding the girl in his arms, he knew she listened intently. Then he realized that he still covered her mouth with his hand. Releasing his hand slowly, he felt her lips, warm and tender, under his palm. The sensation brought sudden desire, hot as flame. He looked at her in the shadows under the plaid, and was sure that her breath came faster, as did his.

"I did not know that *tinneas-an-gradh dubh* was such a plague in this glen," she said in perfectly intoned Gaelic.

"When a beautiful lass visits from the city and leaves the laird brokenhearted, it is the black lovesickness for him," Ranald said.

"You are enjoying it far too much," Dougal said.

"So you've had this plague before," the girl observed.

"Not so often as my kinsmen would have you

believe," he drawled quietly. She laughed, and he heard the reluctance in it, as if she did not want to enjoy any of this, or relax, and yet she did. He smiled a little in the dark, feeling some of that reluctance himself, and aware of its irony.

"The road is clear ahead, but best keep under the blanket until we stop, Dougal."

"Aye." Dougal ducked fully under the plaid, pulling it high over Fiona's head as well.

"I thought your name was Hector," she said.

"Hector MacGregor is my great-great-uncle, who claims to be a hundred years old."

"The officers would have thought Hector to be in perfect health, if they had seen you."

"So they would." He chuckled. "But Hector says it is the fairy magic that keeps him young, so perhaps they would not be so surprised as you think."

"Fairy magic? What do you mean?" She tipped her head, close to his.

"It is said that the MacGregors of Kinloch know a few fairy secrets," he said.

"Do you?" she asked intently.

He shrugged. "More than some, and less than others."

"I find fairy lore quite . . . intriguing."

What he found intriguing was Fiona, he told himself. The feel of her in his arms, his body still stretched halfway over hers, the plaid cocooning them in warmth and strange intimacy; his thoughts were not on fairies, but on far more immediate and tantalizing matters. As the cart rolled along, every jolt and lurch brought him into contact with her, so that he felt increasingly on fire.

He was no boy to be aroused without control, and he was not one to take advantage of a pretty woman for the mere pleasure of it, discounting her feelings in the matter—but by God, he found it hard to endure her warm, firm body under his; her gentle, sweet breath upon his cheek; her heartbeat thumping in her throat so close to his fingertips along her collarbone. He was tempted to pull her closer, taste her, caress her. But none of it suited his purpose.

Then he forced himself to remember what she had said, however odd the remark had seemed under the circumstances. "What is it you want to know about fairies?"

"I am interested in the legends and in sightings. Have you ever seen fairies and such?"

Dougal raised his brows, surprised by her question, particularly considering the situation. "Some of my kinsmen claim to have seen them here and there, and my father—" He stopped.

"Your father has seen them?"

"He is no longer with us," he answered abruptly. "Such strange questions," he said. "I would expect you to complain about smugglers, or at least ask about the school."

"That, too," she said. "But I am fascinated by stories of fairy sightings."

He watched her in the murky darkness beneath

the plaid, where her eyes glimmered like stars, and her breath was soft as a night breeze. "I am looking at a fairy creature even now," he murmured, "and she's the lovely queen of them all."

"That is just silliness. I am serious."

So was he. And just when he should have agreed with her and let it be, he felt her breath soft upon his cheek, and his ear; a devastating jolt of desire went through him—and in that instant the cart lurched and her body shifted against him, her cheek brushing his, her lips perilously close to his. And before he could stop himself, he kissed her.

Her lips softened under his, and her mouth gave way for a moment. Then she pulled away, her chest quickening where she pressed close to him. "Oh," she breathed, "oh—"

She touched her mouth to his then, so that he groaned low in his throat and gave in to the caress of her lips, the press of her body against his beneath the plaid, while the cart rumbled onward. No one but he and the girl knew what the blanket hid, or how one kiss tumbled full into another, as if some magic spell had taken hold of both of them.

He certainly could not account for it, could barely think. He was not drunk, in fact had been his usual sober and wary self that evening. Fully capable in mind and judgment, he was kissing this girl as if he had known her all his life, as if he had loved her forever.

The feeling was like a taste of fairy whisky, or the first burst of the sun at dawn—unexpected, nearly miraculous, something to be savored, something that could change a man within if he let it. When the kiss seemed to renew itself, he touched his tongue to the soft, moist tip of her own, and pressed his body to hers, hard and ready; he heard and felt her soft moan between his own lips.

Sliding his hand along the curve of her hip and waist, sensing the heat of her body, he shaped her luscious curves with his palm, and forced himself to halt. Yet her hands slid along his shoulders to his neck, and he felt her fingers thread into the thickness of his hair.

Slow, sweet, breaths warming, tender exploration—and then the rumbling cart slowed, and he yanked away from her, breathing fast, aware of the quick rhythm of her breathing against his chest. She turned her head away, and Dougal shifted to his side.

"Miss, I—" He hardly knew what to say, or what had happened. "I beg pardon."

She did not answer. He pulled the blanket aside and peered out.

And saw Ranald looking at them over his shoulder through the foggy darkness. "Mrs. MacIan's house is just there in the cove," his uncle said calmly. "We cannot take the cart down there in such a mist. But you can walk."

"Thank you, Mr. MacGregor." The girl spoke as she sat and pulled the blanket down. Hay bits were caught in her hair, and Dougal sat up too, stretching out a hand to pluck them free from her dark hair. He straightened her bonnet, which had slipped askew. Brushing hastily at her skirts, she did not look at him.

Dougal bounded over the side of the cart to the ground, and reached up to her, though she hesitated before finally accepting his assistance. Under his hands, her slim curves fit his hands, feeling so good that he wanted to hold her close again—but he let her slide to the ground. Both of them stepped apart in silence, quickly, as if they had been caught out at mischief.

"My knapsack," she said, turning, acting flustered. Dougal reached past her and grabbed the pack from the cart bed. Then he groped beneath the straw until he felt the hard shapes of the kegs hidden beneath the straw—the revenue officers had nearly discovered those. He drew out one ceramic crock wrapped in thick straw and tied with string. Tucking it beneath his arm, slinging the knapsack over his shoulder, he turned.

"Miss MacCarran, I'll escort you to the house," he said, gesturing for her to precede him. The fog was thick here, so near the water, and the twilight turned it to a sort of lavender mist. He could see the warm glow of brightly lit windows ahead.

She tilted her head, gazing up at him. He could still taste her lips, could sense his heart pounding, and wondered what she was thinking. Then she reached up to yank the knapsack from his shoulder, swinging it to carry it herself, the weight of the thing nearly knocking her off balance.

"No need to go with me," she said, and turned to walk along the road.

"Do not let her go, Kinloch," Ranald said. "She'll break an ankle in the dark and mist on the path in the cove, and Mary MacIan will be after us all to account for it. Ach," he added with a shudder.

"I am bringing Mrs. MacIan the whisky I promised her weeks ago." Dougal shouldered the keg as he turned to follow the girl. He was interested, more so than he could easily admit. She was certainly not just another dull teacher from the city, afraid of smugglers and everything else. She was not only young and lovely, but stubborn, independent, and intelligent.

Perhaps she could even be trusted. But he could not rely on that, or allow her to stay.

Even if he had discovered that she kissed like a fallen angel. Her lips had been sinfully seductive beneath his, and yet innocent as well. He deeply desired her, without question—but he could not bring a woman into his life. Not now, not yet.

Particularly not the sister of a Lowland gauger.

Chapter 4

❧❧❧

Through drifting fog, Fiona could see the cottage ahead, tucked below some trees. Water lapped and shimmered in the distance and mist drifted across the loch, ghostlike and lovely. She could hear footsteps behind her, and she turned to glance over her shoulder.

"I do not need an escort, Mr. MacGregor."

"Rogues about," he said, shifting the weight of the small keg on his shoulder. "And the path down to the cottage is uneven. You could fall, carrying those rocks."

"I can manage. What are you carrying, or should I ask?"

"A gift for Mrs. MacIan and her grandson, the reverend." He caught up to her, his strides long and sure and hers cautious as they left the road for the path into the cove.

"Was the cart full of illicit whisky, sir?"

"It was not my cart," he pointed out.

She sent him a wry glance in the dark. "I suppose you bribe others with whisky so that they will look away from what you and your kinsmen do in the glen."

"It is tradition for the laird to give whisky to the manse. I have a distillery on my estate."

"And you and your kinsmen are smugglers." Though so far he had not admitted it, the fact seemed clear enough to her. "But I will not speak of it to anyone. It is your own business."

"My *business*," he said, "is a licensed distillery. My uncles work with me. This keg holds some of that brew, which I bring to Mrs. MacIan whenever a new batch is ready."

"So the cart was carrying whisky to be shared with others."

"What else would we do with it, Miss MacCarran? Smuggle it, with the law all around?" He sounded amused.

"Mr. MacGregor, I have a bargain for you," she said impulsively. "I promise not to speak of what I have seen, if you promise to never—"

"Never what? Kiss you again?" He stopped, as she did, and she looked up at him through thick, foggy darkness.

"That . . . will not happen again, regardless," she sputtered. She did not fluster easily, and disliked showing any vulnerability. "It is not in my character to behave so."

"Nor mine."

"What about the black lovesickness? Your uncle said it has plagued you before."

He smiled. "And you believed him?"

"I thought it might be true, especially since you stole a kiss from a woman you do not know."

MacGregor leaned forward, so close that she felt his nearness like a rush all through her. "I was not the only one doing the kissing."

Fiona caught her breath. What he said was so true—she could not forget that kiss. Now he hovered near enough to kiss her again, yet did not. Blushing hotly, she stepped away.

"About our bargain, Miss MacCarran," he began. "We could arrange something. If you will consider keeping the evening's adventures to yourself, I will consider . . . never kissing you again."

"Oh," she said. "That sounds like a fairy bargain." As the man chuckled, Fiona glanced toward the cottage and saw the door open, golden light glowing around the dark form of the woman who stood there. "Look, Mrs. MacIan is at the door."

"And gone again," he said, as the door closed once more.

"She must not have seen us out here," Fiona said. "No need to walk me to the door. I can take the keg, too. It is not so large."

"Not large, but heavy."

"I am stronger than you think."

"Aye so." He seemed thoughtful more than amused. "Allow me to play the gentleman."

"Why now, when you did not before?"

"Och," he said teasingly. "Mary MacIan would have my head if I sent you home loaded like a packhorse. And if she knew the rest of it," he added softly, leaning forward, so that a quick shiver went through her, "she would have my head as well, if that is a comfort to you."

"It is, actually." She smiled a little in the darkness.

"And that agreement we discussed?"

"I will think about it." Determined not to let his nearness influence her again, she turned.

"Not for long, if you please. Watch your step, miss, the fog is that thick." He held out a hand, which Fiona ignored as she walked past him.

Soon he was two strides ahead of her, and she watched his wide shoulders and the rhythmic swing of his plaid kilt above strong calves, and thought how wanton she had been in allowing that intimate kiss—and how hungry and fervent she had felt as she returned it. She could not let her impulses lead her astray again, though her heart beat even harder as she considered the possibility.

"Mr. MacGregor," she called.

"Kinloch, if you please. Dougal, if it pleases you more."

"Kinloch," she said firmly. "Let us agree to forget what happened this evening."

"All of it?" He turned to walk backward for a moment, the keg casually propped on his shoulder. "I will remember some of it always, Miss MacCarran."

So would she. "Come now, it was of no consequence to either of us. But if we agree to keep silent about that, and about the free traders out on the road with the laird himself, we will all benefit. The MacIans might be shocked to know."

He shrugged. "Tell them or not, as you like."

"Reverend MacIan would go to the authorities."

"You could try to convince him," he said.

"Do you mean that the reverend is involved in this, too?"

He turned to walk beside her. "Surely your brother has told you that the free trade is common throughout the Highlands, and is found in Glen Kinloch as well. Those who are involved keep it to themselves, and those who encounter it . . . wisely look away."

"So everyone in Glen Kinloch is either a smuggler or knows a smuggler."

"We are hardly a nest of criminals here, Miss MacCarran. The people of this glen are fine and honest folk, and do what they must to survive."

"You seem to be warning me to look away as well."

He paused beside her, and she halted, too, noticing how dark and compelling his gaze seemed in the misty light. "Take it as a fair warning," he murmured. "Your kinsmen work on the side of the law, which will not sit well with the residents of this glen."

"Only one of my brothers is involved with revenue collection, and he is not assigned here."

"Only one? How many brothers do you have?"

"Three. One is a physician in Edinburgh. My twin brother and a cousin of ours both have estates in this part of the Highlands. In terms of Highland hospitality, I believe that makes me less than a stranger here. Besides," she added, "I was invited to come here."

"You have other kinsmen here, besides the gauger?" he asked quickly.

"My twin, James, Viscount Struan, has an estate southeast of here."

"Struan! I had heard that a Lowlander inherited the estate there." He paused. "Did your brother marry a Highland girl, by chance?"

"He did. Miss Elspeth MacArthur of Kilcrennan. Do you know her?"

"Her father, the weaver of Kilcrennan, is a distant cousin." He narrowed his eyes. "Twin brother, is it? You two will be close, then. No doubt he will visit you here."

"He has been in Edinburgh for some months. He is a lecturing professor."

"I see. And what of the cousin?"

"The Earl of Eldin. But we are not so close, he and I."

"Eldin is the one who purchased Auchnashee to turn it into a hotel." He frowned. "We have not met, but I have heard of him. So you are an earl's cousin, the sister of a viscount, and sister to a gauger as well." Frowning thoughtfully, he seemed to assess her.

"So you see, I have ties to the Highlands, as you do," she pointed out.

"Not quite as I do, I will venture to guess. When

were you at Auchnashee last? I hear the hotel is near ready, and is reserving dates for guests on holiday."

"I was there two days ago, and it is coming along. But I suspect it is not Eldin who most concerns you, but Patrick."

"The excise officer." He inclined his head. "Then I assume the gentleman I saw you with earlier was one of your brothers—unless you have a suitor here you have not owned to."

"Of course not. Patrick was walking with me. You saw us there?"

"I keep watch over my mountain and my glen. Where my gaze does not reach, others keep lookout for me." He smiled, but it had an edge. "I wonder if the reverend knew your brother was a revenue officer when he invited you."

"It never came up. Patrick's appointment came after I agreed to the post here. His jurisdiction is south, so you need not worry about that. But he will come here to see me—and to make sure I am safe," she added pointedly.

"Miss MacCarran," he said, "I will guarantee your safety."

Catching her breath at his deep, certain tone, she felt something indefinable, both pleasant and yearning, thrill through her. But she squared her shoulders. "I do not fear any danger in Glen Kinloch. It seems you are the one who needs to be cautious. The king's men were eager to find Dougal MacGregor."

"They know where I am if they want to talk to me. The excise men suspect me of much, but have never been able to prove anything. It is the price of being laird in a glen where, aye, some smuggling does go on. The laird is easy to blame for it."

"Ah. There is a smuggler called the Laird. You are he?"

"I am laird of this glen," he said.

"We were forced to hide while your kinsmen pretended you were another. If you are legitimately the laird of this area, why hide?"

"That was for your protection, Miss MacCarran, not mine. What goes on in this glen is no game. Sometimes the revenue officers are less trustworthy than the rogues they're after." He took her arm again, and she sensed earnestness in him, and intensity. "My kinsmen and tenants will not harm you, but other rascals do come through these hills, and it is good to be wary. If word gets about that your kinsman is an excise man, it could go ill for you, and your brother. I believe it is not in your best interests to stay in this glen, after all."

"Mr. MacGregor, I have been here but a day, and have been hauled about in a most uncommon fashion, threatened with pistols, and exposed to danger—and now you, the laird of the glen himself, want me to leave? Reverend MacIan invited me here through arrangement with the Edinburgh Ladies' Society for the Education and Betterment of the Gaels. And I have agreed—"

"The what?"

She repeated the name. "I have also agreed to teach for several weeks. School begins in a few days. I cannot leave." She drew a breath. "Too much depends on—" She stopped.

He rested a hand on her shoulder, slid his hand down her arm. Fiona caught her breath, feeling the same warm magic that had taken her earlier, capable of melting reason and resistance. He bent his head close to hers, and for an instant she thought he might kiss her again, so that she tilted her head back.

"It is best that you go," he said. "I will speak to the reverend myself. In the morning I will send a gig and driver to take you to Auchnashee. If there are expenses for your return to Edinburgh, I will cover them myself. You may keep the rocks," he added.

"You have neither right nor cause to dismiss me."

"As I have said, it is for your own welfare."

"I believe only Mr. MacIan can excuse me. And I intend to stay." She stepped past him, angry, even panicked—she could not leave the glen. She felt drawn to the place, and now strangely to its laird. And she had to fulfill at least some of the conditions of her grandmother's will, her stay in this glen being the best opportunity for that. "If you wish to protect your smuggling interests, certainly I am no threat to those. Do as you please." She spun away to walk toward the house.

"Fiona, wait." In that deep, mellow voice, her

name sounded different to her, beautiful and warm, in a way she had never quite heard it before. She turned, lured somehow by his voice, his use of her name. MacGregor reached her in one step and took her by the shoulder.

In the misty twilight, as he loomed over her, all else seemed to fade. Wildly, impulsively, she felt as if she were caught in the fairy realm, transfixed by one of the mysterious *Sidhe*. "Listen to me," he said. "This is not the time for you to be here. That is all I can say."

"I will not say a word about this evening. We need not even bargain for it." She stared up at him. Feeling his fingers flex on her shoulder, she leaned forward, could not help it. "That should satisfy your doubt."

"Nothing could satisfy—" He bent toward her. "Damn," he muttered, and pulled back as a woman's voice cut through the darkness and fog.

"Is that you, Miss MacCarran? Who is with you?" Mary MacIan's voice broke the spell that had held Fiona standing in place. She turned to see the elderly woman, once again silhouetted in the door of the cottage, with the firelight behind her.

"It is Fiona, Mrs. MacIan," she returned in Gaelic. "I will be there in a moment."

"It's Kinloch out here as well, Cousin Mary," MacGregor called. "I met your guest while out in the hills, and escorted her back."

"Cousin!" Fiona began walking, and he strode beside her.

"Certainly," he murmured. "We all know each other, and many are related, in the glen."

"Kinloch, you rascal! Come in, both of you," Mrs. MacIan gestured toward them. "Did you bring me a cask? Lovely lad! Is it the fairy sort this time?"

"Sorry, just the usual sort," he answered.

Fiona looked up, curiosity piqued. "The fairy sort of what?"

"Whisky," he murmured. "But that, I assure you, would be quite illegal."

"I want nothing to do with it," she said, and hurried ahead of him.

"Kinloch whisky of any kind is always welcome." Mary MacIan smiled, hands folded in front of her, face crinkling and pleasant. She was a tiny woman with a froth of white hair spilling out from her white cap; a dark dress hung loose on her small frame, and she wrapped a plaid shawl close around her bony shoulders. She stood back as Fiona stepped inside, and MacGregor followed, bending a little to clear the lintel as he entered the house.

Fiona set her knapsack on the floor, and Dougal MacGregor deposited the small keg on a table beneath a window. Standing in the small, simply furnished front room of the cottage, he seemed large, imposing, handsome, and magical. He looked at Mrs. MacIan and bowed his head.

"I am sorry, Cousin Mary, I cannot stay for long."

"Aye, there's gaugers about tonight," Mary said. "The lad was here earlier, and he told me about some officers on the road. Did you meet them?"

"We did. All is well. Give my best to the lad." He stepped toward the door.

"The lad?" Fiona asked.

"My grandson, the reverend," Mrs. MacIan said. "He promised to take you around the glen tomorrow afternoon, Fiona."

"How wonderful," Fiona said, looking at Dougal. "I am so looking forward to it."

"A pity, as Miss MacCarran will be leaving the glen in the morning," he said, gazing intently at her. Fiona narrowed her eyes in defiance.

"But she just got here!" Mary MacIan looked astonished.

"I did, and I just know I will enjoy my stay here." Fiona walked to the door and opened it wide. "Good night, Mr. MacGregor."

"Miss MacCarran." He inclined his head politely, then leaned to kiss Mary MacIan on the cheek. When he stepped outside, Fiona shut the door firmly behind him.

"I wish he could stay longer," Mary MacIan said. "Such a pleasant lad, is Dougal."

Fiona sighed, willing her heart to slow, her hands to stop shaking. The attraction she felt toward him was strong, insistent; yet she told herself it was only the result of an unexpected adventure in the Highlands with a handsome man, and the after-effects of a tender and dangerous kiss. He was a rogue, she reminded herself, and she would do well to avoid him during the time she spent in the glen.

"Och, the dog is barking outside!" Mary said. "She will have heard the laird and come running home again. She loves that lad fierce enough to follow wherever he goes. Has gone all the way to Kinloch House, she has, and he's brought her back. We must get her in for the night, as it may rain again."

Fiona heard Mary's dog faintly barking out in the yard, and she opened the door again. "Maggie!" she called. Peering through the darkness, she saw the black-and-white spaniel in the yard, tail wagging like a quill feather as she greeted the man who walked away from the house.

MacGregor paused then, bending to pet the dog. The mist swirled around him, and as he straightened and shooed Maggie home again, for a moment he stood, gazing toward the house.

Fiona grew still, too. She could almost feel his gaze upon her, and she wondered if he felt her watching him as well. Then he strode away, vanishing into the fog.

She lifted her chin. *I will not leave*, she thought. She did not want to go—already she felt a powerful bond to the glen, despite her strange encounter with the laird.

And no matter what he wanted, she had tasks to accomplish before returning to Edinburgh.

Maggie arrived then, jumping onto the step and over the threshold, her damp tail brushing Fiona's skirts. Stooping to pat her head and welcome her home, Fiona closed the door.

The silvery sheen of dawn woke her, and soon Fiona was pouring steaming cups of tea for herself and Mrs. MacIan. While Mary cooked savory sausages over the fire in the hearth, Fiona looked up, hearing a clattering of hooves and wheels in the distance.

"Is that Hugh, come to take you round the glen?" Mary asked. Fiona went to the door and Maggie launched past her. Stepping outside, Fiona gasped.

A black carriage drawn by two bay horses made the turn from the loch side road and took the earthen pathway into the cove. Wheels creaking, body heaving like a beast, it lumbered toward the kailyard.

"What is that noise?" Mary MacIan set the sausages on a plate and hurried toward the door. "It sounds like a coach!"

"It is." Fiona folded her arms, scowling as she remembered MacGregor's promise.

Mary peered over Fiona's shoulder. "That's the old coach from Kinloch House! It's hardly used—and that's Hamish MacGregor driving," she added. "He's one of the laird's uncles. What does he want here? Well, I am glad Kinloch is putting the old thing to use. That coach has been in the Kinloch stable a long while, ever since the laird's grandfather traded good Kinloch brew for it after a night of playing cards. But fine coaches are not meant for Highland roads," she added. "I wonder if it's carrying a load o' whisky—a coach would hold a good deal, and we'd all make a profit. Oh," she said, glancing suddenly at Fiona, as if she'd said too much.

"I believe Mr. Dougal MacGregor sent the coach for me," Fiona said. "He thinks the glen school does not need a teacher at this time."

"Bah, Kinloch knows how much we need a teacher," Mary muttered. Lifting the hem of her skirt, she stepped into the yard. The coach drew up in front of the house, shuddering to a stop, horses blowing and shaking their heads, thick creamy manes gleaming, the body of the vehicle swaying, its joints and brakes squealing.

"Hamish MacGregor, get down from that seat!" Mary shouted.

"Greetings, Mary MacIan, and I am not getting down," he replied. "I am in a hurry."

"Then I will pull your ears off next time I see you in kirk, for disturbing my morning and ruining my yard," Mary said. The coachman sighed and began to climb off the coach.

While Maggie barked and ran circles around the coach, Fiona called her back and walked into the yard. She waited in silence, lifting a hand to her brow against the morning sun, looking up at the silhouette of driver and coach.

"Good morning, Miss MacCarran," the driver said when he stepped to the ground, the coach's worn springs bouncing beneath his weight. He was a solidly built man of middle age, with a round, mild face and close-cropped silvery hair. He wore a flat dark bonnet, worn jacket, and wrapped plaid over old trousers—the shabby but comfortable outfit common to many Highland men. "I am Hamish MacGregor, uncle to the laird o' Kinloch, who sent me here." He doffed his bonnet briefly.

"Mr. MacGregor, I am Fiona MacCarran. Very nice to meet you."

"What's this about, then?" Mary pointed toward the coach.

"Kinloch sent me to fetch Miss MacCarran. He said she has decided to leave the glen. Pity though, with her just arriving, and we needing a teacher, but still if she wants to go, she shall. Miss," he acknowledged, tipping his bonnet again.

"It is no pity at all," Fiona said. "I am staying."

"Och, the laird will not like to hear that, since he sent me to take you to Auchnashee. Said you would be ready after breakfast. I will wait if you need more time to pack your cases."

"Thank you, but I do not need time," she said. "Please tell Mr. MacGregor of Kinloch that I am content to remain here."

"And tell him to put his coach to better use and carry whisky about in it," Mary said.

"Ha! And attract more attention from gaugers?" Hamish shook his head, then turned to Fiona again, his gaze stern and reproachful. "Miss, are you certain?"

"I am," she answered.

"These are Kinloch's best packhorses," Mary said, walking over to pat the noses of the lead horses, two sturdy bays with heavy white feathering around their ankles. "Groomed very fine, I see, with their tails and manes combed out."

"Aye, and with Andrew's help I greased the wheels and repaired the carriage so the lady could ride in comfort, and no embarrassment at riding in a plain wagon, as she did last night." He glanced at Fiona, who blushed. So he had heard about that; she wondered what else he had heard about last night, and from whom.

"Grease that old wagon all you like, Hamish MacGregor, you cannot make it a comfortable ride," Mary said. "Take it back to Kinloch, and let those horses out to graze. They are not used to harnessing. Just pannier baskets," she added with a twinkle in her eye that made Hamish chuckle.

"Och, very well," he said. "I will tell the laird, but he will not like it."

"Tell him that you did your best, and this is no fault of yours," Fiona said.

"And tell him he will see Miss MacCarran on the first day of school," Mary MacIan said. "The lad is visiting families in the glen to remind them to send their young ones to the glen school to meet the new dominie, Miss MacCarran. I will not tell the lad his visits were in vain!"

"So be it, then. Miss MacCarran, I am sorry to intrude," Hamish said.

"Not at all," she replied. "Will you have tea and sausages? We have oatcakes, too."

"And plenty to spare," Mary said.

"I would like that. And if I may, I will bring some back to the laird, as he likes a bit of Mary's cooking now and then."

"You will take some to him and Lucy, too," Mary said as she accompanied Hamish toward the cottage.

Walking behind them, Fiona wondered if Lucy was the laird's wife. At the thought, her stomach wrenched strangely, as if the name were unwelcome news. If he did have a wife, she thought, the man had been wrong to kiss her the night before.

And she should not have accepted it or enjoyed it; nor should she have dreamed of it at night, as she had done.

"Come, Maggie," she said, turning to whistle the dog inside—but the smell of sausages had already captured the dog's interest, as Maggie rushed past her into the house.

Fiona glanced again over her shoulder, hearing something distant and stirring—the sound of the bagpipes, she realized, but the fleeting melody had grown faint. She saw only the shabby old coach in the yard and two great horses nuzzling the grasses, the hills beyond bleak in early spring. A few sheep ambled, pale dots high on the steep slopes. Their shepherd no doubt played for them.

There, the sound came and went again. She stood for a moment listening, and gazing at the hills. But she saw no one—certainly not a tall, black-haired man dressed in a rumpled jacket and plaid who watched from a distance to see if she had boarded the coach. Likely the handsome, infuriating laird of Kinloch had just assumed that she would do so, and had gone about his day, which no doubt included something underhanded and illegal.

Well then, let Kinloch be surprised to find her still here, she thought as she shut the door firmly. He had no right to expect her to do his bidding, even if it was his glen.

Chapter 5

⎯⎯⎯⎯ ⚬❀❀⚬ ⎯⎯⎯⎯

Drone and melody filled the air, cresting off the mountain and returning fainter but richer, the sound soaring between the hills and out over the glen. It filled him inside, too, so that he need not think, nor stop again to look out past the glen to the loch side road where the coach must surely be rolling now, headed for Auchnashee with the lovely one he would never see again.

But he need not think about her now. Only the music of the pipes, its rich and layered tones ringing out in the air, should concern him now. As the last haunting note faded, he walked higher on the hillside, relaxed for a moment as the wind sifted through his hair. Then he drew breath, propelled air through the blowstick to inflate the woolen bag, inside which was a sheep's stretchable bladder— the set of bag and four chanters was old, having belonged to his own grandfather—and then he tucked the full bag up under his arm and set his fingertips flying over the holes along the main chant pipe. The tune was older than the bagpipe he played, and had been played in these hills by so many pipers over so many generations that the echo had a familiar ring to it, as if the hills themselves knew the song as well.

Dougal had always been a solitary sort of piper, playing mostly for his own listening, and for whatever sheep, cattle, mountain goats, and wandering locals happened to hear. He did not play at weddings or funerals, or for the monthly ceilidhs held alternatively in the two villages in the glen—Garloch at the northern end and Drumcairn at its southernmost point, with the lands of Kinloch, his own estate, set nearly halfway between the two, in the east. The two villages had longtime rivalries enough between them, such as ceilidhs, kirks, ball games, free trading, and fine whisky brews. The lairds of Kinloch had done their best to remain noncommittal. He remembered that his father had played for the people of the glen on local occasions, but he had rarely done so himself, leaving that to his uncle Fergus MacGregor.

Keeping apart from what went on in the glen was not a lesson he had learned from his father before John MacGregor had passed too soon—it was something Dougal had learned on his own, as a boy growing up a laird, with the faith and responsibility of many families on his shoulders. He had learned from his father to be loyal to those folks, and that faith he always kept, though he was not about to play the pipes for them. Truth was, he did not think he was very good at it, though he enjoyed it for himself.

He had learned a good deal from his father, and after John was gone, from his father's brothers, Ranald, Hamish, and Fergus, and from old Hector, too—together his kinsmen had taught Dougal nearly all he knew. He could credit the fine quality of Kinloch whisky to his father and old Hector; the playing of the pipes to the dark-haired blacksmith, Fergus; his knowledge of herding and husbandry to stodgy, calm Ranald; and an ability to fix almost anything that needed repair to Uncle Hamish.

Anything, that was, except that blasted coach, which had confounded both Dougal and Hamish's efforts. As soon as the thing seemed fixed, it began to shimmy and creak once again.

What was broken stayed broken sometimes, he told himself, and he was learning to accept that. But he would rather fix troublesome coaches than his own heart. Once broken, it stayed that way—first with the early loss of his mother, then his father, and finally a girl he would have married, who would have kept a neat house and a kind bed for him. But she had asked him to give up smuggling, and he had refused; and so she had left the glen to marry a shepherd.

And may she be happy with her four small children and her placid husband, he thought. He had learned, in the years since then, that he was better off without a wife.

He glanced toward the loch that stretched for miles beside the glen, with the pale ribbon of the loch side road running alongside it, visible for a long way in either direction. Pausing in the tune he played—the last note rang out like a lamb's bleat—he looked around.

The old coach was nowhere to be seen on the long stretch of the road.

Then he saw his uncle walking over a ridge toward him, with two dogs at his heels, the leggy gray beasts whose forebears had ambled the halls of Kinloch House for generations. Though they looked majestic and formidable, the reality of this lazy pair, Dougal knew, was nothing more ambitious than flopping in doorways. Yet Sorcha and Mhor were good guardians and amiable companions—and their presence now meant that Hamish had returned to Kinloch House.

"So you did not drive down to Auchnashee," Dougal said as Hamish approached. "She refused the offer."

"That she did." Hamish paused beside Dougal on the hilltop, stooped, and picked up a nearby stick, tossing it and hooting to the dogs. They watched the stick fly, then gazed up at Hamish, and settled at his feet. "Useless beasts," Hamish muttered.

"They know fetching only makes them look ridiculously obedient," Dougal said.

"That lass o' yours is not the least obedient," Hamish said.

"*My* lass?" Dougal laughed. "I did not expect her to agree—she has a prickly side—but on the chance she saw the wisdom in leaving the glen, I sent you with the coach. I take it we did not succeed in sending the lady packing." He glanced at Hamish.

His uncle shook his head. "She has a touch of the stubborn to her, like Mary MacIan herself. She could not have learned it in a day or two of visiting. It is natural to her. It is a waste of time and breath to tell her to leave when she intends to stay."

"Her brother is a gauger," Dougal pointed out. "He might bring his comrades into our hills. She has to go," he added quietly, feeling another twist of regret with the words.

"How, Kinloch? She is planning to open the school, and the reverend is going about telling all the families so. Mary told me while I was eating sausages there."

"Sausages?" Dougal raised his brows. "Mary MacIan gave you breakfast?"

Hamish took a parchment bundle from his pocket. "These are for you and Lucy, too."

Setting the bagpipe on the ground, Dougal unwrapped the packet and found several sausages and a stack of oatcakes. He ate a sausage, and the hounds at his feet stood, suddenly interested; he tore a bit away for each dog. "Mary has always been a fine cook, and these are excellent." He licked his fingers.

"The Lowland lady made those for you," Hamish

said. "Just before I left. She cooked more sausages after I ate some, and made fresh oatcakes and good strong tea, too. We three shared a fine breakfast. You should have been there," he added.

Dougal ate another sausage; it was seared, savory, and perfect. Though he wanted more, he wrapped up the rest to take home, and wiped his fingers on his plaid. "So she cooks, eh? That might be enough reason to keep her here."

Hamish chortled. "Wish we could, Kinloch, now that your aunt Jean has run back to her mother again, leaving the household to you and me once more."

"Jean would come back if you both were less stubborn."

"Bah. It's peaceful without her. The Lowland lass can cook. That is enough for me."

"Lucy is getting old enough to help."

"The girl has no interest in domesticity. It comes of being raised by scoundrels."

"We are not so bad," Dougal said. "Aunt Jean taught her to make her bed and keep her clothes neat, to sweep the floors, sew a seam, and cook a little. She learned well."

"She makes salty porridge and tea, and we cannot live on that. And she is too young to tend the fire in the hearth. She needs a mother. You might have married the shepherd's wife," Hamish added.

"She did not want me," Dougal said.

Hamish grunted. "Then you ought to marry this

Lowland lady, and we could have good sausages and more, and she would teach the school and keep quiet about her husband's free trading. And we would all be content."

"You have thought it out," Dougal said. "Jean could not have done better."

"For the sake of our stomachs, someone needs a wife in our house."

"Jean will return," Dougal said, knowing the pattern of Hamish and Jean's stormy, passionate marriage. "Miss MacCarran would expect us to fend for ourselves. It would help none of us if I were to marry a gauger's sister."

"Blast all gaugers." Hamish shrugged. "If she cannot stay, then she must leave. A pity the reverend invited her here now. Had he waited a few weeks, it would be different."

"Perhaps." Dougal bent to pick up his bagpipes. He and Hamish began walking, the dogs following. Aware that he wanted her to stay, he drew in a breath at the strong feeling—a surge of craving, even true need. He barely knew the woman, but the kisses she had returned to him had stirred him so deeply that he had not been able to forget.

He was not desperate for female companionship, he told himself. He dallied now and then with one girl or another—making sure each was willing, and each living beyond the glen. Usually he encountered girls in the larger towns, often the willing sisters or widows of acquaintances when he went with his kinsmen on cattle drives. But in truth, a while had passed. And this Lowland girl was something different, he knew that very well.

Scowling, he looked about for a distraction. Picking up another stick, he threw it. The two deerhounds seemed nonplussed. "Lazy beasts," he said.

"I know how to get the Lowland teacher to leave," Hamish said. "Let the fairies do it."

"What?" Like his other uncles, Hamish was tough as an old ram, and unlike them, was highly skeptical of local tales and fairies and such; his statement surprised Dougal. "I thought you did not believe in the legends of Glen Kinloch."

"Bah, nor do I. But we have legends and haunts enough to frighten any Lowland girl. We'll tell her all about Glen Kinloch's fairies and haunts and the like. She'll run back to Edinburgh, and we will carry on without a visit from the new gauger. But without a cook," he added.

Dougal huffed a laugh. "If I try to convince her to leave again, it would seem suspicious. Her brother would be here the very next day to ask what we are up to in Glen Kinloch."

"And we would have to deal with the ladies— what did Hugh call it? The Edinburgh Society for Ladies Who Fancy Themselves Better Than Highlanders, or suchlike."

"The Edinburgh Ladies' Society for the Education and Betterment of the Gaels."

"Wha's better than us?" Hamish said, and Dougal laughed. "What would scare that lass away from this glen, and none the wiser but us?"

"Very little," Dougal said. "She breaks rocks for amusement."

"*Tcha*," Hamish said, shaking his head. "We will tell her about the sprites who haunt the caves, or the tall ancient race of fairies who live in the hills, or the ghosts—"

"None of it will work. When she first met me on the mountain, she thought I was one of the *Sidhe* or a ghost. I only startled her for a moment."

"Bah," Hamish said again. "Then we will warn her of women stolen away by the fairies."

"Scaring her is not the way," Dougal said. "So do not take your scheme to the other uncles."

"We cannot risk the gaugers learning that we have a supply of whisky long aged, and more valuable than any cargo we have yet taken out of this glen. When we move that down to the loch, we do not need the sister of a gauger wandering the hills breaking rocks."

"True. I hate to sell that cache of whisky, Hamish," Dougal murmured.

"You have no choice. We have all agreed. The sale of that whisky can help you buy back the land that might be sold out from under us." His uncle looked hard at him. "Unless you wish to give up the fairy brew and earn a fortune, as some of us think you should do."

"Never," Dougal said. "My father honored the old traditions, and I will do the same."

"Fairies do not exist, Kinloch," Hamish said. "Your father honored old legends, and that's fine.

But he made a bad bargain that we knew nothing about until recently. Sharing the fairy brew for tradition's sake will not benefit the glen. Selling it will."

"I will not sell the fairy brew." Exhaling, he walked beside Hamish. "We will find another way to stop the risk to the glen."

"What if you told the teacher about the risk? She has a soft heart, that one. I could tell."

"How do we know that she could be trusted with the truth about Glen Kinloch? We have far too many secrets here."

"We do. But sometimes a man must give up one thing to gain something else of worth."

"Tell that to Jean's stubborn old husband," Dougal drawled.

Hamish snorted, and strolled ahead with the deerhounds bounding after him.

Thoughtful, Dougal walked behind them toward Kinloch House. He could think of nothing worthwhile enough to give up the Kinloch secrets. Nothing at all.

"Good evening, Grandmother. Miss MacCarran, how nice to see you." The young man entered the cottage even as he spoke, and removed his black-brimmed hat, bowing a little.

"My lad is here!" Mary MacIan smiled, looking up from setting plates on the table. "Hugh, you are just in time for supper."

"So I hoped," he said with a quick grin, and bent to kiss his grandmother's cheek.

"Mr. MacIan, greetings," Fiona said, crossing to take his black hat. "We have not seen you for a few days. Welcome."

"Thank you. I have been especially busy, though anxious to visit my grandmother and her charming guest again." Hugh MacIan grasped her hand for a moment, bowing, eyes sparkling. Dressed in the old-fashioned black frock coat and white neck cloth commonly worn by Free Church Highland ministers, he nevertheless was a handsome and robust young man; thick sandy hair sifted over his brow as he tilted his head, and his smile was wide and boyish. Yet the quick blush and fluster she felt at his smiling attention was nothing like the powerful reaction she had felt toward Dougal MacGregor during that undeniably exciting encounter, thoughts of which had preoccupied her at times.

"Did you ride far over the glen today, Hugh?" Mary asked.

"I did," he answered, "visiting the good folk to let them know that the school would begin again tomorrow. I rode from Drumcairn to Garloch, and halfway back again just to share supper with you." He smiled at her, then turned to Fiona. "Miss Mac-Carran, I believe I mentioned that I hold the living at the manse near Kinloch House, on the opposite side of the glen," he told her. "Garloch and Drumcairn are the villages at either end of the glen. My father, Rob MacIan, keeps the Knockandoo Inn by Drumcairn bridge, at the lower end of Glen Kinloch. He asked me to send his welcome to you, and invites you to visit the inn for a good meal at his blessing."

"I would be pleased to do so," she said. "There is much of the glen I would like to see."

"Miss MacCarran had an adventure the other night after you left here, Hugh," the old woman said. "Out walking in the mist, she met Kinloch, who brought her back safe."

"Kinloch! I am glad you are safe, Miss Mac-Carran," the reverend said. "He is an interesting fellow to meet on a dark night."

"I was never in danger," she replied. "I am quite accustomed to hill walking."

"You met Kinloch in these hills at night, and did not think yourself in danger?" He laughed. "We've a brave lass for our glen teacher, Grandmother," he added with a wink.

Fiona thought of Dougal MacGregor, who had not been far from her thoughts the last few days. Of course she knew the smuggler might be dangerous—he had nearly kidnapped her, and had kissed her to distraction before she had even known his name.

"I was collecting rock specimens on a hillside," Fiona said. "Mr. MacGregor offered to take me back in a cart driven by his kinsmen, and I accepted, for it was foggy and growing dark. They were traveling through the glen."

"Traveling?" the reverend said, with a glance at his grandmother.

"He introduced himself as the laird of Kinloch, so I felt safe." That was not entirely true—from the first moment she had sensed a risk unlike any she had ever known—not physical danger, but a threat to heart and soul, stirred by a kiss, a smile, a caress in the dark.

"When the Kinloch MacGregors are out and about in the hills, it is best not to notice them, or to know too much about their business," Mrs. MacIan said.

"We are not accusing the laird of anything," the minister said, "but you should be aware that the hills are not quiet at night. There are sometimes revenue officers and smugglers about. This area has some free-trading traffic, like many Highland regions. Nothing to be concerned about, really," he added.

"Thank you for the warning." Fiona turned away to stir another scoop of butter into the mashed turnips that she and Mrs. MacIan had prepared for supper. Both Mrs. MacIan and her grandson knew that Patrick was an excise officer at the other end of Loch Katrine. He had introduced himself as such to them when he had escorted Fiona to the glen. And now the MacGregors knew. She had not anticipated it being a problem, but she would be wary. "I will remember your advice in future," she told Hugh MacIan.

"Good, since you will be staying," Mrs. MacIan said.

The reverend looked puzzled. "Of course she is

staying. She has agreed to teach at the school until summer."

"Kinloch sent Hamish with that wreck of a coach to take her back to Auchnashee, where her kinsmen there could put her on a coach for Edinburgh," Mary said.

"Truly? Miss MacCarran, have you changed your mind?" he asked.

"Not at all. Mr. MacGregor of Kinloch seems to think that a teacher is not needed in the glen just now. We told Mr. Hamish MacGregor that it was just a misunderstanding."

The reverend frowned. "I shall speak to Kinloch."

"It is resolved," Fiona said hastily, as she moved dishes to the table.

"Will you sit for supper with us?" Mary asked her grandson. "There are mashed turnips and mutton stew, very tender. Fiona prepared it herself, and it is quite good."

He nodded and drew out the chairs for the women. When they were seated, they bowed their heads for the grace that Hugh MacIan murmured in a voice more suited to love poems than biblical sermons. Fiona served the turnips and the stew, and as they ate, she glanced around.

The room was the single room common to many Highland cottages, combining parlor, dining room, and the narrow kitchen space with a hearth wall, a cupboard, and a large wooden table. Two small bedrooms were curtained off along the back of the house, and a door between those led out to a small garden.

The house was small and modest but the table was nicely set with Mrs. MacIan's good things—crisp bleached linens, blue-and-white china, and silver pieces. They contrasted with the humble whitewashed and smoke-stained walls, and the old, dark rafter beams overhead, hung with dried herbs. The few pieces of furniture were of very good quality, she had noticed from the beginning—polished woods and velvet cushions—and the windows were draped with beautiful lace curtains in a Belgian pattern. Aware of the smugglers in the area, she wondered just how those things had been acquired.

Hugh smiled at her. "I hope you have cleared your, ah, misunderstanding with the laird, too, for you may see him at the glen school when your class begins."

"Oh? Is he—will he take the class?" Fiona covered her surprise "You did mention in your original letter to the Edinburgh Ladies' Society that there could be adult students in the school."

"There may be, since many in the glen do not have much English." He chuckled. "But not Dougal MacGregor. You will see him indeed. The schoolhouse is part of the Kinloch estate."

"Is it? The laird did not say so, when I met him."

"He keeps a good deal to himself, even something as small as that."

Fiona nodded, and passed the dish of turnips when the reverend requested more. She was astonished that Dougal MacGregor had said nothing to her of his connections with the glen school. But then, she realized, he had wanted her to leave the glen and abandon her obligation to the school—so he had no reason to tell her.

Later, as she drifted to sleep in the enclosed box bed, which she found quaint and surprisingly comfortable, she remembered again how good Dougal MacGregor's arms had felt around her—and how her lips had melded to his when he had kissed her under cover of the old plaid in the back of the pony cart.

And she knew why she had not protested. She had never felt anything so stirring and unforgettable, and she had not wanted that moment, or that feeling, to stop.

Best she forget about it and apply herself to what was real, including her responsibility to the school and her students. She had worked for days to prepare lessons. Unable to sleep now because of the path of her thoughts, she punched the pillow and settled back, ready to go over some vocabulary lists in her mind.

If she did see the laird of Kinloch again, as Reverend MacIan had suggested, then caution would be her watchword.

Chapter 6

❧

In the crystal-clear morning sunshine, Dougal stood in the yard of Kinloch House and looked out over the glen. He felt a sense of anticipation, a keyed nervousness he could not define. Neither the heart-pounding excitement of a smuggling run nor the lusty hunger of lovemaking, whatever it was set his heart thumping, his thoughts racing.

And though he would not readily admit it, he kept glancing across the hills toward the cove by the loch, and the paths leading from it, looking for Fiona MacCarran. She would be heading to Kinloch that morning to begin as the teacher in the glen school.

He could already see people walking through the hills from various directions, approaching the house, set on its hilltop perch in the lee of the pine-covered slopes that formed the bowl sides of the narrow glen. Even from a distance, Dougal recognized them, for they were all his tenants; their families had rented their holdings for generations from the lairds of Kinloch.

Mothers walked carrying their small ones or guiding them along, while the older girls and boys ran ahead; fathers came, too, those who had left their work for a bit. Some of the children ran, leaping runnels and rocks, while their older siblings came after them, no doubt told by their parents to act more sedately and to keep an eye on the younger ones. As they climbed the slopes from the glen floor, they walked past clusters of sheep grazing the slopes; some of the flocks belonged to Kinloch estate and some to the tenants, their flanks marked with blue or red dye.

The wind was cool and the sun bright, and Dougal lifted a hand to his brow. In mid-April, the slopes were greening up, but the heather would not flower for months yet, the evergreen shrubs barely green at the tips; here and there, clumps of gorse bushes showed yellow buds; mingling with the grasses, bluebells and buttery primroses scattered over the slopes and into the glen, soft blurs of color where the grasses grew thick beside the burns that crisscrossed the moorland.

Glen Kinloch was beautiful, he thought, a little wild and more dear to him than he could express—and he would do whatever he must to keep it safe.

"Kinloch!" Glancing over his shoulder, he saw the youngest of his uncles, Fergus MacGregor, coming toward him from the direction of the house. The man waved, hunching forward as he walked in that rushing way he had, swinging arms and fists, his powerful torso and legs, thick black hair and beard reminding Dougal of a black bull, the impression enhanced by the dark leather apron he wore. Dougal waved back and waited, glancing past his uncle toward the house.

Kinloch House was in fact a castle, the old ruined tower house built generations earlier by a Kinloch laird whose cattle-reiving activities were enough to warrant the protection of stout stone walls. After the strife and grief of Culloden had torn Scotland asunder in the middle of the last century, when like so many the MacGregors of Kinloch lost men and fortunes, too, the house had fallen into ill repair, with scant funds to keep its mortared stones together. Two generations later, Kinloch and its tenants had recovered somewhat, being strong Highland stock; Dougal was determined that they would withstand whatever else swept over them, and flourish again.

The latest, and worst, threat to visit the glen was the infiltration of Lowlanders and English who came with wealth and spare time, buying up Scottish land for sheep runs or hunting and holidaying. Against that, Dougal would do whatever he could to protect his glen and its people.

He would never sell the fairy brew; yet if it could be sold for what it was worth, it would save all of them from the brink of this dilemma. The stored cache of good Glen Kinloch whisky would do instead. Aged to a rare degree, it would fetch a good price.

The track of his thoughts changed when he saw

Fiona MacCarran. The memory of kissing her came so quickly that his heart seemed to leap in its place, as if he were a hopeful boy rather than a man, one who had more than enough on his mind already. He had no place for a woman in his life just now—especially the sister of a gauger who could take him and his kinsmen down.

She carried a bound packet of some sort, he saw, clutched against her, one arm across her chest to hold it, probably books or papers for her school session. Sunlight gleamed over her dark hair, which the wind spilled loose from under a plain straw bonnet. Her gown, a deep shade of blue, accentuated her slim shape, and she wore a simple plaid shawl over her shoulders. Oddly and suddenly, it came to him that the blue of her gown would match her eyes.

He frowned, for normally he was not so observant. And it did not serve him now.

Whatever had moved him to kiss her that night, he could not say now. He had apologized for it, and would not apologize again. The night and the mist and the girl's tender beauty had taken him over like a fool, and perhaps the romance of the moment had taken her, too. If he had it to do again he would have tasted that temptation once more, but he did not think she would return it.

Walking beside her was Hugh MacIan, the kirk minister. Miss MacCarran looked trim and small beside the reverend, who had the muscular build of a Highland warrior of ages past, though in his somber black suit he looked like a city man. But MacIan was a clever smuggler; Dougal smiled, wondering what the Lowland teacher would think if she knew it.

He saw her smile up at Hugh as they talked. Dougal frowned; he knew that bright smile, knew the feel of that trim waist under his hands, the scent of that delicate, pale skin. He knew she would smell like lavender and fog, and he could imagine the taste of her lips beneath his, sweet and warm. Suddenly he wondered if she would find the handsome, educated kirk minister more appealing than a Highland laird who had forgone the university in favor of smuggling and illicit distilling.

Then he scowled, and reminded himself that it did not matter. She would soon be gone. Even so, when Hugh took her arm to guide her around some boulders on the hill, Dougal felt a frisson of jealousy roll through him.

"Kinloch!" Fergus joined him. "The lass is ready."

"What lass?" Dougal was startled out of his thoughts.

"Lucy! She's ready at last, and not glad about it."

Glancing toward the house, Dougal saw a boy and a girl standing on the step. His heart gave a tug to see the smaller of the two, his dark-haired niece Lucy—who was in a stormy humor, her hands fisted at her sides.

"The lass does not want to go to school, but Jamie does," Fergus said. Jamie was Fergus's grandchild, the son of his daughter, who had wed a Kinloch shepherd. Tall for his age, with blazing red hair that contrasted with his placid nature, young Jamie put a hand on Lucy's shoulder. She shrugged it off.

"Lucy has decided that smugglers do not go to school," Fergus went on.

Dougal sighed. "And she intends to be one. I sometimes wonder if it is wrong to raise my sister's daughter among kinsmen who think nothing of breaking the laws when it comes to whisky smuggling. Kinloch House is not the place for a wee lass to grow up."

"Oh, it is, for she is treasured among us, and though we be thieves and smugglers sometimes, we are good men for all that," Fergus said. "She's indulged, to be sure, and we can all be more stern with her. But she is blessed with charm, that lass, and she knows it. Still, you and Ellen were reared at Kinloch House by your father and then your uncles and aunts, smugglers all, and you two did well enough," Fergus pointed out. "Jean has been a help, and that was good for Lucy. Until she left," he muttered.

"Aye, now that Aunt Jean has gone, I find it not so easy to raise a girl-child."

"Och, Jean has left Hamish before," Fergus said, "and not for long. She will be back."

Dougal watched as Lucy pushed Jamie off the step. "That lad has the patience of a saint," he said, as Jamie climbed back up and gallantly refrained from pushing back.

"She's a spirited wee creature, lovely as her mother was, but with more courage than Ellen ever had, bless her soul," Fergus said. "When Lucy is a young woman, you will see lads at your door, and hell to pay."

Now Dougal saw Jamie take Lucy's hand, but the girl jerked free and stomped away. "She will be lucky to have anyone knocking at the door for her, least of all Jamie when he's grown."

"The teacher and minister are nearly here. Lucy and Jamie should join the rest at the school. Jamie! Go on!" Fergus called, gesturing.

Dougal noticed the schoolyard filling with a small crowd. Not far from the tower house, the school was a low, rectangular whitewashed building surrounded by an earthen yard and tucked between grassy hillocks chewed neat by sheep and goats. A few students and some glen families, too, had crossed the hills to gather there; those without students had come out of curiosity to see Glen Kinloch's newest teacher. Dougal was more than curious himself, considering he had not seen Fiona MacCarran since he had sent Hamish to offer to drive her back to Auchnashee.

"She will be a fine teacher for the bairns," Fergus said. "We need her here. She's a bonny wee thing. Not like the old one they sent from Edinburgh last time."

"She's a dangerous wee thing," Dougal remarked. "Remember the brother."

"Aye," Fergus agreed. "True, it is not the best time for her to come to our glen." He looked at

Dougal. "I saw Rob MacIan last evening at the tavern. He said Lord Eldin approached him not long ago—he came to the lower end of the glen with the lady's brother—and he told Rob that he's interested in purchasing the very best Highland whisky for his new hotel at Auchnashee. He is willing to pay handsomely, and he let it be known that he does not care if it is illicit."

"Excellent. I hope Rob told him that Glen Kinloch whisky is the best in the Highlands."

"In the whole of Scotland," Fergus said. "Rob declared that he had tasted all of it, from Moray to the Isles, and knew for sure."

"He may be telling the truth," Dougal drawled. "Since he spoke with Eldin, ask him to send discreet word to Auchnashee that there may be some casks available." He named a sum.

"A lord like that one would pay more. And pay a higher price for Highland fairy brew, I suspect, if he knew we had some put away. At Auchnashee, he may hear word of it."

"You know my answer to that," Dougal muttered. "We will get a good price for the usual Glen Kinloch brew once we move it down the loch. Even selling to the buyers I have contacted, we will have some left to sell to Eldin if he wants."

By now Lucy and Jamie were walking across the yard, but the small girl turned toward Dougal, her expression determined. He waved briskly to send her onward. She frowned, and went reluctantly with Jamie.

Fergus laughed. "Lucy thinks smugglers need not learn letters and maths, but should devote their time to distilling whisky and moving kegs through the hills. Reminds me of a lad I knew once," he added, smiling as he glanced at Dougal.

"She is seven years old. Her time should be devoted to her chores, her studies, and running through the hills to play. I've told her that free traders need an education like anyone else."

"She could be a free trader, and a good one—no harm in that when she's older."

"She will get an education," Dougal said with determination. "I will see to it."

"Now you sound like your father."

"Good. I never fulfilled my father's plans for me, but I will see to it for my sister's child."

"Well, thanks to your father, you had a fine education here at the glen school, along with the year and a half in the city before you left. We could not force you back there—"

"Nor afford it," Dougal answered wryly.

"Aye, but I hope someday you will still return to Glasgow and the university."

Dougal shook his head. "I am needed here. For now, the glen school session can wait until we find another dominie—one who is not related to a customs officer." Dougal watched as Fiona climbed the hillside with the reverend.

"And one who will not distract the laird," Fergus murmured in a wry tone.

"Aye," Dougal said without quite listening. He

was watching Hugh MacIan gesture widely to show Fiona the scope of the glen. As Fiona turned, she seemed to look at Dougal across the breadth of the hill. He felt the tug of that gaze. When she set her hand on her upper chest as if she took a deep breath, he wondered if her heart beat faster, as his did.

"Hamish thinks we should scare her off," Fergus said.

"We will not," Dougal said sternly.

"The last society teacher who came here thought we were just a lot of Highland savages. She left quick enough, could not bear us. This one, though—she has a bonny, bold air to her. I told Hamish she will not be frightened of what goes on here."

"I believe you are right."

"But she might meet some dangerous men here, the worst rogue Highlanders in these hills, and think better of being here," Fergus said. "I could send Arthur and Mungo to visit her—"

"I would not trust those two near her." Why the devil had he put it that way?

Fergus shrugged. "Then let her teach here, and we will behave like angels, so that she has no tales to carry to her brother."

"We could do that, I suppose, though it would be easier to send her off," Dougal said. "For now, I'd best go welcome her myself, as the laird."

"Aye. Och, I nearly forgot. The school roof will need some work."

"Again? We repaired it last fall, when it leaked after the rains."

"And we'll work on it again, and again after that," Fergus said. "The structure is old."

"We do need new thatch and new beams," Dougal said.

"We need a new building," Fergus grumbled.

Dougal did not answer. He was distracted again, watching as the girl reached the top of the hill and crossed the long rolling hillocks leading toward Kinloch House and the glen school. She and Hugh were still a good distance away. "I'll go meet them," Dougal said again. "Let the others into the school, if you will."

Fergus nodded. "She is a bonny thing," he said, gazing where Dougal did. "And we have a few days until the cargo must be moved. Let her enjoy some time in our pretty glen before we decide what to do about her."

"Not too much time," Dougal muttered.

"I have no doubt you will enjoy your stay in Glen Kinloch," Reverend MacIan said, as he walked beside Fiona. "We are delighted that you came up from Edinburgh to teach."

Fiona smiled. "Thank you, though I suspect not everyone is glad I am here."

"Kinloch? He has some pressing matters at the moment. Nothing to do with you."

"Mr. MacIan, do not apologize for him. I am grateful to you and your grandmother for welcoming me here. Nothing could spoil such a lovely morning." She lifted her face to the sunshine and cool breeze. "I am looking forward to working with the students. Tell me more about the school. Is it near the castle?"

"Kinloch House is an old tower house, which is a small castle, I suppose. The schoolhouse is beyond it, just there." He pointed toward a long whitewashed building with a thatched roof, situated some distance past the stone tower house, and nestled in the lee of a hillside. The sandstone tower house dominated the hilltop, and beyond it, she saw a few people gathered in the schoolyard.

The laird of Kinloch stood there, too, she had noticed earlier, with an older man, robust with dark hair, whom she did not recognize. Even from that distance, she sensed Dougal MacGregor's gaze, a feeling so keen that she stopped, transfixed, and felt a shiver run through her. Clutching a bound packet of papers in her arms, she held them even closer against her chest, and stared back at him for a moment.

"Ah, there's Kinloch, with one of his uncles," MacIan said.

"Another? How many does he have?"

"Three," the reverend replied. "They all live in the tower house, and have since the laird was a boy and inherited the estate after his father's passing. Well, it looks as if your class is assembling, and school is ready to begin. It is late, since it is mid-April, but in Glen Kinloch, school begins when we have a teacher—and ends on the day the teacher leaves." He smiled.

That would be tomorrow if Kinloch had his way, Fiona thought. "Highland schools are generally in session six months out of the year in most areas."

"True, as they need to take time for planting and harvesting, and allow months for the young people to take the cattle into the hills in the summer to graze on the higher grasses. Here, as in other small glens, we cannot afford a yearly fee to retain a dominie, and rely on the Highland societies to send teachers."

"I understand that there was a lady here from the Edinburgh charity last year who stayed only a few weeks."

"Aye. She changed her mind about the assignment. The glen was . . . too remote for her taste, from what I understood."

"Ah," she said. "The Kinloch smugglers."

He looked startled. "Perhaps. But I heard she also had a terror of ghosts and fairies."

"I am rather interested in those myself. That would not scare me away."

"There are plenty of legends here for you, then. We've had several teachers over the years, and sometimes none at all. For a time, the laird's sister acted as our dominie."

She blinked in surprise. "Dougal MacGregor's sister?"

"Aye. She died a few years ago, a sudden fever. The laird took on the care of his niece, and took more of an interest in the school when the child came of learning age. We had no teacher until we learned about the Edinburgh society that sent you and the others."

"He has a niece in the school?"

"Aye. He is raising her himself—well, he and his uncles. Kinloch, good morning!" MacIan called.

Fiona turned to see Dougal MacGregor approaching them. His stride was brisk enough to set his kilt to swinging, and his dark hair wafted in the breeze, the whole a very attractive picture of a strong Highlander—but his expression was set in a frown that did not match the occasion. "Good morning, sir," she said quietly.

"Miss MacCarran, Hugh," he answered. "I see you are ready to begin this morning."

"Despite attempts to the contrary," she replied, smiling brightly. His scowl deepened.

"Luck to you, then," he said mildly. "I see your scholars have arrived."

"So it seems. It is a beautiful morning," she said as she turned to walk between both men. "I have enjoyed crossing the glen with Mr. MacIan."

"I could have sent the carriage for you," MacGregor said, and tipped a brow.

"No need, as I told your uncle, Hamish MacGregor. I will enjoy walking back and forth to the school. Your glen is lovely, and so peaceful. The Highlands are growing in popularity for a good reason—there is such powerful, yet tranquil beauty in the Highland regions of Scotland."

"Aye." His sudden smile was crooked and appealing. "Glen Kinloch is a small and forgotten place, I suppose, but it is one of those romantical Highland glens that people wax on about—not only for its wild setting and its majestic views, but for its good, hardworking people."

She wondered if he partly teased her for admiring the place like a tourist, for she heard a wryness in his voice—but she could tell that he genuinely loved his glen. "I agree. It has a wonderful quaint aspect. Coming here is a bit like traveling back to an earlier time in the Highlands, if one could do so but in books and paintings."

"Back to the days of cattle thieves and rogues?" MacGregor glanced at her quickly.

"I was thinking of something more idyllic, Mr. MacGregor."

"Ah, she is an idealist," he said softly. His eyes, when the sunlight fell full upon his face, were a soft, mossy green.

"Of course," she said. "Are you, Mr. MacGregor?"

"Not anymore," he answered.

"By idyllic, I believe the lady means the Highlands as described in Sir Walter Scott's grand poem *The Lady of the Lake*," Hugh said.

"I do mean that. Do you know the poem, either of you?" She smiled at him.

"I have read it several times," MacIan said. "Some of the verses remind me of our very own glen." He drew a breath and began to recite.

The wanderer's eye could barely view
The summer heaven's delicious blue;

So wondrous wild, the whole might seem
The scenery of a fairy dream.

"Oh, perfect!" Fiona applauded a little. "I am fascinated by the fairy lore of your lovely glen—" She stopped, wary of giving away her very keen interest.

"Ask Kinloch about our local fairy legends," the reverend said. "He is quite the expert."

"I know no more or less than anyone else here," MacGregor said.

"He knows quite a bit," MacIan told Fiona. "But he is not a boastful fellow. Miss MacCarran, I am inspired to read Sir Walter's magnificent epic again." He swept an arm wide in a grand gesture. "'On this bold brow, a lordly tower; in that soft vale, a lady's bower—'"

"Finish reciting the blasted poem later. There's not time for it," Kinloch said.

Fiona glanced at him. "Do you not like Sir Walter's poem, Mr. MacGregor?"

"I read it once," he replied. "It did not enthrall me. I lacked patience for the length. Though I agree with Hugh, some of the lines remind me of Glen Kinloch. For example—

But hosts may in these wilds abound,
Such as are better missed than found;
To meet with Highland plunderers here
Were worse than loss of steed or deer—

"—or something to that effect." He tilted his head as he looked at her.

"I see." Fiona knew he had quoted exactly, despite his protest, and she understood the implication of the lines he had chosen. "You are right, Mr. MacGregor, we should move along. The scholars are waiting."

Kinloch nodded and set a hand to her elbow, and she felt a sort of gentle lightning go through her. She had not felt anything like that when Hugh MacIan had taken her arm earlier; in fact, she had only felt that way when Dougal MacGregor had touched her.

Nor had she felt much of that sensation in all the while she had been engaged to Archibald MacCarran, her lost fiancé. She gasped a little at the unexpected realization. Flustered, she shifted her bound packet to her other arm, and walked onward, head high.

As they neared the large stone house, Fiona looked up at its turrets and massive walls, and saw a shabbiness she had not seen from a distance—stone blocks crumbling in places, corners covered with ivy, broken trim features, a roof in need of repair.

"There's the school. It was once a weaver's cottage," Hugh MacIan said as they walked down the earthen lane that ran past the tower grounds.

"The place is old," Dougal said. "We've kept it up best we can."

Under the clear blue morning sky, the white

building and greening hills made a lovely picture, but as they came nearer, she saw that the schoolhouse walls showed patches of limewash and plaster, and there were areas of new thatch on the roof. The door sagged a little, and the stone of the threshold step was deeply chipped. A goat and a couple of sheep wandered in the yard chewing the grasses, and the people gathered there moved aside when a ewe settled down on the ground nearby. "It will do nicely," she said.

"The roof leaks," Dougal said.

"We will find buckets if it rains," she said.

"The walls are crumbling in places. Do not lean against the back wall, I warn you."

"Mr. MacGregor, I never lean, nor would I allow my students to do so."

"It is an old place. There may be mice underfoot."

"I will get a cat," she said, laughing. "Mr. MacIan, do you know of a cat I might borrow?"

"I am sure we can find one for you," he answered.

"Miss MacCarran," MacGregor said, bowing a little, "I believe you will fend for yourself in Glen Kinloch, despite all."

She smiled without answer—and as he returned the smile, for a moment she felt as if she saw only him, and he only her. The feeling was so unexpectedly heartwarming that she held his gaze, and then suddenly looked away, blushing.

"The students are all there now, I think," the

reverend said. "Oh, and there is Mrs. Beaton. I promised to speak to her about her daughter's wedding service. Please excuse me." He smiled at Fiona. "The laird, who owns the school, should rightly introduce you."

Fiona nodded, and paused beside MacGregor. "Tomorrow I must be here ahead of the students. I had no idea they would arrive before me. Mr. MacIan said we would be early."

Kinloch smiled. "They are eager today, and curious about the teacher. You would have to rise very early to be here first, since most of the students will be up before dawn to take care of milking and chores, and to take the livestock out to the fields. They head to school for part of the day, glad to escape some of their chores. Come, I'll introduce you."

He took her elbow again, and she felt once again that curious and keen inner tug, and she silently welcomed the strength she sensed in him, though the man was a smuggler and a scoundrel. She walked ahead, determined to let nothing—and no man—distract her further.

Chapter 7

Dougal glanced down at Fiona MacCarran as she smiled, nodded, and carefully repeated each name as she met the glen folk gathered in the schoolyard. She spoke in soft Gaelic, her fluency not perfect, but good enough to please anyone, he thought, even those who were suspicious of outsiders and Lowlanders. He thought each person seemed more at ease after speaking with her.

"This is Pol MacDonald, and my young cousin Jamie Lamont, and another MacGregor—Andrew, Ranald's son," Dougal said, indicating the boys, tall and small, standing together. Expecting Fiona to recognize Andrew after their adventure in the cart, he wondered what she might say.

Greeting the others, she smiled at Andrew as if she had never seen him before, though the boy blushed. Seven-year-old Jamie, his thatch of red hair bright in the morning sun, straightened his small shoulders and shook his new teacher's hand, while Pol MacDonald, with scant new whiskers showing along his jaw, spoke so fast his voice cracked.

Dougal went on to introduce her to all who had arrived that morning to see the teacher; they each murmured a welcome, among them Pol's father, Thomas MacDonald, a farmer with a rough voice and a kind nature; Ranald's wife, Effie, and Fergus's daughter Muriel, with red hair like her son Jamie; and shy Helen MacDonald, cousin to Pol and Thomas, who welcomed Fiona quietly and introduced her daughter, Annabel, who at twelve would join the class, too. The girl was as timid as her mother, with a fairylike appearance and fine, pale hair like sunlight.

Pol's sister, Mairi MacDonald, and Lilias Beaton came forward; the girls were old enough to be married, and Dougal knew that Lilias was promised to a young man who lived in the next glen. It was that wedding that Hugh MacIan discussed with the girl's mother.

Fiona then looked up at Dougal. "I am surprised that boys and girls will be together in the school. Genders are usually separated in other glen schools where I have taught, with classes on alternating days, or in mornings and afternoons, for the two groups."

"We have so few students just now that it is sufficient to put them together," Dougal replied. "It is not always easy for them to find time for school, with chores to do at home. And most of them are kin, and used to being together." Seeing his niece, Lucy, standing with Annabel, he beckoned her to come toward him.

"And who is this?" Fiona asked, smiling.

"My niece, Miss Lucy MacGregor," Dougal said, touching the child's shoulder. Lucy looked up at the teacher, smiling sweetly, her hazel eyes sparkling, dark hair gleaming with brushing, which pleased him to see; impatient Lucy did not always take time with her appearance.

"Good morning, Miss MacCarran, and welcome," Lucy said in perfect English.

"Thank you," Fiona said, greeting her in return. "Your English is very good."

"It is. So I do not need to go to school," Lucy replied. "I speak Gaelic and English, and can read a little of both. Uncle Dougal taught me." Fiona glanced up at him, looking surprised.

"She is a quick study," Dougal explained. "Away with you, Lucy—go inside with the others." The girl scowled, but ran toward the schoolhouse.

Dougal walked with Fiona toward the school, and she glanced at him again. "There are only seven children. I expected to see more."

"The other families will wait," he told her. "Highland people are cautious and practical. They want to know if the lessons will be worth their children's time away from chores. And they wonder if you will stay. Most previous teachers have not remained for long."

"Of course I will stay," Fiona said. "I gave my word to do that."

He nodded in silence, impressed by her calm reply and the steadiness behind it, yet realizing

again that sending her away—due to the unfore-
seen complication of her kinsmen—would not be
an easy thing.

"It is to the benefit of all Highlanders nowadays,"
she went on, "to understand and read English.
And I am glad to see that the laird of this glen
encourages education in his tenants."

"For all his sins," he answered quietly, "he does."

Fiona gazed at him then, long enough that Dougal
felt, once more, that strange sense of being drawn
to her. Despite the logical protests of reason, he felt
oddly protective of her and in need of an intimate
connection with her—he wanted to know her as
a woman, and suddenly, sharply, as a friend. He
wanted her to thrive here; he wanted her to stay.

Without comment, he stepped ahead and held
the door open for her as she entered the schoolroom. Her shoulder brushed his chest in passing.
The clean, womanly scent of her was so enticing—
he closed his eyes, feeling a quick tug within at the
casual touch.

She looked back at him. "I confess I am nervous," she murmured, and half laughed. "Will you
come inside, too?"

He had not planned to do that. But he nodded,
and stepped inside.

While the students settled on benches in the
room, Fiona set her packet down on the sturdy,
somewhat battered table meant to serve as the dominie's desk, with a high-seated stool beside it. She

stood at the front of the room and folded her hands in front of her, forcing herself to at least appear clam. She had taught classes before and was not nervous about that. What distracted her most, even now, was the man who remained in the open doorway—yet she wanted him to be there.

Dougal MacGregor stood with a shoulder leaned against the jamb, the sunlight falling on his wide shoulders and long-limbed body, his dark hair haloed by the light, the colors of his plaid kilt—deep maroon and green—warm, earthy and handsome, like the man himself. She glanced away when he met her gaze.

The children, from small Lucy and Jamie to lanky Andrew and Pol, sat on plain benches, looking awkward and expectant. She smiled and began.

"Good morning," she said in Gaelic, and they murmured in return. Later she intended to speak mostly in English so that they would have to communicate in that language, but now was not the time for it. "Let us bid good morning to Mr. MacGregor of Kinloch as well." The children complied, while Fiona noticed Lucy squirming in her seat and waving to her uncle. Dougal MacGregor walked closer to Fiona.

"Miss MacCarran is your teacher now," he said, also speaking in Gaelic, which Fiona had already noted was the primary language in the glen. "May I remind you of the rules of our schoolroom? We do not want Miss MacCarran to think that Highlanders are savages without manners." Some of the children giggled, and Fiona smiled.

"Obey your teacher," Dougal began, and Fiona recognized the familiar rules given in so many other Highland schools. "Do not run inside, or in the yard. What else?" he asked.

"Neither shout nor stare at others, nor quarrel while you are here," Jamie supplied.

"Be sure to bow or curtsy when you enter, and go quietly to your seat," Lilias Beaton said.

"Good. No doubt Miss MacCarran has rules of her own." MacGregor bowed toward her.

"Thank you, sir." Fiona folded her hands before her. "I expect you to treat others with respect," she said. "Wait your turn to speak and raise your hand when you have something to say. And please pay attention to your schoolwork and to your books."

A hand rose at the back of the room. "Miss, we have no books," Andrew said.

Fiona blinked in surprise. "None?"

"None in English here, and not enough in Gaelic for all of us," Andrew answered.

"There are only seven of you." She walked toward MacGregor so that the class would not overhear her. "Mr. MacGregor, I know that translated texts are scarce for teaching English reading skills to Gaels. But Mr. MacIan gave me the impression that we would have books. The school has been established for a long while."

"Only a few books have been translated into Gaelic, as you no doubt know," he said. "The last teacher who was here took the books I had ordered. I apologize for not having others—your quick arrival was a bit of a surprise. Hugh MacIan made the arrangements, and I am sure he meant to ask me to acquire some books for the schoolroom."

"The Bible and several religious texts have been translated," she said. "Most Highland schools I have visited have several copies of those on hand, at least."

"This is a school, not a kirk."

"Grammar books are not available, and scholars need texts to improve their English skills."

"I own some translations if you would like to look at the library at Kinloch House." He tilted his head. "I own a good copy of the writings of the American Thomas Paine, translated into Gaelic, which I would be happy to lend."

"That is not what I had in mind," she said. "They must have proper texts, or they may as well stay home."

MacGregor nodded, and smiled slowly. "True."

She gasped. "Do you see this as some chance to close the school so I will leave?"

A small frown crossed his brow. "Miss MacCarran," he said, "I am listening, not plotting. And I will take my leave, and wish you luck of the day." He bowed his head and left quietly, and Fiona turned back to the class, aware that her heart was beating a little too fast.

"Can anyone tell me what supplies we have here?" she asked the students.

Mairi MacDonald raised her hand. "There are slates and chalk in the cupboard."

"Thank you. Please fetch them and pass them around." The girl went to an old cupboard beneath a window and removed a stack of slates and a box of cut chalk sticks, which she proceeded to hand to each student before she sat again on the bench beside her friend Lilias.

"We have quills and ink, too, but not much paper," Lucy said. The girl's heart-shaped face, curling brown hair, and wide hazel eyes would make her a beauty one day, Fiona thought, as she glanced toward the girl and nodded.

"Thank you," Fiona said. "Now I would like to know which among you can speak some English, and which ones can read some of it."

A few hands went up, and Fiona soon discovered that only a few of them could read, though some of them could sign their names. Lucy, one of the youngest, claimed the best grasp of both languages, spoken and read. "I can even write in English," the little girl said.

"If we can all sign our names, and the pastor reads the Bible to us at Sunday kirk sessions, why do we have to learn any more than that?" Andrew asked.

"Because you cannot be a smuggler all your life, Andrew MacGregor," Lucy said.

"Lucy, please raise your hand before speaking in class," Fiona said.

"But Andrew is my cousin!"

"And at school he is your fellow scholar," Fiona explained.

Lucy scowled. "When my mother was the dominie, we did not have to ask permission. Well, I did not," she added.

"I am the dominie now," Fiona said gently, realizing that the girl had lost her mother.

Lilias raised her hand. "My father says Highlanders will need the skills of a scholar someday. Lucy is right, the lads in particular must remember they will not always be smugglers, for the changing laws will not permit—*ow*," she finished, as Pol MacDonald elbowed her into silence and the others shushed the both of them.

"Class," Fiona warned. She told the students to write their names on their slates, those who could do so. As she waited, listening to the scrape of chalk, she walked over and looked through the window by the door. The glass was old and hazy, but she could see the yard and beyond.

In the sunlit yard, Dougal MacGregor stood outside the great stone house with two men. They were in earnest conversation, Fiona noticed, recognizing his uncles Ranald and Hamish. After a few moments, the one called Fergus joined them as well.

Then she saw Dougal glance back at the school, while Fergus gestured toward the school building as well, rather insistently. Dougal shook his head in answer.

Sighing, Fiona folded her arms. "MacGregor of

Kinloch," she whispered, "I am here to stay, and you had all best accept it."

"Is there further news from the Glasgow solicitor?" Ranald asked Dougal, who had encountered his three uncles as he walked toward the tower house. Various tasks occupied his uncles in the mornings, so if they gathered now, he knew they had something to say.

"Nothing more than we already know," Dougal answered Ranald. "If we cannot produce the funds to buy back the lands at the south end of the glen— the ten thousand acres of the old Drumcairn estate that my father sold off—the government can sell the rights to the deed. That was the arrangement my father made to stave off losing the glen years ago. Now it's come due."

"We must sell all the kegs we have, and get the best price we can," Hamish said, nodding.

"All of them, aye," Ranald said.

"Not all," Dougal said.

"Aye. The fairies will understand," Ranald said.

Dougal laughed bitterly. "Not according to the legend."

"You cannot believe in legends and spirits at such a time as this," Hamish said.

"But as laird, I have to respect the traditions of kin and glen."

"So much like his father," Hamish said to the others, and though the delivery was brusque, Dougal heard a hint of affection in it.

He glanced at the hills where his father had once taken him to show him the secret of the fairies of Kinloch. "We need sell only what we have stored of our Glen Kinloch brew, and leave the fairy whisky for special gifts, as we have always done. Whatever price we ask will be paid. The quality of our whisky speaks for itself."

"Glen Kinloch malt whisky is without equal in the Highlands," Fergus said, "but the fairy brew is legendary. Men will pay far more just to taste it, and the glen could use that money."

"Whisky is whisky," Hamish pointed out in practical fashion. Dougal knew that his eldest uncle did not believe the tales about the fairy brew—Hamish claimed that its effect on him was no different than any other brew, and he thought the legend a lot of nonsense. "Do not waste time with the fairy ilk. Remember that the government would sell our land out from under us when they sell the right to those land deeds." Most land sales in Scotland, Dougal knew, were nominal, and were in fact rentals—the majority of land in Scotland belonged to king and Crown.

"It is not the fairies who concern me," Dougal said. "We cannot allow customs officers to interfere when we move that batch of Glen Kinloch whisky. If it is noticed that we are transporting so many casks over time, the revenue officers will triple the amount of gaugers in the area."

"When the teacher leaves Kinloch, we can work in better secrecy," Hamish said. His brothers nodded agreement.

Dougal was not keen on that any more than his wrenching decision to sell all the brew they had to hand, even that made by his father and stored away, but he had little choice. "I cannot just order the woman off my land and out of my glen."

"We will find another way," Ranald said. "Frighten her off, and she will run like the last teacher. She was a bit mouse, that one. Easy enough to—" He stopped, and the others glanced around as if they were not listening.

Dougal frowned. "Did you three do something that made the other teacher leave Kinloch? I never knew quite why she departed so quickly." He narrowed his eyes.

"Why would we do such a thing?" Ranald asked innocently.

"She did not like Highlanders, that one. Me, I did not speak to her," Fergus said.

"Tell him the truth," Hamish said, and looked at Dougal. "The lady knew there were thieves in the hills, and then Ranald warned her about wicked fairies who would steal her away as she slept."

"I see. And what did Fergus tell her?" Dougal looked at his brawny uncle.

"Nothing much. I only walked around her cottage at night and whistled."

"So you deliberately frightened that poor wee woman?" Dougal scowled at the three of them.

"Bah, she was a timid thing," Hamish said. "Nor was she bonny. We did not like her."

In part, Dougal wanted to cuff each of them;

and in part, he was amused, but would not show it. "Do not think to do that again. Miss MacCarran is not a timid woman."

"But she is bonny," Fergus said. "And curious. It is a poor quality in the sister of a gauger."

"We have only two weeks or so before we move that whisky," Hamish said. "And it's nearly time for the spring ba' game in the glen. Which side will have you for a player?" he asked Dougal. "Drumcairn or Garloch?"

"Kinloch traditionally stays neutral," Dougal said. "The laird either plays alternate sides or does not take part."

"You should declare a side this time," Fergus said. "If you are there, everyone will come to see. It would be a perfect time for us to safely move so much whisky all at once. We three have talked it over, and we agree. It is a good plan."

"During the ba' game is the best time, with everyone in the glen involved," Ranald said.

"The ba' game? Interesting. It could work." Dougal nodded, thoughtful. The annual spring ball game, played between the rival villages in the glen, could provide enough distraction so that Dougal and his kinsmen would be able to move the casks from the upper hills to the loch. "Otherwise the work might require several trips over several nights. A fine suggestion."

"So you had best send the teacher away before then," Hamish said, "or else . . ." He paused. "Or you had best make her one of us."

"What do you mean?" Dougal frowned. "I doubt she would join us on a midnight trip through the hills with a pistol and a pony."

"He means that a woman of the glen would not talk of what she knows," Ranald said. "Not even to her brother."

"How am I supposed to make her one of—oh no," Dougal said, holding up a hand as he saw the glimmers brightening his uncles' eyes. "You want me to seduce the woman? Or marry her, to bring her into the glen and make her kin? I will not."

"Marry her, aye," Ranald drawled. "I had not thought of that. Interesting that the laird did."

Hamish laughed. "It is a good idea."

"Marriage would be good for the lad, hey," Fergus told his brothers.

"Get him over the black lovesickness." Ranald grinned.

"Enough," Dougal growled. "You rascals do not need another scheme between you."

"Kinloch, the lady is an outsider, come to the glen at the wrong time," Ranald said. "She will not leave easily, and you will not permit her to be scared off. But a woman who was bound to us by loyalty . . . that one would not talk. And a wife would be good for you."

"You do need a wife," Fergus agreed. "So does Hamish, come to that."

"I have one. We disagree with each other," Hamish grumbled.

"Lucy is getting older, Kinloch," Fergus said.

"She needs a mother, and the teacher could be that for her."

"Lucy has female relatives. And I do not need a wife just now. We are talking about managing with the lady over two weeks, not a lifetime. All that need concern us now is moving that cargo through the glen without being stopped."

Hamish clapped Dougal on the shoulder. "All I intended was for you to gain the teacher's loyalty, and swear her to secrecy. By whatever method you like," he added. The others chuckled, while Dougal scowled slightly, skeptically, his arms folded.

"She will fall for your charm," Ranald said. "Did she not the other night?"

"Of course she did," Dougal replied, while they chortled. He wished he knew how the lady regarded him; then he reminded himself that he was thinking far too much about her.

"My wife says no lass can resist the laird of Kinloch, and when he decides to take a wife, girls will knock on his door to offer," Ranald said. "Plenty of lasses have pined for you, though they have never—"

"Oh, they do," Dougal said. "They just say that they never."

Fergus hooted, and Hamish frowned. "Why have you not married one of them? *Tcha!*"

"Am I a fool, with the secrets I have, to marry outside the glen now?" Dougal shook his head. "Besides, each one wanted a lad looking for a wife, and I am not that lad. They have all found what they desired elsewhere, and are happy. I am happy, too—unwed and free to do as I please."

"Well, it is true the Lowland teacher will be gone soon," Fergus said thoughtfully.

"We cannot wait that long. We need the money the whisky cargo will bring," Hamish replied. "There are new leaks in the schoolhouse, and no coin to help us with repairs."

"What if we told her the place is haunted by the ghost of a scholar who did not succeed? City women are nervous sorts. She will pack for home." Ranald nodded in satisfaction. "And we can fix the roof later."

Dougal frowned. "Wait. Think about this. The roof leaks, the walls are crumbling."

"Aha!" Fergus looked pleased. "If the school cannot be used, the problem is solved."

"Perhaps." Dougal turned to look at the school. "A pity, though," he murmured.

Hamish shrugged. "We will find another teacher for the glen."

Dougal nodded, distracted as he glanced toward the school. Behind those windows, behind that worn door with its red, peeling paint, she stood. She had come here to help the children of the glen, including his own niece; he was a beast indeed, as she had called him the night they had met, to scheme for her departure. But his intent, ultimately, was to help the glen.

"I know the children need the glen school and this particular teacher, with her willingness to help," he told them. "I know that." He did not say what came to his mind: that he needed her himself—the strange urgency of it kept returning to him, as if his own heart knew something he did not.

Despite his protests, he wanted her to stay for a while—a lifetime, if he dared dream that far. Instinctively he knew that he could be a better man with her than he might ever be without her.

But the fact of her kinsmen was enough to destroy any dream he had for his glen or himself.

"You have secrets to protect here, lad," Ranald reminded him. "Not just the whisky that must be moved and sold soon, but the fairy brew to be made as well. The time is coming again when you will have to go up the mountain, and see to starting another batch of the brew. As laird, it is your obligation to the fairy agreement each year," he said quietly. Dougal's other uncles nodded.

Sighing, Dougal looked out over the landscape, and the broad flank of the mountain that rose not far from the laird's tower, looming high over Glen Kinloch. "Too much curiosity about our glen is not good now. A Lowland teacher with a gauger for a brother and kinsmen nearby—one with a tourist hotel—could put us in the worst predicament of all."

"Ach," Hamish said, grimacing. "Tourists."

"Aye, tourists might come to Glen Kinloch for its unspoiled beauty," Dougal said. "And for its proximity to Loch Katrine, site of the poem that has brought so much attention to Scotland."

"I never read the thing, and I do not plan to," Ranald said.

"You haven't the skills to read that great beast of a poem," Hamish pointed out. "I have, and did not like it much."

"Dougal read parts of it to me and mine," Fergus said. "I very much liked it, all that chasing about and the noble rescues, and all. But this glen will not remain unspoiled and secret for long if the tourists come up here."

"I still think he could do worse than marry the lass and keep her here, if she makes a solemn promise to honor our secrets, and then sends her kin back to the city, where they belong," Ranald said. "The girl is bonny, the glen needs a teacher, and the laird needs a wife. One as smart as that one will keep him interested, hey."

"It is not so simple as all that." Hamish grunted dubiously. "An educated Lowland lady will not want a poor Highland laird with a small estate and a taste for free trading."

"But if she appreciates the Highlands, as she seems to, she could not find a finer Highland lad or a finer place to live," Fergus replied defensively. "But after a while, she might be more than ready to leave our glen." He sighed.

Listening, Dougal glanced at the schoolhouse door again, and heard laughter coming from inside. He nodded, part regret, part resolve. He turned to face his uncles.

"Tell her about the roof," he said quietly. "The

school must be closed. But first give her a few days
to enjoy our glen."

Fiona sat back on her heels and studied the
sketch she was making. The delicate outline of an
ancient arthropod, a tiny animal with no back-
bone, had left its imprint in limestone eons ago.
She squinted, corrected the pencil drawing here
and there, and then rolled it up firmly to stash it
inside her knapsack. She took another small bit of
paper, torn from a larger page, and laid it over the
stone, rubbing it with the soft graphite to capture
the impression of the minuscule animal remains.

Satisfied, she put her things away again, and stood
to resume walking across the brow of a hill that
overlooked the glen and the loch. The weather was
misted and cool that afternoon, and she had let the
students out earlier than usual, since several of them
said they had chores at home. She understood from
Hugh MacIan that many of the glen children had
a good deal of responsibility in keeping homes and
byres, some of them tending flocks and herds as well.
Having no desire to interfere with that, at times she
was willing to let them go after morning lessons.

The extra hours gave her a chance to walk the
hills in search of fossils for her collection. She had
promised her brother James that she would look
for certain varieties of rock and take notes on her
observations, to assist with a paper he was prepar-
ing on the geological nature of the antediluvian
earth in the Scottish Highlands. Her knowledge of

fossil remains was equal to his, and her ability to sketch them superior, so that her twin often relied on his sister to provide sketches.

But in this and other hours she had walked over the hills in this glen, she had never seen a trace of fairies. She sighed at the seeming impossibility of it. But armed with her knapsack, containing a notepad and a few Conté pencils, she had set out, again hoping to find something of value.

Wanting to look in an area she and Patrick had passed through when she had first come to the glen, she had headed that way, keeping the loch to her right, so that she could easily return to Mary's house in a reasonable amount of time.

Seeing a cluster of graywacke rocks ahead, she climbed that way, and knelt to study them. She bent forward, tapping with the hammer in the knapsack, and turning them in her gloved hands, looking for signs of fossils and the different sorts of rock and minerals that might be mingled in the outcrop. The boulders had thrust out of the ground of the hills, and most of the surroundings were covered with grassy turf and heather, the plants still greening and not yet in bloom.

"That is one devil of an insect you found there," a voice said behind her, and Fiona shrieked, turning to see Dougal MacGregor standing behind her on the hill, studying one of the drawings that had tumbled out of the knapsack.

"Oh!" She set a gloved hand to her chest. "You startled me."

"Pardon, I did not mean to do that," he murmured, and dropped to one knee beside her, looking at the drawings, which had spilled out, unrolling. "Very nice. What are these?"

"Arthropods," she said. "These two are trilobites—the devil of an insect you mentioned, though they were very tiny and probably peaceful enough, just little creatures floating about and eating, procreating, and dying, leaving their impression in forms of mud, which became rock, and preserved them forever."

He nodded. "I've seen these sorts of things before here, but know very little about it." He glanced at her, his eyes a piercing green, very inquisitive. "Floating about, you say?"

"Some geologists believe that much of the earth was covered with water and oceans, eons ago. Scotland was one of those areas—and when one finds marine creatures, fish impressions and so forth, there must be truth to the theory. It is one of the matters my brother James is dedicating himself to studying. He is a professor of natural sciences in Edinburgh," she explained. "When I find things like this, it is sometimes a help to him, and so I make a sketch of it."

"If you cannot walk off with the rock altogether," he said, hefting her knapsack. She laughed a little, nodding her admittance. "Fish on a Scottish mountain—a curious thought," he said.

"This one here," she said, picking up another sheet, "shows the impression of a shrimp." She handed it to him. "And here, a whole row of arthropods, left in limestone. I found this on another hill, and made a rubbing of it with the pencil over paper."

He studied them, turning the page around, and laughed. "Miss MacCarran," he said as he handed the paper back to her, "in the Highlands, we sometimes call these fairy tracks."

Fiona smiled, delighted. "I can see why," she said, tilting her head to study the rubbings, each one vaguely shaped like a tiny footprint.

"It is what my father told me, and what he believed, and I thought so, too, when I was a boy. I have seen engravings of these creatures in books," he said. "And while I had read a little about old fossils, I did not think of them as the fairy feet that I saw in my youth."

"Some of them only occur in bits, rather than whole and complete, so one would not recognize them as . . . well, insectlike. And one needs a keen eye to see them at all, impressed in the rock. There are plants, too, leaves and ferns and even bark, if one looks closely enough." She smiled, rolling up the pages and replacing them in the knapsack. "But I think I much prefer to call them fairy tracks."

"It does sound better than Highland shrimp," he agreed. He stood, wiping his hands on his dark kilt, and held out a hand to her. "Come up to me," he murmured.

Fiona paused, watching him from under the tilt of her straw hat, reminded of the first moment she had seen him on another hillside. She had taken him for one of the Fey then, and he had spoken that same odd phrase that seemed part of him. The smuggler was gone, the scowling laird was gone, too—and once again he seemed to be that man on the mountainside: handsome, compelling, and mysterious, with an aura about him that seemed almost magical.

Yet the one she preferred was the man she was coming gradually to know—the one who seemed so real and strangely familiar to her, the one who laughed easily and did not tell her to go home. Smiling, she raised her gloved hand. He braced her fingers as she rose to her feet.

Brushing dirt and grass from her dark blue skirt, adjusting the drape of her creamy woven shawl, which had fallen from her shoulders, she looked up at him. "What brings you to this hillside this afternoon, sir? Not fossil collecting."

"Flowers, Miss MacCarran." He lifted her knapsack and they began to walk, companionably and in step. "I am roaming the hills looking for wildflowers." He inclined his head a little.

"For your ladylove?" she asked. "It appears that you have not found any—no bouquets, Mr. MacGregor?"

"Oh, my ladylove is not waiting for bouquets," he said. "She is a great belching thing with steam coming off her, very fussy and demanding. But, oh, she gives great comfort when she is ready. A copper still," he explained, glancing at her with a quick twinkle in his hazel-green eyes. "I came out here to look for the first flowers of spring. I need to know which are growing along the course of the burn that feeds the stills farther down the slope."

"How fascinating. I had no idea such things were involved in illicit whisky distilling."

"All manner of interesting factors are taken into account when distilling the pot whisky."

"Why the flowers?"

"They flavor the water—what grows nearby might make the water taste sweeter, lighter, give it a hint of fragrance, or in some cases, give it a tart or a bitter taste. Grass, wild onion, and garlic, even the rocks that the water flows over can affect the whisky, too. So I come out regularly to check the burns and streams. The most important ingredients," he said, "are the barley, the peat, and the water—and what affects those helps determine the character of the whisky."

"It sounds almost like an art," she said.

"It is," he replied, and looked at her for a moment. "More an art than a crime."

"I see," she murmured, and returned his gaze openly. She wanted to know more about him for so many reasons, she thought; his devotion to the whisky, every detail of it, was a revelation to her.

He inclined his head. "If you do not mind, Miss MacCarran, though I would not mind escorting you in your search, my own takes me in another direction today. My kinsmen are waiting." He gestured with a thumb.

Fiona glanced that way, and saw two men waiting for him, a young one she did not recognize, and an older one who looked like his uncle Ranald. "Please, do not let me delay you further," she said. "I am quite content to wander. How nice to chat with you," she said.

"Miss," he murmured. "Do not wander too far. Keep the road and the loch in sight."

"I will," she said.

"And safe home before dark," he said.

"I will remember."

"Just so." He handed the knapsack to her, and his hand grazed hers in the transfer. Even through her glove, she felt the stun of that small contact. And as he walked away, long strides over the sloping, tufted hill, his favored kilt swinging over the tops of his calves as he descended, she watched him for a long moment before turning away, back to her rocks and ancient fossilized creatures.

Her life and interests seemed so dull, so safe and intellectual in that moment. She longed to turn and run to join MacGregor of Kinloch, to spend the day searching out wildflowers along the banks of the burn to please a belching old copper still; she yearned to taste with him the whisky that resulted, and laugh again about fish in the mountains, and the strange tracks of fairies through the Highlands.

Chapter 8

〰️〰️

Under the unsteady flicker of a lantern, Fiona dipped pen into ink and resumed writing. The scratching of nib over paper was the loudest sound in the front room of Mary MacIan's cozy house, so late at night; only the low crackle of the peat fire, the tick of an old clock, and the soft sounds of Mary snoring in a back bedroom could be heard. Fiona sighed, enjoying the peacefulness, intent on the letter she wrote. She had already finished her lessons for the week, several verses written out in Gaelic and then English, which she would present to her students soon. Now she concentrated on a reply to the letter her brother James had recently sent.

Outside, another gust of wind rattled the windowpanes and pushed at the door so that it wobbled slightly on its hinges. Since Mrs. MacIan's habit was to retire early in the evenings, Fiona had ample time to plan lessons or write out vocabulary words, or tend to some of her other work, such as making careful drawings of the fossils she had so far collected, or writing letters to her kin in Edinburgh.

She also owed a dutiful weekly letter to her great-aunt, Lady Rankin, but she was glad to postpone that. Fiona had much affection for Lady Rankin, who had raised James and Fiona after their parents had died, drowned in a shipwreck, with their younger brothers gone to other relatives. Yet Fiona knew what little regard the stuffy viscountess had for her great-niece's "charitable work among the savages," as she called the teaching assignments in the Highlands; the lady wanted her to make a good marriage and get over pining for the lost Archie MacCarran. And she was outspoken in her opinion that her late sister's demanding will, requiring "fairy nonsense," was patently ridiculous.

But even at this late hour, Fiona was happy to take time to write to James. Her twin brother, of all her kin and friends, was nearest her heart, and she knew he waited to hear how she fared in the glen.

I am delighted to learn that your Elspeth is feeling so well,

she wrote, having already reported on the glen, the school, and her students;

and I look forward to becoming an aunt, though my anticipation cannot match the joy of the babe's dear parents. How wonderful that Elspeth is weaving a new blanket for the little one. The pretty green plaid she made for me keeps me warm here in Glen Kinloch.

I hope you will have this reply soon. The mail travels back and forth to Callander with Mr. Hamish MacGregor, an uncle of the laird of this glen (a cousin to your wife and a gentleman of good intelligence and spirit, whose whisky is celebrated in the region, and whose secrets, I suspect, are many—I dare not say more, even to you!). Callander is as far as the weekly mail coach will come, bringing letters and packages from Edinburgh or Glasgow via Stirling into the Highlands. Hamish drives the mail south in an old black coach, very creaky and antique, which has as much character as the driver himself.

To answer your question, I have not yet made drawings of fairies for your revisions of Grandmother's book. The idea still seems so far-fetched to me, but I will endeavor further. Patrick thinks I should simply invent some sprites, commit images to paper, and have done with it. But Sir Walter Scott is a canny gentleman who has my utmost respect, and he will decide the worth of the fairy pictures by the conditions of the will. Nor do I have it in me to betray Grandmother's belief in fairies! How could any of us succeed in our tasks as well as you have done, having found your *sweet wife with her legacy of rumored fairy blood and knowledge of fairy lore?*

While wandering the hills in search of pesky but nonexistent sprites, I have discovered excellent specimens of trilobites set in good limestone, and evidence of a thick quartzite layer beneath Old Red Sandstone, which you will find very interesting, and I have learned something more of the lore of this glen from its very interesting laird—

The door banged again in the wind, startling Fiona so that she jumped, ink smearing on the page. Sighing, she sanded over it and blew, and then rose from the chair. Going to the door to make sure it was secure—the hinges and handle old enough that she wondered if it might blow open—she heard Mary's dog barking somewhere outside. Fiona stopped to listen, hearing warning and agitation in the dog's incessant bark.

She did not want Mary to wake, for the old woman had seemed tired that evening, and had asked Fiona to let the dog in before going to bed. Maggie often tracked rabbits in the darkness, though she stayed close enough to the house to return when called.

Grabbing her shawl from a hook beside the door—she kept the dark plaid woven by her sister-in-law there—Fiona also snatched up the rope lead used for the dog. Then she pulled open the door and stepped outside.

"Maggie!" she called, looking around, but did not see the black-and-white spaniel anywhere nearby. "Maggie, come!"

She walked farther out into the yard, clutching the shawl about her in the wind, chilled by a hint of rain. The fat knot of her hair, already unkempt after a long day, loosened and fluttered to her shoulders. She pulled the plaid over her head like a hood and walked farther, calling the dog.

Clouds drifted across the night sky, and the surface of the loch reflected the moonlight. Fiona paused to take in the dark, sparkling beauty of the water at night, edged by black mountains against an indigo sky, with the pale wafer of the moon floating above, appearing and vanishing behind swift-sailing clouds. She lifted her face to the wind, closing her eyes, listening to the gentle lapping of water against the pebbled shores of the cove.

Hearing the dog bark again, frantically this time, she opened her eyes. The moon shone bright between cloud drifts, and for a moment she saw a boat sailing from the south end of the loch, its elegant black silhouette just visible in the darkness.

Instinctively she drew her dark plaid close about her and stepped back, feeling a need to hide. When clouds veiled the moon once again, the ship seemed to vanish. She turned, determined to fetch the dog inside; the hour was late, and she had no desire to be seen by anyone aboard a smuggling vessel. She knew of no other reason for a ship to sail at this time of night toward the quiet shoreline of this remote glen.

Walking, half running, she headed past the house searching for the spaniel, taking the earthen lane that led from the cove to the main road. She called out softly, wary of being heard. Whatever went on in Glen Kinloch that night was none of her business, she told herself, and she was better off going inside than learning more than she should.

A flash of black and white ran past the lane where it met the main road, and she hurried that way with the dog's rope leash ready in her hand. Maggie barked repeatedly as if she spied something out there—but it was neither rabbit nor fox, which the dog usually pursued in silence. This was a warning bark, protective of her territory.

A chill ran up and down Fiona's spine, and her heart thumped. Slowing, she glanced warily around in the darkness as she moved up the earthen path. "Maggie," she whispered, "come!"

Setting foot on the main road, uncertain which way to turn, she paused while the wind scudded clouds past the moon in a new cluster, bathing all in silvery light once again. Another bark sounded, and she glimpsed a patchy white coat heading up a hillside opposite the road. Fiona turned left to pursue her quarry, running now.

Something was in the air, an urgency that made her hurry, made her glance around furtively, though she saw only the shimmering loch in the distance when she turned that way, and the long slopes rising, massive and rocky, beside the road. She did not want to walk far up those hills after the dog, not in darkness; in daylight it was possible to find her way over the terrain.

Still she could hear Maggie higher on the slope, barking frantically now, and the sound alarmed her so that she headed that way, clutching her shawl with one hand and the rope in the other. Walking a little way up the slope in unreliable moonlight, she looked about.

"Maggie!" she called, but the dog barked incessantly, intent on something. Fiona sighed and walked farther up. "Come *here!*"

A burst of wind whipped at her plaid and then blew her hair free, and she put a hand to her head. In the next moment, the clouds, swept by the wind, extinguished the moonlight like a candle flame. The sudden darkness was so complete that Fiona stopped, poised on the slope, seeing little but the dark mass of the hillside, scattered with the paler shapes of stones. The ground was thick with heather, juniper, and tufted grass, and she dared not move quickly for fear of losing her footing, until the moonlight returned.

As she stood there, she saw what seemed to be starlight, and turned that way. The stars seemed to shift then, dropping like sparkling bits of bright fire, or will-o'-the-wisps caught in a sudden updraft. Fiona stared, and saw them swirl and begin to coalesce into something that made her catch her breath—something ghostly. She gasped, stepped back. The lights spun and rushed away, and she saw then a group of standing stones not far away, behind which the moving starlight seemed to disappear.

Then, over the whistling wind, she heard distinct sounds—thumping footfalls and hooves, and the jingle of harness coming from somewhere above and to her left as she stood on the hillside. Her blood ran chill in her veins, and she went motionless. The sounds grew louder, and Fiona dared not move. Higher on the slope, the dog barked crazily in the dark.

She sensed a group of men and horses coming toward her, though she had not yet seen them. Now she heard the breath and bluster of the horses, and the low murmurs of men. And in the glimmer of scant light—starlight or moonlight, or something more mysterious, she did not know what—she saw them.

But the men were not the Fey, she thought, riding toward her in a cavalcade, as she had heard in so many legends; nor were they the ghosts of men in battle. They were solid and real, grim and determined, walking the hills by night. A few of them were mounted, and all of them led pack ponies. Surely they were smugglers—and there she stood in the open, easily seen and in danger of her life.

Clouds shifted overhead, and she glanced around. The lights, not long ago, had showed the cluster of standing stones not far away, and without thinking further, concerned for her immediate safety, she ran there, slipping behind the tallest menhir. Standing stones were not uncommon in fields and on hillsides, abandoned ages ago, their meaning lost. Now she was grateful for their presence. She drew the dark plaid around her, hoping to blend with the shadows while the men traversed the slope.

Lanterns swung like golden drops of fire in the midnight gloom as the men came closer. Fiona stood motionless behind the stone, legs trembling, breaths shallow; and she peered out, curiosity and fear mingling as she watched them descend slowly. They were about to pass right over the spot where she had been standing, not far from the tall stone.

While Maggie barked incessantly, untroubled and bold, Fiona cringed for the dog's sake. The smugglers might decide to silence the relentless noise to protect their secret progress. Then the moonlight returned, and Fiona saw Maggie— a black-and-white blur chasing up and down the slope alongside the group.

The men and horses were clearly visible now: several horses and twice as many men, with the glowing lanterns scattered among them. Cold fear slid through her, and Fiona shrank back behind the stone. She could hear the thunk of hobnail boots over rocky terrain, the clop of the horses' hooves, even the slosh of liquid in the kegs strapped to the ponies' backs. The rumble of male voices sounded as well: a question, a reply, a curt laugh.

Maggie bolted down the hill and came toward her, circling the stone. Fiona hissed at her to stop, but the dog raced off. Pressing close to the stone, Fiona waited, heart pounding, and peered out again. She could not risk being discovered. Smugglers were a dangerous lot, she knew that well enough, and even if she had met some of them personally, crossing paths with them under such circumstances meant taking a terrible chance.

Beware the hills when the Laird is about with his men . . . we always keep clear . . . so Mary MacIan had insisted more than once.

The men's faces were indistinct in the moonlight, their garments dark. The horses carried either pannier baskets or wooden kegs roped to their backs. Some of the smugglers, Fiona was sure, looked in the direction of the standing stone—but as she caught her breath anxiously, they moved on. A minute longer, and they would pass by completely; another few minutes and they would reach the road, and be gone.

Her heart still slammed, but a stubborn courage came over her, calming her. She watched the men and horses go past, hearing the chink of metal harness fittings and the steady footfalls creating persistent rhythms.

One man, holding the reins of a horse, broke away from the rest and came toward the stone, so that Fiona drew back, pressed behind it, fingers taut on cool rock, rooted there by fear. A moment later a hand snatched her arm, and as she cried out a man covered her mouth with his hand. His eyes gleamed in the darkness, but the shape of his face, his shoulders, the swing of his dark hair were familiar. Oh, she knew him so well. And then, pausing, he bent close.

"*Fiona*," he whispered, "go home and lock the door." The caress of his breath along her cheek, close to her ear, nearly melted her, set her limbs to shaking. His hand lifted away from her lips, his fingers tracing her cheek.

"Dougal," she whispered, taking hold of his jacket.

His fingers supported her chin now, his breath traced along her cheek, and then his lips touched hers. Fiona caught her breath, slid her arms around his neck, and he kissed her full then, deep, hidden with her behind the stone. She felt his body press close to hers, and felt herself falter a little in his arms from the pounding beat of her heart, and the sudden passions, body and soul, that filled her—the kiss, the darkness, the danger, the potent feelings that arose in her.

"*A Dhia*," he murmured against her lips. "What is it you do to me? We neither of us need this now. You do not need a rogue in your life, and I—"

"What if I do?" She pressed close to him, splayed her hands on his chest. "What if I do need this—want this?" Her own questions surprised her, shook her very spirit. What these men did was wrong, yet she craved to be with him. How could that be right?

He stepped back, his fingers sliding away from her face. "Go," he whispered. Then he turned.

Heart tumbling, she watched him return to the group. The strong rhythm of his stride seemed so familiar, and her body ached suddenly, strangely after that compelling, unexpected encounter. The men and horses walked onward, the quiet sounds of their passing eerie, as the wind stirred through the night. They reached the road and turned along it.

Gasping out, Fiona ran then, regardless of the uneven terrain, stumbling a couple of times before reaching the road. Maggie ran toward her, and Fiona reached for the dog's collar to lash the rope to it. "Come here. Good girl," she murmured.

Then a low whistle sounded, and the dog whirled and ran after the smugglers. Fiona realized that the dog had not been defending territory, but greeting friends familiar to her, men she often met out on the hills and moors at night—one of them, at least, known at Mary MacIan's house.

Looking toward the lanterns that flashed like yellow stars, Fiona sensed her own choice. She could cross the road and return to the house and safety—or turn and follow Dougal—and follow the urge so powerful that it took breath and logic full away.

Her life was dull and limited, she saw then, even given her Highland travels; she longed for adventure, for a bold spark of passion in her life; she longed for love again, something wilder than the tame love she had known. And what she felt with Dougal hinted at something more powerful than she might ever have imagined for herself, if only she could find the courage to move in that direction.

Yet smuggling was wrong, was criminal, no matter how he might explain it away. Her own brother was part of the law effort against such men. And she was only a dreamer, she told herself. There could be nothing permanent, nothing right in this—Dougal himself agreed, for he had told her to go home, to lock the door and keep safe.

Yet his lips had said something altogether different; his kiss had been tempting and hopeful. And she did not know what to do, what was right. Adventure was one thing, folly another.

While she stood in the road, the clouds dispersed once again, and in the blue glow of moonlight, she saw the flare of more lanterns, and saw two men on horseback appear along the road, not far from where the larger group walked. Shouts sounded in the distance. Without thinking, she hastened toward them, to see what was happening.

"Customs and excise!" a man bellowed. "Stop there!"

Fiona recognized the voice as belonging to Tam MacIntyre, one of the men who had stopped Ranald MacGregor's cart the first night she had met Dougal. Hearing the dog bark, Fiona saw Maggie dashing back toward her as if frightened, whimpering a little.

Lashing the rope to the dog's collar, Fiona patted her. "Good girl," she murmured.

Knowing she should go, Fiona lingered in the darkness, holding the dog's leash, keeping to the side of the road. She could see a little way down the road. The dog began a low rumbling growl in her throat. "Hush," Fiona said. "Stay."

"Dougal MacGregor," Tam said, and the sound carried toward where Fiona stood unseen in the darkness. "I am not surprised to find you and your men out here tonight."

"Ah, Tam," Dougal said, confirming her suspicion. "And who is with you?"

"A deputy. What is in those baskets, Kinloch? MacCarran, take a look in those panniers."

MacCarran. Oh God, Fiona thought; her brother was with them. Her hand tightened on the dog's leash, and she crouched beside Maggie, petting her, listening, trembling.

Dougal crossed his arms and surveyed the gaugers who had so suddenly appeared in the road. "Smuggling? You are mistaken," he said calmly.

"What else would bring the lot of you out here tonight, with packhorses?"

"Allow me to ask what you are doing here in Glen Kinloch, on my land? It is out of your jurisdiction," Dougal countered.

"The stink of peat reek whisky from Highland stills, carried in the panniers of those horses, brought us here," Tam said. "That, and the fact that there is no customs and excise man here—the one who had this northern post died a while back. Curious, that."

Fergus stepped forward. "That excise man died in his bed a few months back, and well you know it. He was not fit for chasing about these hills. He was bred in the south, and too old."

"Even. so," Tam said, "here we all are, and I would bet you lot are carrying illicit peat reek."

"Call it the best of the Highland brews, as it deserves," Dougal said. "Though I doubt you can prove it is illegal. Good night." He took the reins of his horse and began to walk away—heart pounding at the chance he took. Every basket carried by the dozen horses with them that night was filled with whisky in bottles and kegs, from his own stills and those of others. But it was true that no gauger could easily distinguish the whisky of different stills.

Fergus fell into step beside him. "What are you doing?" he hissed.

"Taking a righteous path," Dougal muttered. "Something I learned from the reverend."

"Ah. We're insulted, and we've the legal amount?"

"Something like that," Dougal murmured. He glanced back to see the rest of his comrades falling into place behind him, walking down the road, while the gaugers sat their horses in the middle of the road. "Where did that devil come from tonight? How did he learn about this run?"

Fergus shrugged in silent answer.

"Kinloch!" Tam called. The sound of a cocking pistol cracked in the silence.

Dougal turned, lifting his hand to the gun hidden beneath the swag of plaid draped over his shoulder. "Mr. MacIntyre, still disturbing the peace of my quiet glen?" he asked mildly.

"Bold lad," Tam growled. He and his deputy urged their horses forward. "So you're moving peat reek down to meet a ship on the loch," Tam said. "One was spied out there earlier."

"Was it? For all you know, we might be moving whisky that was produced in lawful amounts, taking it from one household to another."

"Innocent, hey? I am not likely to believe that."

"As it happens, we do not have illicit whisky with us, nor any spirits. We are carrying barley that has been kept over the winter, taking it to some households in the glen that are sorely in need of extra stores."

"Lawful amounts of whisky, and barley to feed the poor?" Tam spat. "MacCarran, check those panniers. Do it quick."

The man riding beside Tam got down from his horse and came forward. He glanced at Dougal and nodded curtly. "Mr. MacGregor," he murmured.

"Mr. MacCarran," Dougal replied. Fiona's brother was a tall, fine-looking young man, Dougal saw, with dark hair and a face whose features, resembling his sister's, seemed oddly familiar.

"Sir, if I may," MacCarran said, and reached toward the horse.

Dougal stepped back to allow MacCarran to look inside the baskets. The young man's expression did not alter as he shifted aside small sacks of barley, used for packing to stifle the clink of glass bottles as the cargo was moved.

Dougal leaned forward. "Patrick MacCarran? Good to meet you, sir."

Patrick looked up, startled. "Have we met?" he murmured.

"Your sister is teaching in the school here," Dougal said. "Teaching my niece, and the others."

The young man frowned. "We have no need to discuss my sister, sir."

"We do not, nor should we," Dougal agreed. "Let me only say that she is well thought of here."

Patrick's hand stilled on the barley sacks, his fingers inches from the bottles. "Say what you mean to say," he growled, low.

"MacCarran! Hurry up there!" Tam shouted.

"Take your sister away from here," Dougal said quickly. "There is too much risk for her, and for you, in this glen."

"I should keep her away from rogues like you," Patrick said.

"I will keep the rogues away from her, including myself. Just get her gone from here. She is as stubborn a girl as I have ever met. Insists on staying, no matter what I—" He stopped.

Patrick tilted his head. "Aye, sir, that is my sister," he whispered.

"Does MacIntyre know she is here?"

"I do not discuss family business with him."

"See that he keeps ignorant of it. Do not trust the man in anything."

"Why should I trust you?" Patrick asked, low.

"Trust me or not, as you like. Just get Fiona out of here. It is not safe for her."

Patrick's frown deepened. "Best if we all part ways peaceably this evening, I think."

"Just so," Dougal murmured. "You will not regret that decision."

Without a word, Patrick MacCarran moved to the next horse, and the next, checking each basket. When he was done, he went back to Fergus's pony, opened the panniers and lifted the contents, and carried that back toward his waiting comrade.

"What have you found?" Tam said.

"Only a few bottles," Patrick said. "The panniers are all carrying barley sacks."

Fergus, standing with Dougal, huffed quietly. "Smart lad," he muttered.

Tam laughed. "Transporting barley is no crime, though they will just make more whisky from it. What about the bottles?"

"Most of them are like this one, sir," Patrick said. He stretched up an arm and gave the bottle to Tam, who took it, opened it, sniffed it, and upended it.

"Bah, empty!"

"Mr. MacIntyre, my guess is that these men are transporting barley for their own use, and as you say, that is no crime. As for the whisky they're carrying—most of it is in their bellies already. I would guess they're fou, most of them. Drunk as can be."

"Fou," Tam growled, and looked at Dougal. "You devil, Kinloch."

Dougal grinned, crossing his arms. Fergus did his best to wobble just then, grabbing hold of his horse's bridle. Another one of the men—Thomas MacDonald's eldest son, Neill, Dougal noticed—leaned over and pretended to retch.

"I will check those damn panniers myself," Tam said, and began to dismount.

"I wish you would take my word for it, sir," Patrick said. "It would look better on the report for both you and me. I always do my utmost, sir."

"So far," Tam said in a snide tone. "But you're an idiot if you think those sneakbaits are not transporting peat reek tonight."

"Here, I also took this," Patrick said, and handed Tam what more he held—two full bottles of Glen Kinloch's finest, Dougal noticed. "I thought you might find a use for it."

"Ha, I will," Tam said. "But I had better take a look myself—what the devil!" he said, looking past the group and down the road. Patrick turned, and his mouth dropped open.

Dougal turned, too, and swore.

A woman walked toward them along the road, leading a dog on a rope. A dark plaid draped over her head covered most of her, but for her skirt hiked high, and bare feet. The dog trotted obediently beside her as she neared the men clustered on the road. She kept her head down.

Though the woman looked like a Highland Gael, Dougal recognized Fiona immediately, along with Maggie; the dog had followed the men through the hills, for she loved the sport of smuggling runs. And Fiona, he saw, had not gone home as he had advised her. He stepped forward, but Fergus put up a hand to stop him.

Patrick MacCarran walked toward her, speaking quietly to her for a moment. She shook her head and passed by him, and moments later approached Dougal, while the dog trotted beside her.

"Ah, Kinloch, is it you?" she asked in Gaelic.

"You know damn well it is," he growled in that language. Maggie looked up hopefully for the petting he would not give her just then. "What are you doing here?"

"Speak in English, then?" She smiled as if he had actually asked that of her. "I will try. Are you bringing the barley you promised us for our soup?"

"We are," he said, scowling furiously at her.

"*Tapadh leat*," she said. "Thank you. My grandmother will be pleased," she continued in Gaelic. "*Oidhche mhath*, good night, sirs." She walked toward Tam MacIntyre, the dog pulling on the leash, beginning to growl.

Dougal, watching, felt as if his heart had leaped into his throat.

"Good evening, sir," she told Tam. "A thousand wishes for your long health and happy life." And she smiled radiantly at the excise man, Dougal noticed. She had never yet smiled at him that way, luminous and innocent, and he felt the pang of that—and alarm for the risk she was taking. Once again he stepped forward, but Fergus blocked him firmly with an outthrust elbow.

Then Fiona turned to her brother as if she had never seen him before, bid him good night as well, and walked past all of them down the road, pulling the dog with her.

Tam's horse sidestepped, and MacIntyre tightened the reins. He snapped something to MacCarran, who walked toward Dougal.

"Tam says he has no time for this nonsense with you lot," MacCarran said.

"Ah," Dougal remarked. "What did your sister say to you?" he asked, quick and low.

"She asked what I found in the baskets and I told her barley and some whisky. Then she told me to make sure you lot were safe—and for me to leave her be, as she has no intention of leaving the glen anytime soon." Patrick looked hard at him. "MacGregor, keep a care for my sister," he said, "and watch your own activities in this glen, or I swear your life is forfeit."

Dougal returned his gaze evenly. "I will keep a care for her," he said. "Do not doubt it."

"You, sir—take the barley stores to the young miss and her grandmother," Patrick said loudly, for Tam's benefit, Dougal guessed. "See to it quick, and go back to your homes."

He turned and went back to his horse, mounting again, while Tam snapped that he was taking too damn long. Then Tam McIntyre looked toward Dougal, and pointed.

"We will not see you out in these hills again, MacGregor, by moonlight or darkness, is that clear? Next time I will bring more men. Be sure of it."

"In my glen I do as I please," Dougal answered. "Good night, sirs."

Tam growled something under his breath, and he and MacCarran rode away.

Dougal let out a long breath, and Fergus glanced at him. "I like the wee teacher," his uncle said. "I think she should stay out the contract Hugh gave her."

"Two months? I may throttle her before that time is up," Dougal growled.

Chapter 9

Rain drummed on the windows of the school-house, and the soft squeak and scratch of the chalk added another layer of sound as Fiona wrote on a large, framed slate that was hung on a wall, its weight supported by a heavy shelf beneath. She glanced over her shoulder. The students were seated on their benches, working on the assignment she had given them, copying lists of words from the slate on the wall to the slates they held.

They were all busy and seemed to concentrate on their work, without any of the rowdy behavior she sometimes saw; they had listened intently that morning, and had seemed happy to be there, laughing and chatting while two girls passed the slates and chalks around and the others found their seats.

Fiona smiled to herself, and turned back to the large slate to add a few more English words. Beside *cat*, she drew a cat; beside *chair*, she drew one of those; for *cradle*, she drew that, too. Behind her, chalks squeaked over slates as they copied the list.

The glen school was flourishing, which pleased and surprised her a little, for she was not certain how that would progress, with MacGregor of Kinloch and his uncles apparently eager for her to leave the glen—and after the events of a moonlit night only a few days before, she knew why. Now it was abundantly clear that their business in the glen would not allow for the presence of a gauger's sister.

She had been surprised to see Patrick that night—and perplexed the next day by a note from him, delivered to Mary MacIan's house by a man who had sailed up the loch in a small boat manned by another. Beaching in the cove, he had come up to knock on the door, handing her a sealed note with scarcely a word to her or Mary MacIan.

Dearest Fiona, Patrick had written, *if you would leave Glen Kinloch soon, send word by the bearer of this note, Eldin's man, that you are ready to leave. The carriage will arrive for you within the week.*

If, as I suspect, you have formed an affectionate bond with the glen folk and wish to stay—then indicate to Eldin's man that you are content where you are. But if your circumstances are dangerous in any way, let Eldin's man know that. He is instructed to wait while you gather your things, and fetch you back to Auchnashee by boat this day.

*Fiona, may I remind you that in our broth-
ers' absence, it is my responsibility to ensure
your well-being and perfect safety. James and
William would do the same, were they in my
place.*

She had read Patrick's note while Eldin's man
sat at the table drinking a cup of the good brown
beer that Mary had made. "Please tell my brother
that I am content to stay," she told him. "And that
I will take responsibility for my well-being. He will
know what I mean," she said. Giving him a keg of
Mary's brown beer, which was stored in quantity,
she had walked him down to the cove.

Then she had gone back to her studies, writing
out the lessons for the next day.

Wrong or right, smugglers or gaugers, she felt
strongly that she followed her best judgment by
staying. She was not ready to leave Glen Kinloch,
despite pressure from the laird and now her own
brother—and those two stood on opposing sides,
with Fiona caught in the middle. Both were stubborn men, but she was resolute and would have to
prevail. She had not yet completed her obligation
to her grandmother, or to herself, for she had given
her word to teach here.

Fleetingly she wondered if she had given her
heart, too, quickly and unexpectedly, for that she
had never planned. But she could hardly fulfill her
grandmother's wishes, and help her brothers obtain
their much-needed inheritance, if she fell in love with

a poor Highland smuggler who lacked title, fortune, and all her grandmother had wanted for her.

Love, she thought, bowing her head for a moment, pausing her chalk tip on the board. Could she truly feel that again, after so long? Though she wanted home and family, she had never really expected to know again feelings such as she had held for Archie.

Surely it was just fancy, she told herself; just the romantic appeal of a smuggler on a moonlit night, a man unlike any she would ever find in Edinburgh or elsewhere; surely this was a daydream with no more substance than a wisp of fog. And she would not think about it again.

Likely he did not share her burgeoning feelings; likely his heart did not beat faster when she was near; and very likely he truly did want her to leave. She lifted her head and began to write again on the large slate, chalk squeaking in earnest.

But she was more determined than ever to stay for the sake of her students. Each day she learned more about their abilities with both Gaelic and English, while they had learned, she hoped, that she could be calm and kind, yet had a stern side. She did not tolerate disruption or distraction, and there had been some fierce scrubbing of slates by Lucy MacGregor and one or two others for talking out of turn or daydreaming when there was work to be done.

She had spent evenings writing not only letters home, but lists of vocabulary by lantern light until her eyes burned from the oil smoke and her fingers were ink-stained. All the scholars in her school were quick-witted, and most of them learned new English words so quickly that each day she needed more vocabulary lists and fresh ideas. She taught a little mathematics, too, and planned to teach some geography, having found a dusty book of maps in a cupboard in the school. But her most important task was helping them improve their skills in reading and speaking English.

She had been involved in her teaching duties, but not too busy to think about Dougal MacGregor, and to notice that each day she passed his tower house going to the school and home again, yet she had not seen him, even though she glanced about curious and half hoping. But she reminded herself again that he wanted her out of Glen Kinloch and away from his secrets. Twice already, she had come upon his smuggling activities—no wonder he likely thought her troublesome. She caught him out more often than the gaugers themselves. She almost smiled.

Now she turned, hearing some low chattering. "Lucy MacGregor, that will be enough," she said sternly, seeing Lucy whispering to her cousin Jamie. The girl smiled sweetly as the boy handed her his last bit of chalk, though now he lacked some for his own use.

Fiona walked over to them. "Lucy, please fetch some chalks from the basket and hand them to everyone," she said quietly and firmly. Lucy nodded willingly and stood to comply. There was no malice in the child, she knew, just a willful spirit; Lucy was more than a bit smitten with Jamie Lamont, so that she could not leave him be.

While Lucy walked around the class with an apron full of chalk pieces, Fiona saw that the two new students who had arrived that morning were sitting quietly, hands folded, gazes forward in anticipation. New students had arrived each day or so, and the class now numbered over a dozen. Duncan and Sarah Lamont, cousins of Jamie, had arrived before class asking to be admitted. Shaking Fiona's hand solemnly, they answered her questions before finding seats on one of the long benches.

Returning to her table, Fiona took up a quill and dipped it in a bottle of ink to write the new names on the student list she had prepared; then she added notations. *Cousins of the laird*, she wrote; *father is the miller at Drumcairn. Duncan ten, Sarah eight. They speak little English.* On the next line she noted: *Lucy MacGregor needs more activities to occupy her time.*

She looked up when the class was quiet. Walking forward, she folded her hands calmly. "We have a shortage of lesson books, and we have gone through lists of words, so today we will do something new," she said in Gaelic.

Tomorrow she would speak to them in English as much as possible, she thought; but for now she wanted them to feel comfortable and grow accustomed to regular hours in school. Picking up the packet she had brought with her, bound in plain paper and string, she opened it to remove a thick sheaf of papers.

"I have some translations for you," she told the students. "When I was a girl, I loved to sing the Gaelic songs that my Highland nurse taught me. I translated some of them into English, thinking that many of you will know the verses and songs, too. I have only a few copies, so some of you will have to share." She looked up. "Jamie, please hand the pages around."

The redheaded boy jumped up to pass the hand-written sheaves to the other students. When the copies had been distributed, Fiona noticed Lucy sharing with Annabel, and the Lamont siblings sharing another page. Taking up her own set of copied pages, she looked up at the class.

"We will try reciting these. If you cannot read the English very well, just follow along as we say each word, and place your finger there, to help you recognize the words again," she said. "I will say them first in Gaelic, then in English.

"Dear Lord, shield the house, the fire, the kine, and everyone who dwells here tonight," she read, and then continued in a soft singsong while they listened.

> *Shield myself and my dear ones*
> *Preserve us from harm*
> *For the sake of the angels*
> *Who watch over us this night*

Mairi MacDonald raised her hand. "Miss, my grandmother says this verse every night. She calls it the prayer before resting."

"My mother says it every night, too," Lilias said. Others murmured agreement.

"I know this one, too," Lucy said. "My aunt Jean taught it to me, and now that she is gone, my uncle says it to me every night before I sleep."

"Very good," Fiona said, feeling a quick twinge of sympathy to learn that small Lucy had lost both mother and, apparently, an aunt who had cared for her; she was touched, too, to know that MacGregor of Kinloch took time to recite a comforting Gaelic prayer. "Let us say it together in Gaelic and then English," she continued. "Next verse."

Taking up a stick she had found outside, she pointed to the words she had chalked on the large slate hung on the wall.

Air an oidhche nochd's gach aon oidhche,
An oidhche nochd's gach aon oidhche.
On this night and every night,
On this night and every night.

Her students already knew the verses, and she was pleased with her decision to try something new. As they recited the verses with her, the sound was rich and soft upon the air. Fiona smiled, feeling a thrill that sometimes came to her when she listened to the Gaelic language, as if there was magic and power in even its most ordinary words.

"Excellent," she said. "Again, please, and follow the words with your finger or your pencil. Sing if you like, and if you know the melody." She closed her eyes for a moment listening as a shy harmony of spoken and sung words swelled in the room. Then one voice, sweet and silver clear, rose above the rest.

Fiona glanced toward the side, and saw Annabel sitting straight, chin lifted as she sang out. Her voice had an astonishing purity and strength, despite her youth. As the other students finished their recitation, the girl's last note rang out true in the silence.

"That was lovely, Annabel," Fiona said.

The girl blushed, her silver-blond hair slipping down to hide much of her face. "Thank you, Miss MacCarran," she said softly, shoulders hunched. Someone laughed and there were whispers, but Fiona could not tell, in the slanting sunshine and shadow that came through the small windows, who was responsible. Not wanting to embarrass the girl further, she said nothing and turned away, but listened intently.

She resumed the lesson, reciting the verses in English, the students following. Annabel did not sing this time, though Fiona hoped to hear the child's hauntingly lovely voice again.

For the rest of the morning, the students learned quickly, soon reading a few English words from the Gaelic, and Fiona was impressed by their progress. She excused them for luncheon, noticing that the rain had stopped, although air and earth were still damp. Some of the children sat under trees and some on the large rocks that studded the hillside. Each had brought something from home to eat, unwrapping cheese slabs or oatcakes, and filling the wooden cups that Fiona provided with clear water from a burn that bubbled over rocks down the hillside.

Mrs. MacIan had given Fiona a packet of food wrapped in a cloth, as she had done each morning; today Fiona found barley cake and a slice of cold bacon. She set it aside to work a little at the table while the students stayed outside, eating and running about.

"Miss MacCarran," a voice said.

Looking up, she saw Ranald MacGregor peering through the doorway, and just behind him, his brother Fergus, the blacksmith whom she had met only briefly. Rising from her tall stool, she went to the door to greet them. "Mr. MacGregor, and . . . Mr. MacGregor," she said with a smile. "What can I do for you?"

"If you will excuse us, miss," Ranald said, "we have come to check the roof. With the bairns outside, we thought it might be a good time."

She stepped back to allow them to enter. "I did not know there was a problem with the roof."

"Och aye," Ranald said solemnly. "Are you done with the schoolwork for the day?"

"We sometimes work for a little while after luncheon, though if they complete their assignments, I sometimes release them earlier. Today we have a lesson yet to finish."

Ranald nodded. "How will they learn all their lessons if they do not work all day long?"

"I know that most of them have chores and tasks at home, so they need afternoons free for whatever must be done at home."

"Some have tasks only when the laird asks them to do something," Fergus said.

"Ah," Fiona said. "Do the older lads help the laird . . . at night, in the hills?"

"Och, and why would they do that?" Ranald asked quickly.

"Perhaps he moves things about in carts at night," she said, and smiled.

"We brought a cask to the reverend's mother the night you saw us, miss," he replied.

"That is what I meant, of course," she said. "If the older lads are sometimes busy in the evenings, though, I would like to know about it."

"Why?" Fergus snapped, and glanced at Ranald.

"They might be particularly weary some mornings, or without time to do their home lessons the night before. It would help me to assess their work as scholars."

"Ah." Ranald nodded. "My son Andrew, is he a good scholar?"

"Very bright, and a fast learner, Mr. MacGregor. So is Jamie," she added.

"Jamie is my grandson," Fergus said proudly. "A good lad."

"Andrew has his mother's wit," Ranald said. "Not mine. I do not read English."

"Yet you speak it very well. And you are undoubtedly a clever man, which your son has inherited from you," she answered.

"That is true," Ranald said, puffing proudly.

"Huh," Fergus said, as if he doubted it. "Miss, you are a good teacher and a charming lass, I am thinking. What of our great-niece, Lucy, how does she in the school? The laird will want to know."

"The laird should ask me himself, but I have not seen him all this week. She is a bit spirited, and also very bright. She's an enjoyable child."

"The laird has been very busy with matters in the glen," Fergus said.

"I am sure of it," she said with a little spice in her tone.

Fergus huffed. "As for Lucy, do not seat her with Jamie. She torments the lad."

"A little, but I suspect it is a form of affection."

The men looked surprised. "She does not want to be in school, though Jamie likes the lessons," Ranald said.

"So it goes with some children," Fiona replied. "Sooner or later, they learn what they need to learn, and leave the rest."

"She is a good dominie, this one," Fergus told Ranald. "Perhaps the roof can wait a bit."

"The roof?" Fiona looked up. "I noticed some damp spots on the ceiling, but nothing concerning."

"Let us take a look," Ranald said. "We have not always had a teacher here at the glen school," he continued. "Some years a traveling dominie would come to the glen and stay a season, going from house to house so the bairns could learn their reading and maths at home. That did well enough. We learned that way," he said, glancing at Fergus, who shrugged.

"We did not learn much," he said. "John—that was our oldest brother, miss, and the father of the current laird—was more interested in learning than we three. He studied on his own, and took an interest in books and learning for his tenants and his son, too. Wanted him to have an education."

"As every laird needs, these days especially," Fiona said. "I have heard of the practice of traveling dominie. Sometimes it is the best solution when the glen is large and distances are too great for the students to walk to the only school for miles." She saw the men nod and glance at each other. "If more children want to come to the school from the far ends of Glen Kinloch, I will speak to Reverend MacIan about hiring a traveling dominie to help out."

"We cannot afford to hire another teacher. We are a poor glen," Fergus said. "One teacher, that is you."

"And the roof is leaking," Ranald said, without glancing up. "Leaking bad."

"How do you know, without looking at it?" she asked. "At any rate, I am only prepared to teach reading and writing here, and I plan to return to Edinburgh soon."

"How soon?" Fergus asked.

"A few weeks. Can the roof not wait until then?"

The men only looked at each other, then walked to a shadowy corner behind the rows of benches. There they ran their hands over the walls and stooped to check the planked wooden floor for dampness and cracks. The level of the ceiling, which comprised roof beams topped by thick bound thatch, was within Fergus's long reach. They stood gazing upward for so long, and murmuring, that Fiona walked back to join them.

"I hope it is nothing serious," she said.

"It shows the damp," Fergus said. "See there." He indicated some stains and cracks.

"Could you patch it for now?"

"A patch will not do. It needs a new roof, slates like our other buildings here, or at least a new thatching," Ranald told her. "And the rooftree needs replacing. There is some rot up there, see." He indicated the roof beams overhead.

"Can you not repair it now, and replace it properly later?"

"We cannot wait that long," Ranald said quickly. "A week, no more."

She glanced up at the ceiling, where the underside of the sturdy thatch roof showed above bare roof beams, for the building was that old. "Are we in danger from this?"

"Och, could be," Ranald said.

"Oh dear!" Fiona glanced through the window, hearing shouts outside. Most of the students had finished eating, and the boys were gathered in the center of the yard, kicking a ball among them. She turned back. "But we are just getting started with our lessons. It would not do to interrupt them now."

"It would not do for the roof to fall on their heads, miss," Fergus pointed out.

"Perhaps you can return to Glen Kinloch later for the teaching," Ranald added.

Suddenly suspicious, she folded her arms. "Did the laird send you here to tell me this?"

"Not at all. We knew the roof had some damage," Ranald said.

"Then why were we allowed to start up school sessions again?" she asked.

Fergus shrugged. "It is not for us to say. You must ask the laird."

"I will," she said firmly. The shouts from the yard were growing louder, distracting her with thoughts of her class. She stepped back. "It is time for the scholars to come inside. Thank you, sirs. May we talk about this later?"

As Fiona opened door, the MacGregors behind her, she saw that near pandemonium had taken hold in the yard, as the students—boys and girls— still kicked the ball among them, yet seemed to have lost any sense of manners and decorum. Shoving and shouting, some of them fighting and tugging on one another, they jammed together in a group, tussling over the ball, so that Fiona could barely identify each one.

And she stared, feeling a quick excitement that she recalled from childhood, when she and her brothers had played similar games with the children on their Perthshire estate. But as teacher, she could not let it continue. "It is time for class," she said, stepping outside quickly. "Time for this to end!"

Ranald and Fergus ran past her toward the group, and she waited, thinking they would quickly end the rough play. Instead they joined in, laughing and calling out.

And then, in the midst of the group, Fiona recognized the laird of Kinloch huddled with the boys, striving with the rest for the ball.

"Where is that ba'!" Ranald shouted as he shoved his way into the thick of the group, and Dougal looked up to see two of his uncles shouldering their way through.

"Watch the girls," he growled to Ranald, putting up an arm to protect Pol's sister Mairi as the expanding group jostled and enlarged. He knew how seriously his uncles took any game of football. "Fergus, mind the wee ones. Jamie—Lucy—out with you," he ordered. "The game is too rough now." Ignoring him, the younger ones scrambled on with the rest.

"Da, what side are you on?" Andrew called to his father. "We need more men!"

"What sides do we have today?" Fergus asked.

"Kinnies and Glennies," Pol answered. "Those related to Kinloch, and those not."

"Then we are all on the same side," Ranald

called, amid laughter. He hunkered down and swept at the ball with his booted toe. "Nearly had it—damn!"

"What is this?" Hearing the female voice, Dougal glanced up to see Fiona MacCarran standing at the outskirts of the circle. "Watch the little ones, if you please!" she called.

He straightened, looking toward her, seeing her distress—she was pink in the cheeks from shouting. Blasting out a sigh, he stretched out his arm to slow down those nearest him, including Andrew and Mairi. "Stop," he said. "Enough."

"But we only started—" Pol began, looked up, and stopped.

Fiona clasped her hands in front of her. "Time for class to resume," she said. "Come inside." Around Dougal, the others slowed, stared, and did not respond. A few of them still pushed the ball around with their feet. She walked forward to the edge of the cluster.

"It is time for class," she said sternly, hands folded.

"Och, just a bit longer," Fergus said, and one of the younger ones laughed—Duncan Lamont from down the glen side had joined in, Dougal saw, while his sister Sarah and Annabel MacDonald hung back, not taking part. "Please," Fergus said, to more laughter.

Fiona's frown grew, hands folded. "It is time for lessons to start, or the day will be very long," she said.

"Enough, lads, lasses," Dougal said, and stepped back, drawing with him the ones standing nearest to him. The ball, abandoned for a moment in the center, rolled. He shooed the students away. "Listen to your dominie," he said, and looked at his uncles. "You, too."

"Back to work for us and to lessons for you," Fergus said, and ruffled his grandson Jamie's red hair. "Good work at the football, lad."

Jamie grinned and ran forward with the others as the students trudged past their teacher, who stood silently in the middle of the yard, hands folded, mouth set in a prim line as they filed into the school.

Dougal fisted his hand at his waist and watched her. "Good day, Miss MacCarran," he called. "It is a fine day for a game of the football."

"It is," she said, "but far better done after school, or on a Saturday. There are lessons to be learned, and hard play comes later."

"Just as in life—work first, play later," he drawled. "Until later, then, Miss MacCarran."

"Mr. MacGregor." A smile quirked her lips, the luscious lips he had tasted and wanted to again; the feeling tugged at him, as often happened when he saw her, was close to her.

The ball was at his foot. He kicked it with his toe and sent it toward her.

Quickly she raised her skirt hems and punted the ball back to him with ease, scooping the ball with the top of her foot and sending it upward to land softly, just at his feet. Dougal halted the ball with his toe and looked up at her, impressed.

"You see, Kinloch," she said, "I am not afraid of the games you play here in the glen."

"So I see," he murmured, and inclined his head. "But are you equal to them?"

"I believe so. Do you?" She turned away, smiling. Once again, wistful and quick, Dougal wished that smile was for him, but this time it seemed hers alone. The lovely expression disappeared as she entered the classroom, in its stead a stern dominie who would no doubt treat her scholars to an extra lesson.

Dougal chuckled to himself, picked up the ball, and walked back toward Kinloch House. He saw Ranald and Fergus standing in the yard there, waiting for him.

"That's a good lass," Ranald grunted.

Dougal threw the ball toward him. "Keep this, we will need it," he told his uncles, both of them. "And start spreading the word—we want to form a game. A serious one."

"When, and played by whom?" Fergus asked.

"Soon enough, and everyone," Dougal said, and went into the house.

Once the students were settled in their seats, Fiona asked Lilias Beaton to pass around a second set of pages that Fiona had copied the previous evening.

"This is a new verse for us to try," Fiona told the class. "It is called a *fith-fath*."

"*Fith-faths!* They are old charms," Mairi said. "My grandmother recites them. Why should we learn those in English?"

"Because these verses contain lists of words that are easy to learn in translation. Listen," she said, and began in Gaelic:

> *Fith-fath ni mi ort*
> *Bho chire, bho ruta,*
> *Bho mhise, bho bhuc. . .*

"A *fith-fath* I make on you," she then said in English, "from sheep, from ram, from goat, from stag . . ." She had chosen the ancient Gaelic household blessing for its common form—lists of animal names and plain nouns that were simple enough to teach in English, both verbally and written. And she had counted on the fact that many of the students would find the verses familiar and the form quick to absorb.

Now she wished that she knew a blessing charm for a roof; it seemed they could use one. She glanced up at the ceiling uneasily, not sure if it was indeed so precarious, or if Ranald and Fergus MacGregor were leading her on in another scheme.

As the students repeated the lines, Fiona heard the thunk of boots on the step. Thinking Ranald and Fergus had returned, she turned, intending to ask them to wait until the class was excused.

Dougal MacGregor stood in the doorway, arms folded as he quietly listened. Fiona felt her heart leap in her chest, but she squared her shoulders. Still in the middle of the lesson, she did not want to interrupt the students, and when MacGregor motioned for her to continue, she calmly turned back to her class and finished the word lists, aware all the while that he was watching.

She walked toward him. "Mr. MacGregor," she said warily.

"Pardon the interruption, Miss MacCarran." He inclined his head. "I thought class might be ended by now. I would like a word with you."

Her heart gave a little fillip of excitement and dread—she surely needed a word with him, and beyond that, she would admit no need where he was concerned. Then she nodded. "Very well. We are not done with our lesson yet. Can it wait until after class?"

"Let it be another day," he said. "I have some business to tend to very shortly."

"Another day, then," she murmured, wondering if that business had to do with smuggling, and silent treks over the hills at night. "I will be here tomorrow, as always."

"Tomorrow, then, after class. I have something to discuss with you."

Excitement stirred in her again. "Oh? Do you want to look at the roof, too?"

"Not that. Other matters."

She leaned forward. "Illicit ones?"

"You," he said, leaning toward her, "are far too eager."

"I rather enjoyed myself the other night," she murmured, and felt herself blush.

"Did you?" He smiled down at her, and she suddenly wished for more from him, hoped he would return the interest that was ever-increasing within her. She wanted him to take her into his confidence—and into his arms again. "I am glad."

"Did you?" she asked. "Enjoy . . . the other night?"

"Watching you stroll between gaugers and smugglers?" he hissed. "I did not."

"Not that!" She dropped her voice to a whisper. "Besides, my brother would never have arrested you."

"He would not have had a choice, if Tam had ordered it done, or had done it himself. There would have been a skirmish, and you in the middle. I did not enjoy that," he said, low and urgent.

"What of the . . . other, the—" She stopped glancing away.

"Ah, the kiss," he whispered. "That was a taste of heaven, Miss MacCarran."

She looked up at him in silence, blushing furiously, astonished with herself for even asking him, and now feeling her breath quicken. She nodded.

"But you should not be here, should you, with a smuggler tempted to kiss you again, and bring no good to your life. No doubt your brothers would agree that you ought to be safe in Edinburgh, behaving yourself. Until later, miss," he said, and inclined his head. "A *fith-fath* on you and yours."

She leaned forward through the gap in the door, close enough to feel the powerful draw the man had on her, despite his words, which had turned her around like a top. His eyes seemed so green, reflecting the forest hues in the plaid wrapped about him, one end draped over the shoulder of his jacket. Under dark brows drawn together, his gaze was striking, unfathomable.

She felt, wildly, suddenly, as if he spun a spell around her with just a look—like a man of the Fey rather than of the earth. She remembered again the kiss behind that standing stone, and drew a breath. Taste of heaven, indeed.

And yet, even when she had helped the smugglers, he had not spoken of it until now. He had avoided her, she realized, and now wanted to speak with her at last. Clearly he was determined to send her away from the glen. She squared her shoulders against the sudden hurt of the sensation.

"Sir," she said, "if you and your uncles are set on being rid of me, I have need of a *fith-fath* of protection." She kept her tone crisp to prove to him—and to herself—that she did not care if he would not.

"Being rid of you? Fiona," he murmured, "tomorrow I want to show you something. Go inside now," he said, his tone gone gentle. "They are waiting for you."

Chapter 10

D ougal sat alone at one of the four tables in the front room of the small inn kept by Rob MacIan. The only patrons other than himself were three of his tenants gathered around a front table, discussing how soon they could send their cattle into the glen's higher slopes to graze on the sweet hill grass there. The winter had been harsher than usual, Dougal overheard them say; the cattle were thin still, though it was nearly May.

His own cattle were also in need of the better nutrition of the higher slopes, where sunlight and clear mountain streams fed the grasses and flowers, and livestock could grow healthy after a long winter and a wet spring. The Highlands of Scotland did not produce good hay for cattle, though there were oats and barley for them.

Soon enough, the daughters and wives of these men, and some of the younger men, would drive the cattle into the hills to stay in shieling huts, modest cottages used in spring and summer by those who brought the cattle to the high slopes for weeks at a time. With the hills more populated than usual, moving great lots of whisky kegs about would not be as conveniently managed as now, before the shieling time began.

The men had invited Dougal to join them earlier, but he had smiled and declined. He had agreed to meet someone at Rob MacIan's inn, but the man had not arrived as yet. He sipped a tankard of ale in silence, watching through the small window near his corner seat. Along the road, he saw a black coach—not the shabby beast that Hamish drove, but a trim barouche pulled by four sleek bay horses.

He nodded to himself. Hamish would be disappointed to miss seeing such an excellent vehicle, he thought. Outside, the black coach drew up in front of the inn rather grandly, and while the tenants stopped their chat to look out the window, Rob MacIan emerged from an inner room. The innkeeper—who like his son the reverend was a tall, fair sort, though age and ale had made him big and ruddy—hurried to open the door and step out into the yard. Dougal heard Rob call to one of his sons to see to coach, horses, and driver; Rob would escort the passenger inside, offering his guest food, drink, and lodging if needed.

Sipping the ale again, a fine and fresh brew—by its taste, he knew the household in the glen where it was made—Dougal waited.

When Rob returned, he was accompanied by a tall, lean, dark-haired man in a black double-breasted frock coat, neat gray trousers, and high black boots. As he entered, he removed his tall black hat, holding its curved brim, and ducked his head slightly beneath the lintel. He carried a cane that he clearly had no need of, as he had an athletic, restrained fitness in both form and movement.

The tenants watched in surprise and then glanced at one another. One of them looked outside again, probably expecting a tourist party, or perhaps a pack of revenue agents. He shot a look toward Dougal that expressed doubt and suspicion, and the laird nodded once.

The Earl of Eldin was certainly a handsome fellow, Dougal observed; striking really, his eyes piercing enough to take in the room and assess everything and everyone in it with a swift glance. Seeing Dougal seated alone, he advanced to the table.

"MacGregor of Kinloch, I presume," he said.

"Lord Eldin," Dougal said in greeting, and rose to his feet, for Eldin seemed to expect some sort of fancy greeting. He offered his bare, rough hand, gripping the earl's gloved fingers, and was surprised by the strong handshake he got in return.

As they sat on opposite benches, Eldin put his hat on the table. Rob came toward them. "Sir, you must be thirsty after your journey," he said, setting down a tankard of ale.

"From Auchnashee to here is not that far," Eldin said, looking at the tankard with mild disdain. "I will have a dram of whisky, if you please. That local brew you recommended once before to me—ah. Kinloch. It is the finest in the Highlands, I hear."

Dougal tipped his head as Rob hurried away. "My thanks," he said.

"No thanks necessary," Eldin said. "I am not flattering you, sir. If the brew is indeed that good, then I am merely stating a fact."

"Indeed," Dougal said. He sipped his ale again.

Eldin lifted his own tankard to drink as well, then set it down. "I am quite surprised," he said. "That's more than passable stuff."

"Far more," Dougal said. "A cousin of mine, Helen MacDonald, makes it."

The earl swallowed from the tankard again. "It is light for an ale, and . . . delicate. Quite refreshing. I've never had the like. What makes the difference in the brew?"

"Heather flowers, I believe. Helen uses an old recipe known to the family."

"Ah, heather ale! I've heard of it. This is excellent. Does she sell it?" he asked quickly.

"She does," Dougal answered. "Though she does not produce it in much quantity, so of course the price goes higher for that."

"No matter. I will seek out the woman and request that she provide ale for my hotel."

"I will ask her," Dougal said cautiously, "and send her answer to you."

Rob returned quickly with a dark bottle and two glasses, which he poured out, the liquid golden, its familiar fragrance wafting as the drinks were poured.

"*Sláinte*," Dougal said, lifting his glass as Eldin

lifted his. The earl sipped the whisky, and Dougal studied him: wealth and elegant lifestyle were apparent even in the smallest immaculate details of the man's garment, from the snowy linen neck cloth tied high and close, stuffed beneath the high lapels of the woolen coat, whose precise cut flattered a wide-shouldered torso and narrow waist, to the polished beaver hat set on the table, and the gold-headed cane leaned beside it.

Unconsciously Dougal straightened his shoulders, his jacket the same brown wool he favored, his plaid in the MacGregor hues of burgundy and green, his shirt plain linen with a simple open-throated collar, his hair unkempt, windblown, too long. Lord Eldin was a man of obvious means and sophistication, had probably been raised with luxury and ease, and Dougal felt the differences keenly.

But he felt no lack. Rather, he was more aware of his own solid, plain, reliable nature, and was satisfied with it. He suspected that Eldin was not as content as his expensive garments and shining black barouche might make him seem. The man had shadows beneath his eyes, and a grim set to his mouth. And he downed the whisky rather quickly, reaching for the bottle to pour another inch or so in the glass.

"Excellent," Eldin said. "This is from your own distillery?"

"It is," Dougal answered. He had not finished his own dram, and set the glass down.

"Legal or illicit?"

"Does it matter?"

"It might," Eldin answered.

"You sent a message requesting that we meet here, Eldin," he said. "What is on your mind?"

Eldin turned the small, thick-stemmed glass in his hand. "This is a coaching inn," he said. "But it does not seem busy. Does it do much trade?"

"Rob MacIan's inn has been here a long while," Dougal answered. "His father and grandfather tended it before him. Most days its patrons are local men of the glen. Occasionally a coach will come by, filled with tourists who have read Sir Walter Scott and have come to take a look at the scenery of Loch Katrine and the surrounding hills."

"And they are treated to this fine whisky?"

"If they order more than ale or wine, aye," Dougal said. "Providing Rob has a store of Kinloch brew. Other local whiskies are available here as well. The MacDonald family in this glen make a particularly fine one, too, as well as the Lamonts, and MacIan himself produces a few hundred gallons a year of his own whisky."

"Near everyone in this glen makes it, from what I hear," Eldin said, "and most of it is illicit."

Dougal sniffed, leaned back, propped a foot on the opposite bench, beneath the table. He regarded the man across from him. "What is it you want of me, sir?"

"You are the laird of this glen."

"I am."

"So you know all that goes on here."

"Within reason. Why?"

"I have a hotel at Auchnashee, ready to open to tourists and travelers by summer," Eldin said. "I would like to obtain good whisky for that establishment."

Dougal nodded. "There is plenty of good whisky obtainable in this glen. If it is Glen Kinloch brew you want, then tell me what quantities you have in mind, and we can come to some bargain."

Eldin sipped again, stared at the glass, considered something. "What is the finest you have ready for purchase? The *very* finest," he added with slight but noticeable emphasis.

Dougal leaned forward, tapping his fingers on the table as he studied the gentleman. This was Fiona's cousin, he reminded himself, and he narrowed his eyes, seeing a resemblance, despite the differences gender made, in the fine cut of the features, the dark glossy hair, the direct, intelligent stare, the warning hint of stubbornness in the lean, firm jaw. But he saw something more in this fellow's eyes that he had never seen in Fiona—a cunning, calculating layer of thought behind the polish of courtesy. Eldin might be a decent sort, but there was something Dougal did not trust about him—something secretive.

"The finest we have," he said then, "depends on what price is offered."

"A handsome price," Eldin said. "Name it."

"We have a batch that has been stored three years in oak casks," Dougal said, and mentioned a price that was high, but not exorbitant.

"Is it legal, that brew?"

"From a licensed still," Dougal said. The distillery had recently obtained its license, a detail he did not bother to add.

Eldin made a dismissive gesture. "What more do you have? I expected to hear about something more . . . valuable."

"Something illicit?" Dougal cocked one brow and waited.

Eldin leaned forward. "Sir, I do not care a whit about the law. If the whisky is the best you can claim, then how it is obtained is of no matter to me," he said, very low.

"We have something else," Dougal said, making a quick decision. "Twenty years if it is a day, made with barley grown in fields my father planted, and with clear Highland water passed through heather blooms plucked at their height. Proofed to perfection, this spirit has been stored in sherry casks turned regularly, so that the richness of the old Spanish Shiraz, and the passage of the years that it takes a babe to become a man, mellows the whisky to an exquisite degree."

"And?" Eldin waited.

"Very expensive," Dougal said. Dipping a finger in the whisky, he wrote what seemed a considerable number on the table with the tip of his finger.

Eldin waved a hand. "Affordable. Is the revenue paid?"

Dougal stared at him. "What do you think?"

"I see. Too good for the government, a typical Highland sentiment. How many casks?"

"Seven are available." Dougal had more, but would not let on.

Eldin sat back. "I will think about it."

"Think all you like," Dougal said. "Within the month, it will be gone."

"Into England?" Eldin asked quickly.

"London is a lively market for good Highland whisky," Dougal said.

"The blight in the French vineyards has reduced the amount of wine a man can obtain there," Eldin agreed. "And the grain whisky made in England and Lowland Scotland is poor indeed, once one has tasted Highland malt whisky. A whisky that is hand nurtured and aged, kept in store as long as twenty years, and still has not been found by the revenue men—that is rare stuff."

"Thus my price," Dougal said.

Eldin nodded, played with the brim of his hat, then looked at Dougal. "And my cousin, Miss MacCarran? Have you met her? How does my fair Fiona, there in Glen Kinloch?"

"Well enough, I suppose," Dougal said, startled. *His fair Fiona?* What the devil did that mean? "We have met. The schoolhouse is on my estate. My niece and cousins attend there."

"She is quite busy with the teaching, I imagine."

"Miss MacCarran seems dedicated to her work."

Eldin asked. "Does she wander the hills much?"

"She has a hobby of rock collecting, I understand," Dougal said carefully. He did not want to reveal his interest in the lady, given the way Eldin watched him.

"Has she asked you about fairies?"

Dougal blinked. "She expressed curiosity about our local legends and folklore."

"Tell her nothing," Eldin said. "If you know fairy legends, do not share them with her."

"I see no harm in it."

"Be wary, nonetheless," Eldin said. "Do you have a personal fortune, sir?"

Dougal bristled. "I find it none of your concern, with due respect, Lord Eldin."

"It is of no interest to me," he said. "But to Fiona . . . do not let on if you have wealth. Play the pauper."

"Why?" Dougal asked sharply.

"She has other reasons to come to the glen besides teaching the children. That is sincere enough, do not doubt it," he added. "But she has an undue interest in . . . fairy treasure, shall we say, gold in particular. And she has it fixed in her head that she will marry a wealthy Highland man, and none other." He laughed. "Lofty aspirations for a girl whose family has little legitimate fortune of its own."

Dougal leaned forward, feeling a sudden urge to throttle the man. "I find it surprising that a man would blacken the reputation of his own lady cousin," he said. "And I would gladly blacken your face with my boot, sir, if you give me but half an invitation." He stared at him, poised to rise.

Eldin smiled, shrugged. "I am merely warning you, sir. I am offering advice."

"I hardly know her," Dougal said. "I have no interest in the lady."

"That," Eldin said, "is not quite the truth, is it."

"Whether it is or not, I do not see it as your concern."

"She is my cousin."

"Then treat her with the respect due her, or any woman."

"Well," the man said, "I rest assured in your sense of honor, and I am certain that imbues your whisky as well. Will we bargain further?"

"I may not sell it to you," Dougal said.

"Excellent, the honor is of a righteous kind. All the better for the whisky the man makes," Eldin said, while Dougal stared, eyes narrowed. The earl leaned toward him. "I suspect the pauper status is the true one," he said then. "I will pay your price for the Kinloch twenty-year, all seven casks of it."

"It's more than you can pay," Dougal said. "Priceless, now."

"Indeed? That whisky is not the most priceless you have, is it," Eldin said.

"Twenty-year-old whisky is rare, as you have said yourself."

"I have heard of a legend of another sort of whisky brew," Eldin said. "An ancient secret given to the MacGregors by the fairy ilk themselves."

Dougal huffed. "Legends," he said, "do not produce marketable whisky."

"I hear that the lairds of Kinloch have always produced this secret brew. If you do have any of that sort, I would be willing to pay . . . whatever amount you need."

"Need?" Dougal frowned.

"To free your glen."

For a moment, Dougal stared hard at him. "My glen and its tenants," he said, "have always been free."

"The government deed office does not think so." Eldin stood then, lifting his hat and snatching his cane. "Think on it, Kinloch." He inclined his head, then opened his hand to deposit several coins on the table—Dougal saw the glint of gold sovereigns and silver shillings. The earl turned away and left the inn, shutting the door behind him.

Rob approached. "He wanted no supper? But we have a fine roast ready—"

"No supper," Dougal said, standing. Through the window, he saw the black barouche leaving the yard, driver leaning forward, whip cracking, and the silhouette of a tall man in a tall hat visible inside the carriage. "He came here to bargain. Serve supper to our friends with the compliments of the earl," he said, pushing the coins toward Rob, the amount far more than the price of food, drink, and lodging, too.

Going toward the window, he looked out at the vivid sunset over the mountains. What the devil did Lord Eldin want with fairy whisky, and what had he heard about it?

And he wondered, as he returned to his seat, what Eldin had meant by such sly remarks about Fiona MacCarran. Sighing, he drank the rest of the Kinloch whisky on the table. The batch he had sold to Rob for the inn's patrons was good—but not the finest that Kinloch's stills produced.

He did not understand Eldin's warning about Fiona, but the effect was the opposite of what the earl might have intended. Dougal's sympathy warmed to her; Fiona had a devil of a cousin in her life. He could not imagine the schoolteacher, so serene, intelligent, forthright—and so damnably alluring—ever scheming to marry wealth. Particularly Highland wealth.

He nearly laughed aloud. If wealth and Highland life were what she wanted, she would have to look elsewhere. Marry that blasted cousin of hers, for example.

But if the schoolteacher should ever decide that a Highland laird, one as poor, plain, and solid as the gray rocks that studded his land, was to her taste—he would be there for her, waiting and ready.

That thought was more revelation to him than anything Eldin could have said.

Late the next afternoon, when the door to the schoolhouse opened and the students poured out, Dougal waited in the yard. He had just come up from the nearby distillery, which was hidden behind a thickness of evergreens on a hillside. All was progressing well in the stillhouse, with Fergus working on the new batch of whisky started that week, and Hamish's sons, Will and John, testing the proof on another batch. Dougal had stayed long enough to approve the batch with his cousins before heading toward Kinloch House and the school situated on the farthest edge of the vast yard.

Ever since the first day school sessions had begun, he had intended to speak with Fiona MacCarran, but other matters had come along, and he had let them interfere. The barley laid down to germinate for the new batch required shoveling and turning, though Hamish had two grown sons capable of doing that; and he had traveled out of the glen for two days to go to an inn alongside Loch Lomond, for a previously agreed and discreet meetings with English clients interested in his next shipment.

Yesterday, when Ranald and Fergus had told him of their awkward attempt to oust the lady from the school, he knew he would have to talk with her. He had avoided her ever since school had begun, though she walked past his tower house each morning and afternoon.

More than once he had watched from a window as she went past, his heart thumping as if he was a half-bearded youth. Her graceful movement and lush figure, her face lifted to sunlight or bowed in rain, every sight of her stirred him. He had denied his interest, and though his desire to be near her grew keen and intense, he found excuses to keep away—accounts to be checked in the distillery office, though that had been done days before; a pressing task at the distillery, despite his competent, vigilant kinsmen; tenants to visit; herds to count despite shepherds to do it.

Even yesterday, he had put off waiting for her, instead heading for his arranged meeting with Eldin. Dougal was glad, now, that he had met Fiona's cousin. Some mysteries had cleared for him, although others had deepened.

There seemed little question that she should leave Glen Kinloch. Yet Dougal felt torn over that—compelled to be near her, and turned about as well. His body was responsive and craving, his mind and heart resistant, his loneliness profound.

He wanted her, and now, perversely after talking to Eldin, he wanted to protect her from that one's cunning—and he wanted to know why the earl had said such things about her.

Shaking his head, he turned, almost tempted to walk away. Leave the matter of the teacher to his uncles, he told himself. If they bumbled it, so be it, so long as the girl was gone, and with her the threat of her brother's presence in Glen Kinloch.

But just then, she emerged from the school, and walked toward him.

He watched her, his heart thumping. She wore, once again, the gray gown, jacket, and bonnet she had worn when he had first seen her on the hillside. The wind blowing against the fabrics revealed her curving and womanly form; she moved with subtle rhythm and airy confidence, head lifted, shoulders slight but square, hips swaying. He smiled, folded his arms, waited.

"Mr. MacGregor," she said. "You wanted a word with me today?"

"I do," he said smoothly. "I understand my uncles came by the school."

"They say there is something amiss with the roof. I asked them to postpone repairs and patch things in the meantime, until my weeks here are done." She lifted her chin.

"And when will that be?" he asked mildly, knowing the question might rile her.

"Two months at least, unless you have your way with—" She stopped, blushing under the golden shadow of her gray bonnet. Her eyes were a clear blue, snapping really, and he saw the stubbornness in her gaze.

"If I was to have my way with you, Miss Mac-Carran," he murmured, "we would not be talking about a roof right now."

She blinked, and her cheeks glowed like pink fire under the sunlit hat. But she turned her head and pinched back a smile; he was sure of it. Where tendrils of her hair escaped the bonnet, the locks had a warm walnut sheen, and he felt a sudden urge to remove the hat and loosen her hair—and then pull her long-legged, lush body close—

"About the repairs," she reminded him.

"Aye," he said, recovering. "The thatch needs replacing. But we had planned to give the schoolhouse a slate roof, and that would take some time."

"It will have to wait until school is done for the year."

"But some basic repair must be done before then, if it is leaking. Another good rainstorm, and you will have the roof down over your heads."

"If you knew the schoolhouse was in such condition, why was I invited to teach there? Why were repairs not made beforehand?"

"My uncles assured me that adequate repairs had been made to the school last month. We did not expect you so soon," he added.

"Perhaps the need for a new roof is another way of telling me that I am not wanted here in Glen Kinloch."

"You are wanted," he said, "here in the glen."

She tilted her head. "But not by you, sir."

He drew breath. "As I told you, the glen is not safe for the sister of a gauger. It can be, in fact, quite a dangerous place. You saw that last week," he added.

"There was no danger to me that night, except from those who want me gone. Do not send me away when I do not want to go," she added bluntly.

Dougal sighed. "I will admit that you are a fine teacher, and needed here at the school."

"Thank you." She glanced at him.

"Lucy has told me and her great-uncles, too, about her school lessons. She is truly enjoying the class, as are the others, I understand."

"She is a bright child, and quite delightful."

"But she has always loathed school until now."

"At first she claimed to need no lessons, but since then she seems content to learn. Though I must find more for her to do. She works quickly, then sets to bothering Jamie, who is an easygoing lad and puts up with her pestering."

"I know," he said, feeling a bit helpless, having little idea how to manage a small girl as bright and willful as Lucy. "Poor Jamie adores the lass."

"And she knows it, which only makes it worse. And she adores him as well."

"Does she?" He tipped his head, watching her steadily.

"Otherwise she would ignore him altogether."

"I will speak to her about it again, though I have tried before. Someday Jamie will decide to give Lucy a reckoning. It may be worth the wait if she learns it from him."

"True. What interests her most? If I knew, that might help."

"I am not sure you want to hear it." Dougal paused. "She intends to be a smuggler when she grows up, and she is convinced they have no need of studies."

"Ah. And what have you told her about that?"

"Of course I want to set a fine example," he said wryly. "So we are reading a little poetry at home. Sir Walter Scott," he added, looking at her. "A few verses. She enjoys it. But now she is convinced that smugglers may enjoy poetry, but do not need maths."

She laughed outright, and Dougal smiled, finding the sound unexpectedly enchanting. "You ought to know better than I what smugglers need to study."

"Maths, most assuredly, in order to figure the gallons, and the number of ponies and ships needed," he drawled. "And they must accurately count the gaugers sneaking about the hills so as not to get caught."

"Very important. And they should be able to count coin to the last penny," she retorted.

"True. But poetry, alas, they have little use for that."

"Poor Lucy. Will you tell her so?"

"I do not have the heart for it. You tell her."

She laughed again, and Dougal took her elbow. "Come with me." He led her along a path that ribboned between gorse bushes and trees, rather deliberately obscuring a few buildings situated at the base of the gentle slope.

"Where are we going?" she asked.

"Be patient. I wager you will not expect what you are about to see."

"Is it a troupe of lovely fairies—or a pack of clever smugglers?"

"Which would you rather?" he asked.

"Both," she said. "The fairies for me, and the smugglers for—"

"For your brother?"

She frowned, and Dougal felt the lightness leave her mood like light from a candle. "I was thinking of what you might want," she said, "not my brother. But that seems to be much on your mind where I am concerned."

"You are more on my mind than your brother," he said. "Though I will say he seems a decent fellow. It would be a shame for that job to corrupt a good lad."

"That would never happen."

"It could, and has, to good men before him."

She stopped and looked up at him. They stood in the shadow of a thicket of trees, and hidden there with her, Dougal felt a strong urge to take her into his arms, to make all right between them. He wanted no more talk of leaving the glen, or of gaugers and smugglers; he wanted only to set free what he felt for her, and know that she returned it. He wanted life to be simple and blessed, in the fine way that it could be with her.

"Fiona," he murmured, and she leaned toward him, her gaze searching his. He rested his hand on her shoulder. "Listen to me—"

"Aye?" she whispered.

"We were caught, we too, in a moment—" Suddenly he knew he must explain something of his actions the night of the smuggling run, and he certainly meant to ask what she intended by walking so boldly into obvious danger. That had made him afraid for her, distracting him mightily—and yet he had admired her greatly for it. He wanted to know where her loyalty might lie, to the glen or to her brother and the gaugers.

But now, looking at her, he no longer wanted to speak of that. He did not want to talk. He wanted to touch her, hold her, have her here in the green lushness of the pathway, as mad as it seemed, as dangerous—for the laird of Kinloch had no need of such complications in his life. His days were filled with enough risk as it was.

"What is it you wanted to say, Kinloch?" she asked softly.

"Just this," he growled, and tucked his hand against her cheek, tilting her head, and kissed her. She sighed and leaned her head back to allow his mouth to slant upon hers, and he delved his fingers deeper into the snug, glossy mass of her hair, wanting only to let it flow free.

She fell against him, one hand curled on his chest between them, the other sliding up around the back of his neck, pulling him closer, urging him to kiss her again. He did, deeply, fully, his body pressed against hers, his blood beating rhythm within him. His hand cradled her head, and she leaned closer, sighing against his mouth, accepting another kiss—and enticing him with her lips, the wild soft tip of her tongue, so that he groaned low and cupped her face in both his hands now. He held her, lingering his mouth over hers, surprised that she did not pull away. Another kiss, a sequence of them, made him crave, rocked him deep. Stop, he told himself. Stop now, or take her her on the pathway, in the bushes, between the school and the distillery beyond—

"Enough," he growled then, and set her away from him, hands on her shoulders.

"Dougal—" she whispered, her hands rounding over his shoulders, her touch warm and insistent. "Please—I do not mind, I swear it—"

"Enough for now," he amended hoarsely. "We will talk later, you and I." He forced himself to draw back, step back. "Pardon. It is not right for me to—"

"What is that?" She turned, looked over her shoulder. "I thought I heard a child calling."

Dougal looked past her, and saw Lucy at the top of the path, running toward them.

"Uncle Dougal!" she cried. "Wait!"

"Lucy!" He kept a hand on Fiona's arm, his pulsing blood fading to cold as he felt alarm rise up in him. "What is it?"

The little girl ran fast toward them, dark hair flying out behind her, losing its ribbon as she came forward in a panic, waving her arms, spilling to her knees on the path, and scrambling up again. "Uncle!"

He set Fiona aside to run toward his niece, and knew that Fiona was just behind him, as concerned as he was himself. "What is wrong?" Dougal hastened toward her, alarmed.

"I want to go to Annabel's house," the girl replied.

Dougal stopped, dumbfounded. Behind him, Fiona chuckled softly.

Chapter 11

"**I** am going across the glen with Annabel to her house," Lucy said, coming closer. "I am invited to have supper with her and her mother, and stay the night so that you will not have to come get me or send one of the lads after me."

"You gave us a scare," Dougal said, glancing at Fiona, who smiled.

"Tomorrow is Saturday," Lucy said. "There is no school." He saw Fiona nod.

"Very well, then. Go straight there and do not linger along the way," Dougal said with a warning tone.

"Thank you, sir." Lucy smiled brightly, her dimpled expression reminding him keenly of his sister, Ellen. "I promised Annabel we would give her mother some of our fairy brew."

"Did you," he drawled, with a sidelong glance for Fiona. "Then ask Maisie to fetch down a bottle for you to take to her. Maisie is at the house today, cleaning."

"I hope she has not put away my paper and pens, and the poem I am writing!"

"Tell her yourself when you go up. Go on, now." He waved Lucy onward, and she turned to run back to Annabel. The girls joined hands and chattered as they went up the hill.

Dougal turned to walk with Fiona once again, wondering if she thought of that earlier moment as he did. She looked at him, her skin flushed. "Lucy writes poems?"

"Sometimes," he said. "Just now I think she is copying a verse from a book."

"Interesting," she said. "You are a fine guardian for that lass. Some men would not have the patience for a child of such spirit, and one who is not their own."

"She is my ward legally, but I think of her as my own. My sister has been gone three years." That said more than enough, to his thinking. He would not wax on about his affection for the child. The feelings of protectiveness and love that he felt for his niece were stronger he would admit aloud.

"Is her father gone as well, that she lives with her kinsmen?"

"Gone enough," he said gruffly. He did not want to discuss what had happened to his sister Ellen, sweet as a sunbeam, yet wooed and deserted, never married to the father of her child—a disgrace for many, particularly in the south, but quietly accepted and absorbed by many Highland families, despite the rigors of the Free Church. "Lucy is my charge now. My uncles and aunts lend a hand. There are many who care for her—not just myself."

She nodded. "What is fairy brew?"

He sighed. "A kind of spirit traditionally brewed by some Highlanders."

"Ah. Not made by fairies?"

"Of course not. It is just a name," he answered.

"My sister-in-law has a Highland kinsman who makes a type of fairy whisky that the family says possesses genuine magic. They are rather secretive about it."

"You did mention that your brother married a MacArthur girl," he said casually, referring to his own cousin. "One of her MacArthur kinsmen may make a whisky by that name. It is a common name for Highland whiskies made to certain old recipes."

She tipped her head. "Do the recipes contain magical secrets handed down by fairies?"

"The only secret ingredient for any whisky brew is usually something like flowers," he said, and shrugged as if it were all commonplace.

"Ah, the flowers in whisky lend their flavor," she said, nodding. "Is it illegal, this so-called fairy brew?"

"No more than most Highland whiskies. It all depends on the quantity produced. Every Highland household is permitted to distill up to five hundred gallons a year. Any amount after that is considered excessive, and therefore taxable and illegal if the excise is not paid."

"Five hundred gallons seems like quite a lot."

"Not really. What is made is often stored to allow it to age. The rest is consumed by the household. Whisky can be held for years, to increase its flavor and quality."

"And value," she said astutely. "Fairy brew is a lovely name for a whisky, though. So romantic."

"And you seem such a practical lass, what with the teaching, and the collecting of rocks," he said in a teasing voice.

"Rocks have a fascinating mystery about them, which is why I am interested in the geology of the primeval earth. As for fairies—I love the legends," she said softly. "I hope to learn more about local tales here in Glen Kinloch."

He nodded in silence, aware that one of the most fascinating local fairy stories had to do with Kinloch whisky—but he could not share the tale outside the family.

"Is that a clachan up ahead?" She pointed toward the buildings visible beyond the thicket of bushes and trees, where the path skirted a bend and opened in a clearing.

"It does look like a small village," he agreed. "But this is part of the Kinloch estate. That's our distillery."

"I thought most Highland stills were hidden away to keep them safe from the revenue men."

"Sometimes. The Kinloch distillery is not as exciting as an illicit still, I admit. But we've no need to hide our enterprise here."

"That's bold," she said. "Are there many stills in the area?"

Wary, thinking of her gauger brother, he narrowed his eyes. "Why do you ask?"

"The night we met," she said, "the customs man said you would be held accountable for any stills found on Kinloch lands, if the owners were unknown."

"Ah. That new law is now in place, and it is a devil of a thing to put forth," he said.

"It does seem unfair," she replied.

"Along with that provision, the government has also lowered taxes on barley—"

"The tax is on the barley itself?"

"On the wort, actually," he explained. "The mash that is created from boiling and steaming the barley. The wort becomes the heart of the whisky process. The steam from that simmers in a large copper pot, enters some copper coils, and drips down—and that distillation is collected to make the whisky."

"So the wort really is key to making a quantity of whisky," she said.

"Exactly. Any boiled mash that is produced and distilled will be taxed according to how much whisky it might make. We are obligated to report each time a wort is made from barley."

"I do not see how the government can expect you to do that," she said, frowning.

"Just so," he replied. "You see something of the problem now. Highlanders grow the barley themselves, use it for food and sell it as grain. Some is used to produce whisky, too. But if we grow it for our families and our livelihoods, it is ours, and no part of it is owed to the government—or so most Highlanders feel, I assure you."

"No wonder there is such tension between the excise officers and the smugglers."

"True, and with the gaugers making a fee on each bottle confiscated, they are as eager to find it as Highlanders are to hide it. But lowering the tax on the wort may make secretly exporting Highland whisky less profitable, and not worth the effort. Yet despite the newer laws, the king's men will have a devil of a time enforcing them in the Highlands. Regulations like those make good sense to the Session Court in Edinburgh, but here in the hills they can be impossible to carry out."

"Are the stills all hidden? They could arrest you for what they find in Glen Kinloch, even if the stills do not belong to you."

"They could," he admitted. "More often than not, the pot stills are hidden away, and many have been in place for generations. What my tenants produce is their own concern, not mine. If the law does not agree, we will make sure the government never finds out. Not all of it is illicit, though," he said. "More legal distilleries are being opened, encouraged by the lowered taxes. The newer laws will help those who wish to make a legitimate living from distilling fine whiskies."

"But not the smugglers," she said. "That venture will eventually die out."

"We shall see." He gestured onward. "Have you never seen whisky in the making? Let me show you. Come this way."

Entering the glade beside Dougal, Fiona saw a cluster of whitewashed buildings arranged in tidy fashion, with slate roofs and red doors adding to the quaint air. In the middle of the clearing, the path met a wooden footbridge that crossed the burbling stream. The water sluiced under the bridge to channel far into the glen beyond. The distillery was as picturesque and peaceful as a little clachan, yet she knew now it was not that.

"This is a handsome distillery," she said, glancing at Dougal. "I thought Highland whisky was made using small hidden copper stills. But you must produce quite a bit here."

"The private stills serve their purpose. I wanted a larger enterprise at Kinloch."

Fiona blinked at that, wondering at the volume of Kinloch's illegal output.

He strolled with her toward the little bridge. "Originally these were outbuildings for Kinloch House, three hundred years ago when there was a castle on the hill, before the tower house was built," he explained. "The largest building, there, was a stable, and the others were byre, granary, and bakehouse. They were abandoned long ago. My grandfather and father reclaimed them for another purpose."

"I see," she said. As they stepped onto the wooden bridge, Fiona paused to look over the railing at the water, which rushed prettily over rocks and channeled out into the glen. Dougal stopped beside her, just as two young men exited the largest building. They waved at Dougal, glanced at Fiona, and then hastened toward another building, entering that doorway. "It does look a flourishing place," she said.

"We are increasingly busy." He looked pleased, Fiona thought, his slight smile genuine and private. Her brother had once mentioned hundreds of secret stills and casks moved by stealth, and smugglers bold enough to manufacture and move whisky about openly. Kinloch must be one of the bolder ones, she thought, to have so large and organized an operation.

She remembered, then, the moonlit night when she had stood on a hillside and watched the laird and band of smugglers walk past, leading their ponies. *Fiona, go home*, he had said, *and lock the door*. A shivery thrill went through her once again.

"What a rogue you are, Kinloch," she said quietly, impulsively.

He tipped his head. "Miss MacCarran?"

"Making whisky here without apology, and smuggling it out of Scotland."

"I brought you here," he said, "because I want you to understand that we are not all smugglers and rogues in this glen."

She stared as revelation struck—she had been wrong in her assumption. Blushing, she shook her head. "Your enterprise here is legal."

"Just so. This is a licensed distillery."

"Please forgive me. I thought—"

He held up a hand. "I know. But your vision is quite intriguing, a huge smuggling enterprise out in the open. We could pull it off if we plant more trees to better hide the place. We would need more pack ponies, for we produce more here. What do you think?"

"Oh, stop," she said, then laughed sheepishly. "The revenue officers would notice something going on, with so much chimney smoke and activity here."

"They would," he said amiably. "Rest assured that every square inch has been examined and approved. King George himself could be served Kinloch whisky at court one day."

"He asked to be served Glenlivet, a favorite of his, when he visited Edinburgh last summer," she said. "I remember the kerfuffle over it! The king himself requesting illegal spirits, not even aware that what he drank in London was smuggled. People were outraged."

"The Highlanders who told me that story were very amused," he said. "Perhaps I ought to send him some of our own Kinloch brew."

"We have a family friend who could convey a bottle to him, if you mean it. I will ask Sir Walter for you."

"Sir Walter Scott? You have impressive friends, Miss MacCarran. An earl for a cousin, a viscount for a brother, and now the Bard of the North himself. I am surprised you are willing to spend weeks teaching in a Highland glen. You must have a busy life at home."

"Not really. It can be rather dull. Besides, I like your Highland glen." She waved toward the distillery buildings. "My brother did not mention a legal distillery at Kinloch. He told me only to beware the Kinloch smugglers."

"Those rascals," Dougal said wryly. "Your brother is new to his post and perhaps does not know about this place. We were only recently approved by the government."

"If your tenants get licenses, too, there will be an end to smuggling," she said.

"So the government hopes, but it is unlikely to happen for a very long time. And Highland whisky is superior to Lowland, being made from malted barley, rather than the cheaper grain whisky of the south. It comes dear here, so prices will always be high. Especially with more excise officers being sent into the Highlands to find the small stills and put an end to them."

"My brother was given just such a post, after working in Edinburgh as a lawyer. He wanted something with more adventure, and so he came north to Loch Katrine."

"He will find more than enough adventure here, and may he survive it," he drawled. "Why would he want to come here? And you, as well?"

"My brother and I must—" She stopped, realizing she could never explain the reason she was there, and had to stay. "Well, for one reason, our brother James now lives at Struan."

He nodded, accepting that explanation. "Your brother would make a better living in Edinburgh as an advocate. No one needs this adventure. Customs officers do not last long."

"I know it is dangerous. Patrick knows, too."

"The government pays them poorly, but a gauger earns extra coin for every bottle or keg turned over to the government. So they turn sly, and resort to scheming."

"Patrick would not," she insisted. "You simply do not care for any sort of revenue man."

"Gaugers killed my father," he said curtly. "He died for the price that could be collected from the whisky kegs he carried on two ponies."

"I did not know," she murmured.

"He carried whisky made within the limits of the law, not smuggled. They did not care."

She sighed, shook her head, uncertain what to say. "Was it recently?"

"I was nearly fourteen."

"Just a boy!" Heart stirring, she looked up to see a guarded expression fleet over his features, and she realized that he would accept neither sympathy nor fuss.

"So I was. But I became laird of Kinloch that day, and I have learned a great deal since then. Most of it outside the schoolroom," he added.

"As it should be, given the circumstances. Is that all the schooling you had?"

"I went to university for a while—my father wanted that—but I was needed here and came home. This way, Miss MacCarran." He took her arm to guide her over the bridge, their footsteps thudding over the planking. "We've lingered too long, when I intended to show you the distillery. Now it's near gloaming."

"I would rather have talked to you than toured the distillery. Another time, perhaps." She looked at him, feeling a sudden shyness. "I should like to see it, if you will show me."

He waited for her to precede him on the bridge. "We spent the last year repairing and expanding the place. We planned to rebuild the schoolhouse this spring as well. But the Lowland teacher arrived sooner than expected."

Fiona looked over her shoulder toward him. "I have not fit your plans from the start, I think."

"So it would seem," he murmured, standing close to her, his arm brushing her shoulder. She did not move away.

Lifting her head, she detected a sharp, strong odor wafting in the air from the direction of one of the buildings. "The smell reminds me of the beer the servants made when we lived in Perthshire, when I was a girl." Since coming to her great-aunt's estate, where beer was purchased from a local brewer, she had smelled it less often. "It is so distinct—like wet hay and dried flowers." She wrinkled her nose.

"The processes of making whisky and beer are the same, to a point," Dougal answered. "What you smell now is the hot barley mash, being boiled down to produce the wort, from which the whisky will be distilled. It's not a very pleasant smell. But it's not the first step in making whisky. First the barley must sprout, turned for days with shovels. Then it is dried over peat fires, which lends it a smoky flavor. After that, it is boiled down to the wort, distilled and collected, mixed with water from the clearest burns and streams, and set in casks to age. I will show you each stage, if you have the time."

Fiona turned toward him. "I have the time. I will be in Glen Kinloch a long while."

"Will you?" He stood with her on the bridge, the water rushing and frothing below them, and Fiona felt so drawn toward him, so entranced, that at first she did not hear what made Dougal turn, and step away.

Then, hearing a man shout, she looked around. Hamish MacGregor was running toward them, waving his arms.

"What the devil," Dougal muttered. "What is it?"

"Fire!" Hamish shouted in Gaelic. "Fire over at Thomas MacDonald's!"

Kinloch began to run toward his uncle. Without thinking about whether she was welcome, Fiona picked up her skirts and followed.

Chapter 12

Feet pounding, skirt hems lifted, Fiona ran just behind Dougal along the earthen lane that led between two of the buildings along another winding path—the place seemed like a warren of paths, some of them hidden from sight, she noted. The Kinloch distillery was located in a secluded spot that was surrounded by dense stands of trees and evergreens, where the enterprise would not be easily noticed. Hamish had emerged from one of those hidden paths and hurried toward them, waving his arms.

Fearing that someone might have been hurt, she came along, somewhat surprised that Dougal MacGregor did not send her back immediately. He glanced at her and moved ahead.

"Hamish! What is it?" he called.

His uncle came closer, halting to catch his breath. "Fire," he repeated. "The black pot."

Dougal swore. "Is anyone hurt?"

"Not hurt, but the smoke and flames could be seen from afar."

"Black pot?" Fiona asked in Gaelic. *Poit dubh*, she repeated, as Hamish had said.

"A still," Dougal answered in English, and then she wondered if he used English to remind her that she was not one of them. He gestured behind her. "Go back."

"But I want to help," she replied in Gaelic.

"No need." He turned her by the shoulders then, and gave her a little shove toward the distillery. "Go home—go back to Mary MacIan's."

"She cannot go now, Kinloch," Hamish said. "The smoke will be seen by the gaugers, and they will come this way. The lass should not cross the glen alone with that sort about."

"True. And there's no one to escort her back to Mary's just now," Dougal muttered, and glanced at Fiona. "Go back to the school or to Kinloch House, and wait there."

"I will not," she said, continuing in Gaelic as they had done. "I can help if there are injuries, and I am strong enough to carry buckets of water."

"Fiona—" he said quickly, urgently, and his impulsive use of her name sent an unexpected thrill through her. He shook his head. "We have no time."

"Bring the girl," Hamish said. "Pol and Mairi are her students. She wants to help."

"Very well, come along," MacGregor growled. He moved her in front of him, his hands strong yet gentle as he shifted her position with firm intent. That touch was simple yet powerful somehow, and she caught her breath.

"If I cannot be of help, then I will keep out of the way," she told him.

"See that you do. And whatever happens, you must not speak of it to anyone."

She frowned. "You still do not trust me."

"Caution is best in some matters."

"This from a man who so often takes a risk himself?"

"Some risks are . . . safer than others." He glanced at her.

"Do you still think me a threat because of my kinsmen? You saw for yourself how Patrick assisted you that night. I was there, and saw it, too. I did what I could as well. Surely that tells you that you can trust us."

"My girl," he murmured, taking her elbow to move her along with him, "I do not trust so easily, and with good reason."

"Perhaps you might be happier if you did."

"It would take more than that," he drawled. "Besides, there certain aspects of your very person, my dear girl, that pose such a danger that I . . . do not trust myself."

Another thrill went through her then, lovely and heart-pounding. Fiona glanced toward him, but saw only his profile, and no hint of his feelings: good features, firm mouth and lean jaw, a sweep of dark hair, and those beautiful and guarded eyes. "I trust you," she said. "Why do you fear trusting me?"

He smiled, wry and even bitter. "*Tinneas-an-gradh-dubh*," he replied.

"The black lovesickness? Easily cured."

"Is it? Hamish has gone far ahead. We had best hurry," he added.

He rushed her along, his hand briefly touching her shoulder or arm as they negotiated the narrow path, walking tightly together by necessity. The light was dim along the path where it cut up and then down through a wooded slope, and the way was studded with roots and tangled bracken. Fiona reached for Dougal's arm now and then for balance, and once his hand gripped hers, warm and sure, for so long, his fingers lingering over hers, that her heart beat faster. That secret clasping of hands, simple as it was, felt thrilling—then he let go and reached out to push back overhanging branches.

"Again, I want your promise," he murmured, "that you will not speak of what you see." He took her arm again as they left the wooded area to enter the open sweep of the glen floor.

"You have it. Why did we go this way, when we could have crossed the glen?" she asked.

"We do not want to be seen in the open too long if gaugers are about. The distance is shorter this way. We cannot risk leading excise men to where we are going."

The glen lay flat and open ahead, and when they came to a narrow stream winding through the valley floor, they leaped its rushing waters crossing rock to rock—Dougal holding her hand again, and she glad of it.

Ahead, massive, rounded hills rose upward, and along those shoulders, she saw two cottages, sheep grazing the slopes, and the deep track of another stream rushing downward. A patch of pine trees thrust upward on one side of the hill. Above, she saw curls of white smoke too thick and dense to come from a chimney.

"There," Dougal said, pointing. "Run—hurry, we cannot stay out in the open for long." He hastened into a long stride, while Fiona strove to keep up, watching the dark mass of pines ahead, with the smoke rising upward. As she ran, the ribbons of her bonnet loosened and the hat dropped to her shoulders; moments later it blew away, skittering over the glen and quickly out of sight. She stopped for a moment, sighed, and then turned. There were more important matters at hand than wayward bonnets, she knew.

Hurrying to catch up with Dougal, she noticed small, odd lights flitting over the glen, like dust motes glimmering in sunlight. She slowed, glancing toward them. Just motes or reflections of some kind, she told herself, and rushed onward.

Far ahead, Dougal's uncle met two men who ran toward him. Within moments, Dougal joined them, Fiona only footsteps behind. She saw that the newcomers were her student Pol and his father, Thomas MacDonald, who now turned toward Dougal.

"It is Neill's *poit dubh* on fire," he said, with barely a glance for Fiona.

"Is the lad hurt?" Dougal asked quickly.

"He is fine, thanking the Lord. And the fire is nearly out now, but the hut is destroyed, and a good copper still blown to bits. We have moved the casks, but until the rest burns off, there is nothing more we can do."

Dougal nodded. "Any word of gaugers?"

"Always the risk," Hamish grunted. "Thomas sent his other sons out to ask if any have been seen. We'll go look at the still," he told the men.

"What is left of it," Thomas said, and waved them onward. The men walked without hurrying, though Fiona felt anxious about the fire and hastened faster than her companions. She lagged back, not knowing where to go, so that Dougal walked beside her.

"So Neill was testing the proof?" he asked the MacDonald father and son.

"He lit the sample, and it blew," Thomas said. "Too strong," he added with a grunt.

"Your proofs are never too strong," Dougal said.

"It was Neill's own batch," Thomas said.

"Neill?" Fiona asked, looking at Pol, who walked to the other side of her.

"My oldest brother," he said. "I am the youngest of four sons." She nodded, certain that they were all in the whisky smuggling trade.

"Everyone is safe," Thomas assured them. "And Neill has learned more about the power of the whisky brew." He shrugged matter-of-factly, while Dougal laughed, curt and humorless.

Moments later they heard shouts, and the men began to hurry, Fiona going with them. As they looked toward the smoke rising above the pine trees, her attention was caught by a flash below, between the trees. The lights again, she realized, swirling among the trees.

Then she gasped, for a narrow trail of flame snaked down the slope. "Look!" she cried out, running closer. Dougal grabbed her arm to keep her back. "What is that?"

"The stream," he answered after a moment. "It's burning."

She stared in astonishment, and then saw that it was true. Yellow flames licked along the surface of the stream and came flashing downward like a dragon's tail.

And above the stream of fire, she saw tiny round lights that swirled in the air between the fire and where she stood. Sparks, she thought—but these differed from the hot gold of fiery sparks. Instead they were pale and luminous, soft colors floating like bubbles spun out of a rainbow.

Puzzled, she watched the small lights disappear as she walked forward with the others.

The bright ribbon of fire dancing upon the water was so awesome a sight that Dougal slowed, watching its downward course. Sparks flew all about, snapping up into the air. He glanced upward, concerned the trees might catch fire, too, but so far the fire was contained to the area of the stream of water. He knew what could happen—had seen this get out of control before.

Men shouted from above, running downward as Dougal and the others approached. Fiona walked past him and he stopped her with a hand to her arm, keeping her a safe distance away. She stood staring at the burning water, while others gathered along the banks to watch as well.

"There is little we can do," Dougal said, glancing at Fiona. "It will extinguish on its own." She nodded, and coughed a little in the smoky atmosphere, though she seemed transfixed as she watched the water and flame.

He frowned, considering her. There was soot on her cheeks and dusting her dark hair, he saw—and noticed then that she had lost her bonnet, no doubt blown away while they ran.

Hamish came closer and indicated the flames on the water. "You know what it means," he said. "Gaugers about."

"Aye," Dougal said. "Neill dumped a fair amount of brew into the water."

"Is it whisky burning like that? I have never seen anything like this," Fiona said. She coughed, waved her hand a little in front of her face, and he noticed that she blinked as the smoke riding the air stung her eyes. For the most part the smoke was traveling upward, but the odor of burning was strong, and the air hazy with smoke.

"Whisky must have been poured into the stream," Dougal told her. "If there is fire present, the whisky alights, and the stream itself seems to burn until the spirits burn out. If the water is shallow and calm, as it is here, the fire burns the length of the spill—sometimes a long way."

"A beautiful, terrible thing. It looks like the end of the world," Thomas said philosophically.

"A waste of good whisky is what it is," Hamish said practically. "But it will not last long."

"You've seen this before?" Fiona asked. Dougal and the others nodded.

"We've all caused a stream to burn like hellfire now and again," Thomas said. "It is part of the risk. Do not be afraid, miss. We are safe if we keep back."

"I am not afraid. Just . . . amazed."

"Neill must have been told that gaugers were coming," Hamish said, and Dougal nodded.

He had glanced around while they spoke, taking account of those who stood on the banks, and the shadowy forms of others standing among the trees. He knew each of them—his kinsmen, tenants, and comrades, and young Neill MacDonald standing at the top of the stream, near the smoldering remains of the hut that had housed his black pot still.

"I see no gaugers about. I'll talk to Neill," Dougal said, and stepped away. Then he turned back on a quick thought. "Miss MacCarran, please come with me."

She nodded and turned with him, plucking at her skirts, her slim-fingered hands lifting the fabric so that it draped gently around her form. As she moved, he saw narrow-toed boots and the flash of a slender ankle in white silk. He knew well by now that her limbs were long and well-made, and the rest of her was neatly shaped, too. Truly, he had noticed far more about the lady than he would ever let on.

"Can I help?" she asked, as she walked with him.

"Not just now. I must talk to Neill, and I want to know where you are," he replied. "You've seen a bit more than I expected," he admitted, sifting his fingers through his hair, trying to think. He and his kinsmen and friends would have to rely on the girl for silence. But only he knew that the first time he had seen her, she and her brother had been exploring the hillside, while she took notes about the area. He frowned, remembering that.

"Is that Neill MacDonald over there?" she asked. Dougal nodded. "Why did he pour whisky into the stream? Was it damaged somehow in the fire, or did it explode when he was testing it?"

"He would have tested only a small sample, but sometimes accidents occur at that stage, since black powder and flame are used," he explained.

"Gunpowder!" She lifted her brows.

"A common technique for proofing spirits, and not dangerous when handled correctly. If the whisky is too weak or diluted, the gunpowder will not ignite. If the whisky is the proper strength, it will burn clean and go out. But if it is too strong—" He shrugged.

"Then the whisky explodes?"

"Well, it depends on how large the sample, and where the sparks fly. And Neill MacDonald is a young man. The same happened to me when I was near his age," he said, and then held out his left hand, splaying the fingers, where a patch of small scars crisscrossed the fleshy web between thumb and index finger. "But this was the extent of it. Like Neill, I was lucky not to be blinded, or killed outright."

"Oh!" She stopped, and he did, too, and she reached out to take his hand in hers. "This must have been painful enough. I am glad you were not hurt worse than this. And Neill is fortunate he was not killed today."

"True. If all goes well with the process, the batch is considered proofed, then sealed in kegs to age for a bit. Sometimes for years." He looked toward Neill, who waited. "But accidents can all too easily happen with the proofing of strong new whisky." And if he poured a good deal of it into the stream, Dougal thought, Neill must have seen excise men nearby. He intended to find out.

"Stay here, if you please, Miss MacCarran." She nodded, and coughed, covering her mouth with her hand. "Keep away from the building—the smoke is very strong up there."

He walked toward Neill, who turned, looking in shock, eyes wide, soot smeared on his shirt, face, blond hair. The boy shook his head in dismay. Nearby, the stream swept past the charred and smoking hut, the water still appearing to burn in places where whisky pooled on flat rocks in the stream.

"I am sorry, Kinloch," Neill said.

Dougal rested a hand on the boy's shoulder. "I am sorry that you and your father have lost your whisky stores. But we all know the risks, lad."

"I saw MacIntyre coming," Neill said. "I had to pour it out into the stream quick as I could."

"I knew you had a good reason to dump the brew. Where did you see him?"

"After we had been fighting the fire, and it seemed to be burning down, I stepped away to get more water, and I saw the signal—the washing spread out on the hillsides between here and the south end of the glen."

Dougal nodded. He knew, they all did, of the simple system long used in the glen to alert others that excise men were in the area. Bedsheets would be spread on the hillsides as if left to dry and bleach in the sun—just one signaling method among several, so that the gaugers never quite caught on. "And you saw the customs men?"

"I did, after a bit. Three men walking the ridge of a far hill. They were not from Glen Kinloch, and big Tam MacIntyre was with them. I'd not mistake his bulk," he added.

"Then they might still be nearby. Well, if the gaugers come past here, there is no evidence left of a still. Any sort of building could have been here, the way it looks now. That is to your advantage," Dougal said.

"The copper still is destroyed," Neill said. "Blown apart when sparks landed on it. The very fumes seemed to alight. My father paid a good deal for that still and copper coil."

"Fires can happen. Your father knows that, and they can be rebuilt and a new coil purchased. Any copper pieces that can be used again should be hidden away for now."

"Geordie took them," Neill said, referring to another of his brothers. "He will hide them. I am sorry, Kinloch," he said again.

"I exploded a still when I was younger. So it goes. You will make more whisky."

Neill nodded and peered past him. "Is that the schoolteacher? Pol and Mairi like her very much. They talk about lessons at supper. They have never talked of lessons before." He seemed relieved to have another topic to discuss.

Dougal glanced over his shoulder. Fiona waited, looking about; she coughed again, cupping her hand over her mouth. Meeting his glance, she began to walk toward him and Neill.

"Da says he hopes this dominie will stay a long while, so that we can all be better educated," Neill was saying. "He'd like for me to go to school with my brother and sister to learn more. But I told him I am a man now, with no time and no use for schooling."

"Age does not matter when going to school," Dougal said. "It is important to get whatever education you can, and when the opportunity comes to you, do not turn it down."

Fiona nodded agreement, her eyes red-rimmed from smoke, Dougal saw. He introduced her to Neill, and she held out her hand. "I am very sorry for your troubles," she said.

The young man shrugged. "We will get another still and make more whisky, and soon enough have another batch to—"

"Tomorrow or the next day," Dougal said quickly, "once the debris cools enough, my uncles and I will help to clear it. And you and Thomas will decide together about rebuilding. Nothing more can be done today. And Miss MacCarran, you should not be so near the smoldering hut, with that cough."

"I am fine. Neill, you look tired, and should rest," Fiona said quietly. "Come away."

Dougal noticed how calmly she spoke, her tone seeming to reassure Neill, who nodded and relaxed a bit. She had a serenity about her, Dougal thought, a quality he greatly admired yet would never in his life master. Perhaps that was the reason Neill stared at her as if he were under a spell; he could well understand it himself.

"Miss MacCarran," Neill said, "this is not the time to ask, but could I attend your school? Now that I have no still to watch after . . . and it would please my father."

"You are more than welcome," she answered. "If your father agrees, you may begin next week, if you feel ready."

Murmuring thanks, Neill smiled. Standing by,

Dougal knew his own dilemma had deepened, for he and his uncles had agreed the teacher could not stay. Yet now he felt certain that she could not go, either—Neill and others like him needed her. He himself needed her—and then he realized that it was not the first time he had felt that way about her.

"I may as well go to school," Neill told Dougal. "I am not much of a whisky brewer."

"Everyone makes mistakes when they first begin something that they will become expert in doing," he answered. "It will all come right again, lad." Seeing Thomas approach, he took Fiona's arm to guide her away and allow father and son to speak in private.

The stream had absorbed the burning whisky, though sizzle and smoke lingered in the air, and patches still burned. Hamish, Pol, and others stamped out little flames here and there along the bank as Dougal and Fiona walked toward them.

She coughed again, and Dougal, unable to stop himself, rested a hand on her back, thumping a little, rubbing. "Let's get you away from here," he said.

"It is just smoke, and the wind is clearing it a little now—oh!" She gazed upward, eyes wide. "Look!"

"What is it?" He peered upward, expecting to see smoke or flame; yet what he saw was unexpected, and entrancing. Small orbs of light floated overhead.

"Tiny lights," she said, very low. "I saw them earlier. I thought they were sparks, or a reflection from something. Do you see them?"

He did not want to admit it, though he knew very well they were not sparks. "I am not sure what you are seeing," he said carefully.

"They look like fireflies or sparks," she whispered, leaning close, her shoulder touching his arm. "They are so lovely!"

Lovely indeed, he thought, staring down at her, and then glancing toward the lights again, which swirled and glittered like dabs of sunlight. He had seen them earlier, when he and Fiona had crossed the glen. The flitting, sparkly things had swirled toward the woodland, as if beckoning them toward the fire and the burning stream—whether it was meant as a warning or a lure, he could not tell. Perhaps the fairies were not happy that the stream had been set afire—and perhaps like the humans, they found it a fascinating spectacle.

He had seen them a few times in his life. Once he had seen them with his father, who had explained that the tiny lights were visible only to the special few who could perceive them. The lights marked the presence of fairies—they were not fairies themselves, but proof of their magical presence. The Fey hid their true forms, so legend claimed, showing themselves only rarely.

And Fiona could see the orbs. Dougal looked at her, puzzled. She smiled up at him. "Do you not see them?" she repeated. "What are they?"

"It is an odd reflection coming off the water," he said. "The sunset is filtering through the trees, and that could cause odd effects. The hour is late, Miss MacCarran. We should not linger. The smoke is bothering you, and fresh air will help. Pol can walk you back to Mary MacIan's."

He took her arm to guide her away from there, away from the Fey, who were not only calling to him, but to the schoolteacher as well. And what the devil that was all about, he could not say.

Chapter 13

❧

"**P**ol has gone with his brother to hide the parts of the copper still, so Thomas said," Hamish told them when Fiona and Dougal returned. "The lass cannot walk home alone, not with Tam MacIntyre and his men out there."

Dougal frowned, talking to his uncle in private, while Fiona stood a little distance away, watching those who stood along the banks of the stream. She was still coughing, holding a kerchief over her mouth. "The smoke is affecting her. She should rest before walking across the glen. I will take her up to Kinloch House for a bit."

"I wonder if we could ask her to cook us some supper," Hamish said, peering past him. "She's a fine cook."

"And a guest, Hamish," Dougal reminded him. "If Maisie is still there, we will need her to stay, though Lucy has gone to Helen MacDonald's for the evening. We cannot have it said that the teacher stayed at Kinloch House with only the laird and his kinsmen in residence. Jean has left you again, and Ranald's Effie is visiting her sister—it would not be proper to have the teacher there now, without a woman in the house."

"Maisie can stay the night, then, she often does for Lucy," Hamish suggested. "See to it, and hurry back. We have work to do this night."

Dougal nodded. "Miss MacCarran," he called, walking toward her. She turned, and the sunset poured golden light over her face and hair, and illuminated the gentle curves of her body. For a moment, she seemed such a vision of grace and beauty that he stopped, lost his bearings, forgot his resolve. He wanted her, the feeling sharp and deep—a desperate need of body and soul out of keeping with the time and place.

"Mr. MacGregor?" she asked, walking toward him.

"May I invite you to rest at Kinloch House? You've inhaled some smoke, and to be honest, cough or not, it is not wise for you to cross the glen just now."

"Stay at Kinloch House alone. . . . with you?" she asked, looking up, eyes wide, clear, so beautiful and—somehow hopeful, he thought—that it took his breath away.

"I will be back very late. We must help the MacDonalds tonight. A serving girl is at the house, a daughter of another MacDonald family, who often helps to watch Lucy. So you will not be alone . . . there. You are welcome to stay the night."

"Thank you, but I should not. What of Mrs. MacIan?"

"I will send someone to tell her that you are safe at Kinloch House for the night."

"I do not want to be any trouble. I can make my way back to Mrs. MacIan's."

"Not tonight," he said, taking her arm. "I assure you, it is too dangerous."

"Do you mean gaugers? I am not afraid of excise men."

"You should be," he said. "They are not all like your brother."

She frowned thoughtfully. "Then perhaps I will rest at Kinloch House for a bit."

Dougal took her arm and escorted her out of the smoky woodland, out into the wide glen. That in itself was dangerous, once they were in the open, and he hurried her without any conversation. Though she coughed and sniffled some, she did not complain and kept up with him. Glancing behind him now and then, he could see the smoke rising above the trees; surely Tam MacIntyre and his men would see that, and want to know what was going on in the forested hills. Dougal intended to hurry back to the MacDonalds' property quickly.

"This way," he said, guiding Fiona past the patch of trees that guarded the distillery, and toward a broader path that led toward Kinloch House. As they crossed a rough bit of terrain, rocks and uneven turf, and then a narrow burn, he took her hand to aid her over the water, stepping from stone to stone. She grasped his hand, and when they reached the other side, neither of them let go, though he knew she no longer needed the support.

Fiona glanced over her shoulder. "The lights," she said. "I still see them. How odd!"

"Just the sunset," he said without looking back, tightening his fingers over hers.

The moment she entered Kinloch House, climbing a few steps to its plain entry door, Fiona felt curiously at home, though so far she had seen only the crumbling exterior of the tall peel tower, formed by two rectangular sections joined at an angle to each other. The door opened into a stone-floored foyer, with a curving stone stair to the left, and a series of doors to the right.

Sunset light poured into the hall from windows along the turning stair, turning whitewash and wood to golden tones. A quick glance ahead through open doors in the corridor revealed small rooms, quaintly furnished with old pieces, worn patterned rugs, wood floors, and walls that were either paneled or whitewashed. The place seemed simple, clean, comfortable, and inviting.

"It's lovely," she said, turning to look at Dougal as he shut the door behind them. Just then two large hounds careened around a corner and loped toward her so fast that she stepped back, stumbling. Dougal took her arm.

"Steady," he said, and she did not know if he spoke to her or the dogs—tall and gray, the sort of noble beasts that she had seen in old portraits.

Despite their majestic appearance, they were clumsy gluttons for Dougal's affection; he rubbed their heads and shoulders vigorously. She did, too, laughing when the dogs butted against her seeking more petting.

The laughter made her start coughing; the irritation would not clear, and Dougal patted her back, too. When he rubbed her shoulder, she felt a soft tickling sensation all through her, a feeling so wonderful and indulgent that she sighed, rolled her head a little, and wanted more. He bent toward her, his hands warm on her shoulders and neck, and for a moment Fiona felt tempted to turn into his arms.

But he drew his hands away and gave his attention to the dogs again. "This is Sorcha and Mhor," he said. "They are useless creatures, but so congenial that we keep them around. Let me show you the house. There's not much to it; the plan is very simple," he said, as he gestured forward. She went with him, the dogs bumping between them, turning a corner. "Two upright towers with a turning stair between them. This is the parlor," he said.

She peered inside, seeing a modest wood-paneled room with a worn Oriental rug on the bare planked floor, a settee upholstered in faded green, a pair of cane-seated chairs, old tables, and a Jacobean cupboard under a window. The fireplace crackled with reddish flames and the musky scent of peat.

"This is the dining room," Dougal said then, pointing to the room beside it, along a hallway that angled into shadows. The dining room held a table and a few chairs on another shabby Oriental rug, and corner cupboards were crammed with mismatched porcelain; shelves and walls were painted pale green. The fireplace was cold, the room silent.

He showed her a small kitchen with high stone walls and an arched fireplace taking up one wall; a stout table filled the center of the room. A second parlor served as a study; there, a large desk held a jumble of papers and books, and two chairs held more books.

"I do accounts here for rents, livestock, and the distillery," he said, and led her back to the foyer. "On the upper floors there are several bedrooms and a library, separated by floors, with only a few rooms downstairs. The house is very old," he added, sounding almost apologetic.

Fiona nodded. One of the deerhounds nudged her, and she rubbed its head. "Kinloch House was once a castle?" she asked.

"A peel tower," he explained. "Most of them are like this, simple block shapes with two sections joined in an L or a Z shape. The straightforward design provided solid protection, centuries ago. My ancestors needed to defend against cattle reivers and king's men in the past. We also have a priest's hole, which my father opened up so that it could be used as a storage room."

"How fascinating it must have been to grow up in a place like this."

"Fascinating, aye. The place is supposedly frequented by ghosts and visited by fairies, too."

Fiona felt a kindled interest. "Fairies? Have you seen any yourself?"

He shrugged. "As a boy I thought I saw something, now and then. A child's imagination," he added with a half laugh. "The house is a bit of a shambles now, being so old. Parts of it are always in need of repair. Some days the whole thing seems likely to fall down around our heads, but it has always been a good home," he finished quietly.

"I can tell," she said. "It is a warm and welcoming house." She felt relaxed and reassured standing beside Dougal in the house he so clearly loved. "In a way, I felt at home the moment I entered, though it may seem fanciful."

"Not at all," he murmured. "Kinloch affects people that way sometimes. They say the fairies of the estate determine who is welcome, and who is not." He tilted his head, looking at her. "I think they approve of you."

She brightened. "I would love to know more about your fairy traditions. My grandmother wrote books about Highland lore, so my brothers and I were raised on such stories."

"Ah," he said, nodding to himself. "You could probably tell me more fairy legends than I could tell you. There are only one or two legends in Glen Kinloch that I can recall."

"I think you know more than you let on," she answered.

He smiled. "I nearly forgot that you came here to rest after the fire. You can warm yourself by the hearth in the parlor—Maisie sets a good fire in there. Or you may use the library upstairs. It is small, though with some good books, including a few in Gaelic. If you feel tired, you are welcome to rest in one of the bedrooms, and stay the night. Maisie will be here to assist you."

"Will you be here?" she asked.

"Likely not. I will go back to the MacDonalds' to offer my help."

"I need not stay long, truly. I do not want to be any trouble to you, or to Maisie."

"You would be safer here than crossing the glen this evening," he murmured.

"Would I?" She tilted her head, looking up at him. He made her feel solidly safe and yet enticingly vulnerable, all at once. "Do you really expect trouble this evening?"

"Possibly." He stared down at her for a moment too long, so that Fiona caught her breath. "Sit in the parlor. I will find Maisie," he said, as he guided her into the room. Then he left, footsteps echoing down the corridor.

Wandering about the room, Fiona looked at two portraits hung over the settee—a man and a woman, the male with a striking resemblance to Dougal—and she sat on an old, creaky chair with a flat cushion. The fire burned low in the grate and gave off a lovely warmth and the sweetish smell of peat, and though she coughed, she felt that she was improving, as if the inviting, relaxing atmosphere of Dougal's simple home had its own sort of healing influence.

When footsteps sounded again, she looked up to see a young woman carrying a silver tray with tea things on it. She was plump and red-faced, with soft coppery hair spiraling out from under a soft white cap. Her apron was mussed and stained, her dark blue gown patched at the hem, and she did not curtsy, as a Lowland serving girl might have done, but smiled, her expression pretty and bright. Fiona could not help but smile in response.

"I am Maisie MacDonald," the girl said in Gaelic. "The laird said to fetch you some tea. Here it is, with some oatcakes, butter and jam, all we had this day. Not expecting guests," she added, and Fiona heard a slight reproach in it.

"Thank you, Maisie." Fiona peered toward the door. "Where is the laird?"

"Gone to help my cousins with their troubles. Oh, what a terrible fire!"

Fiona agreed, looking again toward the door, feeling disappointed that Kinloch had left. She turned as Maisie filled a blue-and-white china cup with steaming tea and handed it to her. "Thank the Lord, no one was hurt in the blaze."

"True. But the loss of the building, and so much whisky, is a hardship for them. They have plenty stored away, though." She frowned. "I heard you coughing, miss."

"There was thick smoke when we went to investigate the fire," Fiona said. "It seems to have irritated my throat and chest. I'm sure it will clear."

"My mother taught me a good remedy for coughs—whisky with honey and hot water. There's a good store here, as in every Highland home, and it's a fine quality. Will you take a wee dram? Some ladies think it improper, but whisky is very good for the health of the body. Many Highland ladies take some *uisge beatha* every evening—some more than that." She grinned.

"Thank you, Maisie," Fiona said, stifling the tickling cough. "I remember the whisky and honey remedy from my childhood in Perthshire. It will help clear the rest of this."

"Perthshire, is it? Very good, miss. I will see to it. Will you be staying the night?"

"I believe so." She made up mind quickly. "Kinloch extended the invitation, and I am a bit tired. Will someone bring word to Mrs. MacIan, so she will not worry?"

"The laird promised to send one of the lads who help at the distillery to do that."

Fiona nodded her thanks and sipped some tea; it soothed her throat, which felt sore from breathing smoke, and her voice was a bit hoarse, so the thought of a whisky remedy was not unwelcome. She noticed, then, that her hair and garments smelled strongly of smoke. "I would like to wash up," she told Maisie.

"I can prepare a bath for you if you like, though

it is nothing fancy here, just a plain hot bath with a good soap, which my own mother makes from lavender and heather bells. If you do not mind me saying it, miss, you do smell of the char." She wrinkled her nose.

Fiona laughed, not used to such frankness in serving girls—her great-aunt Lady Rankin never tolerated opinion in the household staff—but she found Maisie charming rather than rude. When the girl left the room, Fiona heard one of the dogs barking outside. Setting down her teacup, she walked to the window.

On the far side of the acres surrounding Kinloch House, she glimpsed, through trees and distance, a man running at a steady pace. Despite the sunset fading to darkness, she recognized Dougal MacGregor—she was surprised how very familiar the rhythm of his stride, the set of his shoulders, the dark banner of hair seemed to her. And she realized that he was not heading for the slope that led to the distillery and the short route to Neill MacDonald's burned-out still.

He moved in another direction, heading diagonally up a slope that would take him to the mountainside where she had first met him.

Fiona wandered the hallway, looking in on the dining room and study, exploring the foyer with its large walnut sideboard and oil portraits in gilt frames hung on the whitewashed walls. Then she ventured upstairs, taking the turning steps carefully; the worn stone wedges had been much used over the centuries, and she was grateful for the handhold of a thick rope slung around a central pillar. Each floor, four in all, was marked by a wide landing in the stairs, faced by one or two doors to the rooms on those levels. Most of the doors were open, and Fiona peered into dim interiors, seeing old furniture, walls covered in wood paneling, and sturdy poster beds hung with canopies and curtains. Like the main floor, the rooms spoke of quality and simplicity, hinting at the genteel poverty common to many aristocratic Highland families, particularly since the events of the Forty-five, the year of rebellion that had changed Scotland's fortunes for generations to come.

Aware that poverty was all too real in Glen Kinloch, she shook her head at the irony of her grandmother's request that she marry a wealthy Highland laird. Surely there was a more reasonable way to help her siblings to earn their inheritance, she thought; for according to the lawyers, Mr. Browne and Sir Walter himself, the funds would not be released to them until each one of them met the terms of Grandmother's rather outlandish will.

In her heart, she knew it could be a wonderful prospect to marry a laird like Kinloch, wealthy or not. He was a clear rogue, true—but he possessed qualities that had drawn her from the beginning, a charismatic and mysterious aura that she had even attributed to magic at first. She had been wildly wrong about that, but even so, he had an undeniable beauty and masculine power that she found compelling, attractive, utterly fascinating.

And his kisses, the first night she had met him, were unforgettable. She craved to be kissed like that again, by the same man. She had loved another man, who had kissed and held her often in the months of their engagement before he went to war, never to return.

Yet somehow that dear and much-mourned comfort seemed pale now, compared to the searing, unexpected passion she had felt in Dougal's arms. Indeed, she thought, if she could speak to her grandmother once more, she would tell her that marrying a man like Dougal, having love and adventure, too, in life, was what she wanted—wealth and wills be damned.

Besides, she told herself as she attained another landing and opened the next door, she was utterly in love with the man's house—for in that moment she discovered the library.

A few books, he had said. She nearly laughed aloud.

The room was not large, and its ceiling was low, with painted wooden beams; yet the walls were fixed floor to ceiling with oak cases jammed with books. There were a thousand or more books, she thought, interspersed with other treasures— small paintings and figurines, a row of the round, dark bottles and silver flasks that she surmised held brandy, whisky, port, and other spirits. In one corner, she found a small spinning globe of the world. A large table took up the center of the room, scattered with papers and books. A wing chair in faded red, liberally coated with dog hair, was angled by the window.

Fiona explored the shelves with a sense of indulgent delight, surprised and pleased at the contents: old works of Ovid, Boccaccio, Chaucer, Shakespeare, Milton; an encyclopedia from the last century, crammed with fascinating topics; scores of books on sciences and agriculture and practical household matters; a row of what seemed to be journals, bound in leather and tied with ribbon, hand-lettered along the spine with dates, and locked up behind a mesh front; more poetry, including Spenser's *Faerie Queene* and Percy's *Reliques of Ancient Poetry*, and plenty of native Scottish writers, too—Burns and Hogg, Henryson and MacPherson, and several volumes of Sir Walter Scott's works, including his narrative poems, his own studies of Scottish song and verse, and some of his anonymous Waverley novels—Fiona knew that *Ivanhoe* and others were penned by Scott and not publicly owned to by the man himself, yet here the books were grouped with Scott's poems.

She found a slim red leather volume of *The Lady of the Lake*, too. The book had been set aside and lay on the table, with the corners of pages folded. Smiling to herself, surprised, she fingered through some of the pages, noting what he had underlined— surely that was the mark of his hand, in pencil lead—the quiet tracks of a man who cared about writing, books, and poetry, and studied so carefully that he wrote in the very books themselves.

So MacGregor of Kinloch, the smuggler, the man who seemed so mysterious to her for so many reasons, favored poetry and fiction. And—judging by the books on the table, including another volume of Milton and more Scott—he had a taste for the sublime and supernatural as well. Shaking her head a little, bemused, she picked up a piece of paper.

There, in a fat, childish hand, a few lines had been diligently copied in ink from one of Scott's collections of old Scottish verse:

> O hush thee, my babie, thy sire was a
>   knight,
> Thy mother a lady, both lovely and bright;
> The woods and the glens, from the towers
>   which we see,
> They are all belonging, dear babie, to thee.

Fiona easily recognized Lucy's handwriting, which was round and firm, pressing down hard with the nib, as stubborn a hand as the little girl herself. Frowning slightly, puzzled, she set the page aside, and saw that a box beside it had loops of colored threads spilling from it. Flicking it open curiously, she saw a half-rendered embroidery piece with the first line of that same verse stitched in brown on linen weave. Decorative borders with colorful trees, hills, and a castle ran across top and bottom. Painstaking yet clumsy, the needlework probably belonged to Lucy, she realized.

Something touched her deep inside as she looked at the contents of the table. She saw far more than an untidy jumble of books and papers and a child's half-finished embroidery. She saw the love of a man for words and poetry, and his dedicated tutoring of his niece and ward, even to the point of making sure the girl learned needlework.

No wonder the little girl did not think she needed school, Fiona thought. She had a very competent private tutor, the uncle to whom the child was clearly devoted.

She must not spy further, Fiona told herself, for her natural curiosity had taken over. This was their home and their concern, not hers—though she felt suddenly, keenly drawn toward it, wanting so much to be part of this.

She chose a book from a shelf and settled in the red chair by the window, opening Ramsay's *Tea-Table Miscellany*. The collection of verses in song and poetry kept her occupied for a while, though soon she found herself sleepy, and, looking around the library she had already come to love, she began daydreaming, soon imagining herself seated at that large library table with Dougal MacGregor, leaning close, looking over his shoulder as he read aloud to her.

In her fantasy, Dougal read verses written by her family friend Sir Walter Scott, and while he underlined his favorite passages, she imagined him pausing to kiss her brow, her hair, as she leaned on his arm. Lucy sat nearby, stitching her little sampler and humming.

Fiona smiled, eyes closed, and slipped into a dozing state, keeping the warm and wonderful scene in her mind, so that she saw herself produce a letter from Sir Walter himself, praising Dougal's recent poetic verses, and she read aloud Scott's promise to visit Kinloch House soon to see the laird and his new wife—

Feeling a deep sense of love and contentment as she sat in that cozy room, she let the dream spin onward.

Seated on a projection of rock inside the cave, Dougal wiped sweat from his brow with the back of his forearm and surveyed the rocky interior, its irregular walls obscured by stacks of the small whisky kegs that he and his kinsmen had produced over many years—some of which his own father had produced when Dougal had been a boy.

Of over a hundred casks of whisky stored in the cave, one keg at a time, for more than two decades, twenty-seven kegs now remained, by Dougal's latest count. Outside, several more were stacked and ready to be brought inside. For now, he planned to rest for a few minutes and contemplate the next phase of his plan.

That night, he and a few of his kinsmen had moved several casks from the burned-out Mac-

Donald still to this cave for safe storage. And
Dougal had sent men and ponies down the mountain twice that night. His comrades had descended
the hills like a troupe of ghosts, silent, rhythmic;
faces grim, gazes watchful. But unlike ghosts, they
carried glowing lanterns ready to be shuttered, and
kept their pistols loaded.

Swift as they could, they moved more of the
whisky down to the caves by the loch, secret re-
cesses that Dougal knew were known only to some
of the residents of Glen Kinloch, and had never
been discovered by outsiders.

Standing, he went to the cave's entrance, looking down over the night-dark landscape. That same
hill was where he had first seen Fiona, strolling
with her brother, while she looked at the rocks she
claimed to study with such fervor. He could only
hope that she had not been helping her brother to
spy out the area. If the gaugers ever learned the lo-
cation of this cave, with its hidden cache—let alone
found the lower caves, the most guarded secret of
the smugglers of Glen Kinloch—there would be
hell to pay.

Thinking of Fiona now, he crossed his arms as
if he could resist the temptation of her, and gazed
toward the dark, sparkling loch beyond a fringe of
trees, far below. From certain windows in Kinloch
House, Fiona would have a view of the loch, too,
and of the hill where he now stood. He wondered
if she was still awake; he wondered if she thought
of him.

A rush of desire sank through him, hot and heavy, at the awareness that she slept in his house tonight. In part, he hoped she would be waiting for him. What a rare joy that would be, he thought, to find the woman he cared about waiting in his home when he came back at night; what a delight if she were there to talk with him, listen to him. What a privilege and a comfort if she opened her arms to him and accepted his around her, giving and accepting what he had to offer her.

The woman he cared about. He sighed out, rubbed a hand over his face. What the devil had happened to him in the fortnight since her arrival? He did not need a woman in his life, certainly not now; he had settled for the loyalty of kin and friends, and his own love and loyalty for the glen. At Kinloch House, he had the exuberant affection of his dogs and the hearty, gruff greetings of one or more of his uncles, and in the last three years, the delight of a little girl eager to share stories of her day, or her latest poem or drawing.

However unusual the family that surrounded him, he had been content enough. But now he wanted far more—he wanted his own family, wanted that passionately, though it might unsettle the balance of his life. But he had no time to sort out the desire in thought or heart. Not now.

Footsteps crunched on rocks nearby, and Dougal turned to see a tall man approach.

"Kinloch!" Hugh MacIan came toward him. He gestured toward the stacked kegs near the cave's opening. "How far have you gotten with this, then?"

"A good portion of the MacDonald kegs saved from the fire have been moved into the cave," Dougal said. "These kegs are the last of Thomas's stored whisky, which we'll store here until he can rebuild on another site. I will give him a plot of land in the valley between those two hills, there," he said, and pointed outward, toward the mountain where foothills of the glen nudged along its base. "He and Neill can start again, and hide another still there."

"It is good whisky they make, and should continue. What of the rest of your cache?"

"I've sent some men down to the loch side again. Twice is enough for one night."

"More than enough. Going down there too often poses a great risk in more ways than one. We cannot afford to have the lower caves discovered. How much is left up here?"

"Over the past two weeks we've moved a good bit of it to the loch, ready to be shipped out when the time comes," Dougal said evasively. Much as he trusted Hugh and his kinsmen, he was reticent by habit to give accurate numbers to anyone but his uncles. He kept count of his whisky in his head, and in the journals hidden among the ranks of books in his library. And he never kept his whisky all in one place, but kept moving it around—some in the upper caves, some in the lower, some hidden under the floor of his house and in other places around the glen. Mary MacIan had been particularly helpful in that, as had Helen MacDonald.

"Moving it efficiently. Good," Hugh murmured. "The sales will be made soon, and the glen will have the benefit of it." He took a leather flask from his pocket and offered a drink to Dougal, who swallowed quick and handed it back. "MacDonald whisky," Hugh said. "Not bad. More of a smoky taste than I generally like in a whisky."

"Thomas and Neill add peat from the north glen side when they toast the sprouted barley over the peat fires," Dougal said. "It adds a fine flavor, to my mind."

"You've perfected a more delicate taste for Glen Kinloch stuff," Hugh said, and took another long swig from the flask.

"Flowers," Dougal said. "We added primroses with the heather already in the water this year before we filtered it through. Should be excellent in three years' time, and if we keep it longer, it will be the more excellent yet. Generally the heather gives it the honey flavor that Glen Kinloch has been known for, but the primroses will add something subtle."

"The heather whisky—the twenty-year batch that your father made. Have you set aside the casks for Eldin?"

"I have not yet decided if I will sell it to him," Dougal answered.

"The fellow can be unpleasant to deal with," Hugh said. "Yet he has a basic decency despite his cold manner. The money he is offering could help rescue this glen from the devastation that other regions have suffered."

"With that, we could get together enough coin for the deed, but it may not be enough to save Glen Kinloch in the future. What I want is a guarantee. I want all the deeds back, signed in perpetuity to me and to my heirs."

"A fine dream, Kinloch," Hugh said. "Do not let go of it."

"Just so," Dougal said.

Fiona sat up, stunned by her dream, and a feeling so dear and intimate that she did not want to let go of it. She had dreamed of being in Dougal's arms, of his hands upon her like heaven, playing over her body like a harper caressing strings, so that she burned and sang within, and felt a sense of love so immense that it soared through her—and now she burned with desire yet, felt the heat of it in her cheeks, breasts, as her breath quickened. The light had gone dim in the room; she reached out to turn up the wick of the lantern on the table.

Moments later, she heard footsteps on the stair, and she looked up expectantly, calm and composed by the time Maisie entered, holding a glass in her hand.

"I brought the whisky and honey," the girl said, and crossed the room to set a small glass on the table beside the red chair. "The laird asked me to stay, miss, but my brother has come—he's downstairs. He says our father is doing poorly."

"Oh dear! What is wrong?" Fiona asked.

"Da was helping to fight that fire earlier, and he was overtaken with smoke, just as you were, as the laird said. But Kinloch wants me to stay here with you tonight." As she spoke, one of the dogs came into the room, curious, coming closer. "Try the hot whisky." Fiona saw that the glass held a pale, steaming liquid.

"Thank you. Maisie, you must go to your father," she said, trying a sip of the concoction. The warm remedy slid down her throat, the sudden heat of it spreading, so that she coughed, feeling it clear a little, and set the glass down.

"See, it helps the lungs and throat," Maisie said. "It is what my father needs, and my brother too much of a dimwit to make it for him. My mother is no longer with us."

"I will be fine here; please do not stay on my account," Fiona said. The dog nudged her, and she patted the gray head. "I have Sorcha to protect me."

"This is Mhor, and he's a big coward," Maisie said. "Sorcha, the female, is the braver. But if all is well, miss, I will leave. The bath is filled and hot, and I set a blanket over it to keep the heat in until you are ready."

"Thank you. I'd enjoy a bath."

"Your room is the one upstairs, by the way, top floor. The guest room is ready. I keep a clean house on the days I come here, though the laird and his uncles are a wretched lot to tidy up after when they are all here at once," she went on her breezy way.

"Do they all live here, the laird and his uncles?"

"When the laird was a lad, aye, the families lived together here to help raise him after his father died. Now Dougal himself lives here, and Fergus as well, for his wife died a few years ago. Ranald's wife is Effie, and she has gone to see her kin outside the glen, and he has been staying here until her return—he gets lonesome, does Ranald." Maisie sighed, shook her head. "As for Hamish, his wife Jean has left him again. They do go back and forth, those two. If Jeanie had her own house— but Hamish feels it is his duty as the eldest of the laird's uncles to help the laird with the estate, and the care of young Lucy, too. But someday the laird will marry, as Jean has often told Hamish, and then they will need to find a place."

"I am sure the laird would help them . . . when he marries."

"If," Maisie said, and sighed again. "He does not seem like to settle down soon, though his uncles tell him he must, for the sake of all, and Glen Kinloch too."

"I see," Fiona said.

"And Hamish would stay," Maisie said. "Kinloch has offered him a house nearby, but Hamish likes this old ruin of a place."

Fiona looked around. "I think it is very nice, hardly a ruin. All the charm of a castle, and very well kept."

"All the work of a drafty old castle, too," Maisie grumbled. "The tub is down in the kitchen, Miss. I would not be dragging buckets of hot water up those wicked steps for anyone, and no offense. Well, I do it for wee Lucy, but a child needs less water in a bath, and the laird and his uncles help with the buckets. Not for me, all that work."

Fiona bit her lip to hold back a smile. "Is the kitchen private enough for a bath with so many living here?"

"You are alone here tonight, for they are all gone and will be away until dawn or later, I think. Set the dogs outside the door for a guard, if you like. For supper, there's porridge and soup in the kettles, which you are welcome to," Maisie went on. "I did not cook a meal for the evening, with the men busy on account of the fire, and even before that they would not be here tonight, for when they make a run they are out until dawn, and those nights, I leave cold meats and cheese before I go home, and—" She stopped, and stepped back hastily, as if realizing she had said too much. "I will go, then, if you are all right here."

Fiona stood. If Dougal was planning a run, she thought, that surely meant smuggling. "Thank you. Will I see you tomorrow?"

Maisie shook her head. "I will stay with my da. I left clean garments for you in the guest room." She went to the door and turned. "Miss, please do not go out tonight. It is wise to stay inside when the moon is out, and the men are out as well." Then she left the room.

Turning, Fiona saw Mhor curled on the rug by the hearth, resting his head on his paws as if contemplating her. "What shall we do, you and I?" she asked. "I wonder what your master is up to tonight. It is all so secret," she added plaintively. "I wish he trusted me." The dog thumped his tail.

Picking up another book from the table, she sat down to read a little of James MacPherson's *Ossian*, a stirring but controversial collection of ancient Celtic tales, which her brother William had once read with her. Despite his physician's pragmatism, William was fascinated by ancient myths and legends.

How intriguing, she thought, to find this book, and so many others, in the keeping of a Highland laird who claimed to have little formal education, and a modest library of a few books.

But Dougal MacGregor was far more than a mere smuggler, she knew that now. The laird of Kinloch fascinated her, compelled her, so that she wanted to know more about him—all about him. Yet Maisie claimed he was not interested in marrying; besides, Fiona reminded herself sternly, according to her grandmother's will she could not consider marrying a poor Highland landowner.

Fiona set the book down thoughtfully. She was not safe at Kinloch House—not at all.

Chapter 14

After a hot, soothing bath, while the dogs kept watch in the outer hall, Fiona dried herself and put on the linen nightshirt and a dressing gown of dark red brocade that Maisie had left for her. Both were large and cut in a style suited to a man. Her own things would air overnight, she thought, and she could wear them again in the morning.

From the robe she caught a scent of the man who had worn it before her, a blend of pine and spice and something indefinably masculine; she knew, somehow, that Dougal had worn the garment before her, and she could not resist pulling it snug around her. Rubbing her wet hair with the towel, she left the water in the bath, unable to empty it herself, and hoping it would not be inconvenient for Maisie to see to in the morning.

Hungry, she made a quick supper of the salted porridge and barley soup Maisie had left, with a cup of water poured from a jug. Then, realizing that not much was left for the MacGregors who would return later, she looked around for something to leave them.

In the larder she found sliced cold meat, stored vegetables, seasonings, and barley, which she prepared and tossed in the soup pot, adding water from the jug, and soon a thick stew simmered in the kettle. Then she went upstairs, followed by the deerhounds.

In the library, she found an old encyclopedia and took one of the three volumes with her to the red chair, settling to read articles on natural physics and geological sciences, looking for more information to help in her continuing study of fossils. She was not as intent a geological scholar as her brother James, but found the subject of great interest, and resolved to go into the hills to search for more fossils soon.

And, she reminded herself, she would still have to find some actual fairies to sketch for the book that was with the publisher, awaiting the drawings that would complete the book. She wondered how she could ever supply those, with no fairies to sit for portraits. Scowling at the ridiculousness of that, she wished she understood why her grandmother had made the decisions that had caused so much trouble for all of them.

The dogs curled at her feet, snoring quietly, and she began to cough again. Picking up the glass of whisky and honey, having had a little earlier, she tasted it again, for a few sips of Maisie's remedy had helped clear her throat and chest nicely.

She returned to the encyclopedia, but soon was bored. Checking the bookshelves, she discovered one of her grandmother's own early books, a slim volume entitled *Fairy Tales of Scotland and Ireland*. The book was familiar to her from childhood, and she settled down, delighted to explore it again.

She picked up the glass once more, took a swallow, and turned a page, reading about the pookahs of Ireland. As she reached out to set the glass down, the dogs leaped to their feet, woofing loudly.

Startled, Fiona missed the table; the glass tilted and crashed to the floor, shattering, liquid spilling into the carpet. And as the dogs loped out of the room, she heard footsteps below and a deep voice murmuring to the animals.

Heart hammering, she ran to the library door, but could see little from the landing. The dogs had disappeared around the turn in the stairs, and she heard the timbre of a male voice speaking to the animals. The voice faded, as if the man walked back toward the kitchen with the dogs.

Anxious to get to her room—she did not want to be caught so improperly dressed while cleaning a mess of broken glass and wet carpet—Fiona ran back to crouch and pick up the shards, then realized she had nothing with which to mop up the liquid. Whirling, she yanked open drawers in a side cupboard and a table, finding only paper, ink, and sundry items. Frustrated, tempted to use the hem of her night rail for a mop, she turned, and gasped.

Dougal MacGregor stood in the doorway, bowl in one hand, spoon in the other. Lounging a shoulder against the doorjamb, he regarded her in silence. She saw quickly that his hair seemed damp, curling a little along his brow and the strong column of his throat. He wore a shirt that seemed clean, its folds still neat; open at the neck, sleeves rolled, it was tucked inside a plaid in a pattern she had not seen before, so that seemed to be a fresh garment, too, as did his woolen patterned stockings pulled to the knee, and his leather shoes.

"You have changed your clothes," she said impulsively, then realized how silly it sounded to blurt that out as soon as she saw him.

"So have you," he said, and lifted a brow, as his gaze moved up, then down and up again.

Fiona felt a strange and wonderful thrill go through her. She drew the robe around her, folded her arms. "I washed and changed, since I smelled like the smoke of the fire," she said.

"I did the same."

"Where are your uncles?" she asked, glancing past him toward the silent stairwell. "Did they come home with you? I really ought to go to my room. I should not be here, like this—"

"My uncles are still with the MacDonalds," he said. "The immediate work was done for now, and some of the men decided that it would be a practical thing to consume the whisky in the damaged kegs. It should not be wasted, I suppose. But I doubt we will see my kinsmen for a while, perhaps not until morning, judging by the way the lot of them, my uncles and the rest, were being practical about that whisky. I came back . . . to be sure that all was well here."

"It has been peaceful here. Thank you once again for offering me shelter for the night."

He nodded, holding the bowl in one hand. Then he took another spoonful of what Fiona realized was the stew she had made.

"This is excellent," he said. "Far too good to be Maisie's work. But she tries, bless the girl, which we do not. I assume you made this? All the more reason to keep you in the glen," he added. "Cooking is a skill most welcome at Kinloch House, especially since Hamish's wife Jean left."

"Why did she leave?"

"She and Hamish go round now and then about his smuggling, and her desire for him to be a legitimate whisky maker." He grinned. "He is a stodgy sort, but loves the free trading. And she has a temper. She will be back—or so we hope. I thought you would be asleep by now," he finished.

"I was going to bed, but—oh, I do apologize for the broken glass." She pointed toward the shards, and pulled the red robe close about her, folding her arms over it, too aware of her improper attire. "I hope the glass is not irreplaceable. I could not find a cloth to clean—"

"Fiona, it is no matter," he said quietly, and came forward. "Use this," he said, and gave her a cloth napkin, which had been supporting the hot bowl he held.

Kneeling, she wiped the carpet with the cloth and picked up the rest of the shards, her hands shaking. His unexpected arrival, as well as his nearness, flustered her. As she hastily gathered the pieces together, one of the sharp glass angles jabbed her finger, slicing the skin in an instant, so that she cried out at the sting of it.

"Damn," she muttered, the word slipping out before she knew it. "Pardon—it is a habit I learned from my brothers," she said, then sucked on her finger.

Dougal laughed under his breath, then set his bowl and spoon down and dropped to one knee beside her. Picking up the broken pieces, he set them on the small table, then reached for her hand. He turned her fingers to examine the cut. "That needs a bandage," he said.

"The bleeding has almost stopped," she said, and rose to her feet quickly, just when Dougal stood, and her head knocked against his audibly. "Oh," she gasped, feeling embarrassment more than pain.

"Are you hurt?" Dougal touched her head, brushing his thumb over the sore place, sending shivers through her that erased the ache. His fingers slid downward to cup her cheek, lingered, traced down to brush over her shoulder.

As if entranced, Fiona reached out with her un-injured hand and touched her fingers to the edge of his forehead, where his head had met hers. His dark hair felt cool and silken rich under her fingertips, still damp from the washing he had done earlier. He smelled so clean, she thought; so warm and inviting, a mingling of a trace of soap and a measure of the masculine scent that was his own. She closed her eyes, sighed, opened them. He watched her.

Then she traced her fingers over his brow and down to the jut of his cheekbone and his jaw, its firm shape roughened by a few days' beard growth. Yet she did not mind the texture, bristly yet soft, masculine and somehow so intimate, so meaningful, to touch it with freedom, with curiosity. She ran her hand along his bearded cheek, surprised a little by her own boldness—something in her drove her forward, made her want to do this, regardless of propriety, or the differences between them.

He watched her in silence, his eyes greenish and startlingly beautiful in the lamplight, ringed in black lashes beneath black brows. She leaned so close, and he toward her, that she could feel the warmth of his body, and the gentle drift of his breath upon her wrist. He bent close, and she felt herself move toward him in a natural curve.

She had felt his kisses before, heart-thumping and bold, and the possibility of it drew her closer still, logic slipping away—she did not know him, he was more smuggler than he would ever admit to her, she suspected. And she was a guest in his house, and only partially clothed—and yet as the blood in her veins began to pulse, an urge within her body grew stronger, subtle at first, then powerful. She caught her breath against it, her only resistance.

Closer still, she leaned in toward him as he seemed to incline toward her, his breath soft upon her lips, and then his nose nudging hers—and she tilted her head back, a pulsing desire sinking deep into her body. She forgot the sting of the cut, the aching head, even her keen anguish at seeming clumsy, foolish, vulnerable. She lost awareness of where she was, what little she wore, or that she touched a strange man in an inviting, tender way as her hand lingered along his jaw.

He drew back. "We are forgetting that your cut still needs tending," he said.

She glanced down. The sliced skin along the side of her index finger still bled. "It is fine," she said, and sucked on it, but it still seeped. "I could use a bandaging cloth," she admitted.

Dougal went to a narrow cupboard near the shelf of bottled whiskies and spirits, and drew open a drawer to remove a small folded cloth. "Maisie keeps napkins here, since we have whisky and other spirits in the library for a dram or a drink now and then." He tore the cloth into strips, returning. "Give me your hand, my girl," he said.

Fiona opened her hand on his palm, and let him wrap her finger with a narrow strip of cloth. Simple enough, and soon done, but even that touch sent shivers through her. She found herself watching him, wanting more, breathing deeply and tingling throughout.

"I apologize for breaking the glass," she said, to fill the silence.

"No matter. We are not fussy here, but for Maisie, who stores napkins in odd places all over the house," he said casually. "We sometimes eat meals in here or in the study, and my uncles like a dram and a meat pie in the parlor or a bedroom as much as the dining room or kitchen. They put their feet on the tables and spill food on the furniture, and I have personally broken more cups than you can imagine." He smiled.

She laughed. "Thank you for telling me so."

He finished the small bandage and tucked his hand around her finger, holding it as he glanced at her. "Recovery is certain, I think. What was in the glass?"

"Whisky and honey," she said.

"Ah, Maisie's favorite remedy. We are dosed often around here with that. Did it help?"

"Help what?" she asked, staring at him. Were his eyes so green, or was it a trick of the lamplight, and the contrast of his thick black lashes, beautiful enough to envy?

"Did the whisky help your cough?" he clarified.

"I drank only a little, then spilled it. But it seemed to help."

"The smoke of that fire was very thick. A number of others were overcome and coughing. I should not have let you come with us."

"But I wanted to be there," she said.

He nodded, watching her. "If you want a bit more whisky to help the cough, we have more in the bottles here. I do not know Maisie's recipe, but it should be simple enough—what is that commotion?" He turned as the dogs began barking downstairs. "I had best go see what is bothering them. The spirits are kept over there. Pour a dram for yourself. The Kinloch whisky is just there." He pointed toward the shelf, and left the room.

Some of the bottles lined up on the shelf, Fiona saw as she went there, bore handwritten labels, strips of paper glued to the bottles. *Brandy*, she read; *MacDonald's Whisky*, read another; *Port*, *Claret*, *Sherry*, read others. A brown bottle said *Glen Kinloch*. Three silver flasks and two green bottles, all in a row, were labeled *Uisge beatha an Kinloch*.

Kinloch whisky in the Gaelic, she thought; that must have been what Maisie gave her, minus honey and hot water. She plucked up the first silver flask, along with a glass from several set there to be used for drams, and poured out a little liquid, sipping it.

The whisky was slightly sweet, delicate, and had a seductive simplicity that was quite unlike any whisky she had ever tasted—its heat spread through her quickly, the smallest sip sinking gently, then creating an unexpected heat all through her. But she felt her tickly throat clear, and her chest felt better, almost expansive, a warm and wonderful sense.

She took another sip, seeking more of that sweetness, which seemed honeylike now, changing with the next sip to spicy, and the next sweet again, in a strange, alluring way. The brew had a wildness to it, a fleeting charm that she just had to taste again. Carrying the glass, she sat in the wing chair while the mellow warmth spread all through her. Her tickling cough seemed to vanish, and the pain in her finger was completely gone as well.

Waiting for Dougal, she picked up her grandmother's book and skimmed the stories, thinking once more about the assignment that Lady Struan had given her. So far, in Glen Kinloch, she had seen no fairies. Finally she heard sounds on the stairs, and the dogs came inside first, loping gracefully as they came toward her. Dougal followed.

"Are your uncles back?" she asked. "I should go," she added, half sitting up.

"The noise was just some gusts of wind that made the dogs nervous. My uncles are out for much of the night. After the fire, there may be . . . a good deal of activity in the glen tonight."

She tilted her head. "To do with the revenue men?"

He frowned. "To do with avoiding them."

She was glad to hear his frank answer, which seemed a step toward the trust she wished he would grant her. "They will find nothing, I know," she said. "You are always careful."

"Of course." Seeming thoughtful, he went to the bookshelf, picked up the brown bottle, and poured himself a slight dram of whisky.

"You came back sooner than I expected," she said. "Maisie said you would be out the night."

"I was a bit concerned about you here, alone. I saw Maisie's brother when I was out tonight, and he told me that she had gone to help their father."

"Why concerned about me?"

"With the gaugers out, and your stubborn nature—" He shrugged. "I thought perhaps you might decide to go back to Mary MacIan's."

"I am fine, and I am here, as you see." She smiled a little. "I did not expect anyone, or I would have—" She pulled the red dressing gown around her; aware that her feet were bare, she tucked those under her. "This is quite improper. If we were in Edinburgh, it would never happen. My great-aunt would never have allowed me to end up in such a situation." She smiled more brightly. "I suppose that is why my life has been so dull."

He huffed a laugh. "So you live with your great-aunt?"

"Aye, Lady Rankin," she replied. "She is a dear, really. A bit stiff in her attitudes, and she prefers that I behave that way as well, though—" She stopped.

"Though it is not like you," he remarked, as if he knew that about her. She smiled.

"I suppose that is why I like to go on teaching assignments in the Highlands whenever the chance comes along. I can get away from Edinburgh, and some rather boring people in my aunt's social circles." Fiona lifted her head. "I rather like adventure, and romance, and . . . well, a little wildness in life. I am not as dull as people think," she said defensively.

"Not dull at all. Serene, I would say. Calm and capable. Sure of yourself."

"I am always said to be the calm and capable one," she said, and frowned.

"What would you prefer?" he asked.

She flung a hand outward. "A bit of wildness, but I do not think I have it in me. Dear Fiona, always so capable, does what she must, though she longs to be more adventurous, and a more interesting person. Well," she said, "here she sits in a man's dressing gown, all alone with the man who owns it. I suppose that is adventurous."

He quirked a smile. "Dear Fiona," he said, "seems just right to me. I would not change her."

She blinked at that, felt her heart thump harder. She sipped the whisky, licked her lips, sipped again. "This is sweet," she said. "Light. It's very good."

"I am glad you like Glen Kinloch brew." He came closer, and half sat on the table, resting a hip there. Again he wore the kilt in the MacGregor pattern he favored, with a dark jacket, the shirt beneath open at the throat, without the fussiness of a knotted neck cloth—she liked seeing the strong column of his throat. She liked, too, the sight of his bare and muscled legs, the strong, flat knees and well-shaped calves, the woven socks and low boots.

"I have always thought that the costume of a Highlander gives a man an air of masculinity that is very attractive," she said. "To see a man's muscular limbs and hints of the rest of the hard beauty of the male form is so enjoyable. The kilt brings out the confidence and ease of the natural character of a strong male. Females quite like it," she said, and then felt a moment of sudden chagrin at her words. She felt almost wanton, having expressed herself so, and she looked up at Dougal MacGregor, wondering if he agreed.

"Thank you. I rather like my dressing gown and nightshirt on you," he drawled. "It brings out the enjoyable contrasts between the male character and the female body. You look fetching in that thing—vulnerable, whimsical, and just very bonny."

"My thanks, sir," she said, tilting her head. "My brothers rarely wear the kilt, even at functions. A bit of the plaid while out hunting, for William and sometimes James. Patrick likes a more modern and sophisticated look, he says. But I have always liked the plaid."

"I find it pleasingly simple myself," he said, and took a sip from the glass.

Fiona drank from her own glass again. "This is lovely whisky. *Uisge beatha an Kinloch*," she rolled off her tongue in Gaelic. "Oh dear," she said, putting a hand to her head. Suddenly she felt flushed, dizzy—and quite content to be sitting there with Dougal, together in the library where she had dreamed so tantalizingly of him. "Oh dear," she said again, feeling her cheeks blush hot. "This is strong whisky, and sweet, too. I like it."

"A little is enough where whisky goes," he said. "I rather think this batch has a mellow, spicy taste." He looked at her, frowning. "How much have you had?"

"I had some earlier with honey and hot water. And about half this glass now. My cough is gone, I think. But I do feel a bit . . . light-headed." She raised her brows, blinked.

"You have probably had more than enough," he observed. "And an Edinburgh lady may well have no head for strong drink. Highland women are more accustomed to it. I apologize, I should not have suggested a second dram for you after Maisie's dose. May I?" He reached out for her glass, but she set it on the table.

"I am fine," she insisted. A strange sense of complete well-being, even joyfulness, was coming over her rather quickly, she realized. She stood, and wobbled a little, setting a hand to the arm of the chair. As she looked up, she saw lights and rainbows flitting about the top of the room. Reflections of the lamplight, she thought, watching them. Her head was definitely spinning. She set a hand to her brow.

"How do you feel?" he asked.

She straightened, and looked at him, and a lovely sense of warmth came over her. "I feel . . . wonderfully, marvelously well."

"Do you," he said wryly, regarding her. "So in addition to sitting here with you alone, and you in a state of undress, I am now responsible for your becoming fou."

"I am not fou," she said. "But if I was fou, I did that myself."

"We are not fou—well, not *that* fou," he quoted softly, and she laughed.

"Burns! Just so," she said, using the turn of phrase because he sometimes did. "And if I am in a state of undress," she went on, "I made myself that way, when I took a bath."

"Fiona," he said, standing. "It might be best for you to go upstairs to bed."

"Not yet." She smiled. "I like your company." She really did, she thought, and smiled again, tipping her head. But that made her dizzy, too, she realized.

"I like the company also. But those brothers of yours will come after me for this night."

"That depends on what you decide to do this night," she said. She picked up the glass and sipped again, and Dougal leaned forward and took it from her.

"Decide to do about what?" he asked, setting it on the table beside his own.

She felt a little wicked suddenly, and tipped her head. "Your black lovesickness. I am sure we could cure it."

"How so?" he asked, leaning toward her. He lifted a hand, brushed it over her hair, and she closed her eyes, tilted her head, waited. He did not kiss her, but hovered close, and she wanted it—oh, she wanted it, and nearly said so, biting her lip, licking it then.

"What do you suggest?" he whispered again, his face very close to hers.

"Mmm," she said, as his touch created shivers all through her. "Maisie's potion fixes all."

"I can think of other cures. But none of those would be the gentlemanly thing just now."

"You are a gentleman, a laird—and a rascally smuggler," she emphasized.

"Just so," he said, and took her arm when she wobbled against him. Glad for the support, she wrapped her arm around his waist. He stepped back a little, put an arm around her. "Here we go, my girl, and off to bed with you." He began to walk her forward.

"I am not your girl," she said. "Am I?"

"Not so far," he murmured quietly.

"You know, I have a touch of the black lovesickness myself." She regarded him.

"Do you? I am glad I am not alone in that."

"We are both in this," she said, and tipped forward, so that he caught her again, and she leaned into his chest.

"Oh aye, it's upstairs for you, my dear," he said.

"The book I am reading! I forgot it," she said then, as the thought occurred and she reacted without thinking, dragging him back toward the table where she had left the book.

He picked it up and glanced at the cover. "*Fairy Tales of Scotland and Ireland*. I have read this. An excellent collection by . . . Mrs. Rankin," he read on the spine. "With your interest in fairy legends, you will find this one illuminating."

"I read it years ago, and must read it again. My grandmother wrote it."

He lifted a brow. "Mrs. Rankin is your grandmother?"

She nodded. "She was Lady Struan, but wrote as Mrs. Rankin, using her sister's name, which appalled my great-aunt." She smiled a little ruefully at the memory. "Most of her books had to do with fairy lore. I read them when I was younger."

"So you learned your interest in fairy lore from your grandmother?"

"Oh, quite," she answered evasively, and glanced away. Seeing her whisky glass on the table, she picked it up again and sipped. The heat sank through her, relaxing her even more.

"Truly, I think the whisky has done its work for you," he said.

"It has not cured my black lovesickness," she said.

He lifted a brow. "Good night, Fiona. Best we say that."

"So stern! I have been enjoying your library. I was surprised to find such a handsome collection here, when you had said there were just a few books."

"A few compared to some collections," he answered. "I am not a scholar, and when I was younger, I disliked studying. I wanted to—well," he said, "later I realized the importance of education, and book knowledge. I could not complete my years at university, but I have taught myself something through reading." He spread a hand wide.

"Taught yourself a great deal, it seems. Did you collect all these books?"

"Some of them. My father and grandfather acquired most of them. My father felt strongly about my education, and wanted me to complete a university degree and become a lawyer like your brother. It was different than I wanted for myself."

"What was it you wanted, Dougal MacGregor," she asked, leaning toward him.

"I wanted to be a smuggler," he said.

"And so you got your wish."

When he did not answer, she realized that he had never outright admitted it to her, though she was certain. Then she put her hand to her brow and looked up, as lights swirled and floated overhead. Some even seemed to encircle Dougal's head, and sat upon his shoulders. "Oh my," she said, and giggled. "That is a fine whisky, sir. I am seeing the lights again—dancing little lights!"

Dougal frowned. He picked up her glass and sniffed it. "Fiona," he said slowly, "which bottle did you choose for your dram?"

"That one," she said, pointing. The room spun. "That silver flask there—"

"Silver flask!" he said, low and thunderous.

"Oh, the lights, do you not see them?" She blinked as the dazzling rainbow glimmers began to spin, faster and faster, and began to take on shape, sparkling like colored stars, forming a column, then the contours of a head, shoulders, body—

"Oh look!" she breathed. A woman appeared to be formed by the lights. She was exquisitely beautiful. Fiona sighed out and stepped close to Dougal, wanting the strength of his nearness. She put her hand on his shoulder. "Dougal, look!"

"What?" He glanced over his shoulder.

The woman smiled at Fiona and tipped her head, so that her golden hair slid over her shoulders in a spill of sunlight. Her eyes glittered like diamonds; her gown was like golden starlight and gossamer. She reached out a hand, her fingers sparkling with rings and a natural luminosity, and she touched Dougal's arm, slid her hand along it. Then she looked at Fiona and set a finger to her lips, and moved away. Dougal did not move.

Heart beating fast, the wild thrill of it almost too much to bear, Fiona gasped and leaned toward Dougal. "There—she is standing by the center bookshelf now. Do you not see her?"

"What are you talking about?"

"I need paper and ink." She leaned toward him, so close she could feel his hair brush her cheek as he turned his head to listen. "I must make a drawing."

"Now? Of what?"

"The fairy in the room," Fiona whispered.

"Good God," he said, looking at her. "You are seeing things."

"I have seen what I most needed to find when I came to Glen Kinloch," she confided.

"What do you mean?" He drew his brows together. "Did you come here for something besides the teaching assignment?"

"I did, but—oh, she is gone now." She looked once again toward the slight, beautiful woman in gold and gossamer, but she had vanished. Fiona frowned, disappointed. "I do not think I imagined her, but I suppose you will say so."

He glanced over his shoulder again. "I see no one."

"The fairy was just there. I did see her, I swear it."

He was watching her. "Tell me why you came to Glen Kinloch."

"To see fairies, to get the money. And to find— well, to find you. Only you are not quite what my grandmother had in mind, or Sir Walter Scott, either. But my brothers will like you, if you will have me."

"Have you—good God," he said. "What about Sir Walter Scott? What money?"

She had blathered on, she knew, but could not seem to stop it. The whisky had loosened her tongue, opened her vision to the Otherworld, and her thoughts seemed to race in some strange way. This was unlike the effect of any dram of spirits or glass of wine she had ever had. "I did not have that much whisky," she said. "What was in it?" She put a hand to her head.

"A special brew is in the silver flask, and I should have thought to put it away—Fiona, why did you come here to this glen? What did you mean about the money?"

She looked at him, and her attention, which seemed scattered, now focused wholly on him. "Do you know, you are a beautiful man," she said. "And I think I want to kiss you."

"What—" he said, and caught her by the upper arms as she lifted on her toes to do just that, kiss him as she had wanted to do for so long.

As she pressed her mouth to his, he resisted for a moment, squeezing her arms—and then he murmured something under his breath and took command of the kiss she had begun, so that it turned hard and sure.

Fiona sighed, and felt as if she tumbled from a height—surely it was dizziness from the whisky—yet in that moment she felt her heart bloom full—and then she knew, fou or sober, bold or shy, capable or wild, that she had begun to fall in love.

Along with that sense of falling, stunned by her realization, she felt safe in his arms. The feeling was divine; she could think of no other word for it. He kissed her again, soothing and gentle, and she slipped her hands along his back to his shoulders, and he cupped her face in his hands and kissed her into breathlessness, tilting her head to fit his lips over hers.

Each new kiss, a warm, luscious chain of them, made her knees tremble, her body ripple with desire. A feeling sparked inside her like a candle, a sense of joy—and love. She combed her fingers through his hair, the warm, heavy dark silk of it, and he dropped his head to trace his mouth along her jaw and her throat, and she moaned softly, desperate for more, her heart pounding.

"Dougal," she whispered, and then he lifted his head and held her close in a deep embrace. And she faltered a little in his arms, felt her knees go out, overtaken by whisky, and love newly realized within herself—she did not think that he felt a similar revelation. And when he pulled back, she was sure of it, for he was frowning.

"My dear girl," he murmured. "I did not mean to—"

"I am glad you did." She closed her eyes, rested against his shoulder. "Oh! I feel dizzy."

"No wonder. Best get you upstairs. Fiona, tell me again—what did you see, just now, in this room?"

"A lovely creature, all sparkles and gold. She looked like a fairy. I started to tell you, but—we were distracted. Something came over me," she said. "I cannot explain it. The kiss, I mean."

"Do not try," he said. "How much did you pour from the silver flask?"

"Not so much. It said *uisge beatha an Kinloch*," she said. "Kinloch whisky. As you said."

"I said Glen Kinloch. One of the bottles. The silver flasks hold *uisge beatha an Kinloch an Sìth*— the fairy whisky of Kinloch."

"Fairy whisky!" She stared up at him. "But you said there is no such thing, that the brew is only a legend."

"We, ah, do make what is called fairy whisky from an old family recipe. It has been made in our family for generations, and we keep it secret, sharing it only among kin and friends." Frowning, thoughtful, he watched her.

"And I drank some?" She was delighted. "Fairy whisky, how grand!"

"Not always," he murmured. "It can be potent stuff for some people."

"That is the brew my brother tasted once," she said. "His wife, your cousin Elspeth, said her kinsman made it. Is that you?"

"Aye. And of those who taste it, only a few feel its strange power. Elspeth's grandfather is one of them."

"I certainly felt something," she said, widening her eyes, shaking her head.

"What was it you thought you saw in the room?"

"I do not think, I know. I saw a fairy woman," Fiona said. "And she was there, just behind you. She touched you, but you did not seem to feel it."

"I knew she was there," he said. "In fact, I have seen her before."

Fiona stared at him.

Chapter 15

"**Y**ou saw her?" Fiona stared up at him.

He regretted saying it so quickly; he rarely gave away so much of himself, never impulsively. The girl's effect on him astonished him at times. "I have seen something like that, when I have tasted the fairy whisky."

"You said you saw her just now!" Her blue eyes were wide in her pale, lovely face, and she looked alluring enough to distract him. A flush brought on by kissing—and the drink—enhanced her natural beauty, her skin like cream, eyes sparkling blue, dark hair sheened like silk. He wanted to touch her, kiss her, and more. He did not want to talk.

"I sensed she was there," he said. "It is an ability I seem to have inherited from generations back. Now and then it happens." He shrugged, as if it were nothing much.

But Fiona had felt the rare, extraordinary response to the fairy brew, and he owed her an explanation. Reaching out, he brushed his fingers over her hair. "I am careful about giving away the fairy brew, since it can have an effect on some people."

"What sort of effect?"

"The drink can give a person the power to see into the fairy realm."

She made a wry little face. "I think they call that belladonna."

"Let me clarify. It is not the drink, according to our family legend, but the Fey themselves who grant the power to a select few who taste it. For others, the drink is a decent, rather unique whisky, and nothing more."

"Do the Fey make the brew? I thought you made it."

"I do, as all lairds of Kinloch have done. The ingredients come from . . . an unusual source. We keep the details of the legend, and the recipe, secret for the most part."

"Is that because the Fey require it, or because it all sounds quite mad?"

"It does sound strange," he admitted. "The legend asks for secrecy outside the laird's own family." Suddenly he wanted very much to tell her, wanted her to be part of that circle.

"We have an old legend in our family that sounds a bit lunatic, I suppose. And now my grandmother's will—" She lifted her shoulders, drew the brocade robe more snugly about her, though it gapped at the neck in a most delicious way, which Dougal noticed. "Well," she said then, "I can understand perfectly about fairy legends causing a kerfuffle in a family."

"The Kinloch legend asks that we give away the fairy whisky that we make. We use a recipe that supposedly was given to us by a fairy, long ago, when her life was saved by a dram of whisky given to her by the laird of Kinloch at the time." He told her as much as he could. "We must never sell the brew, and the rest of the details are known by the laird and his closest family members. Yet the drink's power is known, and so there is something of a reputation for Kinloch fairy whisky." He smiled a little ruefully. "If the source of the fairy whisky was known, there are some people who would want to make some romantic spectacle out of it."

"And your beautiful glen would no longer be private, but filled with those who want to make the whisky, too."

He was pleased that she understood so quickly. "Aye. Tourists might come here, too, in droves, as they do along the southern end of the loch."

"You do not like strangers in your glen," she observed.

"Not much. But I find that I can tolerate teachers." He smiled a little.

"You have been anxious to be rid of one teacher in particular," she pointed out.

"I am rethinking that," he said. "Tell me about your family legend."

"Like yours, we have kept it quiet and within the family. There is a golden cup in the family seat at Duncrieff. Around its band is written a motto that was given to us by a fairy ancestor long ago. The cup and its sentiment give us an obligation—" She stopped, and he saw a blush fill her cheeks. She shrugged. "You will think it silly."

"I doubt it. I have lived with a legend of fairy whisky all my life."

"The cup was the gift of a fairy bride who married into our clan. The motto says, 'Love makes its own magic.'"

"Nothing silly about that," he murmured, and touched her arm, drawing his fingers along to her elbow, his touch lingering, then dropping away. She gasped softly, watching him.

"Members of the clan are sometimes expected to marry others with a touch of fairy blood," she said quietly.

"Now that is a bit harder to find in a mate. I have a little fairy blood, so it is said—should that interest you." He smiled quickly, saw her blush. "And you have some fairy blood, too. I knew it already just by the way the *uisge beatha an Kinloch* affected you."

She looked surprised. "How did you know?"

"Kinloch's fairy brew bestows a magical ability to see the world of the Fey, but only in some people," he said. "Those with fairy blood in their veins, in their family tree, even just a hint of it, have the wildness in their blood awakened by the whisky."

"So to others without the 'fairy taint,' as my great-aunt calls it—she says it is all nonsense, but she is not a MacCarran—it seems like any other whisky."

He nodded. "The fairies choose who will see them and feel magic, and who will not. And so they chose you. It must be the fairy blood."

"There is another reason," she said softly, then looked up. "No matter. It is too much talking. I feel the delights of the fairy whisky wearing off. And the fairy herself has vanished," she said, glancing over his shoulder. "What if I drink it again, so that she will come back? I need to see her again. I want to make a drawing of her. But I suppose that seems foolish."

"You remember what you saw," he said. "Draw it from that. You could drink your fill of the whisky now, and still she might not reappear. She allowed herself to be seen once. The Fey are fickle and easily bored with our games."

"You *have* seen her?"

"That one, and others, over the years, when I was a boy. Nothing much since then."

"I would love to know where one can find the fairy ilk in Glen Kinloch. Can you say?"

"They are everywhere," he said, reaching out to pull her close. "It is commonplace here."

"Then I came to the right glen after all," she said.

"I hope so." He wondered why she still spoke of fairies. Drawing her closer, aware of the increasing desire and bond he felt with her, he was keenly aware that they were alone. What she had roused in him with those impulsive kisses earlier had taken him by storm. His body still pulsed, the feeling damnably distracting, particularly now that she stood so close.

"Where did you see the fairy woman?" She set her hands on his arms. "Does she help you make the fairy brew?"

"Fiona." He wrapped his arms around her waist to pull her closer. "I do not want to talk about fairies, or fairy brew."

"But I want to know."

"Later," he murmured, tracing a finger along her cheek. "And later you will tell me why you are so very interested in the Fey."

"Some of that I cannot tell anyone," she said.

"Then we both have secrets. Best leave it for now. Come upstairs to rest," he said. "The fairy whisky is still affecting you."

"My head is spinning," she admitted.

He picked up a candle, lit earlier, and took her hand, leading her to the door and out of the library, up the turning stone steps to the uppermost landing. There, he allowed her to step up ahead of him. She reached out a hand and set it on the door latch, then looked back at him.

In that moment, Dougal knew that he could not leave her with a mere good-night, abandoning the promise of what had happened between them— although he ought to do just that. One more kiss, he thought; one last chance to hold her before the night was gone and morning arrived. He would never find time and place to be so close, so alone, with her again.

But his uncles were away for now, and he and Fiona were unchaperoned for the night. If more than a mere good-night occurred, he would owe her marriage. Suddenly it seemed a very attractive idea, and no ill fit for the laird of Kinloch at all. He frowned, surprised, thoughtful.

She stood a step or two above him, here in his house, wearing his dressing gown; she had sipped the fairy whisky and knew part of its precious legend; she filled his arms and his heart so well, and he had confided in her as he never had with anyone. Trusting her felt like pure relief.

"Fiona," he murmured. Still holding the candle, he set it in a niche along the wall. "Wait."

Wordlessly, she stepped toward him and came into his arms, silently and willingly, standing one step above where he stood, their heads on a level. He touched his lips to hers, she complied. Sweet as honey, hot as the burn of whisky, that new kiss, and as it blended into another, she opened her lips beneath his and curved her body against him. Dougal cradled her head in his hand, his fingers sliding through her hair, tumbling its curling softness loose. "Fiona," he murmured, "this is madness—"

"It is magic," she protested, touching her lips to his again.

"It is the whisky," he murmured, drawing back.

"Not all of it," she whispered, sliding deeper into

his arms, the brocade robe falling open so that her body pressed closely, intimately to his, separated only by linen and wool.

"More than you know," he said, and pulled her so close, bending her back in his arms, kissing her deep now, his hand skimming along her body, down her rib cage, to her waist, her hip. Sighing, he let her go. "Up to your room now," he said quietly. "I will not do this when you are fou."

"Not fou, I swear." She reached out for him. "Stay with me."

He shook his head. "Go. This is not right, when you are in this state. Later," he promised, sweeping his fingers along her cheek. He kissed her again, could not help it, his lips dragging over hers, his body pounding for satisfaction and release, so that he could hardly think. Mustering will, he pushed her away gently. "Later, my dearest girl."

She stepped back through the door, and turned. "What if I . . . should see fairies again tonight?"

"You just may, with the whisky still upon you. But you wanted to see them, so you said."

"Not in my bedroom, in the dark, alone." Her face looked pale in the shadowy darkness.

"Go to sleep," he suggested.

"Dougal," she said. "Tell me about the fairies of Kinloch. I must know—it is so important. I wish I could tell you why—but not yet." She put a hand to her head then, the bandaged finger white in the darkness on the stairs, and shook her head slowly. "I am dizzy. So tired."

"The aftermath of the fairy whisky. Go inside."

"But I do not want—" She stopped, a hand on the doorjamb, and looked past him. "Oh!"

"What is it?"

"Lights," she said. "The tiny colored lights—on the stair behind you."

He turned and saw them, the ones who flitted in that form, sometimes appearing at dawn or dusk, and at times when something of significance was about to happen. "Aye, the lights."

"You do see them, too! I wondered about that before—are they . . . the fairy ilk?" she whispered.

"I have seen the wee lights since I was a lad," he said. "They mean no harm, and only appear to let us know that they wish to protect us. It is nothing to fear."

She smiled then, slowly, the radiant, beautiful smile that he had seen before. Now, at last, that smile was for him alone, and he savored it. "Are we the only two who can see them?" she asked.

"That could be. I have never heard anyone other than my father mention them. Yours is a special power indeed, to see the fairy lights of Kinloch."

"Perhaps there is something very special between the two of us."

"There is," Dougal murmured, his heart pounding hard as he realized the full truth of it.

"I do not want to be alone tonight." She held out her hand. "Come up to me."

He did, taking her fingers in his, and pushing open the door.

* * *

The room was small and cozy, with the same plain elegance of the other rooms in the house—the solid bed, heavy four-poster hung with dark green curtains, the simple coverlet quilted white on white, a few pieces of heavy Jacobean furniture, dark walnut, sturdy pieces; an Oriental rug, worn and aged, under a stiff chair and a side table. Fiona folded her hands, stood at the foot of the bed, and turned.

Dougal leaned against the door watching her, the shadows defining the sculpted planes of his face, the beautiful eyes, the strong jaw, the sensuous, mobile lips that had tasted so wonderful against her own lips. Her heart thudded like a storm, yet she felt shy and uncertain now, having invited this—boldly, knowingly invited this. Once again she felt the spell that he seemed to cast over her. She glanced away, and back. He still watched her.

"You are safe here at Kinloch," he said. "I want you to know it."

She nodded. "I do." When he stepped away from the door to open it, he stopped, glanced at her. "Dougal," she said softly. "Come here. Please do not go . . . and do not send me away from here, from the glen."

He crossed the room then, in two strides, and sank down upon the bed beside her, taking her face in his hands, touching his mouth to hers. The kiss was light at first, as if in question, and when she breathed out a moan and looped her arms around his neck, the kiss turned to passion, like a swirling, heated current that pulled them together.

She touched his face, feeling the warm curve of his cheek, his ear, the hard structure of his jaw, the texture of his beard like sand upon his skin. Sliding her hand to the open neck of his linen shirt, she stretched her fingers over his chest, feeling warm, bare skin lightly softened with hair. With a low groan, he pressed against her, and even through layers of linen and wool between them, she felt the hardening urgency of his body.

She let her hand stray—curious and strangely compelled, for she was not so bold as this, yet she felt right, natural, in doing so for him, and for herself. She rounded her fingers over the bulging evidence under his kilt, and he exhaled a muted groan, lifted his mouth from hers.

Breathing harder now, more sure and determined, he traced his lips over her face, small, exquisite kisses, like a butterfly alighting on a flower. She moaned softly, found his lips again, and opened her mouth beneath his to feel warm wetness as his tongue gentled over hers. A plunging heat spun deep inside her, and she pushed closer against him, her hand on his chest sensing the deep bounding of his heart, like her own. Lifting her hand, she slid her fingers through his hair, the black locks slipping sensuously over her hands like cool, thick, silken strands. He spread his hands over her back and pressed her down on the bed, then lay beside her.

Shifting toward him, drawn to his solid strength, she easily fit her body against his, and felt his low groan drift over her lips.

He kissed her, skimming his lips along her arched throat, his breath warm, his beard rasping over her sensitive skin. She sighed and arched closer, slipping her hands over the width of his shoulders, pulling him tightly against her—she needed more, wanted more.

Now his lips slanted over hers fiercely, and she caught her breath as she felt his hand rest on her breast. His touch floated over, so that her nipples rose, stiffened, and stirred against the linen of her shirt, and though she ached for his touch there, he traced his fingers farther down her abdomen, and a strange, wonderful, peculiar flutter began deep within her.

Sighing, she shifted in his arms, kissed him, his lips pliant and insistent over hers, and his other hand now slipped over her breast, his fingers kneading with exquisite care, so that she cried out softly and pushed her hips instinctively against him. Supporting her with his other hand, he held her, caressed her breasts, and she felt the heated, pulsing hardness of him pressing against her. She trembled all through now, felt like flowing water, moved with the wave of what she felt.

Wrapping her arms around him, she sank into the bliss of touch that he gave. She did not want to think—she only wanted to feel his hands on her skin, his lips on hers, his hard body tight against hers, all the warm curves and hollows finding their exquisite, seductive fit.

Soon his hands explored downward, delicate touches that made her gasp, so that his lips upon hers, and his fingers fluttering lower, lower still—made her turn slick within, her body pulsing and ready in deep, craving ways that she had never imagined before. Though she knew she should not do this, should never allow this—she desperately wanted him to touch her in secret places, as he was doing in that very moment—she gasped again, and arched in his arms, compelled by the wildness of the sensations aroused in her body.

And then he drew back, just as her heart was slamming, her body anxious for release, just as her head seemed to be whirling—he drew back, rested his brow against her own, and stilled, his body snug against hers, his arms tight around her.

"Not this way," he said. "Not with the fairy whisky upon you. Much as I want you—dear God, my girl, much as I do—not this way." And he rose from the bed, stood beside her in the darkness. "Rest," he said, and stepped back. "You need to rest."

"Not alone," she whispered. "Not here."

He sighed audibly and sat on the edge of the bed, taking her hand. "Sleep. I will stay."

She did sleep, sinking faster into it than she expected; she slept deep and full, the effects of the whisky still in her blood. Sometime in the night, she woke slightly and felt Dougal beside her in the darkness, his breathing deep and even. His arm looped around her and she leaned against him, resting her head on his shoulder. As she slid into dreaming, she felt his lips against her hair, felt him draw the covers higher over both of them.

She woke again, much later, opening her eyes to see a gray morning light edging the window frame. The air was cool, and she shivered a little, turning, longing for Dougal's solid warmth—but he was gone, the bed cool there. Sitting up, she shoved back her hair and looked around.

He was there, standing in the shadows by the window, staring outward. Silently Fiona slid from the bed and went toward him. As he held out an arm, she tucked into his ready embrace, and she stood with him by the window, looking out over a misted world, a blur of silvery fog.

"On the day I met you," she whispered, "the hills were misted over like this. And I thought you were one of the Fey, come for me."

He laughed softly, turned her in his arms, and kissed her—and she felt, in that moment, a powerful sort of magic stirring between them, a spell that she could not resist, and one that she meant to feed—drawing her hands up his back, feeling the ripple of solid muscle there, she arched in his arms and felt his kisses deepen, felt his lips trace over the curve of her jaw and along her throat. She moaned with it, her body already relaxed from hours of sleep, her head no longer spinning, but her heart turning within her with a depth of emotion—

a depth of love—that she could not deny within herself. Caught between sleeping and waking, in a sense, as if the misty world outside veiled what could happen, what she knew now would happen, between the man and the woman inside.

"My head is clear now," she whispered.

"Is it?" he murmured against her lips, her cheek, her ear. "So is mine."

"I know what I want now," she said, taking his face in her hands, feeling the textured whiskers that roughened his jaw.

"What is that?" he asked, as he bent close, his lips tracing her cheek, her ear.

"Not to think, not to talk," she whispered, kissing him then, the words tumbling even as her lips kneaded his. She felt his hands set about her waist, snugging her close against him. "Not to wonder if we should—we want this, you and I—nor do I want to talk of fairies, or whisky, or what is proper. That may not seem proper, but it feels so to me. This feels right. Promise me," she said, delving into another kiss, nearly breathless. "No word of what should or should not be—"

"Hush," he said, and pulled her tightly against him, his hands at her lower back pressing her against him so that she could feel the hard shape of him that said what words could not. "Hush."

Her heart beat so strongly now, in a rhythm that her body took on as a deep, irresistible, undeniable need. Kissing her, he swept his hand down to catch the hem of the long shirt she wore, and she

gasped as she felt his warm, big hand smoothing
over her hip, her bottom, the sensitive hollow of
her lower back. Pressing against him, she pulled
at his shirt, tugging a little wildly, eager to feel his
skin under her fingertips, wanting to feed further
the urges that now burgeoned and threatened to
burst within her.

His back felt smooth and hard-muscled under
warm skin, and her fingers found the woolen edge
of his wrapped kilt. A sudden boldness came over
her then and she pulled at it, shoved it aside, her fingers rounding over his thigh, massive and taut, and
her hand moved higher, then as he turned slightly,
dropped away, for his hand found hers and moved
it deliberately away.

"Not yet, love," he murmured.

"No words," she reminded, and his lips found
hers again, sudden and swift and hungry, his
tongue teasing her mouth and then meeting the tip
of her own tongue. All the while his hands shaped
her waist, her rib cage, until his fingers found her
breast, traced its softness delicately, found the nub
of her nipple. And at that touch, her knees seemed
to falter, her legs trembled. She grasped his shoulders, moaned a little, and when thumb swept the
sensitive tip, she whimpered, felt herself shudder,
crave, grow impatient for more.

Then he swept her up into his arms and carried her back to the bed, still warm as he laid her
down among the tumble of linens and pillows,
and stretched out beside her. His lips found hers

in the shadowy darkness of the bed, and she drew back to look at him, to pull at the shirt and plaid he wore. She sat back a little, watching as he tore away the plaid, and then the shirt, leaving them in a muddle at the foot of the bed. A moment later her own nightshirt was there, too, for she whipped it free and then fell back into his arms, delighting, wantonly so, in the sensation of his warm, smooth, wonderful body heating against her own.

She arched back, allowing him to touch her however he desired, his hands tracing over her breasts, his lips following. And when his fingers sank downward and found her clefted passage, she cried out, clutched at him as his fingers dipped and delved. Another moment, and wavelets of blissful sensation ripened and then rippled through her. Exploring him with her hands, grasping for him, she found him, hard and ready and nearly hot to the touch, like velvet sheathing iron. She shaped him long with her hands, heard him groan—and then he turned her full to her back and arched over her. She shifted, opened, gasping with the need to have him closer, as close and deep as could be, to ease the tender ache and demand within. A moment later, a gentle press and shift as he moved and she tilted, the knowing clear, somehow, within her—and he slipped into her like glove to hand, the feeling keen and stunning, so that she cried out and surged in welcome, wanting this, wanting him to be part of her in this primal and certain way.

A rhythm began between them, delighting and then quickly overtaking her, so that she rocked with him and then shuddered with an immense and sudden release—it swirled in her like joy itself, and she knew, without thought or words, that she felt love, that she was loved. His breath was deep and in tandem with hers, and she felt the love rise between them like the wild heat of a strong hearth, rousing too hot, then subsiding to comfort.

Moments later, she rolled with him, and he stretched out beside her. Taking her into his arms in silence, he wrapped her against him. Nestled in the warmth of his embrace, with his breath soft on her cheek, and his body so solid and safe against hers, Fiona closed her eyes.

"Fiona," he whispered, his lips against her hair. "We—"

"Do not speak, not yet—for the magic will flee. Let love make its own magic," she said, and in that moment she understood what the motto of her clan truly meant.

He murmured something under his breath, and the words made her heart soar, as he pulled her closer once again. And she feared, as the daylight bloomed paler and she saw more of the room and world outside, that he might never say it again, if the tender magic of that night faded.

As dull a life as she had led, as much as she had believed herself in love with a man years ago, she had never felt like this—and might never again. She did not want the world to intrude on that, but

Fiona had always been practical. She knew very well it would.

Soon her obligation to her clan, with its beautiful, fanciful motto, and her responsibility to her own kin, would take precedence over her dreams.

"If you are going past the laird's tower this early morning, I will walk with you," Mary MacIan said. "I want to see the laird of Kinloch, too," she added with a mischievous smile.

Fiona glanced at the old woman, suppressing her own smile. "I am going to the glen school this morning, that is all."

"Ah," Mary said, nodding, a twinkle in her blue eyes.

Looking away, Fiona knew the old woman must have guessed what Fiona had done her best to hide in the past couple of days. But her feelings thrummed like a revelation within her. She had kept away from Dougal deliberately, difficult as that was, for she was certain that when she spoke to him with others around, everyone would know—would see shining in her eyes—how deeply and intensely she loved the laird of Glen Kinloch.

She was sure of that much, yet knew the complications of her grandmother's will, which she had not yet explained to Dougal. Nor did she know if he even shared her feelings. Since spending the night at Kinloch House, she had avoided him—and the truth—wanting to treasure the feelings that had blossomed in her heart. All too soon she would lose her Highland laird to the pressure of obligations, just as she had lost her first love to sudden, irreparable fate.

"I am going to Kinloch House today, as it is time to pay my rent," Mary was saying. "Usually the laird comes to collect my little fee, which I earn from selling cheeses and beer, though I have never told him I can afford to pay him much more." Mary smiled impishly.

Fiona chuckled. "I would not be surprised if he knows that, and never asks for more from you. When does he collect the rental fee?"

"That should have been this week, but he did not come by." Mary's quick glance was so keen that Fiona looked away. "And he always brings me a bottle of something fine when he visits. But I do not mind bringing my payment to Kinloch. It is a good day for a walk. Come, Maggie," Mary called to the dog who trotted behind them. "She could use a long walk on a sunny morning."

"She gets plenty of exercise at night, roaming about," Fiona said. "Which sort of whisky does the laird usually give you?"

"Any sort of Glen Kinloch brew is excellent," Mary said. "Dougal gives me the very best of Kinloch whisky but once a year, at Christmas time."

"Is that the fairy whisky?" Fiona asked quickly.

"Och, no! That stuff is not so good. I have tried it and do not see the fuss. Too sweet, and flat. No strength to it." She wrinkled her nose. "I like aged Glen Kinloch best, but the laird is saving that stuff for—well, he has plans for it. How do you know about the fairy brew?"

"Kinloch told me about it," Fiona said.

"Did you taste it when you stayed the night at Kinloch House? Did Maisie give you some? Perhaps the Laird gave you some, eh? Though he was not there, I suppose, with the fire and all."

"I tasted it," Fiona said evasively, "and enjoyed it very much." She felt herself blush.

"Then the fairies favored you. Did you see wee sprites dancing about? They say that the fairies give their blessing to some who drink their whisky. They never blessed me, I can tell you. Did you see them?" She seemed eager to know.

"Oh," Fiona said, "nothing much happened."

"When I have tasted the fairy brew, it is like that," Mary said. "Nothing much."

Fiona smiled without answer. She looked ahead, along the meadow that filled the bowl of the glen, crisscrossed with flowing burns and, in the morning sunlight, scattered with spring wildflowers. On the other side of the glen, a league's walk away straight across the meadow, a hill rose toward the mountains. There, in a shaft of golden sunlight, she could see the tower of Kinloch House, just catching the morning light.

She wondered if Dougal was at Kinloch, or already out at this hour. Two nights ago she had stayed the night with him, after the unexpected events the day of the fire, and that night had been glorious. But in the morning she had insisted on walking back to Mary's house alone, as if nothing had happened between them. She had let the night, the man, and the whisky take her over—and she would cherish and never regret what had happened.

Since then, she had not seen him. She had glimpsed him at the kirk session when she had attended service with Mary to listen to Hugh MacIan's long sermon on the inherent responsibility of all in the glen to think of their neighbors. Restless, she had looked around during the service and had met Dougal's gaze. Her heart near leaped into her throat and she could barely look away, wanting only to go to him. She had forced herself to turn away and give no sign of anything out of the ordinary. But the moment—the spark of gazes touching across that crowded church—had felt as keen and needful as if she had actually touched him as she longed to do.

Later she had seen his uncles with Lucy in the kirkyard, but as she greeted them, and some of her students and their families, she had not seen Dougal again, her spirits falling in disappointment. Everyone had greeted her with warmth and affection, and she had felt truly welcomed in Glen Kinloch perhaps for the first time since she had arrived. Mary MacIan had confided that Fiona's presence at the MacDonald fire, accompanied by the laird himself, had gone a long way toward convincing the glen residents that the new Lowland teacher was truly one of them.

Yet she wanted the acceptance of their laird, too; though she had kept away, something within her needed desperately to be with him again. She had so much to explain—her grandmother's will, her brothers' need for the fortune that could come to them if they all met the conditions. But how could she ever tell him that the will required her to marry a Highland man of wealth and title? For now, she would wait, and keep silent.

If Dougal regretted the evening they had spent together, the dilemma would be solved. But if she did not obey the dictates of the will in the matter of her marriage, what then? Patrick had once suggested contesting the will.

Now her thoughts tumbled with possibilities, though she had precious few answers.

Maggie began to bark, and Mary called out to her, but the dog launched past them and raced ahead toward the slopes that gently rose from the glen floor. "Perhaps she sees some sheep, or a fox, to be so excited," Mary said.

Fiona nodded, then saw several people moving across the slope higher up, running quickly, and she heard their distant shouts and laughter. "What are they doing up there?"

Mary shielded her brow for a moment, watching. "Playing at the ba'."

"The what? Oh, the ball game—they've done so in the schoolyard. I wonder why they are at it so early this morning." As she walked closer with

Mary, she recognized some of her students along with their kinsmen.

"They are practicing," Mary said. "There will be a game soon, for all the glen."

Fiona looked at her in surprise. "The whole glen?"

Mary nodded. "It is a tradition in Glen Kinloch, played on New Year's and again in the spring, usually the first of May. It is nearing May now, so the laird has called for a game."

"He did? I heard nothing of it." Not that she had heard anything from the laird recently, she thought, watching the players as they ran in the characteristic cluster that seemed to mark the form of the football they played in Glen Kinloch.

"The word went round among the men. You are not expected to play, being a lass."

"I played the football with my brothers when I was young."

"Aye," Mary said, "but not like this."

"How is it played here? It seemed the same to me in the schoolyard."

"Practice in a schoolyard or on a hilltop is one thing. The game itself is quite another. They play from the east side of the glen to the west." Mary gestured wide to indicate the whole of the glen as they walked. "It is played by all the men and boys, a hundred and more, with one ball. They form two packs, those from the north end of the glen and those from the south, and they start in the center—there, near where the burn crosses past those rocks," she said, pointing.

"They play over the whole glen?" Fiona asked, incredulous. "All of them?"

"Crossways over the glen," Mary said. "From the fieldstone wall below Kinloch House, across the glen floor, and down near the loch side road, where there is a group of standing stones."

Fiona knew the place. "That's about two miles," she said.

"Aye, not far at all for such a game." Mary nodded as if it was nothing much.

Astonished, Fiona watched the men and boys practicing on the hillside. "With one ball?"

"Just the one. And the two great teams, and the distance over the glen. It goes on all day, into the night. Sometimes into the next day."

"All for a ball?"

"Och," Mary said. "All for the fun of it, you see. The ball is just stuffed with goose feathers. It means nothing to them. The game, that is all of it, and who wins, the North side or the South side."

"Does the laird play too? His house is in the middle. Which side does he take?"

"Other lairds did not always play, but this one does—no one could keep Dougal MacGregor out of it, and he is a very strong at the ba' and both sides want him. So each year he plays a different side. He will play for Garloch and the North this year. The South has more players."

"Are they not even, the two teams?" Fiona said.

"Oh no, it is decided by where a person is born. All but the laird, born in the midst of it."

As they crossed the glen and began to climb the slope toward Kinloch House and the school, Fiona could see the spaniel chasing back and forth, and the men and boys hooting and pushing. Someone in the middle of the pack got the ball, for she saw it thrust triumphantly upward in a pair of hands, only to disappear moments later into the cluster. "When is the game?" she asked.

"Hugh says the laird called for the game on the Thursday, I think."

"Thursday! But the lads have school!"

"Oh, there will be no school that day. All the glen will either be playing the game, or watching it. The laird should have told you."

"He did not," Fiona said. Again she felt a sharp sense of separation from him, and despite her sense of being accepted by the glen folk in the kirkyard the day before, she sighed, feeling very much an outsider again—it suddenly seemed so important for Dougal to include her in what seemed to involve everyone in the glen. Even Mary knew, and had not told her.

"It sounds like great fun. I am sure you will all have a wonderful time." She forced a smile.

"You must come, too," Mary said. "Remember this is what the lads do, and they make their own plans for it. You are welcome to watch and to cheer them on with all the lasses in the glen. None of us would miss seeing a game of the ba'."

"Thank you," Fiona said. "I appreciate you telling me, for I had not heard."

"Did you think the laird would invite you to come? *Tcha*," Mary said. "He knows you will be there, because you are part of Glen Kinloch now. Asking you to come—och, only outsiders would be *invited*," Mary said.

Dougal stood on the hillside above Kinloch House, his pipes tucked under his arm, and he lifted the chanter to blow another series of plaintive, haunting notes. The hour was late in the afternoon, near enough to dusk. He had seen Fiona earlier that day, walking with Mary MacIan toward the house, but he had been out in the hills at the time. Previously he might have hurried to the house to greet them, to accept Mary's rent—he had discovered later that she had come there on that excuse—and to see Fiona again. But something told him to keep his distance for a little while. He suspected she felt the same, for he had not seen her but from afar.

His heart and hers would have to cool a little, he told himself, like the embers in a blazing hearthfire, before he could know for certain that the love he wanted, after that initial fiery burst of feeling, indeed existed. Instinct told him that what had begun between them would burn steadily for a very long time.

But he had to know for sure. Lifting the chanter again, taking a breath and filling the great rounded bag under his arm, he set his mouth to the reed and blew, long and steadily. The sound built and grew, rising and lingering as it echoed around the hills. Burgeoning, flooding, the sound stirred a powerful emotion in him.

What he wanted with Fiona was the sort of love that would last forever, and he hoped she wanted the same. He would seek her out to talk to her as soon as they could be alone together.

In his heart, he felt that this was right not only for him, but for the people of the glen as well. The fairies, after all, had shown the way. Fiona could see them; they had appeared to her. And that was fair proof for the laird of Kinloch.

Chapter 16

"When we play the ba' this time," Dougal told his uncles, while they stood at the cave entrance watching over the hills, "we must all know our parts so that all will go well."

"Aye, we each go into the game, play for a bit, then get out and go off to the caves," Fergus said. "With so many playing and all the rest watching, no one will notice who is in and who is out. What of the gaugers?"

Hamish looked toward them, arms folded. "They have been much about in the glen lately, between the gauger's sister being here, and now the fire. The young customs man may have told the others that his sister is here—and perhaps she has told her brother what she has seen here."

Dougal frowned. "She would not do that."

"We do not know for sure," Hamish said, "and there are more gaugers now than before."

"True," Dougal admitted. He had not told his uncles that he trusted Fiona now, though he rarely felt sure of anyone's loyalty, outside of his closest kin.

Ever since his father's death, Dougal had found it difficult to trust anyone. But he was ready to trust Fiona implicitly, as well as to love her. He was ready to give himself over to dreams of a wife, a family. But his uncles, as yet, did not know that; he wondered if any of them suspected it, from looks they had given him and comments they had made about the teacher, and the night she had spent at Kinloch House, though he had said as little as possible about that.

He ought to marry the girl—and now that he had taken time to sort out his feelings, he knew he had begun to love her. That was clear. But he had devoted his life to the glen, to the production of whisky, and the freetrading of it. What did he have to offer a Lowland lady? He had no fortune, no title to share, no great accomplishments: just the glen, his simple life, and himself.

Not long ago he had been determined to send her from the glen, yet he had fallen to her indefinable magic, spun about by feelings and needs he had scarcely known were there. Now he could not imagine life in Glen Kinloch without her.

Yet unanswered questions still unsettled him. Why was Fiona so concerned about fairy drawings, which seemed somehow connected to money and to Sir Walter Scott? Had she babbled a little due to the whisky, or did she have some other purpose besides teaching while in Glen Kinloch? And he wondered if any of it had to do with her brother.

He could not allow any customs officer to disrupt the transport of the valuable cache of whisky he had stored away. Soon that lot would be moved and sold, for on the day of the ba' game, a cutter was expected to sail up the loch. He and his men only had to wait until then.

"Hugh is in the glen, I can see him from here," Hamish announced from the cave entrance. "And he is not alone."

"Who is with him?" Dougal asked, walking toward the opening to stand beside Hamish and look out. From that vantage point, he could see straight down the slopes toward the road and the loch beyond. In the glen, not far from the lochside road, he saw two men walking over the meadowland. "What the devil—it is Eldin."

"Why is the reverend talking with Eldin?" Fergus asked, as he and Ranald came to look.

"Shooting," Ranald said. "I thought I heard something earlier. Looks like Eldin is carrying a gun. He's come up to the glen for a little sport."

"Interesting," Dougal growled, and stepped outside, making his way down the slopes at a good pace. Within ten minutes or so he lit out across the glen floor, hearing another shot ring out. Hailing the reverend with a raised arm, he hurried toward them. Eldin and Hugh walked together, talking, while a lad followed, leading a horse. Slung over the saddle was a brace of hares and another of birds. Three hounds trotted along between the groom and the men who strolled ahead.

Dougal strode toward them, and Eldin turned.

"Kinloch! Nearly shot you, man." The earl propped the butt of his long gun against the ground. Looking less formal than at their previous meeting, he wore a long brown coat, buff trousers and high boots, and a trim waistcoat with a standing collar and a neat neck cloth. Hat in one hand, gun in the other, Eldin looked at Dougal.

"Greetings, sir. I hope you do not mind—I met the reverend at the coaching inn the other day, and told him I wanted to come out for a bit of hunting."

Hugh nodded, looking uncomfortable. "Eldin took down a couple of hares earlier," he said. "The curlew are flying today, returning for the summer, nesting in the hills. He's got two already—he's a wicked shot, is the earl," he added. The reverend's deep, quick frown told Dougal to beware, that Hugh did not trust the earl and did not like the situation. Nor did Dougal.

He walked closer to Hugh. "On my land, in my glen," he said in a low, fierce voice, "my permission was needed for this."

"Sorry, Kinloch," Hugh murmured, glancing away. "Truly."

"Pardon, sir, but this lower section of the glen is mine, I believe," Eldin cut in. "I am purchasing the government deed to the southern part of the glen, which became available."

"Not until next month," Dougal said. "This is a peaceful glen, and I will not condone hunting for sport, with the glen folk going about their daily business here, and no warning given."

"Glen Kinloch is known for its idyllic atmosphere, and will please the tourists who come up to look at the famous loch," Eldin said. "Though I have heard it said that in the dead of night, it is not so peaceful here as you would have us believe." He tilted a brow.

"Tourists are not about in the dead of night, so you need not be concerned," Dougal drawled.

"Nonetheless, I have applied for the deed rights, and as there was no offer made from another quarter, they are granted to me. You have not applied, I understand, to buy back your own deed."

"Not yet," Dougal said. He did not add that he was waiting for the funds from a profitable source, sending a ship for more than seventy kegs of whisky at a generous price.

"Recently," Eldin said, "I offered to buy a portion of your excellent whisky for a handsome sum. You would have had enough to buy the deed that was cleared after twenty years, which I can now claim. By the way, you never sent word as to when you will sell those casks to me," he added mildly.

"I know that," Dougal said. "This is still my land, and there is no hunting today." Nodding curtly, he turned and strode away.

The main parlor of Mary's house was quiet that night, the little mantel clock ticking, the fire crackling, and soft rain falling outside, a peaceful harmony of sound as Fiona sat at the table. She leaned forward, her hair sliding loose over her shoulder, her notepad open on the table, the pencil in her hand. She tapped the point thoughtfully against the table, studied what she had done, then pursed her mouth and tried again. Rubbing at it with her fingertip, smudging here, adding a light, airy line there, and a darker line there, she worked at the drawing.

The image almost looked like the fairy she had seen in Kinloch House. Almost, yet something essential was missing. Perhaps, she thought, it was because the portrait she was drawing from memory was flat, done in gray pencil tones, lifeless compared to the sparkling, translucent, dimensional vision of the lady who had appeared in the library.

She sighed, turned to a fresh page, and began again, sketching loosely, quickly, as if coaxing the image out of the page with the strokes of the pencil. But still, it did not seem quite right. Over the last few days, she had made several sketches, mostly of the fairy lights, bright bits done in pale watercolor over pencil, floating over flowers and streams, some with small faces within them, an additional detail spurred by imagination—and she had tried more than once to sketch the beautiful ethereal creature she had seen in the library.

Sighing, she set her pencil down, and picked up the folded letter that lay near to hand on the table. She opened the letter and read it yet again.

Dear Fiona, Patrick wrote,

I was pleased to have your letter, and cannot adequately express how reassured I feel to know that you are well, that your teaching duties are rewarding, and that life in Glen Kinloch agrees with you. If, as you say, you have not seen or heard of untoward activities among certain glen residents, that, too, is reassuring.

I find it difficult to believe there is naught afoot in the glen at all—as you insist—but can easily believe that you remain unaware of mischief. The laird of that glen seemed quite sincere in his desire to keep you safe from harm of any sort. He seems a good fellow over all, despite an unfortunate habit of wandering the hills at night.

I will be coming north in a few days, and will call on you at that time. Though I do not know the time and day, Mr. MacIntyre means for us to ride to the north end of the loch, as we must do from time to time. If you should see your laird, please tell him that his hearth may be the safest evening star to view this week.

In answer to your question, I have written to William and James regarding a protest of the will's conditions, but have not yet heard from them. Certainly if the conditions can be met to satisfaction, all the better, but if the demands seem untenable, I shall vigorously pursue another solution. I have no desire to chase a wild goose myself.

At least it is good news that you have dis-
covered a way to produce drawings for the
wee book that James is finishing. It is a pity
that you have not found the prospective hus-
band you came there to find, but Kinloch is
a poor glen, and your chances will be better
elsewhere.

Yrs with great affection, Patrick

Maggie, sleeping by the fireside, suddenly lifted her head and woofed softly, then stood. Fiona set the letter down just as a tapping sounded at the door. She rose, heart thumping, and went to the door. So did Maggie, tense and snorting, head and tail up and alert.

The knocking sounded again, stronger now. Fiona leaned toward the door. "Who's there?"

"Kinloch." His voice was quiet but clear, and her heart bounded. She released the latch and opened the door.

Dougal stepped inside, rain blowing in with him, and the dog leaping up to greet him. He rubbed her head, patted and praised her, and then looked at Fiona.

"Good evening," he murmured.

She drew a breath, folded her hands. "Mary is sleeping."

"I did not come to see her," he said, and glanced past her. "Schoolwork?"

"I am working on some drawings." She hastened to the table to close the notebook. When she turned, Dougal was there, pulling out a chair for her.

"Sit, please," he said. "We must talk."

"Would you like tea?" she asked. "Ale, or . . . whisky?"

"Nothing. Sit, Fiona," he said, and pushed down on her shoulder. "I have something to say."

"Say it, then," she said, glancing away. The days he had let go by without speaking to her after their blissful night together had hurt her increasingly with each passing hour. Now that he was here, the tension that emanated from him did not bode well; she expected an expression of regret and murmurs of gentlemanly apology; and a new, stronger suggestion that she leave Glen Kinloch. She looked down, hands fisted—and then lifted her chin, opened her hands, mustered dignity. Whatever he had to say, she could endure it. Perhaps she did not belong in the glen after all.

But her pounding, longing heart told her otherwise. *Love is not enough reason to stay*, she told herself, *if it is not returned.*

Dougal sighed. "I owe something to you."

"No apology is necessary," she said in anticipation.

He turned the chair beside her and sat, leaning forward to take her hand in his. For a moment he stroked the back of her hand with his thumbs, and began to speak once or twice, subsiding as if gathering his thoughts. Fiona would not look at him. Could not.

"I owe you marriage," he said simply, "after the night we spent at Kinloch. I should have shown better behavior than to disgrace you so."

Surprised, she stared at him. "You never disgraced me. I wanted that, as I thought you did. And there is no obligation," she said hastily. "Perhaps it is better for me to leave the glen soon, as you have wanted, but I would like to finish the teaching first."

"Leave? Fiona—"

"I will always remember that evening, but I do not need a marriage proposal. There is nothing to make up to me."

"That is not my intent." Holding her hand in his, he turned her fingers thoughtfully. "When I was a lad," he said, "my father taught me the way of making the fairy brew, which is a bit different than the usual. He told me that the lairds of Kinloch must keep the process secret, and share it only with the laird's children. Even the closest of kin are not told all the laird knows."

Fiona listened, waited, frowned, for she did not understand the track of his thoughts. Silent for a moment, Dougal entwined his fingers in hers, sending delicious shivers through her. She closed her eyes, yearning deep, aware that she might never feel this sort of tenderness again, when this interview was over.

"My father never told his brothers the full truth of the fairy whisky, which he had from his father— but I have told them some of it over the years. Not all," he said, "but a good deal. But now I find that it is burning in me to tell you. Not now," he said, "but someday. I feel it strongly within me that you—" He stopped.

She leaned closer. "That I understand what it is to live with the fairy lore in one's family?"

"That you are the woman I want," he said, looking up, his eyes so green and sincere that it took her breath away to meet his gaze. "And one day we will bring our children to the place in the glen where my father brought me, the day I learned the secret of the fairy whisky of Kinloch."

She stared, heart pounding. "Oh, Dougal," she whispered, stunned, touched deeply. Her heart filled with love, poured with it, for him, and yet she said nothing, words swept away by emotion.

He looked down at their entwined fingers. "So you see, it is not duty that brought me here," he said, "but affection. I will leave the decision to you." He let go of her hand, and stood.

Fiona caught her breath, wanting desperately to accept, wanting to stand and loop her arms around his neck. Yet she sat, looking down. "There is something I have not told you." What she had left unsaid weighed upon her.

"I know you have secrets, and that there is a reason you came here, beyond teaching. If it has nothing to do with me or my glen, Fiona, you need not tell me."

She reached for the notebook and opened it to show him the drawings of the fairies that she had attempted. "I have been working on these tonight, trying to get them just so," she said. "This one is drawn from memory as you suggested, the night that we—"

"She is beautiful," Dougal said.

"There is something not quite right about it. I have not captured her," she said. "Dougal, I have made promises that I must keep. You should know that."

"What promises?"

"My grandmother made a will with certain conditions that my brothers and I must meet. I am bound by it—bound in ways that I must explain, before you say anything more."

He looked at her patiently, and nodded. Fiona stood, and quickly, quietly, told him about Lady Struan's will and how it asked something unique from Fiona and each of her brothers, each request involving fairies and certain conditions before the siblings could win a combined inheritance. "I am to make drawings of fairies for the book my brother is finishing, which our grandmother began. I came here for that—I could have gone anywhere, but fate, and the Edinburgh Ladies' Society, led me here to Glen Kinloch. When I return home, our friend Sir Walter will judge the genuineness of what I have accomplished."

"I am sure these drawings will please Sir Walter and fulfill any conditions."

"There is . . . something else I must do if my brothers and I are to win our fortune," she said.

"The final condition requires me to find a Highland husband."

"We could solve that, Fiona," he murmured.

She looked away. "The clause says I must find a wealthy Highland laird."

"Ah," he said. "I see."

She moved toward him, but he stepped back—and her heart seemed to sink when she saw that caution, that distance. "Wealth comes in all forms," she said. "I know that now, deep in my heart. You have so much here in this place—the lairdship of this beautiful glen, the loyalty of your kin and friends, even the rare secrets of the fairy realm. So much," she said fervently.

"But that will not win your inheritance."

She sighed out. "Truly, I do not know."

"Of course you do," he said. He studied her for a moment, then leaned past her and picked up the Conté pencil. A stroke here, there, and suddenly Fiona saw the drawing spark to life under his hand—reminding her that she, too, had come to life in his arms. "There," he said softly. "She looks a little like you. That was what was missing." He stepped back.

"Dougal—" Fiona stretched out her hand.

He went to the door, placed a hand on the latch, stopped. "Fiona, you know best what you must do. I cannot tell you that. As for me—whatever happens, my life will not change, either way. Life goes on in the glen. Hearts endure somehow. I learned that, years ago." He opened the door, stepped out, and shut it firmly behind him.

Fiona ran to the door, placing her hand on the latch, leaning her head against the door frame. *Hearts endure somehow.* She realized that he had learned that after his father's death; she knew it herself, for after Archie's death, she had spent eight years simply enduring.

Now they each had a chance for happiness. Yet if she chose him, and the humble yet adventurous life he led in this glen, she would set her own family up for ruin.

In the weeks since she had come to Glen Kinloch, the impossible had happened. She had seen a fairy and sketched her; and she had fallen in love with a Highland laird who would not do, according to the will's tenets.

Hearing a whimper, Fiona looked down to see Maggie beside the door, pawing at it to be let out. Fiona opened the door. "Go find him," she murmured, watching the dog dash off. "Go on!"

Fiona longed to run through the darkness to find the laird, too, and claim what she wanted most in the world. But her choice seemed clear.

She closed the door and returned to her drawing. It seemed beautiful now, after the touches Dougal had made, but she herself felt dull and restricted once again. She had tasted freedom for a while in Glen Kinloch, finding it as sweet and potent as fairy whisky. And soon she would leave.

Chapter 17

❦❦❦❦❦❦❦

"**T**he game is going well," Fergus said, as someone shoved into him hard, causing the powerful blacksmith to push back, straining, his face red. "Very well, I think," he ground out.

"So far," Dougal agreed, his shoulders engaged against the shoulders of other men as they huddled together. He watched his feet, as did many, for a sight of the feather-stuffed leather ball that eluded most of them as it darted and rolled amid a forest of legs.

He and Fergus hovered on the outer part of the great press of men and boys, near a hundred of them crammed together in a great, wicked beast of a crowd, grunting and shoving and sweating as they vied to find, snatch, and direct the ball between one goal and the next: the North side claimed an old, crumbling stone wall on the hill below Kinloch House; the South side claimed the standing stones near the loch side road. No quarter was offered and none given, and whenever the ball was in sight, each man was determined to take control over it.

And here they all were toward the end of a long day, Dougal thought—still stuck somewhere along the

glen floor. They had been up the glen side and down
the loch side, through byres, houses, and burns, and
now were back again on the low, boggy meadow.

They were exhausted to a man, after hours of
shoving, pushing, running the ball in packs from one
point to the next. They had endured pummelings
and hardships for the sake of the ball, so that most
of them were bruised, aching, thirsty, and uncomfortable; they were crowing, swearing, taunting, and
shouting, those who had the breath for it; the ball had
been stolen from gripping hands, hidden under shirts,
rolled under torn wads of turf or sunk in a stream
while men looked elsewhere for it, and yet each time
it was found, claimed, lost, and pursued again.

The day had begun in a civilized enough way,
with the teams assembled, North and South, at a
middle point in the glen. Dougal had played a tune
on his bagpipes, and rousing cheers had bounced
off the hills, shouted by the men about to play and
the people ready to watch. Rob MacIan, the innkeeper, who had brought two carts loaded with
ale and tankards, had thrown the leather ball up,
and the game had begun, with no particular rules
beyond no deliberate harm done to another, and
no particular time set to end the match. The only
thing sure was the existence of the two goals.

Near a hundred men in clusters had gathered
around the ball, chasing it, though most of them
had no idea where it was, moment to moment, but
for the greatest shouts and scrambling. They had
chased through houses and byres, and some had

broken away to run through the schoolhouse after the renegade ball, so that one of the weakened walls now bore a great hole; they had shoved their way past more than one illicit still, stealing swallows of illicit peat reek from kegs opened for the purpose, or had guzzled fresh ale on their way through or around other houses—including Helen MacDonald's house, where she had set beer in great tankards and jugs on a table outside her home— and all of it was considered fair play. Anything that stood in the ball's path was open for the game, according to the rules—or lack of the same—set out for the tradition generations ago.

Laughing, Dougal watched now as the ball somehow popped free of the crowd, and one fellow went for it, with another hopping on his back while they spun about, while the ball was snatched off by a third man, then pursued with hooting goodwill by the sturdy pack.

Earlier that afternoon, they had crossed the glen floor, coming to the loch side road but diverted to the cove by the wayward path of the ball batted about. Dozens of men had thundered in a steady stream through Mary MacIan's little house when the ball was kicked through her open door; they had tumbled over chairs and knocked her ticking clock from the mantel. Maggie had barked and leaped about and risked being squashed in the fray—but Dougal had snatched her up and tossed her to Hugh MacIan, who had shouted he was free. And though he meant the ball, he got the dog, to great guffaws of laughter.

More than one man had taken a dunking in one of the burns that crisscrossed the glen, but they all knew that if the ball reached the shores of the cove, it could be lost in the loch, and they would all be splashing about in the water, nearly drowning themselves to get the ball back. So to avoid that calamity—a little logic prevailing—they had driven their leathery prize inland again, and back to the moor that separated the North goal from the South. The players were coated with sweat and mud, some of them were bloodied, all of them were bruised. And yet, for the sake of the battered ball, they struggled onward.

And they were each enjoying it to the hilt, Dougal knew. He grinned at Fergus, wiped his brow with a forearm, and shouldered his way back into the press. He had made it to the center of the cluster more than once that day, had even taken possession of the ball three times, a greater accomplishment than many could claim. Once more he wanted to delve into the center of it all, shouting and shoving, each of them sharing a bond of effort and boyish, lunatic joy, together with his kin and his tenants and even some strangers from the south he did not know, but who were now his brothers in the ba'.

And soon enough, he would ease his way out, and duck away with Fergus or another of his uncles to do what they had planned all along. But for now, each man there strived to the best of his ability, regardless of age or shape, to defend turf and find that blasted ball.

Luck was with him this time, for as Dougal bent

to avoid a thrusting elbow, he spied the ball rolling between the feet of the man in front of him. Reaching out, he scooped it up and had it between his knees, then under his shirt—the linen had long ago come untucked from his kilt waist—and he was away, diving out of the eye of the storm. Dozens of men were after him, but for now, this moment, that bit of leather clutched against him was his, and he would not let go.

Not yet. As soon as he reached the outskirts—no mean feat, and took some time, with the others pulling at him once they knew he had the ball—he grabbed it out of his shirt and threw it high over head. Shouts and arms reaching up, and men leaping like salmon, and then the thing disappeared, swallowed once more into the cluster.

Dougal looked about and saw Ranald and Hamish. "Let's away," he said, breathing hard.

"Aye," Ranald growled, and Dougal turned with them to slip free of the ragged edges of the great crowd. Looking back, he saw that Fergus was in the thick of it once again, swearing like a savage; he did not seem ready yet to give up the game for a bit of smuggling.

"Where are the gaugers, have you seen them?" he asked Hamish, who had kept back from the heavier part of the game to keep watch with Thomas Mac-Donald and others. Pol, Neill, Andrew and the rest of the lads had been unable to resist the lure of the ba' and had not kept watch as promised.

"Aye, all about, the game has brought them up

here, just as we thought—but they are watching, and some are playing by now," he said, tilting his head to indicate the throng. "Patrick MacCarran is there now, as is Tam's son. Tam himself I have seen about, but he and the other gaugers with him are watching the scrimmage and are not concerned with what we might do."

"Huh," Ranald said, "because they think we are all in the thick of it with the rest."

"Just so," Dougal said. "Come ahead."

The darkness was gathering as he ran toward the loch side road with his uncles. There were enough men scattered about the moor, along with spectators, that they were not particularly noticeable. They could be going down to the loch for a dip in the water, as some players had done throughout the day.

The air felt fresh and particularly cool now that he was outside the close, sweaty throng. He breathed deep, felt the relief as air fluttered his shirt and damp hair, and he paused to tuck his shirt back into the waist of his kilt and straighten the swath of plaid over his shoulder.

Once again he looked about for Fiona, as he had done often during the day. Earlier he had seen her with Mary MacIan, and later she stood with Lucy and others. The sight of her had bolstered his stamina, given him reserves of strength he had thought exhausted.

But after the old woman's house had taken a bit of a pounding, Fiona and the others had disappeared from the group of spectators. Later he intended to apologize to Mary and offer repairs and a cask of his very best whisky; but he did not know how to make up to Fiona the damage that fate had wrought between them.

He wondered if she was done with the unruly lads of Glen Kinloch and their laird, who vastly preferred mucking about in a rough game, smuggling whisky at night, tending herds of sheep, and examining sheaves of barley to suiting up in a black frock coat in the city. He would not discount book learning, for he savored that himself, on his own. But he was different from the educated rich men who followed a human herd, of a sort, in social circles and business. Dougal would always choose roaming free over that, regardless of the level of his wealth. He could not blame Fiona if she left the glen to return to the city.

Tonight, though, he had other matters on his mind, and had best get to work.

Standing on a hill overlooking the glen, Fiona tucked her shawl around her shoulders as a cool breeze wafted past. The ruckus of the game continued, and she watched for a little while. Nearby, Lucy gathered flowers, humming to herself, and Fiona glanced toward her, smiling to see the girl well occupied with creating a bouquet of the primroses, buttercups, and bluebells that scattered the hills here in blurs of color.

Fiona had spent much of the day with several of the women in the glen—Mary MacIan, Helen, and some of the others, as well the girls from the school. Lucy had come with Maisie to watch her kinsmen play, and Jamie and Annabel were with them, too. As the day wore on, women and children drifted away in small groups, some following the men who ranged about the glen in pursuit of the hapless ball, while others returned home to tend to practical matters.

Lucy, Jamie, and Annabel had stayed with Fiona, exploring for rocks. Together they had kept to the ridges of the lower hills, watching the football scramble. The day was sunny, breezy, and brisk, and Fiona had removed her straw bonnet, letting it hang behind her from its ribbons; she wore a lightweight shawl over her dark blue gown, a patterned cotton, its easy style and layered skirts wide enough to allow her freedom as she walked.

Jamie had collected rocks and scouted for insects and small animals; finding a pocket of rabbits, he had wisely let them be. The little girls had gathered flowers, and Lucy had explained to Fiona the importance of flowers to the end result of the whisky-making process. Impressed with Lucy's understanding of the steps, Fiona felt sure that Dougal, with his good sense as a surrogate father, would make sure that years passed before the girl tasted the whisky she discussed with such innocent expertise now. Annabel, whose mother was a brewer, had some knowledge herself, and added to the discussion. As the shy girl walked with them, she began to sing a little in her clear, beautiful voice. Fiona smiled, listening, and asked to hear another song.

High on the hill, Fiona had discovered an outcrop of limestone that contained several fossils, including rare ammonites, shell remains, which she
showed to the children. Having brought her knapsack and tools, she took out her small hammer to
carefully break away some stone bits. Lucy, finding a particularly fine spiraling shell impression,
had taken a rubbing of it with Annabel, and Jamie
found a fat trilobite petrified in stone, which he
proclaimed a true beastie. After more rubbings,
Fiona had split away the stone so that the boy
could carry his treasure in his pocket.

And all the while that she walked about with the
children, she watched down the hill hoping for a
glimpse of Dougal. The game continued as the men
edged ever closer toward the loch side goal.

"The Southies will win," Jamie said, "they
have more players. And besides, the gaugers will
be happy then, and will pay no attention to what
Cousin Dougal is doing."

Pausing as she sketched the ammonites, Fiona
looked up. "What would Kinloch be doing today,
other than playing the ba' game?"

"Smuggling," Lucy said. She was sorting flowers
now, laying them out in groups on a sun-warmed
rock. "He and my other uncles are smuggling tonight, and as soon as it gets dark, they will be meeting a great secret ship from France or Ireland, come
to take their load of whisky and give them good coin
in payment. We will be rich," she said, looking up.

"It will be a cutter or a sloop, not a ship," Jamie

pointed out. "It is only a loch, and connected to other lochs by rivers, and so only fast boats can come up here for the whisky runs."

"Is it so?" Fiona asked. "Only fast boats on the loch?"

He nodded. "They sail up here and then down, and when they reach Loch Lomond, they take the river route to the sea. Dougal MacGregor showed me on a map," he said. "I have seen the cutters coming up the loch."

Fiona had seen one, too, she remembered. Frowning, she glanced toward the game, with the great clog of men at one part of the meadow, and spectators and other players standing or walking about. It seemed as if the men would never give up and go to their homes. Some of the women had told her that the game could go on for a day or two, even near a week, it was said, generations back. Men came and went in shifts, giving each one a chance to eat some and rest a little before diving back into the fray.

Women, being more sensible creatures, Mary MacIan had said, soon went about their business at home or tended to whatever wounds needed it. Now and then, women would dive into the throng, too, welcomed like any player, to give as good as they got, and then some.

Now Fiona saw men walking over the moorland, and she recognized the one in the lead. She knew the set of those shoulders, the rhythm of that walk, the swing of the dark-sheened hair. Her heart quickened to see Dougal, and she wondered if he had seen her, too, standing on the hill with the children. He was not coming toward them, but rather walked toward the loch along with his uncles. No doubt they knew that the game was thrusting toward the lochside goal.

Smuggling, Lucy had said her uncle was doing today, despite the game.

Or because of it, Fiona thought then. Narrowing her eyes, she lifted a hand to her brow. What an opportunity for distraction the raucous game provided—and Dougal himself had suggested that the game be played this week, earlier than the usual first of May. What was he planning?

Hearing a shout and Lucy's quick answer, she saw Hugh MacIan climbing the hill toward them. He waved, smiled a greeting for Fiona, and admired the children's collected items before turning to watch the glen beside Fiona.

"The Southies look to win it," Hugh said. "We are all moving toward the loch. Do you want to come down and watch?"

"We want to see!" Jamie said, and within moments, the children were racing down the hillside, while Fiona laughed and called to them to slow down. Gathering her things, she walked with Hugh.

"Is the game over then?" she asked. "It is late afternoon, and twilight is coming."

"They will play until there is resolution, even after dark. We have attracted the attention of some outsiders with this day's work," he added, gesturing toward the glen.

"Customs officers?" she asked, seeing a few strangers on horseback and on foot.

"Aye, including your brother," he said. "I spoke to him—he will meet us down by the loch. Lord Eldin is here, too. He heard of the game at the inn, and came to watch. Dougal had best be careful," he added, low.

Fiona shot him a glance. "What do you mean?"

"The ship," Hugh said, nodding as they reached the meadow and began to cross its rolling ground. "Dougal has arranged for a trade tonight. Did he not tell you?" He looked at her with surprise as Fiona shook her head. "I understood he might be courting you."

"We are not courting," she said quickly, and lifted her chin.

"Miss MacCarran," he said. "Fiona. I must ask—as kirk minister in the glen, concerned for all the souls in it—when you stayed at Kinloch House, I hope all was well that night between you and the laird. In such a situation there would be a chance of scandalous behavior, especially between two people with such . . . passionate natures."

She shook her head, looking away to hide her blush. "Of course all was well."

"Maisie—who will be my intended one day, I hope—said that there were whisky glasses and a broken glass in the library when she returned next day."

The glasses, Fiona thought; she had forgotten

completely about them. "I had a cough after being near the smoke of the fire at the MacDonalds, and at Kinloch House I took a little whisky for it. I dropped the glass and it broke, so I got another."

"Was it the fairy whisky?" He glanced at her. "Maisie said that flask was open. The laird takes very little whisky, though he brews it. I confess I am curious—did you try the fairy whisky, and if so, did you feel any effect from it?"

Startled, she nodded. "I did, and found it a very nice whisky. If there was any magic result, I did not notice. On the whole . . . it was a lovely evening."

They were nearing the lochside road, walking toward the crowd, as the game headed toward the standing stones on the slope beside the road, where Fiona had met Dougal on the night he had given her an unforgettable kiss. Now she called the children closer, anxious about their safety with the rough game going on nearby. Hugh took her arm, drawing her away from the horde, and calling the children to follow.

"Come this way," he told them. "I will take you to meet Dougal."

She glanced at him, surprised. "I thought we would be watching the rest of the ball game."

"Not quite," he said, and pulled her along. "Come," he said, beckoning to the children.

Frowning as she went with him, Fiona felt the pressure of the reverend's grip as he led them all to the shoreline of the loch. A massive section of limestone layered with red sandstone rose almost straight up from the loch, the sections near the water screened from view by a thicket of bushes and trees, which sprouted close along the shore. A narrow path wound its way there, she saw, and the shoreline followed a deep curve, cutting into the gigantic wedge of rock that thrust upward. In places the water flowed within an arm's length of the cliffs.

"Mr. MacIan, where are we going?" Fiona asked with growing concern. "Children, hold hands and stay by the wall. The way along the shore is narrow through here," she called to them. Perhaps the reverend wanted to show her some rock formations by the loch, she told herself; yet a feeling deep in her gut told her that something was wrong. "Is there some trouble?"

"Dougal promised to meet us here," Hugh said, but her sense of dread only increased.

Within moments, her practiced eye for geological forms told her that there were caves along the narrow shoreline, and soon she saw dark crevices splitting the rock face, hidden in part by bushes and trees. As Hugh shepherded them forward, his manner even more insistent, she wondered what made him so anxious, and why he continually looked over his shoulder.

"In here," he finally said, and shoved them ahead into one of the triangular crevices that split the rock. They had to duck their heads to go inside, but once in, could stand easily. Jamie and Lucy jumped about, delighted to be inside a cave they had never seen before, while Annabel turned in circles, looking in awe at the shadowed ceiling and sloping gray walls just overhead.

Lucy looked up. "It is not very big," she said. "And it is empty. Why are we here?"

"An excellent question." Fiona yanked her arm from Hugh's grip. Then she saw that a few footprints in some light dust on the floor led toward a shadowed wall. "Well, Mr. MacIan?"

"This way," he said without explanation, and led them toward the wall. Now Fiona saw that overlapping walls formed a crevice, with a floor sloping downward into shadow.

"But I want to watch the ba' game," Jamie protested, as Hugh guided each of them into the second cave, Fiona going first, the children guarded between her and Hugh, who then took up a lantern from some unseen shelf and turned up the wick, shedding light on their descending path.

Following the narrow path formed between one cave and the next, Fiona saw immediately that there were more caves under the original—several, in fact, like cells in a honeycomb, formed by bubbles in the ancient liquid material that had turned, over eons, to limestone.

By habit she looked at the quality and nature of the stone, and saw patches of other strata—sandstone, some graywacke, the sparkle of thousands of crystal particles as the lantern light caught them, all common enough stones and so deeply embedded that removal would be difficult, though there were veins of lead, she saw, that could even be mined out. But the stone itself was not what caught her attention in the series of caves.

"This is astonishing," she said, her voice echoing. "So many cave cells progressing eastward, I believe, from the entrance above us. So these caves go under the loch!"

Hugh nodded. "They go deep into the earth, with the loch sitting above us," he agreed, as they continued a downward trek.

"Under the loch!" Jamie hooted his delight, as did Lucy, their voices echoing.

"Hush," the reverend said sharply.

"Will we drown?" Annabel seemed so nervous that Fiona took her hand.

"This is perfectly safe," she told her. "The rock layers overhead are very thick, and have been here for a very long time. A millennium," she said, and explained the word to the children, and told them something about the limestone. Only Annabel listened, the younger two chasing about.

Fiona paused, slowly turning, peering in one cell after another as the lantern light swung and spread. Every small cave contained whisky kegs.

There were hundreds, she thought, most small enough to be carried on a man's shoulder; the larger ones could be rolled up and down the sloped pathways. Transporting the casks into these caves would be the trickier part of the enterprise, she realized. Once brought out of the upper cave, the loch was so close that waiting rowboats could take cargo to a larger cutter or sloop, and away down the loch, before being seen.

"This is Dougal's smuggled whisky cache," she said. "So that is why the game is going on today." She looked at Hugh.

"That could be," he said.

"Smuggler's caves!" Jamie said, as he and Lucy ran about, yelling so that Hugh snapped at them to be quiet.

"I regret bringing them with us," he grumbled.

"We could hardly leave them. Why are we here?" Fiona asked pointedly.

"I know you are interested in fossils. This place must be is thick with them."

"That is not your reason," she said, both puzzled and wary, now.

"I also want you to know what Dougal is doing. If you are considering courtship or marriage, you need to know what a rogue he is."

"I know he cares about his glen and the people in it, and smuggles to protect them from the bite of taxes. And I know he makes legal whisky. This must be a cache of Glen Kinloch brew."

"This," he said, gesturing, "is all aged whisky, made by him and his kinsmen as well. He will make a fortune on the shipment."

"Where is he?" she asked. "You said he would meet us here."

"Soon. Come this way." He turned left to follow a natural corridor in the stone, and Fiona, feeling even more unsettled, gathered the children close, then turned and began to run with them.

Hugh whirled and grabbed for them. As they struggled, the children kicking and screaming, another man stepped out of the shadows. He snatched Fiona by the waist, dragging her away, while Hugh grabbed the two younger children and barked at Annabel to go ahead of him. She obeyed.

Fiona twisted to see that Eldin was holding her. "Nick! What is this all about?"

"Go inside," Eldin said, dragging her toward a small cave, while Hugh pushed the children into it as well. To her amazement, the reverend slammed an iron grate shut, forming a cage. Until then, Fiona had not noticed the metal framework, which was hinged into the very rock.

"What are you doing?" she called, while the children shrieked, Annabel whimpering. "These are just children. Let them go, and Annabel will lead them back to the glen. You are very brave," she encouraged the older girl, "and I know you will watch after the young ones."

"We will hold all of you for a little while, and release you soon," Hugh said. "For now, we need the insurance."

Golden lamplight bloomed where the walkway sloped upward, and footfalls sounded brisk over stone. "What sort of insurance?"

Fiona gasped to see Dougal, his expression a fierce glower in the light, as he descended toward them. Then she saw Patrick walking behind him, carrying a flaming torch.

Chapter 18

"**W**hat the devil, Hugh—and Eldin," Dougal growled. "I should have known you might come after that whisky," he added, glaring at the earl.

"MacGregor," Eldin said smoothly. "And Patrick—what brings you here now?"

"When we heard about the game, I came to the glen with the other officers to watch," Patrick answered his cousin. "I happened to see Dougal, and we noticed the reverend heading this way with my sister and the children."

"But we did not expect this," Dougal said. Beside him, Patrick held the torch high, revealing the two men standing near the cell that had been fitted with an iron grate decades ago, when other smugglers had used these caves.

Behind the rusted iron bars, Fiona stood with the children, her face oval and pale and perfect as she looked through the bars at him. All of them were so achingly beautiful to him, in that moment, that the urge to protect them, even to tear the bars open and send men flying, made his muscles clench, his nostrils flare. He would have to be cautious, and make no move just yet.

He suspected what they wanted—the fools. He would not put it past Eldin, but he could not so easily understand Hugh's involvement. Meanwhile Patrick MacCarran, whom he had been ready to mistrust all along, stood at his shoulder like a stalwart and trusted comrade.

"Where are the other gaugers?" Hugh asked Patrick quietly.

"Out in the glen, watching the game," Patrick said. "They do not know we are here. We are on our own with this, Kinloch," he added under his breath, and Dougal nodded.

"Eldin, why bother to take children and a woman captive?" Dougal asked. "Is it complete cowardice you mean to prove here, or something more serious?" He stepped closer, surreptitiously sliding his hand to the butt of the pistol hidden under the drape of his plaid.

Quickly the earl produced a pistol from inside his frock coat, and cocked the thing; it echoed, and Fiona jumped, and Annabel shrieked a little. "Stay where you are, Kinloch," Eldin said. "Patrick, you too. Move, and you will both regret it."

"Nick," Patrick said, holding the torch high. "Stop this. What is it you want?"

"Kinloch knows exactly what I want," he answered.

"Not seven casks of twenty-year-old whisky," Dougal said.

"Not that," Eldin confirmed. "The other sort of whisky will do."

"Nicholas," Fiona said, and Dougal glanced toward her. "I have known you all my life, and I have seen you change from a kind boy to a smug, cold youth, for some reason of your own. But this . . . is reprehensible. How could you?"

"He seems eager to inherit Grandmother's fortune," Patrick said.

"Ah." Dougal frowned. "The cousin who will take it all—Fiona mentioned that to me when she explained about the will."

"Did she tell you?" Patrick said, raising a brow. "Interesting. She trusts you implicitly, then."

"I would hope so," Dougal replied, with a quick, grim glance toward her.

"Then you know Eldin gets it all if we do not find fairies and suchlike," Patrick muttered.

"By all means, find those damn fairies," Dougal murmured.

"Be quiet," Eldin said.

"Nič, in all the time we have known each other," Fiona said, "I never thought you capable of evil . . . until now."

"Evil, my dear, is a harsh term," Eldin said. "I have my reasons, as you astutely said."

"You are a wicked man," Lucy said.

"Hush it," Eldin hissed, glancing toward the cage.

Dougal stepped forward. "Do not," he warned Eldin.

"I have no interest in the children," the earl said. "Nor do I wish harm to my cousins, though they think ill of me. Once I have what I want, you are all free to go. With some exceptions." He stared, flat and cold, at Dougal. "But that depends on what you decide to do."

"And you?" Dougal looked at Hugh. "What is your part in this?"

"I want you to sell the whisky to Eldin," Hugh said. "Do not bother with the ship."

"It is a cutter, not a ship," Jamie spoke up.

"Hush," Fiona said gently, and rested a hand on Jamie's head. She pulled the children close to her to stand in a huddle by the iron bars. "What is it you both want?" she asked. "Hugh, I hope your grandmother does not know about this!"

"She does not," Hugh answered, without looking at her. "And if she did, she might agree. I only want Dougal to realize that he can make a bigger fortune selling the aged whisky to Eldin and his contacts in England. I have tried to discuss it with him. Eldin's offer for the lot is greater than we could earn from the French and Irish merchants. It could save this glen. That is my concern."

"Save the glen from me," Eldin offered in a mocking tone, "as I hold the deeds now. Not all of them, but enough to control the south end of the glen."

"Who won the ba'?" Jamie asked.

"Southies," Patrick said. "They had more players."

"Exactly," Eldin agreed. "And there will be

tourists and hotels, and barges along the loch here in Glen Kinloch . . . but you could stop all of that, sir," he told Dougal. "With the profit you make from my own pocket, I will allow you to buy me out, and keep the glen to yourselves again."

"Generous of you," Dougal said. He still rested his hand on the butt of his gun, but Eldin held his own pistol steady. No doubt the earl already guessed that Dougal would hesitate to fire the gun in this space, with the woman and children nearby. But he would be wrong in that guess—for Dougal was an excellent shot and would take any chance at all to save them.

"Listen to him," Hugh said. "We could all profit from this."

"Hugh, do you not realize—Eldin does not want the aged whiskies," Dougal said. "He does not care about that. If he had the lot, he would stock the larders of the hotel and sell the rest to his cronies in the Lowlands and England, and make himself a profit on highly valued, illicit, rarer-than-gold Highland whisky. Am I right?"

"Absolutely," Eldin said. "It is not really what I want."

"Then why did you bring me here?" Hugh asked Eldin. "We agreed on a profit for the glen, and for you. You never mentioned wanting something more. What is it?"

Dougal had never thought his cousin a stupid and naïve man, but he believed it possible now. "He wants the fairy whisky," he explained.

"The—but that stuff is only legend," Hugh sputtered. "I have tasted it. Nothing to it, a plain whisky. Nothing like the quality of the aged casks. Eldin, you cannot want that."

"I do," Eldin replied. "I will pay any price for it."

"I cannot think why," Hugh said. "It is a disappointment, that brew."

"It is the genuine stuff made by the fairy ilk," Eldin said. "I have searched the Highlands for something indisputably connected to the fairy world. And this is it—Kinloch fairy brew."

"You're mad," Hugh said, gaping. "Why would you want the fairy brew?"

"I am something of a collector of fairy lore and any magical thing," Eldin said. "I have heard enough tales of fairy brew to convince me that I want it. Sell me all you have—I am offering good money for it, and I think you must accept, since you no doubt want to protect the ones you love. Either way, I want all that you have, and I want the rights to what you make in future. Or," he went on, "you will not see these lovely creatures again." He gestured toward Fiona and the children. He took a step back, lifting his pistol to point it at Hugh, standing nearest him.

"The fairy brew will do you no good. It tastes like an ordinary whisky, but for a few," Dougal said. "The legends are exaggerated."

"I am one of the few," Eldin replied. "And I want to be sure no one else will have the stuff. I want the rights to it, and the exclusive privileges of the source water that you use to make it."

"Nick, that's madness," Patrick said.

"Madness to one man," Eldin said, "is genius to another."

"What water source?" Fiona asked.

"A spring in the hills," Eldin said. "I have pieced that much together from asking around, and learning whatever I could of the Kinloch legend. The lairds of Kinloch will not say all of it, but some of it is known. I want the rights to that spring, and I want to know where it is," he told Dougal. "You can have the rest of the glen, and you will be a rich man. Fiona would like that." He glanced toward her. "She is desperate to find a wealthy Highland man, so I hear."

"I have found the one I want," she said quietly. "I am going to marry Dougal MacGregor."

"A Highland laird with no fortune whatsoever? Excellent," Eldin said. "That will break the conditions of the will, and the bulk of Lady Struan's accounts will come to me."

"He has more wealth than you can possibly imagine, or ever accrue in your life," she said. "The bottomless wealth of the heart—and endless good fortune from the loyalty and love that surround him." She looked at Dougal then, her eyes wide and sheened with tears. He did not move, but caught her gaze, held it, felt his heart opening wide in that moment, filling to the brim.

"What nonsense," Eldin answered. "It is not a bad bargain I offer you, Kinloch. Take it." He waved the pistol. "Agree to give me the fairy whisky and the rights to the spring, and I will let Fiona and the children go. I will pay you handsomely, as I said."

"I cannot sell the fairy brew," Dougal said. "It would undo the magic."

"What?" Eldin leveled the pistol. "You lie. It has a potent and powerful magic."

"And would be rendered to poor quality peat reek if I took money for it. The spring would cease to bubble, and would never again produce water for the whisky, so says the legend."

"I have never heard that," Eldin said.

"Because it is a *secret*," Lucy said with disdain. "We all know it in our family."

Fiona quickly covered the child's mouth, leaning to whisper to her. She pulled the children to the back of the cave, in the shadows. As she did, Dougal gestured for her to stay back there, where they would be safer, and he could better concentrate on the matter at hand.

"Enough, Eldin," he said. "You cannot win this bargain. Give over the gun"—and he drew his own pistol, cocked it—"or I will shoot it from your hand."

"Kinloch is a perfect marksman," Hugh told Eldin. "I would beware."

"He would be guilty of maiming a gauger, then," Eldin said, and lifted the pistol once more. "I am one of the many customs and revenue officers named to this area. I can arrest you in the name of the king, MacGregor of Kinloch, for smuggling and a treasonous plot to take revenue from the Crown. Put away your gun, or I will shoot you—and the others if I must—and call it a good bargain indeed, to catch a bunch of smuggling scoundrels."

"Did you know this?" Dougal demanded of Patrick.

"He is named an officer by document only—he never rides out. It is a formal title he paid to have." Patrick scowled. "But he has the authority."

"You are a fool, Eldin," Dougal said. "I would not have thought it."

"Not a fool, Kinloch. I simply do not care—I ceased to care long ago, when the heart was taken out of me. It needs fairy magic to replace it," he said in a low and dangerous voice. "Fairy magic of great strength, or I shall never feel again, in my heart, in my soul. And I want that," he said. "I want to feel as I once did." He glanced toward Fiona. "I want to care again."

Dougal looked toward Fiona, too, and then stared. The back of the cave was dark—and empty. She was gone, and the children with her.

"Fiona!" Eldin said, stepping toward the cage. As he turned away, unthinking, Patrick threw the torch toward his cousin, striking him on the shoulder.

Eldin turned and fired the pistol. The ball buzzed past Dougal, and hit the rock wall. And then he heard the walls begin to split and crack, and a great rumbling noise began.

"*Fiona!*" he called out, just as Patrick and Hugh

both threw themselves on him in a heavy tackle, taking all of them back toward the walkway as the walls began to collapse, spitting rocks and shards of stone.

"This way," Fiona whispered frantically, leading the children along. "Quickly, before we are seen!" She glanced back over her shoulder, through the narrow crevice she had discovered in the back wall of the cave. The golden glow of the torch Patrick held was still visible, and she could hear the men arguing.

Hurrying the children, she guided them through the slim, high channel she had found in the rock. Scant light glistened on the walls from the torch-light behind them, and she could feel the dampness on the walls. The floor of the passageway was damp, so that here and there she stepped ankle-deep in water, heard it rushing past her. "Walk carefully," she whispered.

The sound of water had first attracted her when she and the children were trapped in the cave, and she had quietly investigated, seeing the crevice, and a little trickling stream running through it. The walls were so honeycombed with cells and passages, formed the cooling bubbles in the original lava, that she was not surprised to find water leaking and pouring here and there—possibly it came from the loch far overhead.

Where the passage would lead them now, she could not say. But if she could get the children out of danger, and remove all of them as bargaining pieces for Eldin, she could help speed the resolution of their argument.

"There's light ahead, Miss Fiona," Annabel said, pointing. They had to walk sideways in this part of the passage, edging along with their backs to the wall; their feet, hands, hair and clothing were increasingly damp.

Fiona saw a pale blue glow ahead, and felt a burst of relief. Although the channel seemed impossibly narrow, they managed to pass through, step by sliding step. As the light grew brighter, she saw more than the glisten of wet limestone walls.

She saw the unmistakable gleam of gold veining the rock.

As they edged along, the water became a stronger flow, and Jamie whispered mischievously that the loch would fall down around their heads any second, which made the girls whimper. While Fiona assured them it would not, she smiled in spite of herself at Jamie's antics.

"We are perfectly safe," she said as they continued. "The channel in the rock is moving upward, see. Climb with me, now, and go carefully, for it is slippery."

"We are walking through a stream," Lucy said. "It is so deep that my skirts are wet."

"When we are out, I will come back to mine this gold," Jamie said. "It is inside these walls, isn't that so, Miss Fiona?"

"Aye, very good," she answered. "Gold indeed,

and the stream rushes right through the channel, adding the flavor of the gold to the water." Realizing what that meant, she gasped.

"That would make excellent whisky," Lucy said, echoing her thoughts. "I will tell Uncle Dougal. He will want to know."

"I think he may already know," Fiona said, and smiled so widely that she nearly laughed. "Look where this leads!" Ahead, the water rushed and pooled, propelled upward toward the opening.

"Water does not flow upward," Jamie said. "How can it be?"

"It is an artesian well," Fiona said. "It bubbles up from below, and bursts forth like a fountain. This one comes up away from the loch, and through the hill, and out on the hillside in a well. I think that is what we will find. Come ahead, and watch your step."

Through the opening, she saw a bright sunset sky in glorious colors—purple and red below wide streaks of amber cloud—and the exit, edged with thick grass. Climbing through the tight opening, where the water rushed out, took an effort that soon had each of them soaked. For a moment Fiona thought it was a little like being birthed into a new life, a new place. Into Glen Kinloch, where she would always stay.

Stepping out, she reached down to help the children out, one by one. "Come up to me," she said, and they did, and then all fell to the ground, exhausted, wet, and laughing a little.

"Look," Lucy said. "Oh, look! Bluebells!"

Fiona looked around, and saw them—thousands of them, covering the ground like a haze of purple-blue, the most beautiful sight she had ever seen.

"This water will make a fine whisky, between the gold and the bluebells," Lucy said, sounding so much like her uncle that Fiona smiled.

"Very fine," Fiona agreed, brushing off her skirts. "The perfect fairy brew, I suspect," she added, while the three young ones stared at her in astonishment.

This little glade and spring had to be the place, she thought, looking around, where Dougal and his father before him had collected water for the fairy whisky. He had never told her the whole of it, not yet—but she cherished his hint that he would tell her, and their children, someday.

She gathered the children near and looked around for the way out of the glade. Then she heard a rumble beneath their feet, a sound like deep thunder. The well burst forth, soaking them as it rose upward, past the rim of the well.

"Dougal," she cried. "Patrick—the others—they are still in the caves!"

Turning, she began to run down the hillside with the children behind her.

Dougal and the others ran from the cave at last, having gone back to drag Eldin free of the rubble—he was hurt, but not badly, and limped with them, silent and as stunned as they were. Stepping out into the sunset light, coated with dust from the limestone, they hurried around the narrow loch side pathway as the rumbling continued underground.

"Fiona," Patrick said, running alongside Dougal. "And the children—trapped!"

"I think they made it through," Dougal said. "Fiona is a brilliant girl, she found the old water channel back there. I had forgotten it. She got the children out safely."

"What if the walls collapsed on them?" Hugh asked, catching up to them, still giving Eldin a hand as the earl limped beside him. "We will have to get help and go back—"

"I think I know where they are," Dougal said.

"The whisky—" Eldin said. "All that whisky—gone, too, if the walls fell."

"Not gone," Hugh said, breathless. "The collapse was in the back of the caves—not where the kegs are stored. We may be able to go back and dig it out. Most of the kegs should be fine. It is Fiona and the children we should be concerned about."

"Fiona is fine. I know it," Eldin said. "I feel it when she is not safe."

Dougal turned to look at him, then met Patrick's grim gaze in silence.

"Where is the fairy brew?" Eldin asked.

"Kept elsewhere, not here," Dougal answered. "And I will never sell it. Patrick—keep pace with them. I will find Fiona and the children—I think I know where they went."

He hurried ahead through a gap between two

hills and headed upward, while the other men fell far behind. As he climbed a hill, though he was deeply weary, after the day of football and the events in the cave, he found strength to keep going. He could not rest until he knew Fiona was safe, and that Lucy and the others were safe with her. Behind him, at one point, he heard shouts and turned to look down the slopes. Men on horseback rode across the glen, waving Patrick and the others to a halt. Recognizing Tam MacIntyre with other gaugers, he knew then that the law officers had caught up with Eldin, and he felt sure, pausing there for a moment, that Patrick would know just what to say. He hoped that Hugh MacIan would not be implicated—the reverend was not a bad man, only grievously misled by Eldin. Turning away, he felt sure that he could trust Patrick MacCarran to handle it properly. One day Patrick might well be his brother-in-law.

Fiona had to be safe and unharmed, he thought, growing desperate, frantic. A burst of strength came over him and he climbed onward, breathing hard, coated with dust, running upward as if he had not played to exhaustion at the ba' or clambered from a cave. He ran as if his life, and the lives of those he loved, depended on his effort now.

But still he did not see them. If the tunnel had indeed collapsed—he could not bear the thought, and ran onward. "Fiona!" he called out in sudden panic.

Then, breathing hard as he paused to look around, he saw her just along the rim of the uppermost hill. She was holding hands with Lucy and Jamie, while Annabel walked beside them. The golden red sunset poured down over them, and Dougal noticed then that Fiona and the children all looked wet and exhausted. Lucy clutched bluebells in her hands.

Bluebells. He laughed outright as he ran toward them. So the tunnel had led safely to the hidden spring, just as he had hoped. And Fiona, recognizing the geological structure of the place, had taken the children that way. The fairies, he was sure, had watched over them.

As Fiona came closer, he reached out and grabbed her, lifted her up and spun her about. Her arms encircled his neck, and her laughter was sweet in his ears, her cheek soft against his.

Setting her down, he kissed her, tasting heaven upon her lips in that slow, soft, endless kiss. She opened her lips under his, telling him that her feelings matched his own, relief and deep love, warm and washing over him. He held her close, wrapped his arms around her, moved his lips over hers, and felt his very soul ripple and awaken fully, keen to be with her.

"Oh, my dearest girl," he murmured against her mouth, her cheek, her damp hair. "I am indeed a rich man."

"Very rich, Uncle Dougal," Lucy said. He pulled back and looked down, reaching out to touch the child's head, pulling her close, while he smiled at the others, too. Lucy held up the bluebells. "We found these for the whisky. And there's gold, too," she said.

"Gold?" He frowned a little, looking around, seeing them nod all at once.

"We saw it," Jamie said. "Lots of it!"

Fiona pulled Dougal close, reaching up to rest her hand against her cheek. "And even if that gold stays there forever," she whispered, "we are so fortunate, so blessed and wealthy. We need nothing else to make it so."

"Nothing?" He smiled. "Oh, there are always needs, my love." He dipped his head to kiss her again. "Needs, and dreams, and desires."

"Obligations, too," she said, and gave him that bright and luminous smile that he had once coveted, that beautiful smile meant for him, now.

"Ah, those as well," he murmured, bending close again. "And they will be easily, and happily, fulfilled."

Epilogue

Fiona read another rhyme aloud for her students, and paused to listen to them recite it back to her—Gaelic to English, and English to Gaelic—and then she glanced at the door, hearing a commotion outside. Lessons had begun but half an hour ago, and it was early yet, though she had thrown open a window to the cool spring air. Hearing the rumble of voices outside, she excused herself and went to the door to open it.

Several people stood out in the yard, men and women, some older children and adolescents. She recognized Neill MacDonald and his father, along with Helen MacDonald, Annabel's mother, and several others whose names she did not know.

"Good morning," she said, heart thumping anxiously, having no idea why they had gathered outside the schoolhouse. She wondered, with a sudden ache, if they had come to send her away, for her time in the glen was nearly up, her teaching contract done. "What can I do for you?"

She saw Mary MacIan now, walking through

the little crowd. Mary had been saddened and disappointed to learn of Hugh's involvement in what had happened in the caves, and she had blistered him with her opinion. Hugh had apologized to her, and to Dougal and Fiona, and had kept to his side of the glen—but few knew the real details of that ordeal. Dougal had seemed inclined to forgive his cousin, at least eventually, and had not told his uncles the whole truth of it. But they had guessed what Hugh had wanted, once they learned of Eldin's wishes that day.

Fiona caught her breath as Dougal appeared just behind Mary. Her heart bounded a little to see him there. For an instant, he was the only one she saw in that group, her gaze intent on his, questioning, pleading.

She did not want to leave the glen, if that was why they had all gathered here. Perhaps word had gone out about what had happened that day—perhaps they had all decided she must go, that her cousin Lord Eldin was a terrible man who would bring not only ruin but tourism to the glen. But he had sailed for the Continent, so Patrick had sent word, and likely would not return for a long time.

A few days had passed since the ba' game, and Fiona had resumed teaching, guiding her students through their lessons, and comforting their fears over some of the events that had happened in the glen. Everyone had heard about the collapse of the caves under the loch, a natural phenomenon that she explained away with a few geological terms.

The few who had had been present kept the rest of it a strict secret, including the children, who were pleased to be entrusted with knowledge of the hidden caches of whisky as well as gold.

Dougal had been busy rescuing whisky kegs from the collapsed cave, selling some to the promised merchants by night, when the cutters came, as he had agreed. The rest he had sold to Eldin for an exorbitant amount. Before he left for his holiday abroad, her cousin, keenly aware of the value of his reputation as an earl and peer, had realized that it would be best if no one ever knew about his disgraceful behavior in the caves under Loch Katrine.

He was trying, Fiona thought; Nick was trying to make amends, though she would never trust him. He was like an untamed raptor, she knew, a powerful hawk or raven that could be cooperative, though its loyalty would never be certain.

Now she looked at the group gathered before her. Dougal glanced away as the woman who stood beside him murmured something. He leaned down to listen. Fiona did not recognize the woman, who was handsome and sturdy, with thick brown hair under the drape of her plaid. When the woman turned to look at Hamish standing beside her, and when Hamish took her hand in both of his, Fiona realized then that Jean MacGregor had come back to her husband.

And suddenly she wanted very much to stay in Glen Kinloch, so that she could come to know Jean, whose warm, laughing glance made her feel welcome—all their smiling faces did. And yet she frowned, nervous, twisting her hands behind her. Her teaching contract was over, but Dougal had not yet told her completely what was in his heart, and though she hoped . . . she did not know for certain.

"Fiona MacCarran," Mary said then, addressing her in Gaelic, as was so often the case. "These people would like a word with you."

She nodded and looked again at Dougal, who now watched her with a calm expression that revealed none of his thoughts. Behind her, the students had left their seats to come to the door, too. "Aye, what is it?" she asked.

"We would like to know if you will teach us," Mary said.

Fiona blinked. "Teach you?" she repeated in surprise.

"We want to learn to read English," Mary said. "Some of us should learn to sign our names, and some of us need more words in English. And a couple of these rascals ought to be able to read their own arrest warrants." A ripple of laughter followed. "And so we want to join your class."

Stunned, Fiona glanced at Dougal, who nodded slowly, silently.

"I would love to teach you," she answered, and several of the people nodded. "But the schoolhouse is nearly full now, with twelve scholars. The roof leaks, and the wall is damaged. It needs replacing soon or it may fall upon our heads. And I . . . my teaching arrangement will end soon. According to that, I need no longer stay in the glen," she added, glancing again at Dougal.

He tilted his head, watching her, and said nothing. She could not read his expression.

"You could stay," Mary MacIan said. "Teach here at the school as long as you like."

Fiona fastened her gaze to Dougal's own. "I would like that."

He nodded slowly. "What else would you like, Miss MacCarran?"

"You know very well," she said then, crisply and quickly, unable to hold back. Mary MacIan laughed, as did Jean and Hamish, and some of the others. Dougal's lips twitched.

"You could stay," he said. "And teach us . . . what we most need to learn."

"What is it you would like to learn, Dougal MacGregor?" Fiona asked. Her heart bounded.

He smiled then, widely. More people turned to stare at him, then at her. "I think you know, Miss MacCarran."

"Will you be joining the class, too, Kinloch?" Thomas MacDonald asked.

"I might. I will need to read some of those warrants," Dougal drawled, amid laughter.

"He can read those well enough, he has done it before," Thomas said, and turned toward Fiona. "Miss, we can help rebuild the school, if that will convince you."

"That would be very nice." Fiona could not speak for the quick tightening in her throat.

Dougal walked forward then through the throng. "You could marry the laird," he said quietly, "and stay forever."

She caught her breath, and watched him come closer. Though she heard gasps and saw smiles in the crowd, she held Dougal's intent gaze. "I could," she said then. "I could marry the laird, if he will have me."

"Will he meet the approval of your kin, and your lawyers?" he asked quietly.

"That does not matter," she murmured, and held out her hands. "I will tell them that I will marry a rogue, regardless of his fortune. Unless it matters to the laird himself—"

"Not at all," he replied, and laughed, deep and mellow. He was close then, and stepped through the crowd, lifting her off the step and to the ground, taking her into his arms.

When he kissed her, she heard cheers and laughter all around—and then only the strong, steady thump of his heart against hers, and the pulse of her blood, gone to wildness, within her.

"Fiona," he murmured in her ear, and kissed her again. "Tell those lawyers of yours that we shall marry soon, and invite your brothers and your kinfolk to our glen. We shall have a wedding to rival any your family could give you in the Lowlands."

She pulled back, looking up at him. "Why so quickly? There is no need for haste. Well," she said, blushing, "not that I know about, yet."

He rested his brow against hers. "It is nearly time

to go up into the hills," he murmured, so that only she could hear, "to the place where the bluebells grow. I want to take you there as my wife. I have a story to tell you—the whole of the legend of Glen Kinloch."

She drew back to look at him. "I thought the tradition was for fathers to tell their sons."

"I am changing the tradition," he said. "We will improve upon it, you and I. The Fey will be glad of it. They love you, as I do."

Fiona slipped closer into his embrace, her lips upon his cheek, her whisper in his ear. "I want to know more about it—and I promise to keep the secret all my life."

"I will see that you do," he whispered. "Every day of it."

Behind her, Fiona felt a pull at her skirts. She turned and saw Lucy, her small face flushed and her smile wide. "You could have bluebells for your wedding bouquet," she said.

"What a lovely idea," Fiona said. "I hope you will carry them for me." Laughing, she gathered the little girl close, and Dougal rested a hand on Lucy's shoulder. The child wrapped her arms around both of them as best she could—and then Fiona smiled again, for Lucy reached out impulsively to snatch Jamie by the arm and drag him into the shared embrace.

Dougal chuckled in her ear. "She does torment the lad."

"Someday," Fiona said, "that will surely change."